THE SELECTED LETTERS
OF SOMERVILLE AND ROSS

THE SELECTED LETTERS OF

Somerville
and Ross

Edited by Gifford Lewis

Foreword by Molly Keane

faber and faber
LONDON · BOSTON

First published in 1989
by Faber and Faber Limited
3 Queen Square London WC1N 3AU

Phototyeset by Input Typesetting Ltd, London
Printed in Great Britain by
Richard Clay Ltd, Bungay, Suffolk

British Library Cataloguing in Publication Data is available.

ISBN 0-571-15348-8

In memory of Katharine ('K') Johnston
and Diana Somerville

Contents

List of Illustrations

List of facsimiles appearing
in the text

Reviews of *An Irish Cousin* (1889): *Athenaeum*, 31 August 1889;
Morning Post, 12 September 1889, *pages 146, 148*
The Zetlands in the West: *The World*, 22 April 1891; *The Daily
Express*, 14 April 1891, *pages 173–4*
Reviews of *Naboth's Vineyard* (1891): *Daily Graphic*, 5 October 1891;
Black and White, 28 November 1891, *page 178*
Review of *Through Connemara in a Governess Cart* (1891): *Morning
Post*, 16 November 1892, *page 180*
Review of *In the Vine Country* (1893): source unknown, *page 183*
Reviews of *The Real Charlotte* (1894): *Lady's Pictorial*, 19 May 1894;
and another, source unknown, *pages 200, 201*
Reviews of *All on the Irish Shore* (1903): *The Spectator*, 18 April
1903, *page 261. Outlook*, 6 June 1903, *page 266. The Independent*,
no date, *page 269*
Biographical notice: *The Gentlewoman*, 8 October 1904, *page 272*
Reviews of *Some Irish Yesterdays* (1906): *Times Literary Supplement*,
26 October 1906; *Weekly Sun*, 20 October 1906, *pages 280–1*

Acknowledgements

These letters between Edith Anna Œnone Somerville and Violet Florence Martin are reproduced with the kind permission of the Henry W. and Albert A. Berg Collections, the New York Public Library, Astor, Lenox and Tilden Foundations, and the executor of the literary estate of Somerville and Ross, Sir Toby Coghill.

I am most grateful to the following for their help and patience: the late Canon Claude Chavasse; the late Sir Patrick Coghill; Sir Toby Coghill; the late Katharine (Coghill) Johnston; the late Diana Somerville.

I have to thank these relatives of Edith Somerville for illustrations: the late Katharine Johnston for 1, 3, 6, 7, 8 and 9; the late Colonel Brian Somerville for 2, 12 and 5; Christopher Somerville for 4, 14, and 17; and Sir Toby Coghill for 10, 13, 15, 16 and 18.

I thank the President and Fellows of Magdalen College, Oxford, for permission to reproduce the photograph of Herbert Greene from their archives.

The Somerville Family Tree

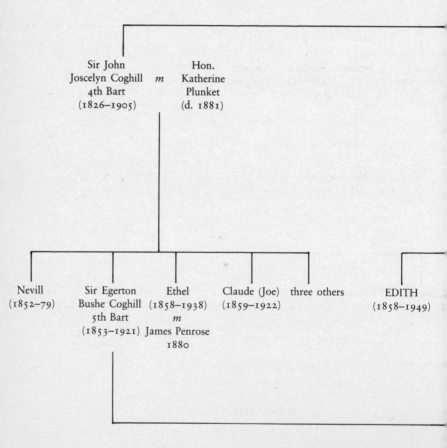

Sir John
Joscelyn Coghill   *m*   Hon.
4th Bart   Katherine
(1826–1905)   Plunket
                                  (d. 1881)

Nevill   Sir Egerton   Ethel   Claude (Joe)   three others   EDITH
(1852–79)   Bushe Coghill   (1858–1938)   (1859–1922)   (1858–1949)
                    5th Bart   *m*
                    (1853–1921)   James Penrose
                                          1880

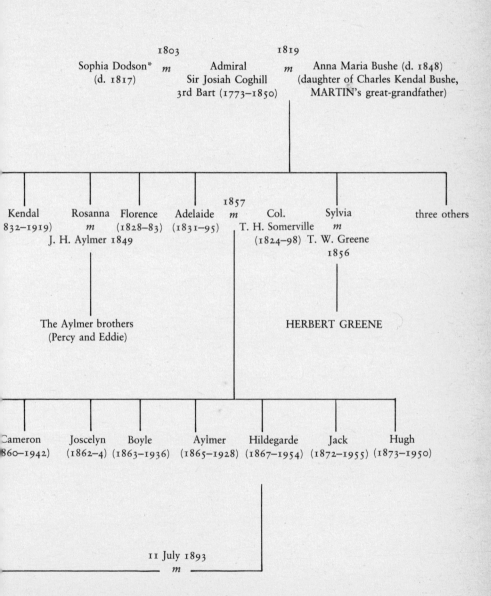

                    1803   1819
    Sophia Dodson*   m   Admiral   m   Anna Maria Bushe (d. 1848)
       (d. 1817)   Sir Josiah Coghill   (daughter of Charles Kendal Bushe,
                          3rd Bart (1773–1850)   MARTIN's great-grandfather)

                                              1857
Kendal   Rosanna   Florence   Adelaide   m   Col.   Sylvia   three others
832–1919)   m   (1828–83)   (1831–95)   T. H. Somerville   m
            J. H. Aylmer 1849   (1824–98) T. W. Greene
                                                                  1856

            The Aylmer brothers   HERBERT GREENE
            (Percy and Eddie)

Cameron   Joscelyn   Boyle   Aylmer   Hildegarde   Jack   Hugh
860–1942)   (1862–4)   (1863–1936) (1865–1928) (1867–1954) (1872–1955) (1873–1950)

                        11 July 1893
                             m

* Who had daughters Caroline, Josephine and Emmeline. Emmeline m. 1839 Rev. Charles Bushe,
son of Charles Kendal Bushe, Rector of Castlehaven.

The Martin Family Tree

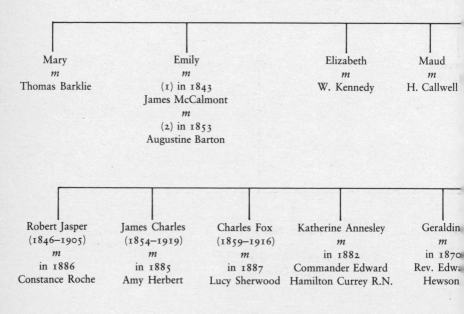

(1) in 1824 Anne, dau.
Thomas Higinbotham

Mary
m
Thomas Barklie

Emily
m
(1) in 1843
James McCalmont
m
(2) in 1853
Augustine Barton

Elizabeth
m
W. Kennedy

Maud
m
H. Callwell

Robert Jasper
(1846–1905)
m
in 1886
Constance Roche

James Charles
(1854–1919)
m
in 1885
Amy Herbert

Charles Fox
(1859–1916)
m
in 1887
Lucy Sherwood

Katherine Annesley
m
in 1882
Commander Edward
Hamilton Currey R.N.

Geraldin
m
in 1870
Rev. Edwa
Hewson

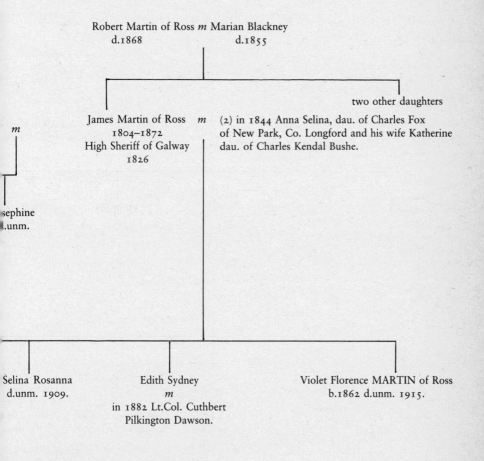

Robert Martin of Ross *m* Marian Blackney
d.1868   d.1855

two other daughters

James Martin of Ross   *m*   (2) in 1844 Anna Selina, dau. of Charles Fox
1804–1872   of New Park, Co. Longford and his wife Katherine
High Sheriff of Galway   dau. of Charles Kendal Bushe.
1826

m

sephine
.unm.

Selina Rosanna   Edith Sydney   Violet Florence MARTIN of Ross
d.unm. 1909.   *m*   b.1862 d.unm. 1915.
                    in 1882 Lt.Col. Cuthbert
                    Pilkington Dawson.

Foreword
by Molly Keane

In her introduction to *The Selected Letters of Somerville and Ross* Gifford Lewis gives us a piercingly accurate description of the times and circumstances in which Edith Somerville and Violet Martin of Ross wrote these wonderful letters – letters conveying a sense of the period so intense that, as we read, ghosts walk. As well as this, we get fascinating insights into the inspirations, although not the constructions, of their books.

Those were the great days of letter-writing. The absence of sons and lovers in faraway continents and corners of the Empire was accepted by their families with total resignation, and with it a tolerance for the lengthy homeward voyages – arrivals long delayed by weeks, even months, of bad weather. My grandmother, steaming back from Mauritius, gave birth to her baby before the end of the voyage – the baby did not survive. These trials and changes, accepted by their victims as inevitabilities, account largely for the potency and importance of letter-writing. Letters and photographs were as flesh and blood to close affectionate friends and to long-parted lovers. Familiarity lived on in them – their recipients would not meet again as strangers.

Sisters and friends, living at distances of fifty miles or less, wrote to each other regularly. Fifty miles was too far for the carriage and too short for a train service. To write a letter was as natural and necessary a communication as a telephone call is today. Had there been a telephone service then, how barren and shadowy for us would seem the background of Edith's and Martin's youth. All would be lost in long, and long-forgotten, telephone conversations; the joys and troubles of their lives expired for always in myth and misplaced curiosity.

Their letters reflect wonderful long playtimes – hunting, sailing, tennis, dancing, amateur theatricals – their pleasures seem endless as a summer's day, thrilling as an historic run with the hounds. These accounts mask something touching, not on poverty, but on a conscientious acceptance of a shortage of money when the consideration of a journey between Dublin and Galway (a rail ticket was nineteen shillings, second class; twelve shillings, third) was a serious impediment to constant meetings.

This considered economy contrasts strangely with the lengthy hospitality shown unquestioningly to large contingents of family, including cousins, near and distant, loved and unloved, but always to be welcomed as part of 'the Family'. Aside from personal economies, the entertainment of friends, and friends of friends, was an unquestioned responsibility and, very nearly always, a pleasure. Edith gives a wonderful account of a luncheon party at Castletownshend where life, although not affluent, was rather easier than at Ross. She writes: 'Four chickens and a turkey, ham, tongue, lobsters, fish (from Cork) were laid in, besides sweets innumerable . . . Bessie went a mucker and had three glasses of champagne and a wineglass of Benedictine which had the effect of making her talk endlessly and abusively . . .'

Edith and Martin wrote to each other letters long as short stories, every one of them an entertainment; discretion mercifully lost in gossip, not always kind but always with an undercurrent of tolerance. They did not suffer fools gladly. Their respect for language, their intricate use of it in their most private letters and confidences was an accepted, considered importance, and no short cuts were taken. Only for small vulgarities of speech in others is their snobbery evident. Martin's liking for a neighbouring family was a little frustrated when she heard the local village spoken of as 'town'. They transferred this pathetic pomposity to the refined society depicted devastatingly in a long short story, 'A Conspiracy of Silence'. The fact that Edith and Martin would have spoken good colloquial English together and with their friends would lend an intense vulnerability to their ear for every subtle difference in social accents.

I can remember a previous generation to our mothers with wonderful voices, not of the peasants or middle classes, but belonging strictly to their own social set. They said 'me dear', and 'well, m'dear', when embarking on any information. Their daughters, our mothers, had English and French governesses and tutors. They went abroad to study languages. They spoke 'proper' English and insisted on their children doing the same. There was fierce correction for 'speaking like the servants'. Edith and Martin would have shared in these constrictions and concepts; their use of English is evident even in their most casual letters.

In contrast with their repulsion towards the refined is their delight in the language of the country people; its poetry and its absurdities alike echo for us through their hearing and memory. They recognize the lively stuff of Elizabethan English, entirely different from the beautiful languors of Yeats and Synge. The Celtic revival was not their favourite literary movement. They did not entirely approve of Lady Gregory. Their appreciation of Sean O'Casey must have represented quite closely the alarmed repulsion later to be felt for John Osborne and *Look Back in Anger* by a younger generation of writers. There is no smell of the literary world in their letters. When their own books were published, they had a severely practical view of the proceeds, scarcely commenting to each other on the dazzling notices. They wrote to each other of the daily happenings in their lives and of the fortunes and misfortunes in the vast family circles, seldom of their own feelings and sensibilities.

In that nearly miraculous collaboration over the books, Edith, me feels, is the more emotional writer of the two; Martin the remorseless censor. 'Once more the critic dips his pen in gall,' and so she did, tearing apart every line of the poem – where is it? – that Edith sent her. They accepted that the characters in their books were mainly derived from the strata of society they knew best – 'let us take Carbery and grind its bones to make our bread'. But in the letters, especially in those telling of her return to Ross, where neglect and decay were consequent on fifteen years of absence, Martin's letters express without reserve her deepest feelings. The welcome of the ex-tenants breaks her heart in its emotional falsity. Their disloyalty to her father is still too near, too raw, yet, for her practical sense and her loving heart to allow her to accept their present kindness to the family, now fallen from the almost royal state it had held, and from which favour and disfavour had been dispensed for several hundred years. It was not snobbery or vanity that made such hapless successors as Martin cling to the preservation of the Old Place. It was something more like a sexual love for the house and its demesnes as well as an abiding affection for the local families who had been in the service of Ross for past generations. It took longer for her affection and understanding to regenerate towards the ex-land tenants, but the change came with her acceptance of the many kindnesses constantly given by the New Order to the Late Ascendancy.

The viewpoint in her letters to Edith at this time is that of the dispossessed. Understanding or acceptance of the realities of past deprivations and injustices suffered by the dependants on absentee landlords and British non-comprehending rulers are frustrated and lost in memories of sacrifices made and losses accepted by great landlords such as the Martins of Ross – usurpers perhaps, in a conquered country, but conscientious and self-sacrificing during their long ascendancy.

Present tragedy and sorrow was to link Martin again in a strong accord with her people. She was deeply moved when a mentally disturbed boy drowned himself in the lake below Ross House. Here, her reaction to the finality of death seems hopelessly divergent from Edith's acceptance of her cousin's presence after death. Martin involved herself practically in every aspect of the suicide, from the scapula left on the bank (no one can drown with a holy scapula round his neck) to the discovery of the body tangled in the sunken dead branches of a tree that had fallen to the furthest depths of the water. While part of the tragedy was used later in a short story, in her letter to Edith it was far removed from any voyeuristic or journalistic angle. Her involvement in the event, and in all the circumstances leading to it, pervaded her physically. This invasion and terrible understanding provoked much of the writing of books such as *The Real Charlotte*.

Martin's letters are often poignant accounts of the traumas as well as the delights she experienced in the rehabilitation of Ross. Edith's are dramatizations of the daily life, a comfortable, very social, life at Drishane, far distanced from the barren Great House of Ross, its present shadowed by glories and dramas from its past. Romantic affairs and attachments, happy or otherwise, are not confided in any of their letters. Both Edith and Martin seem more than fully occupied in recounting the events – often startling enough – of the day-by-day happenings in their lives. One of the limitations they treat with the lightest possible touch is the indulgent obedience to Mama, taken as a natural part of the air breathed by upper-class daughters. Bright souls like Edith might laugh behind their hands at Mama's absurdities but, to a large extent, they had to attend to the words of her lips. Martin's difficulties with her mother are shrouded in a tactful tolerance, but Edith, though never spiteful, is eloquent on the subject of her mother's absurdities. What is more surprising is that she should read the joint, unfinished, manuscripts of the books aloud to the whole family, and accept their criticisms, condemnations and suggestions quite seriously – or so it seems. Even after publication, and rave reviews from the most respected literary critics of the day, she could still consider the comments of her mother and her mother's friends with indulgent understanding.

One's mental pictures of the young Edith and Martin can rely only on photographers' perceptions. We read of Martin's enchanting and provocative looks: amateur photographs show us a soft expressionless face, its only discernible feature the slightly prominent teeth; quite wispy hair escapes from the cruelties of an awful hat. Perhaps it is because the pictures are so inadequate, and her life so short, that so much of the real Martin fills our imaginations.

In contrast, one's clear idea of the young Edith is of a woman wonderfully and correctly turned out for hunting: dark habit, perfectly tied white stock, hunting crop held in a gloved hand, her hat, never, I think, a huntsman's velvet cap. In all the years when she was Master of Fox

Hounds, her hair was glazed to her head in tidiness beneath the silk of the bowler hat. It is delightful to contrast this picture with her account to Martin of the comments on 'a black and white velveteen blouse' made up by a French friend whose sartorial taste she respected. ' "*May* I ask, Paris or London?" I said "Skibbereen" – "Ah, alors c'est le façon de le mettre!" It was highly gratifying.' At the summit of their success, when the 'RM' had swept the reading public into a sort of rhapsody, she is still in difficulties and contrivances over a proper outfit for celebratory parties.

Music was a second life to Edith and its effects described with the same passion that went into an account of a marvellous day with the hounds. Martin was her equal in devotion to hunting, but less well versed in its rituals. When Aylmer Somerville had the hounds, she writes to Edith of a cub-hunting morning in the woodlands, when hounds rioted on deer, unrated and unstopped. All that mattered to her was the full chorus of their music flooding the hot morning air. No one seems to have considered this to be a strange introduction for a young novice to the disciplines of fox-hunting. The echo in the woodlands was glory enough, and the hours live on in every word she wrote.

Later, when Edith was Master of the West Carbery, she hunted the county in a more orthodox style. Her description to Martin of a long blank day conveys all the melancholy and disappointment persisting through every hour until, late in the evening, hounds found and were away on a screaming scent, and over an impossible line of country. Edith, in the first flight, is just about to give a lead to a friend's refusing horse when . . . the rest of the letter is lost. That we never know just what happened leaves us with an unrequited curiosity that preserves every moment of that long grey day to its last hour when tired hounds and tired horses are lit as by magic.

Edith's knowledge of fox hounds and fox-hunting went far beyond Martin's. But Martin could put the inexplicable into words conveying the power and the glory that goes past all sensible recognition. After a long enforced abstinence she writes of a day's hunting: 'I have tasted of the wine of life again.' With her lyricism and Edith's knowledge, in their compacted writing they come closer than any author, dead or living, to imparting to the reader a share in the passion and mystique of fox-hunting.

Though their letters to each other do tell of everyday exasperation and exhaustion, they tell more often of the comedies, high and low, that move them to delighted laughter. When they write of disasters, personal distress or physical pain are minimized in importance. Other tragedies are enlarged on with the unquestioning certainty of understanding and sympathy from the other. We read with growing wonder and respect for the strength, tolerance and perseverance they show so clearly in their acceptance of life as it was for them.

Above all else, their letters are provocative of our curiosity concerning those past years. It is a beguiling curiosity that excites interest far beyond the fanciful and lends us a share in those enchanted spaces of leisure that we have lost and they knew so well how to occupy. But from within that distanced and enchanted area, and without malign intention, another and different door is opened for us on the cruel limitations beyond our sufferance today.

Introduction

Being physically separated for a large part of their life as a literary 'partnership', Edith Somerville and Violet Martin (known as Martin Ross) exchanged hundreds of letters. They did not live and work at the same address until 1906, twenty years after setting forth on a career together. They were family women, rooted to their family homes: Somerville to Drishane in County Cork and Martin to Ross in County Galway. Martin remained tied to Ross until her mother's death in 1906; only then did she feel free to remove to Drishane which remained her base until her death in 1915. The hundreds of miles between Drishane and Ross did not dim the intensity and quality of their work, and their letters crackle with the full charge of a perfect line of communication. The postal service of those days was excellent and their career was not hindered by the fact that manuscripts oscillated between Drishane and Ross for six months or so before clean-copying and the journey eastwards to their publishers in London.

The letters between them are a patchy collection of fragments, and relative to other series of Somerville's letters, insignificant in size. Ninety-seven letters survive from Edith to Martin, on 571 pages; 139 letters survive from Martin to Edith, on 996 pages. The tone of these letters is flippant, very rarely touching upon intimate subjects like Irish politics, as Martin wished to preserve peace with Edith at all costs; it is a tone peculiar to these off-the-cuff communications between them. We find more polished letter-writing in the surviving complete series of letters from Edith to her brother Jack – 1033 letters on 4,150 pages – written over sixty years, or the series to Ethel Smyth – 300 letters on 1,047 pages – where she expresses herself fully on Irish politics and current affairs. But however unpolished and fragmentary they are the letters between them still give us the interchange of voices and ideas, and the balance of power between these two women who made their double-barrelled mark with a peerless right and left: the best Irish novel of the nineteenth century and the best set of comic tales of Irish life in the last days of the Ascendancy.

When their letters begin we are in the company of a facetious pair of dizzy girls who were astonished by their breakthrough into 'literature'. Edith's diary entry for the day that their first novel was accepted runs: 'Wrote a dizzy letter of acceptance. Went to church twice in a glorified trance . . .' While Martin's reads: 'Got a letter from Richard Bentley and Son announcing that the birthday of our lives has come and that he was prepared to publish the Shocker giving us £25 on publication and £25 on sale of 500 copies. All comment is inadequate. Went dizzily to church twice. Wrote accepting terms with dignity.' It took them ten years to find their commercially rewarding form in the RM stories, and during that time they became hardened dealers and professional writers, conscious of the value of their work. Far ahead of their time, they were proud of being professional women, and were prepared to be affronted if women's work was not considered on equal terms with men's. In 1906, Martin wrote to Edith of Sir A. Henniker Heaton, who was about to publish a biography of her brother Robert: 'The book is to be crown octavo . . . my part is to be about 15000 words! He said "about twelve columns of *The Times* — but write all you like, and we can select what is wanted." I at once said I was too busy to write stuff that might not be wanted and he seemed quite surprised — I don't think that he realizes at all the position, or that I am a professional writer. I shall not put you in a passion by telling more of his recommendations and advice . . .'

Because the Anglo-Irish landlord class to which they belonged was moneyless owing to non-payment of rents, the ability to earn their own living was a matter of life or death, or at least life or marriage to Edith and Martin. They succeeded very well. Their literary agent, Pinker, who was also agent for grandees like Arnold Bennett and Henry James, paid over more than £6,000 to them during the period 1898–1922. During twenty-four years with Pinker Edith Somerville earned £4668 17s 10½d and Violet Martin £1920 11s 3½d from 1898 to her death in 1915. Much of their income was swallowed by the upkeep of their homes. If the Land League had wanted evidence of the damage inflicted by their non-payment-of-rent tactics, these letters would have given much joy. Lack of money, and how to raise it, are perhaps the main recurrent topics, so that it is eventually borne in upon the reader that the Anglo-Irish 'ascendancy' of the end of the nineteenth century and the beginning of the twentieth was an enormous confidence trick, shored up by faithful servants and good horsemanship.

Of the Castletownshend families, the only wealthy one at the opening of this correspondence was the Coghills; but under the mismanagement of Sir Joscelyn and Colonel Kendal we see the Coghill family lose their last substantial sum of capital (and this was after their rents had stopped coming in) in a crazy French investment scheme referred to by the code-name 'Bourget' then 'Bougie'. In consequence Egerton, the heir to the Coghill baronetcy and an out-of-work engineer, has to delay his marriage to Edith's sister Hildegarde because of his lack of money and prospects, and the engaged couple set up their photographic business of selling West Cork seascapes and landscapes to tourists. Resourcefulness was strong in the female line. From Hildegarde selling violets by post to destinations all over the British Isles to Mrs Martin selling her surplus eggs and greengages in Oughterard, there was intense application and agility shown in putting a cheerful face on the fact that there was nothing in the bank.

Outwardly the Anglo-Irish seemed well housed and well dressed. The fact that they still had their houses was what saved the day and appearances, for the big house was put out to rent. Readers of these letters will remark the influx of 'new' people into Castletownshend. These were often holiday tenants of the homes of the Somervilles, Townshends or Coghills, whose real owners visited relations or retired to the Home Farm, or, in the case of the Coghills, moved on to their old schooner-cum-houseboat *Ierne*. *Nouveaux riches* were called 'suburbans' – the old rich but newly impoverished visitors tended to be cousins of some sort and therefore 'Buddh'.* Further supplies of new faces arrived via the barracks at Oughterard and Skibbereen with endless delight in the changing rotas of 'th'Officers'. Many an English officer took home an Anglo-Irish bride to sighs of relief in many a damp drawing-room. With the disappearance of their private income parents had to concentrate on placing their sons well in the Army, the Navy, or the Church. The letters now and then reveal the Martin and Somerville brothers at their various postings around the world when the British Empire was at its greatest extent. The fate of sisters was mostly marriage, or if maiden-aunthood was unavoidable, a grey and empty life like that of Martin's elder sister Selina. Edith and Martin were unusual in that many of their female cousins escaped marriage and made careers for themselves. Violet and Hebe Coghill became doctors (Violet was one of Dr Jex-Blake's first students at Edinburgh), Fanny Currey was a journalist, Rose Barton a noted water-colourist, and even those who married sometimes managed careers as well: Hildegarde had her dairy herd, violet farm and photography; Ethel Coghill, married to Jimmy Penrose, became a writer of children's books. All of these managed to capitalize on some ability that had been inherited and encouraged by their families. In the case of Martin and Edith, when it was seen that they actually earned money by their writing, few obstacles were put in the way of their career, as in this way they remained available to the family and contributed to the upkeep of their homes.

Somerville and Ross excelled in the dramatic use of recorded speech of all classes in Ireland. They had confidence in their own powers of speech and retort, and a remarkable gift for the understanding of dialect and the ability to record it instantly. The exactitude and bulk of their record of Irish speech is unique. Hilary Robinson has shown how little they changed what they had taken down from life when it was sewn into a novel or story. Martin threw away drafts, much to Edith's irritation, but kept notebooks of recorded speech throughout her life. Fellow guests of Martin's at house parties in Ireland became accustomed to her disappearing to her room to write down words that she wanted to use later. Edith had a different system, always carrying pocket-books with her, and sketching or making notes wherever she happened to be.

Edith and Martin happened to be in many unusual places and wrote about aspects of Irish life previously unseen or unnoticed by the centre-stage male; they enjoyed laundries, kitchens, boot cupboards, ashpits – in short, places frequented by servants, most of whom were women. Their frank recognition of the emotions and powers of expression that they found in these women gives their writing a range and depth not found in other Anglo-Irish authors of the time. In Castletownshend there is a parallel street of very poor tumbledown cottages running behind the main street of biggish to grand houses. This was Dirty Lane, much frequented by Edith Somerville, and later to reappear in *The Real Charlotte*. It was the authors' familiarity with the poor, poverty, dirt and ugliness that repelled many readers of *Charlotte*. Here they were in the forefront of 'dirty Irish realism', and it did not sell.

We can see from those letters that are scornful about 'suburbans' that the old gentry refused to be at all familiar with people of the middle classes who were 'not quite'; on the other hand the letters, particularly Martin's from Ross, show an almost bizarre intimacy between gentry and servants in families that had been isolated for generations together. A quotation from a letter of Martin's to Edith illustrates this:

Mama told me tonight to my extreme amusement, of an effort she made before I came home to get Selina out of bed, she having taken up her usual winter residence there. Selina at once announced that no one cared for her but Jim and fell to weeping with great violence. Mama was completely nonplussed, "but" she said with beautiful casualness "Kate Welsh happend to be within hearing, she had come down about something or other, and I think I had got her to sweep the stairs, and she with great cleverness came to the rescue." This meant, I found, that she came in and told Selina she would rather have her than any young lady of the whole of them. The tide of tears began to abate, but was not completely checked till Johnny Welsh was called in – He in some other unexplained way had flown out from his situation in Galway and was probably at that moment making Mama's bed or lacing her stays. To Selina then, seated Niobe-like in bed behold the bold Johnny approached. He also roundly asserted that we were all but blackamoors compared with Selina . . .

Somerville and Ross wrote of a time when the Anglo-Irish gentleman had gone away, or at least was only home on vacation, and the fort was being held by his mother and his sisters and his cousins and his aunts. During this period powerful women came into their own, and in their fictional portraits of this type Edith and Martin excelled. Their most memorable character, Charlotte Mullen, was based on a cousin of Edith's called Emily Herbert, who by cheating Edith of an inheritance gave her the impetus to make a career for herself. What irony lies in Edith's dreadful revenge of her casting of Emily Herbert as the dark centre of their best novel. Several of the letters tell some of Emily Herbert's story, including the gruesome scene at the Point House where she was found lying dead in bed surrounded by her fourteen cats.

Time and again we find in the letters the seeds of their stories. Two letters of Martin's about a suicide at Ross ('It has the makings of a story almost') were worked up twice – once in a story, once in a novel. Letters used in this way have later notations indicating their eventual home in the fiction, or are actually marked at the time of writing 'Save this for me, we can use it later' or 'This has the makings of a story'. One of Martin's very last extant letters is about a visit to Tyrone House and a description of the ill fortunes of the owners, the St George family. She concluded with: 'if we dare to write up that subject!' It was Edith who wrote *The Big House at Inver* after Martin's death.

These letters cover a period during which the Anglo-Irish Ascendancy received two mortal blows: the obvious one being failure of rents, leading to sale of land or the compulsory purchase order, and the other the redundancy of the mounted gentleman. The iron and machinery of the Industrial Revolution slowly closes around the horse-drawn world of the old gentry from the first mention of barbed wire maiming hunters in the letters of the late 1880s to the annihilation of cavalry by the weaponry of the First World War. The type of Anglo-Irish gentleman thus squeezed out of existence was the hunting, shooting and fishing military or naval man – the type of man most familiar to Edith and Martin.

This class of passionate riders had the natural ascendancy of the mounted over the pedestrian, and was traditionally used not only in military engagements, but to control the lower orders. Cavalry was used to control riots in Ireland as well as in England. Charles Kingsley in his *Alton Locke* recalls the Peterloo massacre when he describes his hero at a Chartist rally that turns bad:

> I just recollect the tramp of the yeomanry horses, and the gleam and jingle of their arms, as they galloped into the yard. I caught a glimpse of the tall young officer, as his great grey horse swept through the air over the yard-high pales – a feat to me utterly astonishing. Half-a-dozen long strides – the wretched ruffian, staggering across the field with his booty, was caught up. The clear blade gleamed in the air . . .

Astonishing feats of horsemanship continued to fascinate all classes in Ireland, and country people and townees flocked to watch the West Carbery Hunt in action. Edith acknowledges coolly that the desire to see a rider break his or her neck drew them more than any love of the chase. Irish regiments had, and still have, a very particular swagger, and their riders a particular daring and grace. The renown of Irish horsemen and the 'severity' of Irish hunting country spread far beyond the bounds of the Empire. In *Anna Karenina* the most terrible obstacle in the regimental steeplechase that Vronsky enters, and in which he kills his mare by shifting his weight on her back when she is at full stretch, is the Irish bank.

In Anglo-Irish circles cavalry officers were very open-minded in their admiration for, and emulation of, excellent lady riders. Captain Bidgood, who came from a Sligo family and trained cavalrymen, used to round off training by sending a man cross-country 'after' Miss Gore-Booth (later Countess Markievicz). Both she and Edith rode with an exceptionally long leather to the left stirrup. Hildegarde, Edith's sister, rode with this leather three holes higher than Edith, although she was a taller woman. The long leather enabled daring women riders to make the best use of balance and quick shifting of weight in the many sudden extremities of full-stretch cross-country riding in Ireland.

Many of the letters contain descriptions of runs, later used in their books. Martin wrote lyrically of the chase as well as Edith – this was a lifelong delight and fascination to them both. The length and quality of the chase was their object, not the kill. Living in a society where the more remote peasantry behaved with barbarity to animals, and sometimes to humans, Edith and Martin were satisfied that the kill – what they called 'the chop' was quite scientific and instantaneous. The leading hound, coming up to the fox, broke its neck in a snap of the jaws as it overran the fox. When the hounds ate a fox, it was already dead. When we read the phrase 'he was chopped' in one of these letters the writer means to convey a quick kill.

Numbers of episodes from these letters reappear in the RM stories hardly disguised. Critics who have been uncertain how to classify these stories – patronizing satire? hack Irish ham? – should take into account the type of society at Castletownshend and Ross where vivid speech, the successful telling of tall stories and the carrying-out of elaborate practical jokes enlivened the calm of country life for both sides of the green baize door.

The letters survive more on Martin's side than Edith's. There were two house fires at Ross after Martin's death, and some of Edith's letters may have been lost then. When they are fragmentary they often have their outer sheet missing, probably because some scandalous piece of information had to be destroyed. Because of their humour and liveliness, letters between Edith and Martin were often read aloud at meal-times by popular demand. Only selected parts were read, as Edith and Martin exchanged so much gossip that a great deal had to be censored. Warning signals – to prevent the reader from blundering – consisted of initial words written backwards to slow the reader down, or a phrase in Irish, or simply DO NOT READ ALOUD.

The order of the undated letters is uncertain, as Edith cannibalized the letters extensively after Martin's death, working them into the memoirs particularly. Another large group of undated fragments, kept separate by Sir Patrick Coghill in an alphabetical sequence, has been worked back into the dated letters by means of internal evidence. This reordering helped the letters to reveal the remarkable writing technique of Somerville and Ross whereby they altered drafts after their circulation throughout the family; we see this notably in the case of their first novel *An Irish Cousin*, and two of the early letters from Edith Somerville, previously forlorn in the waste-dump of the alphabetical sequence, have been brought forward to shed light on their first intense session of novel-writing by post.

The letters were brought from Castletownshend after the death of Edith Somerville in 1949 to Sir Patrick Coghill's home in Gloucestershire, and eventually they were sold to the New York Public Library at the Sotheby's sale of Somerville and Ross material in 1968. However, the family kept Edith and Martin's review books and scrap-books and I have keyed in material from these wherever this helped to fix a chronology.

In this edition, reviews of their books, as they were issued, are included whenever possible, as their letters often refer to particular reviews. This also gives the sequence of creative divisions in their lives from the first postal exchanges through their response to their relatives' reactions to the first drafts to the submission of the complete manuscript to the publisher and the retreat on holiday for recuperation after publication day. The substantial letters, dashed off at visitorless times at the dead of night or at the crack of dawn, were called 'bed sheets' because of their inordinate length and were a form of conversation. We frequently find both women referring to their letters as 'talking': for example, Martin writes that she has come up to her room at Ross to write to Edith rather than keep company with deadly visitors, as she would prefer 'to talk to you'. In those days before telephone, radio or television, conversations and letters had a dramatic intensity now lost in a society where television has taken up the free spaces in people's lives, spaces that used to be given to the development of personality and individualism.

One of Edith's and Martin's favourite haunts for the garnering of dramatic flights of speech was the court-house in Skibbereen. The Bantry lawyer, Serjeant A.M. Sullivan, started life fairly humbly on the Munster circuit, and ended as a QC living in Derry House, the old home of the Payne-Townshends, a perfect model of the type of professional Irishman who rose to fill the places vacated by all those redundant Anglo-Irishmen. He opens his memoirs *The Last Serjeant* with a reference to Somerville and Ross and casts his eye back to the days when, as a testy young lawyer, he became aware of the two women: one untidy with straying hair and an engaging manner, the other thin, pale and remote behind pince-nez; and he must have wondered fleetingly what the blazes they were scribbling at. He found out:

The passing of the Kingdom of Ireland caused the disappearance of a great Irish institution. It was something between national pastime and national education. It was 'going to the courts', for in my young days the people went to court to listen to the conduct of the litigation as they now go to the pictures. Entertainment was far superior. The tragedies and comedies were real and the actors living, and there was unfolded day after day the true and intimate life of the people of Ireland.

Among the spectators of my early professional life in the gallery of the County Court of West Cork there used to sit two girls studying

the scene before them, from whose contemplation we have gratefully
received their delineation in the books of Somerville and Ross.

In the scenes that passed before them Somerville and Ross saw the
ousting of the Anglo-Irish Ascendancy by a new, wealthy Irish professional class. In the case of the Martins and Somervilles, as in a large
proportion of other London-orientated, cosmopolitan gentry families in
Ireland, 'Anglo' is misleading. Although the Martins and Somervilles
came from two very different strains of landlord, both were Norman
families who had spent barely a generation in England before settling
respectively in County Galway and the Lowlands of Scotland. The
Somervilles moved to Cork in the late seventeenth century to escape
religious persecution in Galloway. Both families considered themselves
'Irish', and served Ireland with that important intermediary group of
Irish gentry who tried to improve the condition of Ireland and her
relationship with England. Charles Kendal Bushe and Lord Plunket, both
ancestors of Edith and Martin, were prominent in this group; they led
the movement for Catholic emancipation after the death of Grattan, and
Bushe's voice was the most eloquent to plead the case against the Union
with England.

In the year that Edith and Martin met, Gladstone's Home Rule Bill
was defeated on its second reading by thirty votes; Gladstone resigned
to be succeeded by Lord Salisbury and his Conservative and Liberal
Unionist coalition. This great political event was greeted differently by
the Martins and the Somervilles. The Martins were paternalistic, old-
style Unionists. Martin's brother Robert was a boycotted man and a
close associate of Arthur Balfour, Chief Secretary for Ireland. He was
ultimately brought to financial ruin by the stalemate of non-paying
tenants and unleasable farms. Ross had been largely mortgaged during
the Famine – to tide the estate through the period when rents were
waived – and never recovered.

On the other hand the more liberal of the Somervilles were Constitutional Home-Rulers, supporting Isaac Butt – whose family is
mentioned in these letters. Edith Somerville backed Joseph Chamberlain's plans for devolution and national parliaments, an extreme stance
in her family, and was thus referred to as 'Mrs Chamberlain' in family
political rows and in the Buddh Dictionary. Edith's grandfather had
hidden two Fenians in Drishane after a riot in Skibbereen in the year of
her birth.

Edith and Martin consequently had very different political views. They
both felt the effectiveness of Land League tactics during the 1890s:

neighbours were shot (an attempt was made on Robert Martin's life), cattle and horses had their ears cropped, hayricks were burned, rents were not paid. Edith thought the outrages an understandable expression of anger at England's treatment of Ireland, but Martin only saw the misguided deeds of simple people who had fallen under the sway of superficial mob-orators. Perhaps because of their own contrasting natures, their portrait of Ireland is a valuably comprehensive account of a complex transitional period in Irish history. Their letters lay bare the predicament of their class and chronicle the last days of the great house in Ireland, as well as the happy course of a most unusual working collaboration between two gifted women.

The letters are printed here as they were written — with haphazard and quirky spelling and punctuation. Although Somerville and Ross took the utmost care with the proof-reading of their books these private letters are careless, and they were not re-read before being posted, so that the same information may be repeated unconsciously if there was an interval between sections of a letter. Martin Ross used a dash as a general-purpose mark when writing at speed. Irish placenames, rendered into English orthography, may be spelled in three different ways on the same sheet; at that time there was no standard anglicized spelling, and they did not fix on one themselves. The letters selected, less than half of what survives, have also been reproduced as fully as possible, so that acutely observed episodes and personalities crop up in their natural matrix of mundane queries on the whereabouts of relatives, mislaid laundry, pecuniary emergencies and books in the making.

GIFFORD LEWIS

Chronology

1858 Edith Somerville born on Corfu 2 May (father Colonel of the Buffs there).

1862 Violet Martin born at Ross 11 June.

1872 Martin's father dies and her brother Robert closes Ross. He lets it on a fifteen-year lease in the following year. Mrs Martin and Martin live in Dublin.

1884 Edith begins study abroad with Egerton Coghill in Düsseldorf.

1886 January, Edith and Martin meet at Castletownshend. In March Edith goes to Paris; returns in the summer.

1888 Mrs Martin and Martin return to Ross.

1889 *An Irish Cousin* published by Richard Bentley.

1890 *Lady's Pictorial* commission them to tour Connemara.

1891 *Naboth's Vineyard* published by Spencer Blackett. Tour of French vineyards for *In the Vine Country*.

1892 *Through Connemara in a Governess Cart* published by W. H. Allen.

1893 Tour of Wales in June and of Denmark in September. Visit to Herbert Greene in Oxford.

1894 *The Real Charlotte* published by Ward and Downey, followed by a recuperative stay in Paris. Edith back to studio life.

1895 Martin in St Andrews while Edith in Paris, then together to the Aran islands May–June. Electioneering for the Conservative and Unionist, Women's Franchise Association in East Anglia. *Beggars on Horseback* published by Wm. Blackwood. Edith's mother dies.

1897 *The Silver Fox* published by Lawrence and Bullen.

1898 Edith's father dies; they begin the RM stories at Étaples. Martin badly hurt in a fall while hunting with the West Carbery Hunt; ill health follows. The RM out serially in the *Badminton Magazine*.

1899 *Some Experiences of an Irish RM* published by Longman.

1902 *A Patrick's Day Hunt* published by Arch. Constable.

1903 Edith MFH of the West Carbery Hunt; *All on the Irish Shore* and *Slipper's ABC*.

1905 Death of Robert Martin.

1906 Death of Mrs Martin. Martin moves to Cork. *Some Irish Yesterdays* published by Longmans.

1908 *Further Experiences of an Irish RM.*

1911 *Dan Russel the Fox* published by Longmans.

1912 Edith revives the West Carbery Hunt (previous pack destroyed because of rabies); she was MFH 1912 to 1919.

1913 Edith President and Martin Vice-President of the Munster Women's Franchise League.

1915 *In Mr Knox's Country* published by Longmans. Summer in Kerry. Martin suddenly taken ill and rushed to hospital. Dies of brain tumour in Cork, 21 December.

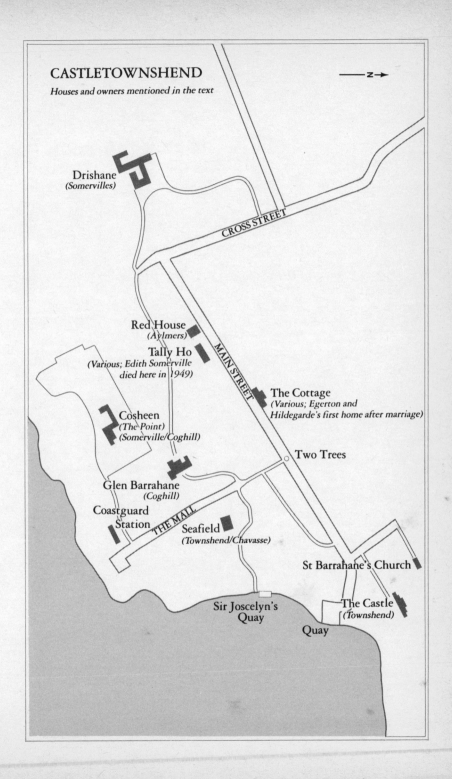

CASTLETOWNSHEND

Houses and owners mentioned in the text

Drishane
(Somervilles)

CROSS STREET

Red House
(Aylmers)

Tally Ho
(Various; Edith Somerville
died here in 1949)

MAIN STREET

The Cottage
(Various; Egerton and
Hildegarde's first home after marriage)

Cosheen
(The Point)
(Somerville/Coghill)

Two Trees

Glen Barrahane
(Coghill)

Coastguard
Station

THE MALL

Seafield
(Townshend/Chavasse)

St Barrahane's Church

Sir Joscelyn's
Quay

The Castle
(Townshend)

Quay

THE LETTERS

Violet Martin of Ross came to Castletownshend in January 1886. She was twenty-four and not yet a strongly formed character. Although she could be an amusing and endearing companion to a chosen few she was also shy, reserved, supercilious and undemonstrative. At Ross she had been left to her own devices by an absent-minded Mama, and in Dublin while she attended Alexandra College she had not shone in society but observed it coolly from a distance.

Castletownshend and its people enchanted her, particularly her cousins Edith and Hildegarde Somerville, and it was partnership with Edith Somerville that was to form the literary personage of 'Martin Ross' – the pen-name that Violet chose for herself. When we meet Martin in these first letters to Edith she is tentative, feeling her way, aiming at something that may elude her grasp. Edith did not trouble to answer any of Martin's first letters to her when she was away in Paris in the spring of 1886, and Martin may well have felt that it was foolish to expect any sort of special relationship with this 'popular person'. But Edith did eventually see special talents in Martin, and as their literary partnership blossomed so did Martin Ross. The tentative girl became 'a genius' as perceived by Nevill Coghill, when he recalled her for a BBC talk in 1948:

When I was a boy I knew Martin Ross as well as any little boy can know a grown-up who is also a genius and a woman. Her real name was Violet Martin, but we all called her 'Martin'. She came of the great family of the Martins of Ross, one of whom, Richard Martin, is known to posterity as 'Humanity Dick' for his work in the prevention of cruelty to animals. Martin had all his humanity and more. She was slender and graceful and intrepid; a lovely rider to hounds, in spite of her short sight – very dangerous to riders in our rough country. She was as kind as she was courageous; the delicate serenity of her manner was the first thing one noticed; yet it would dissolve in an instant into unquenchable laughter, for she had a shattering sense of humour and the gift of sudden wit. Vividness of perception, trenchant

*intelligence and easy grace were the qualities of her life as of her style.
As she lived, she wrote, with unerring felicity of phrase and impulse.
Courage, candour and affection blazed from her.*

Tally Ho
Sunday – March 28 1886

My dear Edith –
Your sister Hildegarde and your brother Aylmer are people of rare
worth. Only for their combined efforts I should have no occasion to
write to you – as it is I have much pleasure in telling you of yesterday's
sport – viewed from the back of your dear Sorcerer. To my astonishment
your parents offered him to me for Friday – I was quite taken aback
by such kindness to which the only drawback was poor Hildegarde's
disappointment at not being allowed to ride him – It was too bad – and
she took it to heart most awfully – even to tears. So you may imagine
my feelings were not all unmixed joy – Friday was perhaps the most
hearty and business like wet day of the large selection that have been
lately offered to us, and after getting up at 7 and going up to Drishane
equipped, the idea of hunting had to be abandoned – On that afternoon
your father and mother went up to Cork, in company with Harry – and
with Harry's horses to Skib, of which more anon –
     Next morning when a little more than out of my bath I heard Aylmer's
jovial tones summonning a parley – and found that he had ridden over
from Lissard to bring me to the hunt at Glen Curragh there being a by
day – It was a noble act – and hearing from him that he and Hilda had
arranged all about sending to Skib for the Corkites, we started in nice
weather – Arrived at Glen Curragh we were received by Mr. d'Avigdor
in carpet slippers, of emerald green, and pale blue stockings – and in
profoundest dignity. I must tell you that before I left Mama had heard
from him about some tea of his – and at the end of the letter came the
awful words "I hope to come over and see you some afternoon, and
will choose a fine afternoon so that Miss Martin may be able to take a
walk as she did last Sunday when I called" – Aylmer and I went in and
had some breakfast (an improper proceeding, which I have not revealed)
and there was a touching scene of explanation and magnanimous
forgiveness – We finally started for Bunalun (the spelling will be phonetic
throughout) with Willie Becher on the chestnut and the old kennel
huntsman on the little horse. We picked up Mr. Maxwell, Dr. Jennings,
the agile and sprightly, and J-a-a-a-ck. I was so sorry the Becher's girls
weren't out – I believe they couldn't manage a mount – We turned to

the left at Bunalun gate and drew a cover up a hill to the right of the road, the hounds working much better without Mr. Beamish. It was about this juncture that we had our first lep – a nasty awkward wall – and the unhappy agile all but gave his horse a lead over it – only for a convulsive clutch of the back of the saddle he certainly would have preceded him into the next field – This was my first experience of what Sorcerer could do – He is a delightful horse – an education for a young rider, and he has the manners of the best society, and in his most excited moments is a gentleman – I can't say enough for him and his fencing. He is so gallant and so judicious – and so perfectly comfortable to sit on. Two covers were drawn blank, and about this time two things were borne in upon me in an unpleasant way. One was that it was raining about as hard as it could, and another was how much I missed your company and protection – One does miss a comrade very much on such occasions – Another gorse was drawn blank in simple torrents and we all got soaked – I could feel drops coursing down my spine and congregating just where I sat down. At Mr. d'Avigdor's suggestion we then turned our streaming faces towards Bunalun house, and had a good deal of lepping on the way – At each jump my hat fell off, being in a state of pulp, and I broke the string of my eyeglasses in putting it on, and all but lost my veil and in this happy state rode into Bunalun yard and was greeted by Captain Morgan and next by Ethel – *She* swept me up to her mother's room without more ado while "the gentlemen" as she called them huddled into the schoolroom – I then stripped myself and was dried with the Morgan bath towel, damp from someone's ablutions! was combed with the Morgan comb and curled with the Morgan tongs – and finally was clothed in Mina's best body[1] over my habit skirt – Ethel's good nature was extraordinary – I never saw the like, but still I don't like to think of that towel or of what my back view must have been in that body without an improver They gave us excellent food which we ravenously devoured – I may add that the Agile was too shy to come in and hovered in the out houses – It would have made you very ill to see Mr. d'Avigdor on his native heath as it were – adored by the whole party and very patronising to them – I somehow like the Morgans, they are passing kind, though they *do* call Skibbereen "town". It got quite fine at 2 and we put on our own things again and went forth to draw Hollybrook – The cover about the house was blank, and we made for a gorse on a hill opposite the gate accompanied by the entire Morgan family – on foot – At this point a very pretty little incident

1 *Body*: a bodice, blousoned top.

took place – I saw Mr. d'Avigdor in the midst of the Morgan throng from which he emerged wearing Ethel's red Tam o'Shanter while on her head was coquettishly placed his huntsman's cap and they both remained so for the rest of the day – My dear if you had been there, we should have forever disgraced ourselves – As it was Aylmer and I laughed loud and long – The hounds at last got onto a hare in that gorse and we hunted her for an hour and a quarter round the hill – 3 times did we fly in at Hollybrook gate, past the house and through the shrubberies, checked at about the same places, and galloped the same fields till it became ridiculous – Twice I believe the hare was within a yard of the leading hound and escaped – and she was finally lost after showing us capital fun – Everyone went well including Aylmer and the mare and Sorcerer took me over at least 3 very big places and about a thousand of sorts – and never made a mistake – We all hunted the hounds, notably Willie Becher – who was most invaluble – for a blissful 5 minutes he and I had the whole thing to ourselves all through Hollybrook – gallop-ping our best a few yards behind the hounds – till a check came and then the red Tam o'Shanter hove in sight – The hare finally got into the gorse she started from, and there she stuck – it being then about 4.30 – We left off and made for Skib and home – once more in torrents of rain – It was a very amusing day all through and not a trying one for the horses I am glad to say – as there were no long severe gallops – Everyone said that run you missed on Friday week was a splendid one – it is a grievous pity you were'nt in it – of course you have heard of the dismal and feeble attempts at capturing a buck here – They are going to try and snare one tomorrow but I suppose they will fail – but if they suceed he will be hunted from Lissard on Friday next – I must tell you that when Harry came home yesterday evening and found that *his* precious horses had been sent to meet him and your father in Skib, he got quite beside himself and was awfully rude to Hilda about having changed the arrangement made that Sorcerer and Connaught were to go in – Hilda is boiling with fury – and justly so – I think Harry is ashamed of himself today but he is a strange and difficult being.

Your letters are largely read in Castle Townshend with varying com-ments – They are received with enthusiasm by all – I am afraid you had not a good passage yesterday – There was a lot of wind here – You are bound to have a good time in London I think – Paris I resent so say nothing about it – I have a feeling that you will meet Seymour[1] – how

1 *Seymour Bushe*: their cousin, a celebrated figure at the Irish Bar, and the 'Saymore Bosh' of Joyce's *Ulysses*.

interesting if you do – In the intervals between downpours we all walk
hastily out to Sandycove headed by Egerton, such is our pastime – that
and the fly pole[1] – I have written much more than I intended but you
brought it on yourself –

Yours afftly

V. Martin

*This is the second letter that Martin wrote to Edith. It has an offended
tone, as Edith had not responded in any way to her first letter of a
month before, written almost the moment that Edith had left for Paris.
Martin put herself forward to be noticed by Edith but it is very unlikely
that a close relationship would have emerged had Martin not been so
persistent. Edith had so many engaging relatives in Castletownshend
and surroundings that one more cousin on a brief visit from distant
Galway could hardly press any special claims.*

*This letter is of particular interest in that it mentions the house sale
at The Point after the death of Emily Herbert, who was to be the model
for* The Real Charlotte *when Edith and Martin first plotted the novel in
November 1889. Martin did meet Emily Herbert, once, in this year of
her death. Diary entry for 1 May: 'Went to see Emily Herbert at the
Point with Mama.'*

*Her meeting with Martin, at the end of January 1886, only became
significant to Edith when she wrote it up many years later for her
memoirs. As we see from the first letters on Martin's side, in which she
is evidently straining to get Edith's attention, Edith was far too busy to
respond personally to Martin. In their accounts, made up at the back
of their diaries which are now all at Queen's University, Belfast, the
expenditure of farthings is noted by both of them. Edith herself had to
earn the money that paid for her tuition in Paris, and she would not
allow writing unnecessary letters to take up any of her valuable, hard-
won time. Her only letters went to her mother, and Adelaide Somerville
read these aloud at meal-times to spread the news of Edith to her
relations. Martin heard these letters and felt left out of things.*

1   *Fly pole*: a construction, something like a maypole, made by Egerton Coghill in the
grounds of Glen Barrahane, from which the agile could swing out and round on
ropes, high off the ground.

Mall House – Castle T
May 19. '86

My dear Edith

You know and you should blush to know that there is no reason in the world why I should write to you – but there are people to whom it interests one to write irrespective of their bad qualities and behaviour – As I have heard each of your letters declaimed I have felt that I should like to make merry with you over many things therein – but have been daunted by the thought of your many correspondents – You have one fatal fault – you are a "popular girl" – a sort that I have always abhorred – so bear in mind that theoretically you are in the highest degree offensive to me. So you see that we are in our new house – I had a high old time over settling it while Mama was staying in Cork – and still have any amount to do – I have come to the conclusion that having to banish kamaks*[1] is better than the absolute dearth of them – The room here is so very unfurnished that I feel a fool when I sit down to read in it – It seems only a place to walk about in – However respice ad finem – if you were not such a popular girl I could say very nice things to you about your coming home – Seriously I shall be delighted to see you back again and so will everyone else – It is possible that I may meet you in London as I have an idea of going over to Kew about then for a fortnight – I have today had an invitation to Chatham there being a large ball on the 4th there with other delights – and I am tempted but somehow the Castle Townshend inertness has me in its grasp – It is so dreadful to think of getting clothes made – I am going up to Drishane this afternoon you will be surprised to hear, and will have a look at the Japanese garments before I send this off – so as to give you my valuable opinion but I am sure the blue is the one for you and the yellow for Hildegarde – I wish you could have seen Hildegarde in her Japanese clothes at Harry's "bal masque" – she looked quite delicious – intensely Japanese – and yet handsome – If you can imagine the two things – Hers was a genuine good fancy dress – with the exception of Egerton the others were rather impromptu charady "Indeed we were all saying it was a great pity your honour was not there – for the liking you had to Driscoll"[2] I daresay they told you that I went in a sheet draped à la greek statue – it looked thoroughly indecent, without being really so

---

1 Asterisked words defined in Glossary, pp. 297–302.
2 An anecdote used twelve years later, when it was put into the mouth of Slipper in *Lisheen Races, Second Hand*.

and was heaven in the way of comfort – I am sure if we all dressed like that we would be more ladylike and more agreeable – that dance was most pleasant and your mother has, I am confident, ideas of another at Drishane when you come back – I was grieved to hear that you had been sick and I daresay the sooner you leave Paris the better for you – You are an unhealthy though not a gross feeder (bar pancakes) and you ought to be looked after – What a good time you will have in London – and probably a good one at Walmer – Our Edith knows the latter place well – I see plainly that the Commander loves you with a reckless ardour – deny it if you can. I believe however he can be a very good friend to his friends.

You have lost almost the prettiest time here – it does look delicious now – and I am deeply enamoured of the place – I came back to it last week with ecstacy after a 2 days stay in Cork – I actually went there for the Races – and had a dissipated time. Some friends of mine were staying with Captain Plunkett, and he was noble enough to invite me – I was given my ticket for the stand and won some monies besides, so that I came back richer than I went – Aylmer came up with me but went back next day disgusted – He could not squander his money going into the enclosure and of course had a bad time outside – The brutal soldiery gave us tea each day and luncheon – and we dined each night at the Country Club – Great dissipations but as I said I returned with the greatest pleasure to the fly pole, the glass room and the business like waste of time – Hilda and Violet play with me very nicely – I am beginning to think they are the nicest and best people I have ever seen – I am glad I am not a Buddh* so that I can freely praise the Buddhs – yesterday the Cobbs swept us in to tennis to meet the Piffs – It rained hard all the time – but as everyone else said it was only a fog I made no comment – I had never seen the Piffs before – They are terrible – dreadful little dwindled dressmakers – at least to look at – they may have all the virtues, but their appearance is against them – and their conversation is emetical – It was refreshing to look at our nice Hildegarde in her white frock – She and Aylmer and Violet had a ride yesterday morning and were late for all meals whereupon Egerton suddenly rose up and slew them with a great slaughter. No one can account for his fury, but it led to him sitting all day at Drishane reading Punch, and refusing to be comforted or to go to the Cobbs or anything – He is a strange person. Harry has been in here while I am writing – neither staying or going away, but just hindering – Whenever I had pulled myself together to say that I *must* finish my letter, he seeing it was coming put in huge flatteries, to which one must make suitable objections leading to lengthy discussions. Altogether he has put off my stroke about writing – Mr. Cobb said a beautiful thing to Violet and me the other day – namely that at the Point Auction no one dared to enter Miss Herbert's room as there were 16 cats confined there – Seeing he meant no harm we all bellowed long and hard – I daresay on thinking it over he took in what he had said, for yesterday he brought me out a cutting from a newspaper, with a decidedly backhair* colonial story therein – I hope my want of appreciation will deter him from wasting any more good stories on me – I am obliged to confess that he really looked handsome at Harry's dance, in his uniform – This sentence looks as if Harry had tripped it inside his own clothes – I am now going to leave all remaining space for comments on the Japanese garments.[1]

I have just seen them and think the blue lovely and just your colour – With something else it will make a beauteous tea gown – but will require anxious thought and a good deal of twine coloured lace –

Yours ever
Violet Martin

Shelbourne House
Ball's Bridge
Dublin
December 14. 1886

[P.S.] I have not sent love to anyone – I hate doing it – I think it's absurd – This is a heavy sort of letter, but I feel rather seedy

My dear Edith
Strange to say I have arrived at the above address – who would have thought it – You will be interested to hear that I had a rather odious and dismal journey – particularly up to Cork, till when I was I may say in a stoon* of cold feet (see definition). There was only just time to hifle* across to the Dublin train owing to some feebleness on the part of the Skib engine – I looked out at Mallow and the Junction for Aunt A – and can only conclude that she and your brothers were released like carrier pigeons and flew to their home – No train passed mine till about Maryborough – I was very drunk but I think I can swear to that – Tell Hildegarde that at every fresh sandwich I rose up and called her blessed – They were delicious and I should suggest some as an entree when you next feed the Broughams – I am pining to know what your mother

---

1 Sent by Boyle to his sisters.

thought of Jane and Ellen and whether the former confided any secrets to her relative to wine and vegetables – I had two awful women in the Dublin train – I am happy to say they both had friends to see them off – and I heard some highly entertaining conversation. "Well for you – going to Kingstown – and you'll have the agent up there" – Bashful titters – "Oh well I'll be looking out for news of *you* too when someone comes." "Oh indeed, much about him" and so on – while the pale distinguished lady in the red hat and grey cloak with fur was apparently sunk in graceful slumber – I felt very seedy in the afternoon – shivery and marookish* – and when the train pelted through Kildare station (where I was to have met Mama) without stopping, I resigned myself to the situation with almost relief – When I got to Kingsbridge I stowed my things, had a cup of tea, and waited for the 6.20 – On the arrival of which Mama was nowhere to be seen – After long search I discovered her strolling down the platform with a pair of enormous spectacles on, and having in attendance upon her a guard and two porters, with whom she was holding airy converse, most probably about "my son's pantomime." I may add that there was a long and most favourable notice of that in yesterday's Irish Times – We found the lodgings awfully comfortably prepared and in every way nice – They have some peculiarities worthy of note – A piano – not at all bad – in the general sitting room – where no one ever sits – A man with a cough like Johnnie Bushe – appallingly like – A cat very like the Manxer – A landlady the image of Frances – and the most extraordinary plethora of furniture – I sleep in Mama's room where there are two excellent beds – and have a dressing room – a most weird place – only lighted by a window looked onto the stairs – It was most clearly intended by Providence for a tweesortir* but only fulfilled its destiny to the extent of having a long bath in it – which frightens me awfully to get into – it is so dark and unfathomable. The other furniture is remarkable & comprises amongst other things 2 large looking glasses, 2 ditto bullock trunks – 1 ditto chest of drawers (every draw locked), 2 ditto ladders – 4 jugs and basons – and something which appears to be the furled dropscene of a large theatre – Miss Myers' lodgers have apparently never any clothes except those on their backs – but I have just created a disturbance and think I shall get something to stow my clothes in – I must tell that Mama is perfectly *delighted* with your pictures – your alterations in the one of me satisfy even her – she is really awfully pleased with it – and particularly likes what she calls "that look of thought" – This morning while dressing I heard Miss Myers say – "I see a picture of Miss Martin there ma'm – Very nice indeed ma'm – I suppose she did it herself" To which proudly my mother "Yes Miss Myers, I think it *is* very good. It was done by Miss Coghill a cousin of mine – " Beatrice has awakened to find herself famous –

It is an awful day of thick rain, but I am just going down to lunch at Mitchell's having had a letter from Violet to say that Ethel was coming up for the day and that they would both lunch there – I shall be awfully glad to see them both again – Violet seems rather sick of things in general I think – but more anon when I have seen her – I forgot to say that Mama was also much enamoured of the landscapes – of course in a worthless and uncritical way but still she represents fairly the B.P.* I cannot say how pleased I was at her liking the portrait – Robert is not staying here, but at Aunt MaryAnne's – I suppose we shall see him today – Let me before I forget it tell you what a woman said to Mama at Gouran – in talking of another woman having lost her husband – "Oh indeed ma'am – there she is – the crayture – and he having left her with one child and the invoice of another" – *Is* this very improper – I feel that it is, but am not sure – I have heard from Rose – rather relieved on the whole that I won't go to Lea – you are a person of sound judgement. I gave many a sympathetic thought to your swelled face yesterday I do hope it has not given you any further puckings – I dont know when I have been more depressed than at leaving Castle T – and more especially Drishane – and more especially you – "but no matter" I think of moos and mashed potatoes – and the monkey's trick as to vermin and feel nothing but relief at escaping from such an atmosphere – I cannot tell you how sorry I am to have missed the Dublin contingent – I wanted to complain to your mother of my ill-treatment while at Drishane – I can't help making dreary jokes – I don't know how to say what I should like and what I feel about the way you all united to spoil the Doll – It would take a Doll of superior mechanism to mine to say it all – I hope Hildegarde was not dead beat by her hard day – and hope you didn't get up and that your breakfast was not quite cold – Mama sends her best love – and deep sense of the moral and physical improvement in me – Red Cardinal very interesting –

Martin

In comparison with Martin's social life, Edith's was multitudinously crammed. Her first surviving letter to Martin describes a ball given by the Maxwell family, and reveals Edith's intense interest in pronunciation as an indicator of class. They were to use this to profound effect in their novels.

Now we meet the family of Dr Jim Somerville, Edith's uncle. He was the local doctor, living in Union Hall at Park Cottage. The accent of the women in the family was refined Anglo-Irish, i.e. the accent that renders Park Cottage as Pork Cottage. Hence the shorthand form for this family, 'The Porks'. They also said 'imawrl' and 'Paw-ris' (the two being connected in their minds). Each family had a voice and accent of its own and Drishane Somerville women, although having rich voices with a great range of expression, avoided the 'aw' sound in that tempting word 'God'. Canon Claude Chavasse wrote down Anglo-Irish pronunciations as he remembered them from before the First World War:

'Girl' we never pronounced gurl it was always more like gay-earl. My mother and her sisters were addressed by their parents as gai-erlies. I remember the shock I felt when as a little boy I first heard Lady Coghill (Hildegarde) pronounce GOD as God and not as Gawd. The late Archbishop Gregg always to the end of his life said 'Gawd'.
(Letter from Canon Chavasse to Gifford Lewis, 9 May 1980.)

In the early 1960s Nevill Coghill's sister Katharine thought that it would be a good thing if her older relatives, who had known Edith Somerville in the nineteenth century, wrote down what they could remember of her. Isabella Somerville recalled:

The first time I went to Drishane was to pay an afternoon call with my Mother and Uncle Tom. I was nine years old at the time [1883] . . . Uncle Tom's phaeton held three. He drove, with my Mother beside him, and I sat with my back to the white horse . . . We left the carriage at the ferry and embarked in the Ferry boat. The holes in the bottom were stuffed with sods to keep the water out, but we thought nothing of this and were soon reaching the end of our sea crossing which was the Castletownshend pier and climbing the hill which forms the village street . . . Soon we were turning in at the gates of Drishane . . . we were entertained by E. Œ. S. How well I remember her standing by the fireplace as were leaving, a tall, straight figure, blue eyes that missed nothing and an emphatic manner that drew my childish attention at once . . .

When Nevill Coghill described his aunt in a BBC talk in 1948 she was still alive. Her manner was still as Isabella described it in 1883: 'Energy, fearlessness and decisiveness characterize whatever she does. You never know what she will say next, but you know it will be emphatic and not *what anyone else would have said; but sharply to the point, and built on opinions firmer than rocks.'*

Drishane
December 29th 86

Though I am a poor wake creature, I am a purfeck lady, and as I said I would try and tell you of the humours of the Maxwell dance, I will keep my word – merely premising that though we left the house of revelry at 2.30 – I was not in bed till past five. So am not over-vigorous in mind and body.

All through the long and bitter day Egerton and I had tried to devise a means of escape, and Hildegarde had abetted us with more or less sincerity. Aylmer had the courage of his opinions, and calmly announced that hail, rain, or snow he and Tom and Vesta would go in the trap. But mother acted a most unworthy part. While assuming the idiot baby's expression of loathing disgust whenever the show was mentioned, she, in reality was as keen to go as Grace Pork or Aylmer. She deftly combatted or ignored all our most ingenious suggestions, and the end of it was that 8.30 o'clock found her, Hildegarde, Egerton and me in the Glen B carriage ploughing our way over the worst possible roads to the dreadful entertainment. As I am nothing if not minute I will give the fullest details. Egerton wore a standup collar [small drawing] of this type, (besides other things) – Mother her black velvet – Hildegarde a black lace skirt with a high hideously-made-by-Driscoll black lace body – on the skirt a yellow Jap petticoat had been draped by the invaluable Anne, who came over and spent the day in decorating us. I had a black net dress, which you *may* remember having seen before, and about my knees and lower person another and green Jap coit* was cast! Aylmer wore his new and dazzling false teeth. The Maxwell avenue was a dream of Arabian Nights' beauty being hung with Chinese lamps. At the door, the Lord of the mansion, Mr. Swanton met us – or rather he darted in and out like the needle of a sewing machine, receding as we advanced and finally – finding that mother took no sort of notice of him he went and hid behind a screen and I saw him hurriedly drinking a cup of strong and excellent coffee to steady his nerve. Big Di Hungerford – who for one awful moment I thought was a strayed away man, had cut her hair very short in the front, parted it at the side, and sleeked it down on her huge red-ridged forehead, while the insignificant remainder was knotted into a tightest doggy behind. With her flangeing* nose and gleaming tusks she was a nightmare. But if you could only have seen

Mrs. Ja-ack De Burgh – my senses slip from me and reel into idiocy as I think of her costume. It was, as Francie observed of Hildegarde's shriek "unearrthly – scarcely human" – You could hardly believe you were looking at a real woman. I will try and draw her back, but know that I am utterly inadequate to the task [drawing] – she is whirling in the polka, the partner is left to the imagination. She was more like some amazing table, or towel horse that had been galvanised into life. I don't know what her awesome garment was made of but it looked exactly like an altar cloth, and the general ecclesiastical effect was enhanced by deep crimson silk gloves.

Old Di was in crisp black satin – on one side of her body was a sort of raw beef steak looking splodge of ribbon – on the other an immense silver lizard was displayed, rampant, and silver jewels of great weight and magnitude jangled all over her person. (I must just try and do Mrs. De Burgh's front, but it is impossible to do it justice). [drawing] Just as we were preparing to go downstairs a perfect ocean of pink-clad Piffs boiled into the room. To Aylmer's joy, K.M. was there in a rather dirty pink frock, but looking very pretty. The dancing room was very well arranged – an *excellent* floor, and the Chips* all sat in an inner room and watched the giddy scene through an immense open double door way. The music was a nice solid little professional pianiste from Cork, who played exceedingly well and didn't doldromise* between the dances for hours, as all amateurs do. Harry had gone via the ferry and then in an inside car with Grace Pork and was there when we arrived. He was perfectly black with fury and came up to me saying "The whole thing is a mistake – I'm going home". When I asked why, he said that Swanton – who was making feverish efforts to show he wasn't hired to attend for the night – had come to him and said whenever he wasn't dancing he – S. – would be very glad to go upstairs and smoke with him!

Poor Harry – he presently trod a measure with Grace that soothed him; and he was not reduced to the necessity of huggermuggering with Mr. Swanton as he danced like mad all the time. There were a good number of people there. The women being those whom you wot of – less the Bechers and the Girlies – but the men were mostly strangers. On the whole a much better lot than the D'Avigdor eggs.* Mr. Maxwell did the honours very well and nicely, and so did she, on the whole, though she was much occupied with a small bald barrister from Dublin called Manders. He looked a good dancer, but I was not introduced to him (nor indeed was anyone else: he was a patent.) Mrs. Maxwell brought up one of the most odious looking bounders you ever saw and introduced him as "My brother". Strange to say – not being well up in

the peerage – I didn't know his name. He said he had nothing before
18 – (we had come rather late) or extras – I promptly said 18, and
asked him what his name was "Mun" – "What?" "M.U.N.N. very few
people catch it" he said – exactly as if it was the measles or some similar
contagious disorder. Then he retired, and we held no further converse
– as I need hardly say we had left before 18 came on. Your own dear
Ja-ack De Burgh was of course there – and failing you he settled upon
me. He was covered with a most strange scent, like crêmes fondants,
which was not nice, but one has a lovely feeling of personal security
while he is conveying you round – which atones for much. He has
developed a new and extraordinary trick in connection with his stutter.
When he cant get hold of a word he scrabbles his fingers up and down
his nose. They canter from his forehead to the end of his nose, as one
makes a spider to alarm children – and sometimes in moments of great
difficulty take a little mad gallop round his eye. No words can express
my anguish of suppressed laughter, while he was trying to tell me that
he knew "La-adies didn't care to dance with maw-aw-aw-ried men"
while his fingers caracoled over his entire face in the agony.

Richard Townshend was the only Myross Wood there and was as
feeble and simpering as usual – Egerton and I were delighted to find on
going upstairs after dance, the most elaborate cooling arrangements. The
jungle was an arid plain compared to them. There was a very wide
landing and one end was mysteriously draped with a large red flag with
a crescent and star, which made the place look exactly like the hot room
of a Turkish bath. I need not say that no druids temple ever had half
the amount of mistletoe that bedecked the place generally, but I believe
– for I did not explore the Turkish bath – that there was more in there
than in all the rest of the house put together – Egerton really made my
blood run cold by describing all he heard, and partially saw in connection
with this considerate institution. Aylmer is very reticent, on the subject,
and wont be drawn; it gave a very degraded tone to the whole camac.*
The Morgans were all there, and mother and Mrs. Morgan discoursed
one another the whole night, imparting much mutual information. In
fact when we were coming away, and turned the corner of the Avenue
to go home mother vowed we were going the wrong way, and it was
only after elaborate explanations that it transpired she thought we were
at Bunalun all the time as she had talked so much to Mrs. Morgan.
Mrs. Maxwell introduced me to a rather nice boy, a sub Inspector in
the R.I.C., who had come from Skull for this dance! His name was
Irwin, and he was a nice simple young creature and a foully bad dancer.
He clasped his partner tightly to his breast and then stooped over so

much that he pressed a burning and moist ear closely to her forehead. I could feel the mark of it during our infrequent pauses. He felt a solemn responsibility on him to dance as much as possible, and fled round and round the room with heavy breathings, gasping "thankyou" at the conclusion of each course. If Hildegarde tells you that she and Egerton saw me proposing to him you need not believe her. They sat out a few dances in order to invent the story – which really is not true, or even amusing. Hildegarde began her career by a Liebarcation* with the Gordon – (vice the Seal). After two dances, running, with her, he asked me for a dance. I coldly assented but really he danced so well that my heart warmed to him, and when afterwards he asked me if I knew Lewis Morris's poetry "Epic of Hades" etc I almost loved him. We thereupon sat out two dances, and I discovered most interesting things about his love of books, and poetry, and the musical glasses[1] generally. He has read a great deal, in the most curious simple kind of way and knows a great deal more than he thinks – I then proceeded to dance two dances on end with him, and finally went into supper, by which time I had promised to lend him some of Howell's novels – Once I was very near making a great mistake. He asked if I had seen a critique upon the revival of an opera. I asked who it was by – he said "he didn't quite know, but he thought the composer's name was Ross-in-I" "*Who*" I said – "Ross-in-I" then I knew, *Rossini!* It sounded like a service – Farrant in D. But I never said a word. There was an excellent supper, and opposite me a huge pie like a Noah's ark with every sort of animal inside it. Hildegarde and I found ourselves at the head of the table, and I may say with modest pride, that we gorged – at least she did – and I did fairly well. Aylmer took in Nina and they remained at supper for an hour and a half, and I believe, mowed like mowing machines from one end of the table to the other, leaving the place bare behind them. We went just as the cotillon was beginning – I daresay it would have afforded much amusement to the observant – Aylmer said that one of the figures consisted in his and Skibbereen Gordon's going into the middle of the room, and tickling each others noses with feathers – the one who laughed first being the looser – Aylmer said he broke down almost at once with a yell, so the Gordon had the privilege of dancing with Mrs. Maxwell . . .

Although the last page of this letter is missing, a postscript survives

---

1 'Musical glasses' were a row of glasses filled to varying levels with water to produce a scale when struck lightly.

written across the head of the letter: 'I got very decent shoes in Skib. Thanks for the trouble you took about them. I hope yr face is better.'

Robert, Martin's eldest brother, was technically Master of Ross but the house and lands had been leased out after the death of his father James in 1872. He earned his living by writing popular songs, light articles and reviewing, and resided at 48 Leinster Square in Bayswater where Mrs Martin and her daughters frequently joined the household en route to anywhere but Ross. He was a diehard Unionist and a boycotted man, unable to think of any new way for Ireland. Martin wrote of him in a memoir:

> London with Robert in it was then, for Robert's family, a place with a different meaning – a place of theatre tickets, of luncheons, of newspaper news from within, of politics and actors reduced to human personalities . . . The hum of London seasons filled his brain . . . four hundred miles away lay Ross in the stillness of its summer woods, and the monotony of its winter winds, producing heavy bags of woodcock after its kind, while its master 'shot folly as she flew' and found his game in the canards of Fleet Street and Westminster. It was inevitable as things stood, but in that alienation both missed much that lay in the power of each to give.

[*From Martin to Edith, early 1887, fragment*]

. . . it – I am writing to her on the subject – Beatrice and Violet have given me Tennyson – a most lovely copy – a great deal too handsome for the likes of me – It was awfully good of them –

Last night the Ronnies[1] and I went to the dress Rehearsal – were there at 7 – and the curtain did not ring up till 8 – Just as we were stumbling into the dark dress circle the orchestra began "Die Blume" – I felt almost faint from the smell and taste of Castle T that it gave – everyone's voices, everyone's dress (notably you in the tea gown – playing it) the look of the room with the lamps lit – a kind of vision – through which it became gradually apparent to me that a large fat man was groping his way up to me – Dr. Power O'Donoughue – effusive and timid –

---

1 *The Ronnies:* Robert Martin and his wife Connie. Martin concealed her ill opinion of Connie, and felt sorry for her when Robert's frequent flirtations with other women made her madly jealous.

Robert in the dark introduced some other man to us – a savage – and after long and tedious talking to them the rag went up on a very good scene – Dr. P. O'D. was joined by some of the strangest people I have ever seen – amongst them his wife – and a lady in what appeared to be a black waterproof over her naked body, and a pot hat – which latter she removed – and evidently considered herself the best dressed woman there – their talk was of Handel, and other exalted themes as far as I could gather – there was quite a good number of private view people in the dress circle – amongst them the Gunns – sitting in judgement – the actors just gabbled their parts throughout – they never *will* let themselves out at rehearsal – The thing is not so much a Pantomime as a burlesque – and if it fails it will be from want of spectacle – Gunn has relied altogether on the dialogue – and I am afraid the actors will not do it justice – However the songs will give it a lift – They are not published yet, tell Aylmer – I have just had a letter from him for which thank him – I will respond in a day or so – We got very tired and stiff from sitting at the rehearsal, and with the greatest readiness accepted the Gunns invitation to supper in a very snug private room – It was a curious feeling altogether – there in the small hours, surrounded by extraordinary theatrical people – to whom it was difficult to talk unless one talked shop – and everyone drinking champagne like milk – Mrs Gunn is an American and was an actress – she was interesting and rather good looking – Her niece whom she introduced me to, was one of the prettiest girls I have ever seen – & a very haughty young person – I became as a grass hopper before her – being conscious of a swelled face, and general inferiority – It appeared to be the rule that only Christian names were used – Robert's being the one most frequently employed – The actors and actresses had supper after we had finished – and I never heard anything like the row they made over it – I have never seen anything more weird and terrific than the transformation scene – In itself it is pretty – a sub-marine scene, grottoes of seaweed and the like – which unfolded gradually till at the very back appeared the usual nymph suspended – and on each side of her another nymph – but these latter were in morning clothes – I never could explain what an effect it had – grotesque is a feeble word for it – with the lime lights playing on them – and to complete the nightmare, the stage manager in a frock coat and tall hat came out from a great shell – Another bewildering effect was that the actresses feeling cold towards the end of the piece put on their coats – imagine a sealskin opening up the back and showing blue tights up to the hips – I hope I haven't fatigued you – *I* was pretty fatigued this morning when I got home – Let me know about . . . [*end of fragment*]

Owing to her lack of funds Edith could not spend more than a month or two in a year at a Paris studio. She worked very hard at her art and responded carefully to the criticism of her tutors, who included some fairly distinguished French painters of that period. Mrs Somerville had overcome her horror at Edith's living in Paris. She had stayed in Paris with Edith, been bored to death by Edith's regime, and decided it was safe for Edith to live in Paris provided she had a companion. An unoccupied gentlewoman called Miss Newstead was employed in this capacity for the second of Edith's stays in Paris after she met Martin.

March 2nd 87
Hotel de la haute Loire, Boulevard d'Enfer 204 Paris

Dear Martin
I have just written home, so feel weak – but I think it is due to you to send you a letter and if you have found Minnies whereabouts in town you might make an occasion to go and declaim its contents to her – As I told you I met Miss Newstead at Victoria allright. She is very tall – about 5 foot 9 – with a small head and with a face like a gentle kindly bird of the Emu tribe. Long deeply fringed semi-prominent dark eyes, a straight projecting nose, and an amiable mouth and small chin. She is thoroughly English and has a terrible way of saying "*indeed*" with brisk intelligence which rather quells any foolish jesting. I think she is a really good sort with no two ways in her,* and not a *touch* of the crossroads.* She has a bad habit of doing nothing after dinner, when I want to write etc – but as she turns in early it doesn't matter. The more I see of her the more I like her, but she is very un Buddh* like, and even if I were to saturate her with the dictionary* I fear it would be of no avail – I am in a very fragile mental state tonight, having been at the poles of hope and despair, and the changes of temperature have made me brittle. First I showed Collin my picture. He thought it poor, badly composed, "pas absolument mauvais" – he had seen worse at the Salon, but – enfin – I ran before I could walk etc. He had had a long morning of correction in the studio, which may have embittered him, but he spoke with awful calm and simple sincerity. I suppose a sicker worm than I seldom crawled up those studio steps. I felt it was all true. He had also said that "I came for two months in the Spring then – vous disparez – that was not serious

work" – The blackness of death was on me, and while my fellow roughs jested, laughed and swore, I could only join with them in the latter amusement, principally at myself for ever having tried to do anything – (don't be microscopic* you brute) Well – M. Blanc – another Master – came after lunch. A big fat black southerner, and one of the girls compelled me to take him down to show him the beastly thing. He was as encouraging as Collin was the reverse – and said he thought it was pretty sure to be "reçu" at the Salon and anyhow I ought to try – and she was "bien intressante – cette bonne femme" and not of the type "Anglais" – and he liked the colour and the tone – but Hang it – I dont think he is as good a man as Collin, and he is far more amiable – one thing however – he is a biggish swell, and knows pretty well what gets hung, and he seemed quite surprised when with shaking voice I asked him if he thought it would have the least chance. A young American man and I had both stuck up pictures to show the Masters in a big empty studio – M. Blanc said – "Ah – one sees that woman Mrs. Norris, is a Catholic and not English" – (I instantly tried to look as if I washed in Holy Water every morning) "the English have a little hypocritical air like this – here he tried in vain to fold his hands across his tum and parade up and down – but they would not reach – and he was too fat to step as stiffly as he wanted to so he and I and the other young man all laughed and Patsey – who early in the performance had tried to misconduct himself and been summarily ejected by me – yelped outside the door. M. Blanc was much kinder to the American than Collin had been but we despair of everything French . . .

Herbert Greene receives his first mention in this letter. He was the son of Edith's Aunt Sylvia, and had spent all his summers at Castletownshend. He fell in love with Edith at about the age of eighteen and remained in that state for the rest of his life. He was an undergraduate at Pembroke College, Oxford, and became a Classics don at Magdalen. He had already proposed to Edith several times before Martin arrived in Castletownshend. His father was Tom Greene, Secretary of the General Synod of the Church of Ireland, and his Uncle Willy was Dean of St Patrick's, Dublin. The Greene home at 49 St Stephen's Green was the Dublin base for Castletownshend society.
    Canon Claude Chavasse gave this description of him:

When I knew him he lived in Stone Buildings, either Gray's Inn or Lincoln's Inn. Like me he was ultra-conservative and when he retired

*from being a Don at Magdalen he vowed he would never look upon
Oxford again because they had abolished compulsory Greek. However he found that as an ex-Don he had dining rights at High Table,
so when he arrived at Oxford station he hired a growler and pulled
down the curtains of the windows. To look at he was so like King
Edward VII that he had to avoid passing near Buckingham Palace to
prevent the sentry on duty from calling the guard and presenting arms.*

(Letter to Gifford Lewis, 18 September 1980.)

*Diana Somerville, daughter of Edith's brother Boyle, also remembered
being taken, as a child, to have tea with Herbert Greene in Lincoln's
Inn. She remembered a big, bearded man with a basso profundo voice
who always greeted her with an operatic address: 'Blessed is Diana
amongst the Ephesians.'*

*In the spring of 1887 Edith was off again to Paris and studio work.
Martin remained in London with her brother. Castletownshend society
began to call on the Martins in Leinster Square, and both Herbert
Greene and Sir Joscelyn Coghill are mentioned as callers in this letter.*

*Sir John Joscelyn Coghill was born 11 February 1826 and died 25
November 1905. He married (1 February 1851) Katherine, daughter of
John, third Lord Plunket. After Rugby he served in the 59th Regiment,
succeeding to the baronetcy in 1850. He had several interests. He was
a founder member of the Society for Psychical Research in 1883. He
had sittings with the remarkable medium Daniel Dunglass Home; of all
the people levitated by Home, complete with chair, Sir Joscelyn was the
only one to keep sufficient presence of mind to sign his name on the
ceiling. He was a noted yachtsman, sailing the Mediterranean and the
Hebrides as well as Irish waters. His schooner Ierne was much photo-
graphed. A fine singer, he wrote operettas for performance by his family.
As a photographer he was noted for his experiments in stereoscopy. He
was the first Secretary and second President of the Photographic Society
of Ireland.*

[From Martin, staying with her brother Robert and his wife Connie, to
Edith]

48 Leinster Square, Bayswater
March 3 1887

What makes you so *awfully* clever? Who but a person with a really
great mind would have thought of writing from Paris and giving no

address – It savours of the fine old tawny crusted Buddh* sell[1] – As I took occasion to remark to Herbert this morning, I believe your address to be Rue de l'Enfer, Quartier Latin, but you will no doubt make arrangements to have your letters sent to Boulevard Mont Parnasse or Maurice's hotel or some such place – I have asked Castle T-ites for your address and hope eventually to send this. I have found a very priceless French phrase book for the use of travellers here – written by a Parisian – and when I land at Dieppe do not anticipate any difficulties – Do I not know the French for "that thou mightest have a shift" or even "that he might have a squirrel" and am fully instructed as to how to converse with my fellow passengers on these topics. I am even ready to remark "Thank God, we have left that hole" when coming out of a tunnel – This is all genuine, and really in the book – with many other *beautiful* things. The French is all right – of course – it is the English that is so enchanting – I hope to make many quotations for your edification – I am very glad you got your sleep that night – you wanted it after your horrible night with me, sitting erect on a sore spine and supporting an inert mass of flesh on your lap and person generally. What did Newstead do – dropped into small decorous dozes I have no doubt – I think I know what her handbag is like – and her belongings generally – also her boots – rather MacDermotty. Like my friend Mr Hannigan the bank clerk, at Punchestown, you are I should think "in your glory" surrounded by American art students with their excellent comic paper jokes and general flavour of the Mariamne. My little dog must have a gallus[2] bad time at the studio and I daresay that taking him down and making him squat in the street every 10 to 12 minutes interferes a little with your painting. But what of that – we must amuse ourselves and it was the way you elected to do so in London. As long as Patsey's inside holds out there is a fund of innocent recreation for you – It is very curious that our Edith also takes delight in this common but enthralling spectacle – After you left I got better and was nearly right next day, though not free from sudden grasps of pain in my head and sick feeling – Now I am in the most blooming condition – I don't know when I have felt so well. Robert and Connie were very sorry you could not have stayed on – You would have just made the right number at dinner on Sunday night – and would have liked it I think. Joscelyn walked in at luncheon on that day, and I went with him down to see the Townshends, who are at 32 Gordon Place, Campden Hill – Kensington. There we were a

1 *Sell*: a successful practical joke.
2 *Gallus* (*deformed Irish*): extremely.

most representative Castle T group – I *was* glad to see Minnie she was as cold water to a thirsty soul – and gave me the most interesting particulars about your mother, Mr Harris, Violet and everything – I gather that Mrs H. has been pretty raw, and falling foul of Aylmer, and all but doing so with everybody – She has now gone to Blarney and probably will perspire it all away – I think poor woman she is very lonesome for her Jim – Minnie had a list of amusements compiled by Mr H which gave me much amusement to read – First a list of churches, then "if not inclined for church" several alternatives followed – Then the week days – Concerts, the Woolwich Arsenal, the advanced Jew's Synagogue, the Aquarium, several restaurants, and at regular intervals, various hospitals. Minnie with a beaming countenance said she hoped to manage all – Silvia looked unkempt and rather bewildered, Harry all there and rather the man about town – I don't suppose any other 3 people in London are enjoying themselves as much. Friday morning I still continue to write in the belief that sometime or other I shall find out where you are. I am going this afternoon with the Townshends to the advanced Jew's Synagogue – to which I must say I look forward very much – and will report on it – On Sunday I go with them and Constance and Sophy to the Carmelite Chapel where the singing is the *best*. I think I said something about the dinner here last Sunday – It was very pleasant – a rather du Maurier dinner – Consisting of ourselves and Mr and Mrs Upperton – she a rather nice wog,* her husband just the man whom du Maurier makes say the smart things – tall, pale with small whiskers. There were besides, Joscelyn, who was a strong tower and a Mr Farrel, a man who lives near Bray whom I have known for some time – an awfully good musician and has been studying music at Cambridge – of course I had a good time talking to him, and Mr Upperton who was on my other side – the latter is delightful – *most* agreeable – I had no idea that Connie would go in for such smart dinners. I mean in the way of doing them – The table was arranged with Lily of the Valley and red geraniums – regular bouquets of the each – and the food was most awfully good – Mr Farrel and Joscelyn stayed till all hours, but Connie and I returned about 12.30. Robert got us a box for the Gaiety on Tuesday night, and we had the Uppertons and Mr Farrel as before. We dined at the Gaiety restaurant next door first. An amusing place – I never saw a prettier show than Monte Cristo, the Gaiety burlesque – As to what it is all about I know no more than you do – It is said the authors once knew the plot, but it had to be cut a good deal – and now no one alive has the faintest idea – nor is it needful that they should – George Edwards the manager was very amusing on the subject to Robert – He said when the authors first brought him the play he thought there were 5 plays in it, it was so enormous "my dear sir we might have played it all day for a week, and not have been done with it then – and when I asked these chaps to write songs for me, they bring me those bally psalms." I must say the songs were not much, dreary political truisms – and only that Nellie Farren sang them, they would have been too putrid – Robert's two songs went like smoke – the first was Ballyhooley – sung just tolerable by a man called Lonnen, who couldn't remember his Irish accent all the time – however the house loved it, and so did I to a certain extent – next came "the jolly little chap all round" sung by Nellie Farren, to whom I here tender my unalterable allegiance – She is a wonder – and when she sang that song I felt just as we do when Patsey gives that intoxicating mad glance showing that delicious bit of white in his eye – quite prostrate from startled admiration – She is not pretty, she has a *hideous* voice, she is rather vulgar – but my word she can act that sort of thing – I don't think the other people felt it as much as I did, but to my mind there is no such burlesque actress – such a face, such expression – and filling up every minute of her time with something new – With her of course Robert's song was bound to be encored and shouted at, & it was *that*. It is a real hit – just beside our box was standing George Barret the jockey, at whom I gazed adoringly through opera glasses, at a distance of two yards – He looks about 16, and has a jolly little healthy plucky face, a contrast to the other men there. The dresses were perfection, but less of them than I have ever seen before. I must say I did open my eyes when I saw an assemblage of plump young women come on in the dress of men in the last century – perfectly skin tight white breeches and long tailed cutaway coats. However it looked very pretty. I am proud to say that Robert has got the order for the Gaiety autumn burlesque which will mean about £400. We shall all be borrowing money from him one of these days – Connie has been very seedy from gout – but is better. The boredom which I anticipated was only a sick headachey vision – it is "far otherwise" here. I am finishing up this on Saturday night – I went to the Synagogue with the Townshends – most interesting. To begin with we saw the Queen in the Park. She looked cold and unhappy. We got to the Synagogue at sunset – which is the time. Harry was swept away from us, and we were skyed up into a gallery from whence we could see him seated in lonely splendour below with his hat on and with a jewish sexton giving him the tips from time to time. The service was all in Hebrew, read by Robert Franks in a square black cap, long ditto gown, and several chairbacks, hung from his shoulders. The music was really fine, so vigorous that it was almost coarse and very wild tunes. The singers were all behind a screen at the back of the Holy of Holies – and were about all the congregation – Today I went off to S. James' Hall for the Sat. Pop. and was to meet the Townshends and Mr Farrel. Arrived there behold no Townshends, not a seat left in the house and Mr Farrel in despair – He and I then took up our parable and cursed – and finally went down street to Picadilly Hall where we saw the great Verbeck, the conjurer and mesmerist – It was all uncanny in the extreme – his magic was beautiful – He spoke all the time in French and I understood most of it – but there was an interpreter for fear of mistakes. The mesmerism consisted of a stupified looking woman being led in by Verbeck, and then doing tricks of sorts. He stuck a pin through her arm, made her write the number of a bank note, he made her balance in most uncomfortable attitudes for any length of time (that is a must for models.) I hated her look, all animal and bewildered. Verbeck's face was delightful – like Philip Smyly and the last Napoleon – my writing gets smaller by degrees, but beyond this sheet . . . [*edge damaged*]

I have just had your letter – I will do your bidding as to the picture – I am much distressed about Mrs Norris – but I sorrow not as those without hope. I cannot offer consolation with any show of sincerity – not having seen the picture – but I don't think it can have deserved what Collin said. Oh the offensiveness of you and Patsey – the shameless indecencies – the unhappy Newstead. With the same gnawing regret have I watched Katie and Edith lose all self respect about their kids. Do you know that Hildegarde is to be at the Butts next week? She will be much nicer to go about with than you. You are too frivolous and captious and indecent about my little dog. So – me dear – your hostelry is in Boulevard [illegible] – very nice – you must pave the street with good intentions as to work in the summer. I will endeavour to send the Dic. things, and will write again soon – at present I am harassed with gaddings. We dine at the McCalmonts tomorrow night – it ought to be interesting – but I think I should prefer a nice little temperance meal with you and Newstead. I have heard from Herbert expressions of regret that we could not visit the University at this time – he hopes we can when you are on your way from Paris . . . I interviewed Mrs Butt all alone and thought your mother's description of Patsey would apply to her – Kitty and Kendal turned up later – Kitty looking as nice as possible – Kendal oozing with suppressed ecstacy. Minnie is rather indignant that the Butts have not looked us up – Sylvia endeavours as much as in her lies to assume the accent of a London bus conductor with some success. It is very funny. However she is on the whole very subdued and

quelled and diffident – I am very glad about that *Magazine of Art* –
they are good solid satisfactory people. Don't mind about Norris even
if the Salon wont have it. Remember Disraeli "The time will come when
you *shall* hear me" and then like the unbelieving lord, Collin will go
into an inner chamber to hide himself. A long letter from Violet – she
thinks Aylmer is really going to America – I can scarcely believe it. Have
you any idea what things of ours Hurley took to Tally Ho? This is an
appalling looking sheet – I pity you for the reading of it – Newstead
must be very unattractive, and if she talks all the evening she ought to
be choked – Good night –
Martin

The Irish Times, *a Conservative and Unionist paper, had organized a*
competition for poets to compose an ode in celebration of Queen Victo-
ria's Jubilee. This was not something that Edith felt like celebrating, but
Martin wrote a sonnet, won a prize, and duly had her ode published in
a volume of selected poems submitted to the Irish Times.

Some previous writers on Somerville and Ross have quite wrongly
imagined a worshipful adoration of the genius Martin by the 'hack and
amanuensis' Edith. This is one of the far-reaching side-effects of the
conception of Somerville and Ross as a beautiful, ultra-feminine genius
paired with a masculine, obtuse hack writer.

Here we see Edith cheerfully describe Martin's fellow odes as 'pukey
rubbish' and quite soon her letters will frankly refer to parts of Martin's
draft articles as 'puke'. Her criticism of Martin's style is acute. At this
stage Martin wrote in a wordy, Carlylean manner that was dense and
lacked movement. The Martin family had a low opinion of her writing
talent – both her father and brother Robert were fluent writers – and
called her, wryly, 'Our Little Carlyle'.

Hell Street, Paris
Friday, March 11th 87

My dear girl
Your letter of this morning was as whisky to a thirsty soul where only
water is. (This is only a metaphor, and its spiritual tendencies may be
attributed to the fact that Newstead and I shared a bottle of beer – at
six pence – this evening.) Really you are a good woman to write to me,
and likewise to send me the papers which I am awfully glad to get –
and was much pleased to see Robert's scratch in the Bat. As for the

Oobilee Jode – never was I seen Jode as like. More pukey rubbish could hardly be conceived, even by the Dublin beanie.*

My dear, I *hope* yours will be clean out of it – I would be ashamed to see you in such company – How I wish you had dollared the collars. I envy you the leprous paper. This imposing home made thoroughbred silk-all-the-way-up stuff is a rank swindle. The ink darts through it as if it were acid . . . Your letter interested me so much that before going on to my own trivial life I will skim through it again – I have scum.

I hope you keep the French phrase book – very precious those remarks you have already culled. I do pity you for having missed the octett. I wish you had heard it – though it might have taken the taste of Hildegarde's and my rendering out of your mouth which would have been a pity. May I ask if Mr. Farrel is a licensed chip* or a licentious chap – I doubt he is the latter. Anyhow if he likes classical music he cannot be very abandoned. I can well fancy Seafield in London – Minnie would be very refreshing, but Harry's assumption of town comportment might be a trifle exhausting till it wore through a bit – you seem to be having times (the infernal Newstead is babbling and I find it rather hard to combine politeness and composition) I am awfully glad Constance's watercolours got a lift – but they certainly are not in it with Rose Barton's – I went to a show here, yesterday, of water colours, pastels and drawings and I saw *nothing* within miles of Rose's. There is another good show which I hope to see on Sunday – but I doubt there will be better work than hers there. About the boxes – I am afraid I know nothing of them if they are not at Tally Ho. My impression was that I sent one or two boxes down from Drishane to Tally Ho by Hurley, last January, at the same time with two very ancient gowns of your mothers (which I subsequently gave to the poor) I will tell mother this when I write on Sunday night. I am most *pleased* that Ronnie is approved of – I was half afraid Mrs. R. might not like it. I will have no more from you about those ridiculous frames – I told you that the frames are always "compris" in all respectable establishments – and as for the rest – my dear child – don't talk nonsense –

I never heard "Noodenafore"* or "Nooden behind"* or whatever the word is, in my whole life – and I believe it to be an elaborate invention of the little Coghills – but it is a good scheme for a word – and it was a place where one is wanted – but we must get it authenticated. *I have written out all D.* so now – though I am up to my eyes in work of sorts – I got a letter from the *Mag. of Art* asking me to alter certain of the drawings, written with a little tone of pleasing levity. Instantly I responded in the most wog-like* manner – the same tone only more so

– and I sent him the woman who wouldn't poke the fire and the words thereof. He has not replied which is a healthy sign. By the by why do you spell this homely word thus "enthutitiastically". It is pretty looking and takes up space – but it doesn't amount to much otherwise ... I have at home the copy of the letter we wrote Herbert, and he doubtlessly has the original, so we can work up a preface out of that. You must write Purlieu,* and send epitome* – and I don't mind how much proverbial philosophy you send me – only dont expect very punctual replies as I have really hardly a minute – Courtois came to correct today, and was rather nice to me – I consequently love him best of all – I took my first fiddle lesson yesterday. An *awfully* good man – I noticed that he abused me for none of the faults of last year, which was very cheering – and was on the whole extremely encouraging. But now I have to leave the studio earlier in order to practise – after dinner I am working for the *Graphic* – I have done four of the Irish set – and think they are fairly successful – I ought to be at them now – but you inveigle me into writing to you – bad scran to you. Now let me whisper in your ear, that Newstead is a bore – an amiable, worthy, well meaning, upright, un-exacting creature, but a bore. She is, in a way interesting – I should like to try and write an exhaustive analysis of her character. She has an amazing capacity for doing nothing – *literally nothing* as I know she doesn't think, but sits in a kind of dwam.* She usually sits till 9 – in my room making little Ti-W* remarks – which when I am drawing I dont mind, but when, as now, I am writing I feel that "my temper line is ... [*piece of letter missing*] ... had no aches or pains, and hardly felt tired even. A Yankee tale of an awfully close boat race between Harvard and Yale colleges – Harvard won by two or three seconds, and promptly sent this telegram to the college. "We win. Yale expected in every minute" – not very funny – but rather a good idea. I know I shall talk in a twang soon. I hear nothing but Amurrican but they are a nice people – I must to bed. I cant help it – I don't seem able to write any sort of a decent letter – but I live in a groove and you must get there too, before I can write of anything that will amuse you – Best love from Steadfast – (and my little tiny thing)

Yours Ever

E.Œ.S.

P.S. Have you ever discovered that I eloped with your Mc Dermott boots and your bottle of Lively Sarah* that you brought that day at the

Stores?[1] I am awfully sorry and if there was parcel post I would send the boots – but as they are too small for me I can't wear them – and now that you are a high toned blue blooded wog* I suppose you wouldn't wear them till you came to these wilds. There was something else I wanted to tell you but I can't remember it now.

E.Œ.S.

This is the first letter to mention Egerton Coghill and Hildegarde together. Egerton and Hildegarde could not marry until the family was assured of financial security. This depended on the success of a mad shares scheme subscribed to by Sir Joscelyn, Egerton's father, and his uncle, Colonel Kendal. This – referred to in these letters as Bourget or Bougie – held up their marriage for years. They were engaged for so long – at least seven years – that Martin eventually christened them 'the Dowager Lovers' (shortened to 'the Dowagers' later).

Egerton Coghill was born 7 February 1853 and died 9 October 1921. He married Hildegarde, sister of Edith Somerville, 11 July 1893. After leaving Haileybury he studied engineering as a Premium Apprentice at Erith Engineering Works. When his elder brother Nevill was killed in action on 22 January 1879, saving the colours of the South Wales Borderers at the Zulu battle of Isandula, he became the heir to the baronetcy and no longer, it was thought optimistically, needed to earn his living. He then studied painting, first in Düsseldorf and then at the Académie Julien where he was a pupil of Bougereau 1881–4. He was an accomplished painter, photographer and singer but quite without ambition. He succeeded his father as baronet in 1905.

Hildegarde Somerville, Lady Coghill, was born 1 August 1867 and died 6 March 1954. She married her cousin Egerton 11 July 1893 and had four children. She ran a dairy farm and a violet farm. She wrote an excellent article on violet farming for the Irish Homestead *17 April 1897, and ran the violet farm remuneratively from 1891 for almost fifteen years. A fund-raiser extraordinary, she instituted a collection for chloroform during the First World War and was awarded a Diploma of Honour by the French Red Cross. She also raised funds for the Blue Cross. A great manager and holder-together of things and people, she was the mainstay, at home and in exile, of Castletownshend society.*

1 *The Stores*: the Army and Navy, where the Coghills and Somervilles bought everything from folding rubber travelling baths to false teeth.

[From Martin to Edith]

48 Leinster Square, Bayswater
Friday March 18 '87

Lady – beneath December snow our year lies chained in icy bands – it does really. The houses and Parks are white, the streets are black. The day I got your letter I spent in bed. There is no place where one so much appreciates a letter I may remark in passing – but I had a cold – and had a day of thorough enjoyment while it snowed like everything – It was not in vain that we said, my heart and I, "Newstead is a bore." I felt it, and feel it for you – Nothing on God's earth has the same power to rouse me to fury as being talked to while I am writing. One of the worst battles I have ever had with Mama was last year when I wasted a goodly evening in writing to you about a day's hunting. I would not answer her conversation – and there was work out of that. If Newstead intends to go round with us I don't go to Paris, that's all – If it were that Ever-Wog girl[1] with the yellow hair I should not mind so much. Tell me more of her humours the next time you write and I think you might at the same time give me a notion of who the other people in the Studio are. It would amuse me, (mark the invalid's querulousness). I really have felt rather seedy this week – from that cold, and biliousness – and late hours.

I went down and called your picture "Midi" yesterday. The ceremony was impressive – and your sister Hildegarde assisted at it – I maintained an attitude of reserve as regards her, for the first few days – and finally we asked her to luncheon here, and she came – The reserve was of course diplomacy as regards the Butts, who I think have not acquired Castle T. habits – I never saw Hildegarde in more fine condition, much fatter than when I saw her last – She is awfully pleased with London and everything amuses her. After lunch I chaperoned her down to Bond St to have her hair shampooed at Douglas' and we then paraded in Regent St and had tea at the Hungarian bread shop and home by Charing Cross – all doings of the deadliest impropriety I have no doubt – but no one knows us – Egerton was about till today but I need not chronicle your sister's doings further – she will tell them to you no doubt – Anyhow I was awfully pleased to see her – and will see her again as soon as possible – She is a very true hearted squaw* – and the songs of Zion in my bedroom nearly lifted the roof off the house – Aunt Georgies

1 Edith's fellow student, Miss Overweg.

must have been too sickeningly dull – *Where do you go to church?* I hear about W.C.[1] shows and Chantilly and Autueil (if such places there be) but nothing about religious instruction on the Sabbath – I may mention in passing that I was too late last Sunday to go to morning church at all – However I am sure Ever-Wog deludes you into evil courses somehow – When she comes back to London I shall question her as to these matters. I wonder that you can talk such offensive rot about your letters and your uninteresting groove – Go to, my dear and invent a better class of falsehood next time. When I find your letters uninteresting I shall cease to correspond with you – you bet – At this moment I have most keenly felt what it is to have to write and talk – Connie having come into the room, and finding me occupied immediately began to tidy Robert's papers with much and exhaustive comment – and I have removed myself to my room, where thank heaven there is always a fire before dinner – It is Connie's only fault, that and the sitting over the relics of her food – she is tremendously good and nice in every other way. She and I are alone now – as Robert has gone down to Derbyshire to speak for the Conservative candidate – He told me a tale of a sub-agent which amused me – "Will you pay me the rents boys" says I. "We will not faith," says they; "Maybe ye'll be that ye'll *have* to pay them" says I. With that they turned about and threwn half the estate at me – It was a rather happy way of putting it.

London is I believe full of good pictures, divil a one have I seen as yet – please goodness next week I shall make a tour with Willie Wills – who is painting away at Penywern – It begins to dawn on me that after all the Coghills had not such a doose of a time over here – however they thought they had, which did just as well – Last week I went to the Butts at-home camac* with the Townshends and saw Janie looking pounds better – awfully pretty – in fact three more goodly women than she, Kitty and Lucy it would not be easy to find in one family – Lucy seems a big amiable heifer with a rather vacuous sweet gaze – Janie has the heels of her in the way of looks I think. When we got into the house I heard singing and we waited on the landing with the servant (the latter much bored) till it was over. Like Mrs Connellan when the wop[2] struck up a tune beneath her "me heart stood still" as I recognized the well known sounds of "Auf deinen blauen Augen" It was very well sung too by a woman called Winthrop, who evidently thought it was an absolute novelty. I longed to say "Pardon me Madam, there is a third verse."

---

1 W.C.: Water Colour.
2 *Wop*: reversion of *po*, for chamber pot.

Not being a Buddh,* I refrained. I went to Westminster Abbey with the Townshends on Sunday afternoon where I remark that we did not get there till the service began – and a policeman waved us back from the door saying "All full here go round to the Poets corner" – many others were also waved back and turned to go round the corner with us – on which Harry in the tones of a brigade general said "Let us outrun them to the Poet's Corner" If you could have seen the people's faces as we ran past them with loud elegant guffaws – Minnie of course at once got a whooping cough spasm and held on to me and shrieked. Harry never drew bridle till into the church & well up the aisle, while we sank on the nearest chairs, and the women whom we had outrun came crowding in. We then spied Harry uplifting a mystic finger from afar, and squaw* like rose to follow – but those outpaced women also saw, and in one compact mass advanced, seeing in me intimation of probable advantage in Harry's husbandly eye – and my dear they bested us – got every available decent seat – and we stood through the whole thing from the word go – We heard very well but the music is not very much – and the sermon was mostly blather of an affected would-be Ultra Broad Church kind – you may observe that the Westminster Abbey part of Sunday is given some prominence – It is done for the sake of style and for fear of causing the weak brother to offend – as truth compels me to chronicle the evening's dissipation. It was not of an alarming nature, being supper with Jennie Lee and her husband who calls himself Mr Burnett, but his real name is Dodds – so it is pretty complicated all round – Let me say at once to allay your anxiety that they are both eminently respectable – The entertainment consisted in sitting round a small back drawing room at the other end of Regent's Park, and having supper in the front room, and returning to the back and hearing a few comic songs. But the other guests my dear – the other guests – shall I ever forget the row of them opposite to me at supper – First a Mrs Levi, a person of fabulous wealth with a house in Piccadilly and without an H in her composition. She was of great bulk, and rather haughty and talked of how she often took 16 or 18 stalls at a time – when Jennie Lee was playing – I add that she was dressed in black satin of the richest – Next her came Robert, whom you have the pleasure of being acquainted with – Next him Miss Levi just home from Melbourne where she had lived all her life and looked like it – a sort of jovial savage with a "merry war." Next her came a most remarkable being – a young man – who to begin with is an artist, who in the next place is stone deaf, and in the third place is nearly dumb. He lost his hearing at 6 years old and only knows how to talk in the voice he had then. He has somehow learnt a few words, but very few. And his presence was depressing in the extreme, he looked something like this [drawing] across the table, to me – I wish you could have seen him and his hair and his aesthetic coat – Finishing the row came old Mrs Dodds, Burnett's mother – a common ordinary domestic madwoman – tall and terrific, with flaming cheeks and hungry eyes. She came to me in the course of the evening and laying awful hands on me remarked that Mr Burnetts mother was a very nice woman – I repressed a shriek and fervently assented. She then applied the spladge* and said something else, I don't know what – as I tore myself from her and fled to Jennie Lee – There were two other men there, the saddest people I have ever seen – and that was the lot – The curious thing is that no one else thinks Mrs Dodds is mad – but I *know* it and I felt all the time like Cuthbert coming down through shrubberies at Folkestone in the dark, when he said "I wish I were safe at home and the bedclothes over my head." Jennie Lee herself is 5 foot nothing and full of talent all the way through. She sang a sort of medley song awfully lively, and is excellent company – but she is *very* histrionic – called me "MY dee-ar" and Robert "Martin" which made me think all the time she wanted me and not him – I must say I have given you a dose of her and her supper – and now I am going to bed, where Connie thinks I have been two hours ago – Saturday morning – Did I tell you that Minnie has not been able to come here, as Connie has taken a panic about the whooping cough. It is unfortunate, but one cant argue with people who have children – at least not on those subjects. Connie asked Harry to dine and go to the theatre the other night, but he was not able to come, having a bad cold – She has asked him again for Monday night, when we are going to see "Modern Wives" at the Royalty – and I hope he can come. He is not the least the man about town now – and is very amusing – I think he is madly jealous of Egerton – old idiot. Sylvia is still piano and silent – London is one too many for her – she wears a high hat and white veil! and skin tight brown coat – Minnie has purchased a new tall bonnet, which suits her awfully well, and she meanders through the streets with nodding plumes, and a face of placid delight.

We dined with most interesting people on Wednesday night – half American, and cousins of Connie's – Their name is Haigh with the g. hard. They consist of a very peculiar girl of 22, and her bachelor Uncle, a barrister of over 40, who looks 30. These two live in comfort together – They are both musical and accompany each other turn about. I wonder if Americans have any strange rules for going to dinner, find out from your Paris friends. When dinner was announced I drew back into a corner & waited for whatever man might be my lot – as besides me the female guests were Connie and two strange married women. To my horror Mr Haigh with the utmost politeness requested me to accompany him, which I did, followed by my elders and betters, and thinking it must be a mistake, but no, there was my name on a card up at the top of the table – while Robert was given Miss Haigh at the other end – though there was some legal bigwig there. For what do they take us – However I tried to look the part and not to frivol and had a delightful time – Mr Haigh being a *most* agreeable man – Robert and I had by a long way the best of it as Kitty Haigh is also very agreeable – Connie had the legal cove, and drave heavily in comparison to her husband and sister-in-law. The wife of the legal boss was a fine genuine specimen of the aesthetic at least in dress – She was swaddled in terra cotta of the brickiest, each of her puffed sleeves would have amply contained the most representative Buddh leg* – and the garment opened over her large chest with the utmost freedom – I say chest advisedly – no other term is applicable in her case. She had a large Roman Matron face and actually and really a white lock à la Whistler. I don't believe it was her own – or she must have bleached it – but there it lay, among a lot of heavy dark hair swept back from her forehead – She was wholly unattractive, as were all the other guests. Mr Haigh sang very well indeed – a dear little German song and Miss Kitty got up and bellowed through a bad style of English ditty – starting fff and just half a note flat, and sticking to it like a man all through – quite awful – The skin disease[1] is not at all what it might be this time, I don't know what has happened to it. Connie gets it at the A and N stores – Wait till you come to write on it and you'll find that it gives you the sensation of rough diseased skin, it did to me at first but I have got over that – You know of course that the boxes with the plate and kitchen things have been found in the pantry at Drishane – I believe there are still 2 small boxes missing but they are sure to turn up – I am sick to death of the subject – and so I should think were the Somerville family. I think the *Mag of Art* is bound to take your fireside woman – Why is it that I don't fancy the idea of those *Graphic* sketches – I know not, but I never did take to the notion – However the English public will no doubt love them . . . The hunt is hunting in Westmeath at present. It is now Saturday night – but all the same I have gone and hunted out Epitome* in spite of fatigue and slight toothache – here it is – "Any peculiar sign or token of Buddh eccentricity,

1 The 'skin disease' was extremely bad writing paper sold by the Army and Navy Stores.

a disregard of the ordinary social conventions is said to be, 'the family Epitome' Deriv. this expression originated in a remark of Mr T Greene's that all the qualities and characteristics of the family might be summed up, or epitomized in their habit of instantly and unseasonably trying on and wearing any new article of personal attire." That is the lot – Hildegarde suggested "Flea shop" a sort of dirty cheap shop like the place you bought your hat. I should think you know the word. The more I think of it the more deeply do I applaud your definition of stitchify* – it was inspiration – I have in snatches got a pretty good notion of the lie of your *Sonnets of Europe* – It appears to me that the French men have it all their own way – perhaps the translators felt more at home with them – One or two of Michael Angelo's take a good deal of beating I must say, but our native sonnets leave them nowhere – though it is not fair to judge them. The papers say you are snowed up in Paris just as we are here – Fancy my little dog's sensation at seeing the familiar bare branches suddenly get hidden with leaves – he has never seen a spring, I believe – I went down to Kew today with the Townshends, sat for ages at the Helps, Harry made a better fist of Lady Helps than anyone I have ever seen . . . A calamity has befallen your picture of me. The day I was in bed I heard a sort of creak from it, and discovered that it had warped and is evidently cracked right across – though the paint has not given way as yet – There is a line straight across my chest and hand – I am grieved very much and feel it is a bad omen –

Yours
Martin

March 22nd 87
Hotel de la haute loire, Boulevard d'Enfer, 203

Dear Girl
Does not this small cramped fist inspire you with a belief that I am going to write forever and forever? If so, I doubt you are filled with a lying spirit as I don't think I am – Your letter came last night – as at this time – and I was very near falling to and answering at once, but had a bit of a head so thought better of it and went to bed. Here is again post, with your newspaper. It is awfully good of you to send these things to the friendless exile, and the *Sporting and Dramatic* was dew to the tender herb (that's me.) This paper will now – so to speak – go back an hundred fold into your bosom as it shall silence the twitterings of Steadfast, whose fairy foot is even now upon my threshold. She is now

in my room and saying in a facetious squeak "tea-tea-beloved tea" because we are about to partake of that drink. I think Ti-W* is really her worst point; fortunately it is not *very* pronounced, but at times gets the better of her, and she wags in a painful manner – but never gives herself away, or causes shame to the partner of her soys and jorrows. So I have no real cause to complain. One of her worst traits is her callousness to the little dog (of whom much more anon) I had to leave him in the court yard – chained like a little mad lunatic dog, while I was at my fiddle lesson, and though she was sitting at home she never took him up to her room, or said a kind word to him. At the Studio it is "far otherwise". He takes after his dear Mother and is extremely Popular, rather too much so in fact – as the way that the average woman manifests her undiscriminating admiration is neither good for man nor beast. Overweg – (I object to ever wog – she is not a wog* – or at least, not much – and you or I pronounce her name Overvay) is an admirable girl. She is tallish, with a nice figure. Her hair is very light bright yellow white – her eyes blue and foolish looking, and her face a dull uniform pastel pink, and rather lower in value than her hair – (to speak technically). She and I rather got a rise out of the Studio the other day. We had gone down to drink black coffee – and on going up again we found that the door had been locked to prevent its being opened and allowing the cold to come in while the model was posing – (there is another back entrance, whereby the wind is tempered to the shorn lamb) We first "beat upon the door" violently in vain, then in a hoarse frightened whisper – though the key hole I said "Monsieur Blanc! Mes dames! Ouvrez" (Monsieur Blanc is our 25 stone Master and was expected that day,) and then Overweg and I timing our steps, tramped as one large man, down stairs. After that we fled round, said we had seen Monsieur Blanc and that he had gone away and more truthfulness that sounded like lies – and I think a good many believed and some trembled. This is the sort of mild game that is very successful especially among the primitive foreign element. There are two or three nice Scotch – one a very dirty plain woman, but a worthy, and a doggy. Another is a splendid creature – six foot high, with a grand head and figure – most awfully classical – and a fine easy going slob at that. I am the only Irish woman, and besides Steadfast there are only two English. One, a decent quiet, sensible woman, who reminds me of a good solid nutritious piece of roast beef (morally, not physically –) and the other is a queer little creature with grey hair and a little consequential air which is the consequence of her having kept a studio and taught art at Reading. I had always looked upon Reading as wholly given over to the construction of biscuits, and it seems a pity that Miss Butcher did not stick to the local industry. She nearly drove me mad the other day – I was trying to make a most putrid composition – at least I was trying to make a composition, but putridity came unthought – for Collin, who gives a subject each week – and this little wretch stood at my elbow and made hints and comments and suggestions until I felt my arm stiffening with fury, and my tongue claved to the roof of my mouth – (and well for her that it did.) But she meant well.

The Americans are a strong, curious, class. They are none of them of the class of my dear Mariamne Adams – and I expect she would regard them with eyes of cold disfavour, as the rankest kinds of vulgarians. But they are very simple and play very fair, and their voices are a joy to me. One Miss King has the most curious voice. She inserts a y, by a sort of nasal effort in the most unexpected places – she says "Wyell I cyall that superyub" and she feels "neryvous" (meaning nervous) – It is really very interesting, and she is exceedingly funny into the bargain . . . [*end of extract*]

Edith's fellow students in Paris were a motley collection of Scandinavian, Middle-European and American women with whom she kept in touch for the rest of her life. Martin visited Paris this year to see what studio life was like, and thought it awful. She did not approve of the type of company that Edith kept, and was particularly amazed by the super-blonde Miss Overweg. She keeps trying to amuse Edith, and in this letter we find the first example of an anecdote followed by the comment 'The whole thing makes quite a nice little story.' The mood of these anecdotes is far removed from the tone of the serious political articles that Martin was writing at this time, and is a foretaste of the humour that she was to develop with Edith in the RM stories.

Edith did not work with feeble amateurs; to most of her student friends it was a matter of great consequence that they should train to a professional level. They wanted to be self-supporting and many went on to become teachers or illustrators. Some talented artists worked in Edith's circle: Rose Barton, her cousin, has just been rediscovered and Egerton Coghill was acknowledged as a supremely gifted painter by his contemporaries. Among these were Adrian and Mariamne Stokes (née Adams), who used to visit Egerton at Castletownshend on landscape-painting holidays. While Edith was in Paris Martin acted as her agent in the editorial offices of London illustrated papers. The upper levels of Anglo-Irish society were markedly cosmopolitan, and 'town' meant London.

Edith composed and illustrated comic-strip stories for journals like the Graphic; *at this stage she was more concerned with illustrating than writing.*

48 Leinster Square
Sunday night March 27 '87

Dear Edith,
There is nothing like making a beginning – Heaven only knows when I shall finish this – such is my state of fashionable flusthration.* Do not attempt to deny it – Overweg has white eyebrows – and eyelashes. I know she has – and you endeavor to slur over the fact – you have depicted a purple faced albino as your friend – I do not know if you are aware of that. Furthermore I think Overweg was at the studio last year. I remember quite well you trying to fire my imagination by the description of a girl whose face was three shades redder than her hair, or whose hair was three shades whiter than her face – I forget which – Also you said that she made the most scathing of jests with the air of one who is half witted and amiably imbecile. She must be the same. What a corrective to the blighting influences of Newstead as brandy and soda to barley water. The next time Overweg incites you to such vulgar practical jokes as the one you described, just say "Dear Miss Overweg, it can never be right to excite the earnest feelings of others needlessly and for your own amusement." This if you will remember I have often had occasion to repeat to you – Let me tell you that I have seen one of the Mariamne's today to wit Mrs Stokes – only from a little distance and with a white veil on so that I could not see very well but she has a delightful way of speaking. Her husband was with her a fair fat fluffy little man – I wish I had been introduced to her, but there wasn't time. I am very sorry to hear of my little dog's seizure it evidently was some nervous thing – Either a bad dream, or your feigned voice, that made him think that he had gone mad. He is very uncanny – a kind of changeling. A dog that I had once was taken in that way one night on seeing me in my bath for the first time – and frightened me awfully – Half flew at me, and then fled to the door and yelled till everyone in the house came to the rescue – while I naked and dripping but safely under the bed clothes, adjured them to stay outside until the paroxysm was over – which it soon was. This animal was a large harrier so it was most alarming. I may add that when I did succeed in getting her out of the

room she immediately proceeded to the kitchen and drank about two quarts of milk which had been set for cream and then perambulated the house all night uttering faint injured cries and clattering on the oil cloth with long nails, and decorating the various landings with a patent kind of fluid outline map. A few days afterwards she was presented to a pack of harriers in Sligo. The whole thing makes quite a nice little story. However I do think your medical inspiration was a genuine one. What is this that I hear about you wanting the whole of Drishane to locate themselves in Paris this autumn? I vaguely resent it why I do not know – but I don't suppose it's likely to come off. Fancy your mother in Paris – she would spend her whole time and income in writing lamentations to her family "the exile, from prison" sort of thing and Egerton would plough the deep most of the time on his way to and fro. I saw him on Friday at the Butts very clean shaven looking and sleek and in a decent black coat but with a turned down collar. I think he seems anxious and bothered about this rotten Brighton scheme – so should I if I wanted to make a living out of it. I have seldom seen a man more demented than he is about Hildegarde – who is absolutely calm – but for all that is keener than I imagined from the way she talked. She is wholly swallowed up by him and the Butts as is only natural and proper She was very seedy indeed last week – had an awful throat and a sort of influenza which the doctor said came from debility – I suppose he knows best, but I never saw her look better than since she has come to town she will have to take care of herself for a little time about catching cold. I know she was going to write to you so I need not further dilate on her doings.

Monday evening – I have been out with Connie paying visits – she says she would take me among other places to see a Miss Cameron who was an artist and up we mounted to her flat – where she was in the midst of most purlieu-ish* cammacs.* There was another woman there who talked – who tackled Connie, so I buckled to with Miss Cameron – "So glad to see your studio what a pretty pastel – you must have studied in Paris" with the actions and gesture of the connoisseur – she had studied in Paris at Colarossi's Studio, and knew you – she said Miss Somerville is very amusing and was very clever with her pencil and was interested to hear you had gone in for the *Graphic*. She then showed me her pictures, and concealed her loathing of the task, and was very nice. It seemed to me that she was tremendously clever with watercolours and pastels – and not so good in oils though she had some sketches done in the latter which were very pretty. She is if possible going over for the Salon so don't be surprised if she and I turn up together at the

Gates of Hell – She is very interesting and must have been very pretty – Connie tells me they are frightfully poor and all clever. She used to lecture at South Kensington on anatomy and turned an honest penny thereby, but her health couldn't hold out and here she is, trying to sell her pictures, and succeeding pretty well only – she has sent two pastels to the Academy and is doubtful as to the reception of that sort of work. I told her you had sent a picture to the Salon on which she said that your studio (I can't spell the proprietor's name again) was a bad one to send from as it had no friends on the jury – Juliennes [sic] was much better in that and in every respect, but was built on tweesortirs* and was consequently unbearable. Altogether I heard many things of interest, and saw many more and was sorry to go away. Her sister came in while I was there, she writes for the *Temple Bar* – I understand – and seemed genuinely interesting. Altogether a family to know – I can't help thinking about your Salon picture – I would give large sums that it might get in – Never mind about it my dear if it doesn't ... I have just heard from Hildegarde about your *Graphic* pictures. It must be the American influence that has made them too broadly comic for that paper. I will go round with her on Wednesday, as it will be an opportunity of jousting about – But otherwise I don't see that I shall do much more. Hildegarde and Kitty are much better than I am at that sort of thing. I do not know if it is a sign of depravity of the blackest, but to get any satisfaction of even the most ordinary male being I find a tête a tête essential. However tomorrow (this is Tuesday night) I will go forth and first go to the *Sporting and Dramatic* armed with a letter to Mr Watson, the Editor – from Robert – and he may at all events give some sound opinion as to the next best place to send them. I will not send this off till tomorrow night and can then report progress – I have had a very nice letter from Mr David Arnott sending back the Jubilee putridity. He begged me to observe that it had scored 90 marks – 95 having collared the prize – rather infuriating to have got so near that nice little 3 pounds. Robert now is nothing but the Duke of Buckingham if that was the gentleman who was poet, fiddler, statesman and buffoon He had a great week campaigning for the Derbyshire Conservative candidate who was defeated I may add – that in the districts that Robert held forth the electors polled three to one against the Radical. The miners and mechanics tried to trip him up all the times he spoke but I am happy to say he was man enough for them. He spoke altogether on Land League topics, and as a Boycotted man, and the Sheffield paper said that he had astonished everyone by his facts. He actually reduced the miners to tears over the outrages. I generally leave politics to your mother and other

competent persons but it seems to me that there must be the devils own
row over this Crimes Bill[1] before it is passed and Balfour is the worst
man in the world to hustle it through but no matter. Robert was housed
and fed in sumptuous manner by Mr Mundy (Lord Shrewsbury's prede-
cessor, at Shipley.) Robert liked him tremendously, as also Mrs Mundy
No. 2 and seems to have had an excellent time in company with Admiral
Bartlett, Stuart Wortley and some others. While he was away, Connie
and I went on the spree more or less – we went to the play three nights
running for one thing. On the first of those nights, Harry Townshend
and Colonel Barton dined here and went with us. Harry having previously gone on with Minauderies* and nonsense about coming at all –
comparable only to Vesta's obstinacy "Robert is away and I have not
the pleasure of Mrs Martin's acquaintance" etc – However he did come
and very early – and when I bundled in to entertain him his question
was "*You* must see me through this" I said "Through what" with
asperity – and received a harangue which you can imagine – Connie
then appeared – On which Harry fixed blood-hound eyes upon her and
made a sort of curtsey – or rather he broke himself in two at the middle
and crouched finally shaking hands – I have never ever seen him shy
before – but he certainly was painfully so then, and scarcely spoke at
dinner – which bothered *me* as it of course was general talk being only
four. Connie took it into her head that he was deaf, from the habit,
which *we* know well, of deliberating before he answers – & bawled at
him with great assiduity throughout. She also thought he was very old
– and rather cracked – and the latter surmise cannot be wondered at –
as in addition to his peculiarity of manner on the occasion he brought
with him an extra pair of boots, a knitted cap, a pot hat (which no-one
wears going to the theatre) and a white knitted shawl – a regular
grimy Seafield one. I have seldom been more astounded than at these
preparations for the road. He became more like himself at the play
("Modern Wives") and assisted me to find likenesses in a most refreshing
manner – and was amusing. Don't give me away on this subject – you
well know the dynamitical nature of the danger. I am glad to say that
Connie has overcome her fear of whooping cough, and went to see
Minnie yesterday. She of course was out. Connie and I went out the
next night for a sort of pennygaff[2] – to two and six-penny places at the
Court – go to see the piece there if ever you get a chance 'Dandy Dick'

---

1 *Crimes Bill*: following the prevention of Crime (Ireland) Act of 1882, it extended
   summary jurdisdiction for offences of conspiracy and intimidation.
2 *Pennygaff*: slang word for any entertainment to which admission was one penny.

is its name and it is delightful. I applauded and bellowed from the gallery with the utmost freedom, and felt an ignoble desire to spit on the people in the stalls. The next night we attired ourselves with befitting splendour & went to a box at the Opera Comique to see the "School for Scandal". We very nearly asked Hildegarde and Egerton to come too and when I got there all I could feel for some time was deep abiding thankfulness that we had not. They have not bowdlerized the play and as you know the dialogue is enough to make your hair stand on end – I could not believe my ears, til I felt them getting crimson – I think Hildegarde and I would each have died if she and Egerton had come. For the rest – Kate Vaughan as Lady Teazle was not up to much, wooden and Kate Vaughanish but her minuet – lovely – she can dance – Forbes Robertson as Charles Surface was a very lovely man. I don't think I did anything else of interest lately except spend an afternoon in bed and go to Olympia with Molly McCalmont. I have I hope made Aylmer happy – I have this day despatched to him Ballyhooley, and the "jolly little chap". They have just been published and I believe are selling away like fun. I wish Robert hadn't parted with the copyright – I said nothing to Aylmer on the subject of enlisting – everything seemed to have been said – and I think he will do it – Wednesday evening. I have just come in from a long day with Hildegarde and let me tell you what happened among the Editors – she and I started at about eleven. I armed with a letter from Robert to Watson, the *Sporting and Dramatic* – recommending you in the highest manner – Robert happened to know him. Having sent up the letter we were presented and bidden to come up – which we did and found a little watery-eyed black man very like Mister Cole and very civil. We proceeded to display the sketches. He at once said that he was afraid they would not do – being in wash – and not in line. His paper never engraved except from lines – He however looked through the whole set and said they were very good and he was very sorry and all the rest of it. He also said they trifled with too serious a subject – We then hussied him all we knew and he showed us round the gallery of the originals of the *Sporting and Dramatic* pictures – mostly Sturgess – and showed us a lot of instantaneous photos of horses etc. Before we left he said he would be delighted to receive anything you might send him on other topics or for their Christmas number and done in lines. Sturgess' are all done in Indian ink. We then proceeded to the *Lady's Pictorial* who sent down for the sketches and returned them saying they were not suited for a Ladies' Paper so we left. I thought it a horrid vulgar place altogether. We next boarded the *Illustrated London News* and having wandered through strange lofts and garrets found the sub-editor. He took the sketches off to the head boss – and returned with the old story – too frivolous – and besides they had had an overdose of Ireland. He also said they would be most happy to see any drawings you might send – reiterated this before we left – but preferred the Indian ink style and no Irish need apply – He was a vulgar dirty creature – but I think he knew what he was about. We left and headed for the *Pictorial World* – and on the way it occurred to me that if you could do some character or other sketches of a French Race Course – it would be the thing – I daresay you are aware that they have prohibited betting with bookmakers in Paris – and there is great interest in the matter over here – and great ructions at Autueil. Of course you know all about it – It next occurred to Hildegarde and me that we should like to go and interview your special property – your own capture – Mr. Williamson. *We did* – as if to inquire from him exactly what he objected to in the sketches. We are both much enamoured – and we think he likes us very much – and we had a great deal of conversation in his little room. He apologised for its smallness and we reassured him. He said all the same things – too frivolous – too Irish – but said that they were always delighted to have your work – It was so original. He hoped that the *Mule Ride* would be out in a few months – but could not be exact as to dates. He seemed very anxious to have some sketches of copyists at the Louvre – He was really keen about them – I said something about the Race Course idea, and he immediately caught at it – and said it would be capital. He said the *Pictorial World* was the last chance, told us the Editor's name, and after fond Adieux we went. The editor of the *Pictorial World* was out so we went and had lunch in a steaming hot little bun shop and returned. He was still out and then Hildegarde and I had to abandon the pursuit, as we were going to a matinée at the Royalty – but Hildegarde will take them tomorrow or the next day and tell you – It seems to my limited intelligence as if the Race Course would come in admirably just at the present for the *Sporting and Dramatic* and you have the London sketches for the *Graphic*. Of course I speak as a fool – and if you want any more interviewing of Editors I am ready to do it. It is no bother – The matinée was a variety entertainment and great fun – Hildegarde admires Robert very much and liked Ballyhooley which was sung – I am dead beat so farewell –

Yours

Martin

Hell
April ? 87
Tuesday – anyway

My dearest child
I have no song to give you but I send eight drawings for you to send
on to the *Graphic*. The reason I give you this needless trouble is because
I want you to see them, and also to change if you think fit – the sub-
titles (I enclose the same, please forward them with the enclosed letter
to Mr. W) I have written the titles in a hurry at past bedtime, so I doubt
they are very bad. I especially dislike number four – and eight is stupid
– so if you get any inspiration, including a joke on *Duty* etc etc send it
to Mr. W instead of what I have written. I like this new drawing paper.
It is most interesting to work on, and I think has a very pretty effect.
Don't tell mother I have sent the sketches to you or she will kill me for
not sending them to her, but they are *very* easily rubbed and stained –
I had to work with tissue paper under my hand, – and besides it is such
a waste of time. I hope the G. will have them. They are not very
interesting – but I should like my little thing to be shown to the public.
Did you hear that the Salon wont have poor "Drunken Norris" – I have
almost come round to being glad – such is the Sanguineous Coghelian*
– because they all say your first picture should be just as full of your
best work as it can hold – and I had only ten days on this – and I know
it ought to have been lots better. Your last letter was deeply interesting
– Overweg and I wept sympathetic tears of much laughter over your
dealings with the insane hen-harrier (why hen I dont know – but there
is such a thing – and it feels like it to me). I have had a horrid cold the
last three days, and cooked it at home. Hence these pictures. Do come
with Miss Cameron if you can, she knows the ropes. Mind you dont
bring any more luggage than you can help – *I want to bring some on
your ticket.* So be careful – I will write more fully on this subject later
– when things begin to crystallize a bit and we know where we are. I
am sending you a thing of Miss Overweg – I shall tell her she must try
to see you, and try not to miss her. She would be able to interest and
amuse you much. I am going to try for Auteuil – but it wont be easy to
work – and I am dubious if we shall succeed in getting there. It is an
excellent idea and I am obliged to you for it. Miss O. will be in town
this day week or there abouts – I will tell her to write to you. She will
tell you all about Steadfast. She has been most supporting and consoling
in the matter. I must go to bed it is every sort of small hour. Steadfast
sought her virtuous couch at nine thirty. Thank the Lord – this is not

profane – but sincere – I do not like them as good as she is. If I had to choose between the poor but saintly curate and the wicked Duke, I would take the Duke at once and I advise you to do the same. Steadfast's morality is too rich for my blood.* She doesn't pretend to be good – she is rather this gay daringly reckless bohemian and she is exceedingly facetious. Anyhow she believes she is these things, and it is pitiable to see her doing her best to be "a little rawscal"* when she has not imagination enough for even the rudiments of villainy. She bores and absolutely exhausts me. I feel myself getting rigid with a kind of dumb bored fury, while she prattles on – as she *will* squat in my room every blessed night, unless I can keep her outside playing the fiddle – and she hears directly I stop and pelts back again. Remind me to tell you about her and Patsy when I see you. Well, goodnight – I could go on for hours, such is the relief of not having "my friend Miss Newstead" here. Of course they all think she is the friend of my bosom – and I writhe under the imputation – but have got to bear it. Thanks *awfully* for the *Grap*. & *Punch* – but dont send the former. Steadfast always gets it so it is a waste of good material. About the middle or end of the month I shall know what will be the best time for you to start. I think you can get a return for 42 shillings. Your grub will cost about 2/6 a day – and if – as seems likely – the hotel is too full to have room for you – you can share mine. I dont think it would be too bad. The bed is really a decent size and there is a little place in which you can wash – but if I can get you one of the small cheap rooms for a week I will – as I am afraid it will be rather a squash in mine – but not too bad. Your room (if you got one) would be about ten francs for a week or twelve or fifteen at the very outside. If I cant get one for ten – you will have to put up with mine – I wont let you squander your money –

Yours

E.Œ.S.

Willie Wills, playwright and man about town, took a benevolent interest in his young cousin Violet. Maurice Collis, in his biography of Somerville and Ross, suggested some kind of romance between this sixty-year-old man and the twenty-four-year-old Martin. But as a man he was not what Martin referred to as 'stirring'. The web of Martin connections-by-marriage laid a strand on Oscar Wilde via the Wills family (Oscar's middle names being Fingall O'Flahertie Wills). Wills men were celebrated for their eccentricity. The DNB, wishing to encapsulate Wills eccentricity, states that Willie Wills' father once boiled his watch, adding helpfully 'in mistake for an egg'.

Willie was foremost among the supporters of the actor Henry Irving in his late days, and it is possible that he actually wrote the anonymous Henry Irving – Actor and Manager: A Criticism of a Critic's Criticism, *a defence of Irving, that he gave to Martin in the early 1880s. It would seem that there was no special personal relationship between them, as Martin recorded that the book was a present from W. G. W. in her own handwriting on the title page.*

48 Leinster Square
Sunday April 17 '87

My dear Edith
I am afraid it is always the case that disappointments do not come singly. Yesterday a letter came for you from the R. A. which I opened and saw the fatal word "regret" – indeed it was what I felt. However we know that neither human beings or bed-bugs can get them all in a minute and it seems to me that you do wonders considering how little real toil you have put into it – Personally, though I should like to have seen the young gentleman on the walls of Burlington House, I shall be very glad to see his dear face back on my own – as you say, he *is* really a spoonful of paint for a big show like that. I don't know how the Bart has fared with his Faust. Willie Wills has sent his two pictures to the Grosvenor and says he means to take up portrait painting and wishes this fact to be generally known. I met him today in an unexpected manner near Minnie's. He was skulking à la conspiritor, and was dressed in *the* coat. This has an immense coachman's collar and cape. The former was turned up until it touched his hat, the latter hung freely back from his shoulders like a hood. He was covered in white smudges, and in this guise did I, in my very best bonnet, white veil and all the rest of it, wander with him down High Street to Gloucester Road – while he affected not to know the way except by the spires of churches and distant trees and the stars and such things. I am so accustomed to this nonsense and so wearied by combating it that I pretend to believe in it now, and follow him when he deliberately takes the wrong turn – no one would believe that a man of his age and ability could be so perverse and foolish – but no matter. I am very sorry to hear of my little thing's distemper – truly grieved – and hope he will be allright when I see him. I can imagine the disconsolate arch of his back and the retiring nature of his tail. You do not mention whether he was of the Auteuil party – but I suppose so –

make the most of your time, for he shall not accompany *my* rambles. I saw in the paper the other day that there was born unto me a grand nephew in the town of Paris last week. Hugh McCalmont's wife has apparently been caught out while travelling by land and water to get home and has come under the next clause of the Litany. I think you were in the highest degree spirited to make that expedition to Auteuil and I know Mr. Williamson will welcome the sketches with rapture which may or may not be due to the fact of their being done by a cousin of mine (I am thinking of sending him some sketches on my own account. There can be no reasonable doubt that he would accept them) I wish I had been at Auteuil with you all if it were only for the fun of trying to invent a bigger lie than you told when you said that you and Overweg picked the three first horses in every race (I forget the exact term which is used in Ballyhooley to describe such tales but will ascertain). Philip sent me concoctions that have already done me heaps of good and I shall be fit to run for my life when I get to Paris – I shall probably do that most of the time – certainly if that old Bedstead is after us. One of the Nostrums is to be taken "when the nerves are excited" so you need put no check on your powers of agreeability. I shall possess an antidote. I have heard nothing from Overweg. People with white eyelashes are always deceitful, however, white or black I should like to see her, and if I knew her address would ask her to tea without more ado. I don't believe that man was her brother. She is just the sort of girl to have . . . [*end of letter missing*]

Hell Street
April 23rd '87

My dear Martin
Your letter of this morning was a shill[1] of the largest and most uplifting kind. Instantly I sat down and wrote to your mother – a letter which combines the subtlety of a diplomatic note with the pathos of Little Nell's deathbed scene in Thackeray's beautiful novel, *The Mill On The Floss*. It will go by the same post as this if you can square your anxious parent and other things are equal it would be well if you could travel over on *Friday* night (April 29th) to arrive here on Saturday – because I find that Sunday 1st is the only day in the month when all the swagger fountains play at Versailles and we were thinking of going to play there

---

1 *Shill*: slang for something that raised the wind.

too. It is a great sight, and worth making the struggle for – and I fear you could never go straight there after your journey – anyhow even if you could – I would not permit you to do so. So try and hurry up and come over on Friday night. (Moreover we shall have to start from here at about the hour your train arrives). It would be a pity for you to miss this show. Try and bring other forces to bear upon your mother – It will be too hard luck if we were to give it up after all. I am afraid you will have to put up with half my room as a room on this étage is impossible, and you would be sure to see spiders and hear Hurley's dog or something if you were away by yourself in the other quarter of the hotel. We can always work it by the one (you) staying in bed while the other (me) gets up and dresses and sometimes washes. I was very nearly sending you my Auteuil sketches – but on the whole decided that it was better to send them direct. I am awfully glad Edith likes your picture I am a good deal elated by both Collin and Blanc approving of a head I painted last week – especially as it is so hard to get a good word out of the former. I have had my teeth quite put to rights and am a new and sound man. The worthy dentist let me off for thirty francs – and as he fixed four teeth I think it is cheapest thing I ever heard of – I had expected forty or fifty at the very lowest. I hear there are lovely little coats to be had at the Louvre for about one pound ten shillings. Only for these vile teeth I might have got one. I tell you of them so that you may hold your hand until you come over, in case you want the lot . . . I had an enchanting letter from mother this morning full of the most eminently Buddh* like and characteristic abuse of the new Harris import-ation – Miss Capes – ending with these soulful words "Oh she is a loathely female, and a vile Radical and Papist" – I will keep the letter to show you. I should think the woman must be a beast – and of course the Harrises keep her permanently out at grass on our tennis ground. I don't feel like writing any more tonight and have got to write home and also to Boyle tomorrow morning so I will shut this up. If you come to Paris will you bring two half pound packets of tea – I suppose two shillings and thruppence a pound. I would . . . [end of letter missing]

Martin's sister Edith married Captain Cuthbert Dawson and travelled with him on his various postings. At the time of writing this letter, Martin was visiting them when Captain Dawson was stationed at Portsmouth. Edith was her favourite sister, and is referred to as 'Edith' throughout Martin's papers; Edith Somerville is 'E.Œ.S.' throughout.

This letter describes an escapade of Jim and Robert Martin's, which was later used as an incident in the life of Florence McCarthy Knox in Occasional Licences.

[*Edith's note*: 'Staying with her sister Edith and Cuthbert Dawson.']

May 23 1887*
Gun Wharf, Portsmouth

This is such an engaging way of dating one's letters – I have picked it up from the best style of people here – and I think it is so original – quite Parisian. I am sure you will like it and perhaps adopt it as an alternative method. There is no doubt that what we loosely term "charm" is made up of these delicate idiosyncracies in manner of speech, gesture and even of writing – I hope you are having as good a day or better than we are having here – I mean for the benefit of Aylmer – I wish I had been there to give him cheer, but I daresay there were many others to do that – I simply love seeing common people running races whether afoot or a-horseback. I have such blissful recollections of the Oughterard horse races at which Jim used to ride, and we used to buy sugar stick in the tents and share it with the coachman – I remember Jim taking out the unhappy carriage horses who had dragged us from Ross, and racing them in turn, to their absolute amazement. Robert's races were a thing apart and belonged altogether to Ross. In one foot race, when they had well started it was seen that the favourite was left at the post and it was observed that his trousers had obeyed the word "go" and had gone to ground or to heel or any other way you'd like to put it – this is true. Has Aylmer absolutely fixed on the 7th Fusiliers as his regiment? It seems to me that it is too good a one for promotion. However I speak as one of the unlearned. I have heard that it is better not to go into a regiment where there are likely to be many other gentlemen . . . In spite of all your clumsy sneers I here proffer my deepest sympathy with that little dog in his affliction. I really feel sorry for him – He hasn't the physique to stand such awful times . . . It amuses me very much that Edith is going to make an expedition to Porchester to buy a goat, and will bring it back with her. Her garden is bounded on the North by sort of blind railway arches and there the goat is to live mostly and yield of her substance for the baby – Cuthbert says he will have a goat carriage to go about in – and a night goat when he goes out much in the evening – and hopes next year in the description of the meet of the Coaching Club to see a mention of Captain Dawson's team

1   She uses roman numerals thus: May XXIII, MDCCCLXXXVII.

of nannys – I don't know why these things should make me laugh but
they do. If you knew Cuthbert you would laugh too. His birthday text
in the Mark Twain Birthday Book (which Edith has got) is excellent
"you are a very proper and soldierly person" . . . Go to Youghal by all
means it would be a beautiful thing to do – was auch die Mutter spricht
– This is German – and singularly aptly quoted or koted as I suppose
you would say – I must say an artist's trade seems to me to be the
pleasantest all around especially when it gives an opening to your cousin
to come and improve her mind in Paris. I think I was a sort of dumb
dog over there, and assumed a sort of aristocratic langour all the time.
So it seems in reflection – but I was inwardly full of enthusiasm and
pleasure – so don't make any mistake about that. Indescribably vile is
the nor'easter which habitually blows here – ditto is the Common where
the aristocracy air themselves. The brutes dress well – but that is all that
is to be said for them. They are an odious class – old girls who have
taken to Southsea as a forlorn hope – Dirty little grubby soldiers – and
their no less dirty little grubby wives – There are of couse notable
exceptions – but the general tone is feeble gadding and going out on the
Common and Pier to meet their horrible carraways* – One of Cuthbert's
brothers in arms in the Gun Wharf has a wife who never by any chance
puts in her H's and today that fool Edith began unconsciously to leave
out hers too and then of course giggled. There are many excellent points
about Southsea a principal one being that the string band of the Marine
Artillery plays twice a week in the pavilion on one of the piers. We went
on Saturday – were admitted for the moderate sum of three pence – and
found with what despair you can imagine that selections from Lohengrin
had just been played – and that there only remained for us such as
'Dorothy' someone's waltz – selections from Norma and the like – but
it was enjoyable. We nearly cast off at the sight of the waltz – some of
them with their backs to the orchestra all of them talking through the
music, not even pretending to listen. Tomorrow night – I shall see them
in their thousands (thousands – me dear – *hundreds*)* as I am going to
the Admiral's reception. It will be very glorious as of course everyone
puts on their Sunday throusier[1] – I wish Boyle were going to be there
in his. Edith and Cuthbert are going on to the General's reception while
I meekly go home. Mrs. General not having asked 'party' which is what
I represent at the other place – Arthur Paget will of course be about.
He is to give us tea on the *Malabar* tomorrow afternoon – and I don't
think I can be ill – as she is in dock – but I am not by any means too

---

1 *Throusier:* hibernicized English for 'trousers'.

sure. Arthur was here yesterday, and says that Sophie has been ordered to some place up about Alsace, in the Vosges – which conveys nothing to me – However she is to go on the 2nd and wants most awfully to find someone to go with her – Arthur asked me if I would go, but as the return ticket is about £8, – you may imagine I did not accept – certainly she ought to have someone with her. A very mysterious thing has happened about my burnt red umbrella. You know that your little dog put his teeth through it – I'm sure you remember the two little holes – Very well – those holes have been mended in a most exquisite way – darned by a skilled hand and I have not the faintest idea whose – I discovered it the day I arrived here – For one moment I thought – Ah Edith, the angel in the house – she has quietly repaired the mischief done by her pet – Dear thoughtful girl – but a closer inspection of the work leads me to think I was mistaken. The burnt holes are as they were – but the puppy's toothmarks are effaced – I here propound another problem on which the youth of Castle T. may exercise their ingenuity (Cuthbert saw it in the *Pink 'Un* last week) a young lady and a ditto gentleman are in a drawing-room – the young lady becomes hysterical, from causes unknown – the young gentleman in his anxiety and confusion thinks he remembers dropping a key down the back is good on such occasions (as it is for a bleeding nose) He accordingly tears the key from the door and shoves it down her back – He then rushes for further help, and finds that in taking out the key he has locked the door – curtain – you will observe the delicacy of his position . . . It is very late and I must to bed – that dress that I bought when casually shopping with you is going to be beautiful. It is being made by a woman who once was Serpolette in *Les Cloches de Corneville* – but lost her voice in scarlatina. Could anyone but Edith have such a dressmaker. We were at a concert last week where a woman called Hemmings played the cello right well and solidly and a boy of 16 in a blue funk played the violin astoundingly – but made a hash of the first thing. He played my beloved Chopin Nocturne very well – Antoinette Sterling was fine—
   Martin

Both Edith and Martin had mothers who were powerful but frustrated women. Nanny Martin had been released from her husband through his death and from most of her children by their marriages, and had become vague and inattentive. Martin's father can only be described as despotic, and it is easy to understand the attractiveness of Castletownshend society to Martin, whose chief knowledge of family life had come from Ross.

Edith's mother, a possessive type unlike Nanny Martin, lived for her family – indeed, engulfed them – and was a sore trial to her children in her larger- and louder-than-life, frankly interfering behaviour.

This letter shows Mrs Somerville determined to intrude upon a family called Harris, who had become tenants of The Point for a holiday let.

Mall House
Lismore
June 2nd 87, Thursday

Dear Martin

As I daresay you are longing to write to me I will mention that my address is as above till Monday and after that Post Office Youghal will be the direction till about Thursday – Hildegarde and I got to these parts yesterday, but before detailing our adventures, let me tell you of the present phase of the Harris row – which I may observe, is now assuming international proportions. Mother considered that by stopping away from the Point for a week she had sufficiently marked her indignation at Mrs. H's kenattiness* to Aylmer and Mr. Snow – but when on Sunday, she resolved to go down, she found that she was in too great a fright to go by herself and she demanded that she should be conveyed, like the colours of a regiment, in the centre of a hollow square, composed of Hildegarde, Violet, me and the Puppy – (I had gone down to see her before and found her "out of home" – and H. had also been there) – Violet refused – and mother put it off till after second Church – i.e. 8.30 at which ridiculous hour we processed down through the garden – Mother "white to the lips" and my eyes and Hildegarde's full of tears – (as Bessy Fleming has said) On arriving at the big window we saw the drawing room was empty. Naturally they were at food of sorts, and equally naturally our proper course was to march on, smiling as we passed the window, and so home. But mother became siezed with unreasoning panic. Regardless of the fact that they must have heard our approach she darted up on the grass and fled back of Glen B. uttering hoarse whispered injunctions not to make a sound, and to hurry, which must have been distinctly audible for miles. Of course H. and I laughed like fools, and H. finally tumbled flat over a small fuchsia tree, driving it into the earth like a tin-tack, and nearly giving mother a fit of apoplexy from the combined effects of rage, terror and laughter. Thus ended the first attempt of the little peacemakers. I was sent out from the ark again on Monday but found no rest for the sole of my claw. On Tuesday – all went to Glen B. for tennis (except the little snowman and I) and there they met the old Cat she cut Aylmer dead, twice. He lifted his hat to her and she took no notice of him – both when she came and when she went. The General was civil enough to him, and she was alright to mother and H. What Aylmer's offence is none of us know except not having put the General on his committee and he explained and apologised to Jim – so why she loathes him is a mystery. This I know – that if she wont know Aylmer I wont know her – so I daresay there will be Ber-lud[1] – Little Mr. Snow and I rode to Lough Ine that day. I in my *new habit*. Alas – too large for me at waist and here [drawing] – I think the skirt is very good and the cloth seems very nice. We got into the fields at Blackstaff's Cross – (just where your nerves received that violent shock from the bedridden mare with an infant foal) and went right along the drag course till we got to the far end of the O'Donovan's lake. We found some elegant fences – big and sound. Do you remember one I had an awful work getting Vesta over – a big fence out of a dry boggy field with a gripe on the far side? We had that from the gripe side, and it would have done your heart good to see how Sorcerer and Ballyhooley jumped it. Very different to Vesta's little unenthusiastic belaboured bucking scramble. By the bye Hildegarde confided me the painful secret that in spite of a beautiful black hunting coat, breeches, boots and spurs the Beany[2] solidly declined to jump for Hal, and his godmother inserted her family hoof* by suggesting to him that Aylmer should be got over to teach her her duty . . . When are you coming? Try and crystallize your ideas and tell me what they amount to –

E.Œ.S.

[Queen Victoria's Jubilee Procession]

Gun Wharf Sunday Evening and I ought to be at church
June 26 1887

My dear Edith

Before anything let me tell you what has just happened to me. The day is not warm, and I have gone out in a skirt without a body, and with a coat. Returning I find Arthur Paget in the drawing-room, and sinking on a chair (I had been rowing) unbuttoned my coat with a run to the very top and flung it open to its widest – and still did not see anything

1 'Ber-lud': comic opera exclamation for 'Blood!'
2 *Beany*: nickname for a horse.

amiss, till the tail of my eye caught a glimpse of skin where skin does not usually show – and I sat revealed, a maid in all her charms – with Arthur opposite in strong convulsions. In that supreme moment I reflected that my stays were highly creditable – almost new, and what was visible of my combination was very neat and that my manly bosom had had its Sunday wash and altogether there were many bright features in the case – but it was awful for all that . . . Thank you very much for the dictionary in which I note some new words and many mistakes – words generally used – one or two wrong definitions etc. All these will I set in order when I come . . . Edith has remembered several of Granny's and Uncle Arthur's words – Partly obsolete but I think it is our high privilege to preserve these for prosperity – Anyhow I will take them down – One of Uncle A's which I have heard many a thousand time is 'outlying deer'* a noun of multitude – meaning his various carroways.* I daresay you have heard it. This lined paper is like the old times – I don't like it but have no other. I am proud of Patsey and the slaying of the rats. I didn't think he had it in him – and what shall I say of your mother and her sporting tendencies.¹ Perhaps it may be given to me to see her engage in the past-time which is undoubtedly a fine old national one. I have long thought that nobody has principles – at least about one in a hundred – and the rest of us are just held together by conventionality and the like – being in reality ready for any crime when put at it straight. Such is the history of the downfall of the Castle Townshend moral standard. How shall I feel this summer when Aunt Adelaide sends out her invitations for her afternoon ratting party "You will kindly bring your own rats if possible" I see Minnie arriving with a few good stable ones in a cage and laying the odds on Stinger – You made mention of a certain sketch which you kindly placed at my disposal – Never say it again – I accept with the greatest pleasure – which will probably be greater still when I see it. I like your landscapes tremendously so don't you go and give that to anyone else as you are quite capable of doing. You will not find anyone who will appreciate it more. Now that I am in the vein for saying pretty little things I may tell some things about Hamilton. All of you are delightful, he says, all of you are talented, all are hospitable – but you (unworthy slut – that I should *have* to tell it!) in your proper person form the apex. He could not say too much of your combined talent and modesty and pleasantness and wound up with "she's as nice as they make them". There – I cannot do better for you than that – and coming from him for whom you have confessed your

1 Mrs Somerville had been rat-hunting.

affection you ought to value it. I think he was perfectly delighted with his time at Castle T. What with the weather and all of you spreading yourselves to make it pleasant for him I cannot be surprised. I have got into a maze of honeyed phrases which strange to say have given me much satisfaction to write – We missed Hamilton on his way back. He anchored at Spithead for a few hours, but as Cuthbert and Edith had not come back all I could do was go down to Arthur Paget to find out what would happen – and then discovered that *Tamar* had sailed at eleven o'clock. We had a delightful evening on board when he left this for Edinburgh – the height of eating and drinking and much high class conversation. There was a nice man called Maxwell whom he, Hamilton, chartered to entertain us – and the Captain – by name Warren – knows all the Penroses – and Castle Townshend and every mortal thing – and has an invigorating brogue – I feel it my duty to make some mention of the Jubilee – which I am bound to say was a very grand sight. As soon as we got to town we felt that we were under its spell in common with everyone in London. The town was something to remember. Countless thousands of people just walking about the street and looking about them not pretending to have any other business – Edith and I went into the Row on Monday evening, and though there were not very many people in it, the crowd at Hyde Park Corner was tremendous – all strangers and country people, come to stare at the quality going into the Park. We couldn't get through for ages Piccadilly was wonderful from the decorations and the throngs. We walked up to the top of the hill in it and from there to Hyde Park Corner looked back at one solid block of carriages – not a move in them as far as we could see nor any prospect of a move – omnibuses and coaches all in a compact mass for a quarter of a mile. This was all the evening before – We left the house at 8 next day and even then there was a tail of people right into the street at the underground so we gave that up and footed it to Charles Street through the Park and the Green Park up to Pall Mall. I never can forget the look of the Park that morning – so beautifully dewy and fresh, with the rhododendrons so lovely that I could scarcely believe it – and the people converging through it in processions from every quarter. It felt like a sort of dream. I never knew before that feeling of a tremendous advance to a common centre – whatever way you looked there were people hurrying in – We had a squashing at the gate of Green Park but got through and fetched up at the Waterfords at about nine – There we found peace and calm, the best of good seats in the balcony, and a breakfast of the most inviting and comprehensive kind. There were about 15 other people there – just about what there was room for in the balcony. We had a perfect view as the drawing-room runs right up to Waterloo Place – or nearly. We had not the sun in our eyes, and it shone straight on the Procession as it came towards us. We ate a great deal from time to time while we were waiting – it being a crossroads we saw some most entertaining fights at corners between police and people. Several times a telegraph boy was handed across the heads of the crowd like a roll of cloth amid the greatest cheering – You know just as much of the Procession as I do from the papers. What struck me most were the Indian people, who looked like the real fine old stage princes, sparkling fit to blind you. The crown prince of Prussia, in a beautiful white uniform (poor fellow I believe he has cancer in the throat and his days are numbered) and I think perhaps the Queen herself was the finest of the whole show. You could not believe what a great lady she looked – neither could you believe how dark it is and how hard to write – no more for the present – I see that I have enthused about the Jubilee in a surprising way – so would you if you had been there. All that remains to be said is that we hifled* out to St. James Street to see them on the way back and wrestled with the filthy mob – A drunken man steadied himself against me to cheer as they passed, and though I could see nothing but the coachmen's heads I bellowed and screamed too – most refreshing it was after the lady-like reserve of the Waterford's balcony. Edith managed to get on to the corner of a chair on which there were three or four other people, and was immediately clasped round the neck by one of them, a man – who apologised – but said he must hold her round the neck or he would fall off – *She* would have fallen off if he hadn't so it was rather fortunate – Cuthbert propped her from below and while in this pleasing position her pocket was picked with great precision – She did not loose much in the way of money – but our return tickets were in the purse also her store ticket. We were nearly dead after it all but it was quite good enough. It is something to remember to have seen London off its head in the way it was – and to have heard the shouting. I believe that in the Abbey the places were ticketed a few days before "Room here for three kings" "Room here for 14 princes" that is to me a strange and amusing thing. Talking of the Jubilee I have received from the *Irish Times* a gift of the book of 50 poems which was presented to the Queen for light reading – Hers was bound in white satin I understand – This is rather a pretty green cloth – a poem to each page – harps and shamrocks in profusion – but not as vulgar as you would think – rather neat on the whole – I was surprised to see mine among them – Having got back the original long ago – and also surprised that they were all better than could have been expected – one or two quite good – and almost any one of them better than the one that collared the prize out of 400. It is great nobility on the Chimps[1] part to come down with the ready as he does – and a nice healthy sentiment that he should like to have a portrait of the house – I suppose that you are doing it from the Conservatory side – It is just as well that I am not at Drishane now. I see that Sylvia would be my only companion what with the painter, the sitters and the engaged people – not that I should want a more entertaining companion I may add. I wish however that Fanny Currey had put off her visit till August. I should like to meet her – to hide about in safe corners and look on while she was with you. As to those tennis shoes I have neither seen nor heard of them – but at Richmond I may – Katy tells me that tennis is a very old-fashioned game now at C.T. Said I not well that you were all both effete and spasmodic – no healthy moderate interests – all is at fever heat, with nauseated reaction . . . By the way it is on the cards that I might bestow myself on your household about the end of July. I cannot be sure but supposing that I did, would it be the same thing to your mother? I wish I could be more exact and satisfactory, but there are wheels within wheels. Edith tells me that she humbly thanked Providence that I was not in Church tonight with her and Cuthbert. There was the most appalling back-hair* sermon – too awful – she simply sat with her eyes fixed and perspiring freely – Cuthbert has a tale of a cousin of his – a very shy young man who went to the Lyceum, and during one of Irving's great soliloquies in "Hamlet" his opera hat opened itself with a pop – that man also perspired and died a thousand deaths inwardly – which is what reminded me – This cousin went on another occasion to visit some relations with discouraging manners and an awe inspiring house. To show that he was quite unembarrassed he began to play with the favourite pug, finally dancing it round on its hind legs – it immediately threw up – and that I think ends the story. Do you know that sailor hats should be tremendously high in the crown now, and rather narrow in the brim. The people here wear them trimmed off at the back – a beastliness I think – They also wear white yachting caps – one of which I have got – and fear I am of surpassing frightfulness in it – but they look very smart on the water. Sophie Paget likes Contrayville very much, and Arthur is more or less moody and forlorn in her absence. Probably if she hated the place he would be quite happy – such are men – Mama talks of Castle T. lodgings with some confidence but I don't know what will come of it – She is almost off her head with delight about Jim coming

1   *Chimp*: Cameron, eldest brother of E.Œ.S.

home and I don't wonder. I don't know whether Katie has left Castle
T. yet – tell me in confidence your candid opinion as to the new chastener* and also in confidence what the humours of that fair fellowship
have been. Evidently the present idea according to Hamilton is that the
Bart hasn't even a look in – that he is tolerated in a friendly way and I
do admire Katie for the way she drove those two in double harness. It
amounts to inspiration. I drivel on into the smallest of hours for no
particular reason – except that my head is alright after being rather a
bother for a few days. My address from tomorrow will be Kew Cottage
– Kew – Surrey – a very delectable place just now in the way of the
trees and river –
Yours
Martin

P.S. I am horrified to find it is daylight – don't give me away

Drishane
Friday night July 15th 87

Dear Martin
You are a good woman not only to do Mother's behests, but to write
letters on the subject. I enclose dollars to the amount of goods as per
invoice. The blue dress hasn't come but it sounds very recherch.* If the
white one is not to be had, don't mind getting another in its place, as
Mother had fondly hoped to get things ready made, which should cost
23 shillings and 4 pence each, and was rather horrified at hearing the
skirt and body was one pound ten shillings or thereabouts. The Dolman
is very nice and exceedingly cheap and looks very well on Mother, it
must have been a most solid shop girl on whom you tried it as it is a
little bit too large even for my parent's ample shoulders. You will be
surprised to hear that she and I are the only two in the house tonight –
Papa is in Cork on the Grand Jury – Aylmer – of course – at Liss Ard,
and Hildegarde is at Glen B. and poor Jane (the house maid of whom
you wot) has been very bad with a tooth and consequent neuralgia; she
is now on leave for a week. So Hildegarde went to Glen B. to lessen the
work for the remaining domestics. Tomorrow however Captain Bourke
and his wife and Aylmer are coming to stay till Monday so poor me
doesn't get much of an easy. The varied shows of last week were pulled
through with fair success. The Rectory at home after the confirmation,
was *direful*. Mad acute boredness possessed us all. These new people

the Lloyds are a very dull lot. She is a good little thing who would have been pleasant and agreeable if she got a show but her husband is a sour mean conceited Kenat* and she is overshadowed by him and a coming infant. His two sisters are more stupid than you could believe to be possible. For instance, one was telling me of her two dogs, pugs – she said "Miss Currey tells me (they come from Fanny Currey's country) that if pugs run among bushes their eyes drop out, but they are attached to a bit of white string and you can generally put them in again". This with a gentle seriousness. I could only sit with a fallen jaw and a glazing eye – but I retained sufficient presence of mind not to go back on the ingenious Fanny.

Of course the object of the Show was the Bishop, who sat large and gloomy and yellow, and was tackled by Buddh* after Buddh in discomfited succession. Hildegarde's was the most pronounced failure. We had thought he looked upon her, his little old convert, with a soldier's eye, and we hurooshed[1] her at him as the Puppy is set at the calves; and with equally reckless vigour Hildegarde advanced to the charge. He praised the choir, she acknowledged the compliment and said with truckling smiles and swayings "an old woman said that indeed, glory be to goodness, the Coghill family would be a great addition to heaven". In one instant the Prelate's huge bare head became blue with passion; with an awful scowl he said "You seem very musical" and then the little convert fled, and left him to brood over her profanity. Rose was also very ghastly. Mother, Violet and I were the victims – and Beatrice who is the Darling of the Rectory, went with the Broughams and the Bishop. The "representatives of sixteen choirs" made as bad a noise as I have ever heard. The only interest of the day was lunch. The Dean (Isaac of that Ilk) had really provided a square meal to which 130 people sat down – Violet and I were nearly carried off to the high table at which the Bishops and Principalities and Powers were placed. In fact I was there, when the gleaming slit of the Squaw* eye conveyed to me that a more lowly station offered greater facilities, and I deftly withdrew. The only drawback to the humbler place was an absence of second plates. We cleaned our meat plates with bread and the table cloth – others seemed to use their pocket handkerchiefs, but mine was too clean. We gorged; after the meal, your respected cousin by marriage made a long speech, describing the Jubilee service in the Abbey. He seemed to have been fetched by the "beautiful gilded seats of the princesses" I am not surprised – I wonder who gilded them. Then he proposed the Queen's

1 *Huroosh:* to cheer on.

health . . . Beatrice – my dear – sat with her hand clasped in the Bishop's – more or less – all the time and went home like Lazarus, reclining in A-Brougham's bosom – it was a picture to see her.

I fancy the little Coghill has told you of the Cobb picnic. Yesterday thirty of the uncircumcised were here for tennis – very exhausting. We had both grounds going and they seemed happy, but it was hard work. Great agitation prevails at New Court just now – "A young Man, dear Adelaide, is very fond of our little girlie Bessy" – a most rank Galoot,[1] I may observe. Richard O'Grady by name. There is division amongst the girlies – Bessy and Suzie loving him and the other two abhorring him (with reason). Our people went there this week and said the excitement was at fever height. Mother, like Mr. Hannigan at Punchestown was "in her glory" – a mixture of airy badinage combined with a most searching cross examination had the effect of bringing to light the minutest details – She has at this moment given me an incident in the courtship which I had not before heard – One of the girlies was sent into the drawing room to do gooseberry, and there she found them, my dear, sitting on a window seat, looking at each other, roaring crying – I naturally asked why – Mother said "Oh I don't know, me dear, Love, I suppose" – I hear the last scene before he left New Court was harrowing in the extreme. He went into the yard and sat down on a water barrel, and weeping, refused to pack his clothes. It seems he has – as yet – said nothing official, and Mrs. Fleming wanted to send him off in order that absence might screw up his courage into writing, as he doesn't dare speak. I wish I could tell you all the facts – they are unspeakably funny – but I haven't time, as even now I ought to be in bed. Mrs. Harris has another niece – Miss Harriet Capes. She seems by far their best importation. She is a large handsome, interesting woman, and has a nice quiet manner. She is like millions of people, which adds to her charm considerably.

You will be glad to hear that Dannyman is coming here, Drishane, for about a fortnight in the beginning of August – I don't know exactly who the Coghills are to have – Fred Barton I think and possibly Willie Lee and Katie Plunket and Constance and Ethel and Jim besides Uncle Jos and the Colonel – I don't know how or where they are all to go, but that is the rough idea . . . I daresay all you say of Gordon is true, but I have as yet only read the *Bab Ballads* and skimmed the others, which certainly seemed to me awfully influenced – to put it mildly – by other people. I thought bits of the *Swimmer* were very good – but I lent

1 *Galoot:* American slang for fool.

Minnie the book and haven't got it back from her. I am much obliged
to you for Mr. St Leger's opinion – I am afraid he must have thought
you wrote those sonnets – hence his good nature – but all the same it
was very good of you to show them to him. If you would only do what
I ask and apply your own heart into rhyming you would do well – Now
bed. *Saturday* – we are all going to Liss Ard today as a kind of scratch
cricket match has been got up – a team was coming from Clonakilty to
play Aylmer's eleven, but wired yesterday to say they couldn't come –
so now – they have gone into the highways and hedges to collect another
eleven, and if they can by any means, – they will have some sort of
cricket or skittles whatever, and we are in any case to eat lunch there.
I have no time to write anymore this morning – Harry Becher is coming
to preach here tomorrow – Thank goodness – the Canon's drivels
become washier and weaker every Sunday – and longer – I may add –
but I can now so completely disengage my mind and hearing from what
he is saying that I have ceased to object to him actively – unless indeed
the church is as hot as it was last Sunday –

Yours

E.Œ.S.

P.S. I suppose you know that Uncle Jos is at Pennybun – my stamp is
like a sunset in water colours.

*While at Castletownshend in the summer of 1887 Edith and Martin
finished compiling the 'Buddh Dictionary', a collection of words and
phrases peculiar to the network of families descended from Charles
Kendal Bushe, Lord Chief Justice of Ireland. Their interest in words was
matched by their interest in pronunciation, and from the beginning we
find them striving to render accent and tone by all manner of means,
even using the notation of the tonic sol-fa system then coming into
popularity for village choirs whose members might not be able to read
music.*

*Noticing their shared facility for writing, Edith suggested that they
might write a story together. It is not difficult to understand why this
idea of collaboration should have sprung into Edith's mind. Since the
age of eighteen she had illustrated texts – sometimes her own, sometimes
other people's – for many different publishers, and had also published
a few humorous 'pieces'. She was perfectly accustomed to the 'poet and
painter' combination, and indeed this term was to be applied by critics*

to their joint writing. What was unusual in their joint venture was that the poet and painter both worked in words.

Theo, their heroine in An Irish Cousin, *is a young Canadian woman. This unusual background was inspired by Mrs Martin's friendship with a Canadian cousin, Archer Martin, who later stayed at Ross, and the fact that part of the Martin family had emigrated to America and Canada after the collapse of the Ballynahinch branch during the Famine years. She is a very modern woman, countered by a very well-drawn male character, Willy, who may well be derived from Edith's cousin Hewitt Poole. The series of letters exchanged by Edith and Martin during the writing of* An Irish Cousin *shows how important the reaction of the family was to them. Their novel was known as* The Shocker.

[From Martin to Edith, ? December 1887: *fragment begins on page 2*]

. . . bawling, prating, unselfsufficing brothers – and I suppose the Chimp to be written to every other day. You may tell Aylmer, the good and trusted, all this abuse, but to Boyle you may just mention what pleasure it is to me to think that you are enjoying the privilege of a little Naval Society. But indeed I give you solemnly the Award of Merit – you are a heaven born correcter – a spy-crack of the most unfailing and the most courageous – a truly reliable coadjutor, a comfort in all aspects Shocking –

You must think of a name for yourself. Two New Writers is every day more odious to me – Gallantly invent something like Currer Bell, George Eliot, or any of them – "Peg o'the Purlieu"* "Miss B. O'Hemia" "Sister Chimpan". The tears are running down my cheeks – It is "Peg o'the Purlieu" and I don't know why it should make me laugh in this way except that there is a grand breezy Scotch feeling about it. It is very weird to hear my own little cackles in the silence – but Oh I seem to see that name in print with Richard Bentley and Son beneath it. B. O'Hemia is really ingenious but scarcely suitable – and the little nunnery suggestion of Sister Chimpan is pleasant – but anyhow *do* try for a name – I have seen a work advertised by "A New Writer" . . . I am going to the church practice, with the faint hope of inducing Miss Roberts not to play the hymns Presto Agitato – I would sneak out of choir if I could, the working of it is so futile, but don't see how, and anyhow I have your Alto to look forward to when you come. Tell Hildegarde her hymn book is a great pleasure to me and an adornment to the Church . . .

[From Martin to Edith, 3 December 1887, *fragment*]

Rossetti had but one idea of life – to be in love – with perhaps religion thrown in – of a glamoury enamoury sort – and I think for all his sonnets he had not the right idea of a woman. I never feel inspired by reading him – inspired I mean to be brisk and candid and interested in common things – Far otherwise – a contrast will explain – For instance the first bit, group of verses or whatever you call it, of *In Memoriam* – that leaves a nice clean taste in ones mouth. Here is indeed the complete letter writer, fresh from quotation hunting – and I shall probably read Rossetti in bed in a few minutes and confess that he is unsurpassable.

I do not dare to think of the hour – but this is last of the midnight scrawls. The proofs never gave me time to write before dinner and after I am bound to play with Mama. I am going now to burn the lot of Shocker things – headings mottos and so forth and feel a faint sentiment in so doing. Any period of good work has a nice honest romance about it. I do not think much of the Shocker all around I am bound to say. It has its points but it is indifferently written – with awkwardness and effort. However the tone is very sound and the sentiment is genuine and it is sincere and unusual. That is my opinion.

You once said a little thing about it and what the writing of it did for us – if you don't remember it I do – that is good enough. Anyhow it was a nice little thing. Goodnight now. Heavy soft rain flopping against the window. Rather a pleasant sound –

Yours
Martin

This letter shows the first novel approaching final manuscript stage. It was Edith who did the clean copying for the typesetter as she had what she referred to disparagingly as 'a clear commercial hand'. Here she has been adding a love scene, knowing that Martin will avoid such. Hildegarde's criticism that Martin wants to write unlike anyone else is very acute. It is clear that from the very beginning they had trouble with the character of Nugent, who never did spring to life like Theo and Willy.

Drishane
January 21st 88
Half eleven of the clock
Saturday night

My dear Martin,
I know I ought to go to my good sleep, but my brain is so be-shocked
that I really can't, and will try if beginning a letter acts as a sedative. I
have finished the copying! and about three of the hardest pencils are
worn to the bone over it. I think I shall have to send it to you by book
post tomorrow as I cannot bear to wait, and for pity's sake try and
write by return of post to say if you like pages 71 and 72. I have always
felt something like that there – *don't* say it is premature – it isn't – and
I do think that that is the kind of thing that seems to me probable. Of
course add, if you like, but I would not sweep or modify – don't anyhow
till you have given it good consideration. H. is enthusiastic and loved it
the instant I read it and said it was just what was wanted – and so did
Minnie. I know you must loathe my sticking in these putrid things and
then fighting for them. I couldn't help it – as I got the feeling of it one
night in bed and wrote it there and then. Please goodness we will have
many a tooth and naily fight next month – but don't let us combat by
post; it is too wearing. I pity you – I was just saying to H how odious
it must be for you having these things jumped upon you. She says you
are ever so much too refined, and too anxious to have anything in your
book that was ever [sic] in anyone else's book; I think that is true.
Mother has complained bitterly of the want of love interest. She read
the last chapter tonight but could not comment more than by saying,
for the first time, with unqualified approval "*very* good!" She was very
amusing this afternoon. She came in as I finished reading it to Minnie,
who said that "Now there was enough love in it" Mother had not then
read the proposal and replied with infinite scorn "only squeezing her
hand me dear!" She went on to say that *she* liked impropriety. I said
that I had urged you in vain to insert many such – and she declared
that you were quite wrong and when I suggested the Family's "remark"
thereon she loudly deplored the fact of our writing being known. This
is rather good seeing that she has blazoned it to the four ends of the
earth and Aunt Georgina – not the story however – only the fact of our
writing. She has just exported a parlour maid to Aunt Louisa, who wrote
lately, gratefully offering the half of her Kingdom. I made mother write
at once and ask her to read the Shocker, and I am sure (in any case) she
will do so. Mother says O'Neill ought not to say to Theo that Mrs

Whelply plays as if the "the devil"[1] was after her – (I wish I was "after" him – he still tarries and demoralises me) I have left a blank – and can only suggest "the Old Gentleman" which is rather odious but the only alternative that I can see. Minnie says that the only part that has in the least struck her as being tedious was Nugent's and Theo's talk in the billiard room – I have always felt that billiard-Jimmy-Barrett-business superfluous, and that a more personal opening, tho less probable would be more interesting to the reader. Minnie is so lenient that I think a lot of any adverse criticism from her, and I certainly found that part both dull in the writing and the reading out. Mother did not object to it and H thought it characteristic of Nugent but I must say that I have from the start thought it dull. However do just as you please about shortening it. We might leave it till February unless you get an inspiration in its place. I should leave the hunt chapters intact (except perhaps a little cutting of geography) and let the Esuols, Ethel etc see what they think of them – I think the beginning of the ball, for example during her dance with O'Neill – is rather garish and his remarks are too isolated, and come in like a Greek chorus – However I made no change – I think an adjective or two might be omitted with advantage – though they are expressive in their little way. Minnie thought the whole ball *excellent* and gave the feeling admirably. None of them see any charm in Nugent, except mother who likes him in contrast to Willy, whom she hates as a "vulgar Aylmer". *He must do some doughty deed* – self abnegation of sorts – moral virtue in connection with a Durrus trouble – or else Theo must enlarge on his magnetic fascination – otherwise he is hardly made attractive enough for her to be made very keen about him. In this next volume he must be as paramount and as vivid as Willy has been! Mind that now – also Moll must be found murderously in Theo's room soon – before all the effect of the "uncanny room has faded from the reader's memory – and also of course, before Willy's marriage to Anstey. She ought not to stop more than a day at Clashmore – both on Nugent's and Moll's account, and W. must have left for Cork so that she can have a good gubbing* with Moll and Dominick. Would you tell Ethel to send it on to your Edith, or to Aunt Louisa? And if the latter, would you send a rough sketch of plot? I think that is a pity, but still you can't expect a working opinion from her without giving her some idea of the whole thing. H says she will gladly, and carefully, copy for us onto foolscap while she is at Glandovan, and would like the occupation. It is a good offer and I know she would put her back into it – and it would

1 *The devil*: the name given to their periods.

save us an awful lot of time and trouble. Please goodness, we shall know about the rents on Tuesday or Wednesday; til then nothing is definite. Minnie says Geraldine's would be a most shrewd intelligent opinion, in spite of her absence of mind. I am quite sure of it too – and it is certainly encouraging that both she and Minnie should like it – and both have heard it badly; as it is a book not to be read aloud. The words are rather too long and peculiar for satisfactory declamation – Now it is 12.25 – I will try to go to sleep – more tomorrow . . . [*letter unsigned*]

Drishane
Sunday 1888

My dear Martin

I was going to have written to you today in any case to announce the sending to you of the first volume of the Shocker – up to the 13th chapter, I don't like to send it on to Ethel until you have had a run over it and corrected it. From the Dominick and Moll chapter. There are only little verbal alterations here and there and you will see that nothing of any importance is changed. I am quite sure you would have felt just the same about the puke of the stable yard chapter. I know we put it in because Aylmer had made those two loose boxes. However I have faithfully preserved all the original M.S. so if you don't approve it is easy to put it in again. If you thought Geraldine would not be bored perhaps you might try it on her, and if she can stand it she might be a valuable bit of the vox populi. In any case send it on to Ethel as soon as you can, as I promised she would have it some time this week. I think I shall have the rest copied by Wednesday, I have yet another book which will more than see it through. Mother's attitude is one of disfavour, but she tries in vain to conceal her interest. Minnie is openly delighted, and even said the other day, when I had finished speaking a piece – "I wish I could say I had written it" she also told Mother it was much better than she had expected. I think if Mother had not begun by saying she loathed it she would not feel bound to continue doing so now – or rather pishoguing[1] it. If you have time, send me a detailed account of what you think of the alterations and if you think they may stand. I thought of one or two things, but had not time or courage to do them. About the illuminator. I believe that Mr. John Gilbert, 120 Patrick Street Cork does that kind of thing very well. I don't remember ever having

---

1 *Pishoguing (Irish):* putting spells on it.

seen any of his work, but I know is always employed to do all the addresses and testimonials and things; I daresay he could send a specimen of his artistic muscle if you ask him. He is a very clever man, and does rather nice water colours. Mother begs Geraldine to let her see Robert's row with Trevelyan. She had seen no Dublin papers since the Coghills went and she swears she will faithfully return whatever she is sent. She was enchanted to hear of your letter from Mr. Hunt – and says you are a "shameless hussy to ply him with love ditties when he is soft and weak with grief". Hildegarde sends thanks for the hat and will send the hems tomorrow; Sunday there is no parcel post. I knew you would be looked upon as the Maharaja's white swan – Bother – church – and hordes of loathely foreign suburbans coming to the gallery – of whom more anon – Of all the suburbans only Aylmer's little lorn love Hilda Pethlum, came to the gallery. Her sisters stayed downstairs, and so did Mrs. Harris's brother Mr. Ratcliffe and his daughter both of whom I had expected upstairs. He is an old buck with a closely clipped grey head and short grey moustache. Rather like a vigorous, big, unghostly Colonel Powell. He is also like Mr. Currey. She is small and trim – aged anything from 25 up – plain, snub-nosed – delicate and intelligent looking. She had a nice little English manner – quiet and intelligent and is *marvellously* clever with her fingers. She makes lots of money by tying flies and her father "is the very best fisherman in the whole of this world" – the General says, and this girl's flies really amount to genius. I believe she can sell as many as she can make. He is rather the aged wagster type, and wearies me by playing the gaw[1] most of the time. But I have only seen him twice. I went to Seafield with Minnie after church and she hurriedly read to herself the last three chapters that I might send it on to you – but Harry came in so I could not hear what she thought – I cannot help misgivings about the hunting chapter being superfluous. I daresay you will be very much amused to hear that as Minnie and I were walking to Seafield we met old Nancy – and I immediately said "Good morning Martin – I had a letter from Nancy this morning" at this screaming joke Minnie and I both sadly smiled and reflected on your probable hysterical seizure had you been there. Hildegarde and I rode to Myross wood yesterday. She rode Sorcerer, and we had a lep or two which she sat exceedingly well. She said the jump was much bigger than she had ever gone over before – so I commend you for your moderation when you were bossing her. Herbert sent me a sonnet –

1 *Gaw:* reversion of 'wag'.

"On a picture" O'Donovan's lake by E.Œ.S.

[*a painting given to Herbert by Edith*]

So late, so late! How fast the hours are flying!
How soon the world, and we therewith, grown older,
Sink into shadow! Night winds breathing colder
Their sad lament across the lake are sighing;
O'er head the melancholy sea bird crying
Sweeps westward, night rolls down the mountain's shoulder
Scarce, should she come now, could mine eyes behold her.
Day dieth fast – and hope with day is dying.
Oh horror of great blackness grimly falling!
No moon shall cleave thy blinding folds asunder,
No star illuminate thy murky cope.
Oh thou that tarriest, hear my passionate calling!
But a brief space, no cry shall sound thereunder.
Still the light lingers, – is there yet a hope? [*end of letter*]

Edith spent a good deal of time toiling around the editorial offices of the 'illustrateds'. She did only moderately well, however, and Oscar Wilde's lukewarm reaction to her work, when he was editor at the Lady's Pictorial, *indicates that a profession solely as an illustrator would have been an uphill struggle for Edith. When she and Martin began to publish their travel books she was the obvious choice as illustrator, so that in more ways than one the joining of forces with Martin was a sound and rewarding move.*

[*Note added later*: 'Placing of *An Irish Cousin* 1887–88']

Wednesday
32 Gordon Place

My dear Martin
Yours to hand in bed this morning – I wont post this till I have seen Mrs. Rivington this afternoon, but I will try and answer your questions. The last page of chapter 13 is 115 – and the dates in diary are as follows. Morgan's dance. February 23rd. Papa went March 10th. Aylmer's return. March 7th. Depart 12th. Mother and H. started March 14th. Papa returned March 22nd. We started 26th. I can safely leave the rest to your fertile imagination. Now I must copy. H. and I went down to

Oscar yesterday (he was out on Monday) sent him a letter and we were marched in. He is a great fat oily beast. He pretended the most enormous interest – by Egerton's advice I said I was the Bart's niece as Oscar knows him well – but it was all of no avail. Neither Carbery, Vernissage (with pictures and I wouldn't give it without,) nor possible Atelier des Dames would he have. He languidly took the sonnets and is to return them by post. He talked great rot that "French subjects should be drawn by French artists" – I was near telling him, as Dr. Johnson said – "who drives fat oxen must himself be fat". He assumed deep interest in the "Miss Martins", asked if they were all married: I said "mostly all". He was kind enough to say that Edith was so pretty and nice – and bulged his long fat red cheeks into an affectionate grin at the thought of her. He then showed me a book of very indifferent French sketches – was foully civil, and so goodbye. I then took Carbery to *Cassells Family Mag.* Office. A dear little intelligent vulgarian in charge – such a relief – He said for eleven or twelve months they were full up [with] descriptive papers. I said that like Smiley's bullpup I would hold on if it was a year. So he kept it to look at, and seemed rather to like the sketches. Send along the chapters as you write them – I think now we must decide to wait until you come to Kew – I will settle with Mrs. Rivington that you shall call on her – She is very pleasant and easy. Her son Kenneth is or was an artist, is now in trade, she is keen about art, and knows the Chimp and is sister of Mrs. General Cameron. So *there is* your map of the country. I hope you will see Mr. R – a very nice man – I could love him if I got time – but go inside me if you get a chance – I will send you the last chaps. As soon as I can – but I hate cutting the book and would rather copy up to them and then send it. Both H. and Minnie like them and even mother approves – and only regrets that "Mee-mee", as she will call Miss Mimi, has "no love story". Saw "Sweet Lavender" last night – Terry ripping – an American, like Aylmer (very good) an Irish Doctor with a good brogue, moderate and unostentatious, a chaperone and her daughter fair, the rest pukes of the first water, and the story pretty pukey too – and slightly back-hairy* – enough so to make H. purple and stiff and Egerton silent and absorbed and gloomy. Before I forget – when you next write tell me the numbers of the chaps; graveyard – etc. Mrs. Rivington just been here – will be delighted to see you when you go through town – 8 Glasbury Road West Kensington. Go to the W. K. Station – turn to your right on leaving, then first to your left (up I think to Trebovir Road) then second or third to the right is Glasbury Road – No fresh news except that no precis is required – I paid Connie a visit after lunch. She said she had heard *nothing* of any of you since you left town – and asked if I had. I told her I had heard on professional business – but I believe she wants a letter. She was very nice and pleasant. I am much worn, on the top of Mrs. Rivington, a Mrs. Morewood (sister of General Cameron) and a small boy, enter to me – Polly Capes – and I have grappled alone with her for the last three quarters of an hour as she squatted on after they left. I have cut a little bit about Roche that I thought puke. I think you said so too – it *must* run to three vols; if you can make any scene about Nugent, do, and send it to me and I will try and add. Don't forget Arthur's picture and tell me if Sophie likes it – I told Mrs. Rivington in a week or ten days I have done three chapters (besides the new bits) but it is slow, and all this afternoon was wasted.

Send what you have to me before Monday next, I go on Tuesday early – (Finghall Rectory, Bedale, Yorks,) and I will leave it all with Constance and she can read it –

Yours ever
E.Œ.S.

P.S. Long visit from Rose on Monday. Very glad to see her. Much talking of sorts.

This is the first mention of Mrs Martin's return to Ross. Martin's mother intended to move back during the coming spring and summer. It is remarkable that she should have asked Edith to join her and Martin there without any idea of the condition of the house. She had taken a great liking to Edith but had never had any idea of housekeeping. She used to have a special hiding place at Ross to avoid the servants when there was nothing to be cooked for dinner. Anna Selina Fox had been the second wife of James Martin, whom she married in March 1844; thereafter, as Martin wrote, 'bringing with her a great deal of energy, both social and literary, a kicking pony, and a profound ignorance of household affairs, my mother entered upon her long career at Ross.' Edith was staying with the Peirse family in Yorkshire.

Sunday April 29th 88
Bedale Hall, Bedale

My dear Martin
This ought just to fetch you before you go to Kew – anyhow it shall try. I sent the MS to Con yesterday. I read it with the deepest and most

careful interest. First of all, I liked *immensely* the bit alluding to her return to Durrus from Clashmore – "jagged sunset showing through patches of cloudy trees etc" – I thought it very good – also the little bits stuck in about "the restless water" – and one or two small things there. I did not quite care for the way she described her drive home with Nugent. It was, I thought, a bit crude and patchy. I recopied that half page, with unimportant alterations and additions that fetched it up to a whole page, I didn't think it worth while sending back to you, as you can easily get it from Con, (in fact you will have to do so in order to page it.) I think it was better – I managed to get a couple of hours on Friday morning and put it through – I liked awfully the little extra Nugentian dialogue, and give you the greatest credit for it. It helps it very much, but why did you not let him call her "Theo" – ? I was very near shoving it in again, but as you hadn't done it – I conclude for some wise and good reason – I left it alone. But I think it was rather a pity – though of course it is rather a stale trick. I shall be going back to Finghall on Thursday, so send the (Nugent) draft of chapter to me there.

I don't mind admitting that I also thought there was too much explanation in the end – but most of it was put in in deference to Minnie's suggestions and questions and as she is a clear headed person, I concluded it must be necessary. Hear first what Edith has got to say before you cut it out. I think I improved Willy's letter. Don't cut-out rashly out of it – I believe you will come to thinking the extra bits are not superfluous. I know what you mean about the last two chapters but if you bring Miss Mimi along you must be moderately funny, and she certainly ought to show again. I think to end with a kiss would be rather cheap – and I like the little human commonplaceness of the finish better than passionate gubbing* of the suicide chapter. It would be too definite a "curtain" – which I think a great mistake. By all means do without a postscript – I hate it – only I was afraid it might be wanted. Mind you tell me word for word what Edith says and also Constance. I am glad you like gibber – it gave a home-like feeling to the book at once and I think your little conceit of cobwebs on all the Drishane walls pretty tho fanciful. I do believe I have got through the Shocker business. Hoo (Uncle Harry) Ray.

Well my dear. I was sent on a very hospitable letter from your mother asking me to Ross – I should like to go and mock at your dirty little Galway scenery very much – few things – if anything better. But I am awfully afraid I don't see any way to it. What with expense (journey) and having been away, and Aylmer and Emmie, I am afraid I haven't a chance of getting there – We would have had I am sure an awfully good

time, but you can see the difficulties in the way and I don't see a chance
of their clearing themselves out of it – worse luck. If there is, you may
expect to see me at Ross. Wait till we begin to collar something out of
the Shocker and then we'll see – I have written about meeting you in
town on the 10th and curiously my letter crossed one from Hildegarde,
in which she (secretly) begged me to write and ask her to go home with
me on the 8th or 10th, it was really very funny. However if I only went
to town on the 10th I shouldn't want to start the same day. Saturday is
the 12th and is one of the Milford boat days so I might try to cross on
the 12th and go to town on the 10th or 11th – (it is as bad as fixing
the days of Owen and Theodore's deaths.)

Cassells' has returned West Carbery. Oscar cleaves silently to the
sonnets, and has doubtless, – in a poetic frenzy – used them to light the
gas. I am late for the Suffolk Street show which grieves me much – I
have heard no more of the Anglo-Daneries, or the Irish Exhibition at
Olympia, or anything else, which is discouraging.

We are having a very good and gay time here. It is a perfectly ripping
old house. Full of enchanting old pictures, notably a beautiful Romney,
and some delightful old fashioned pastels. The furniture is all old and
genuine. In fact it is a typical fine old English country house, where they
give you clean towels every morning. Alice and I share an enormous
room, full of things that I should put, respectfully, into the drawing
room, and the rest of the house is to match. Sir H. B. P. Bart – is an
exceedingly nice man – nice looking, with a long sad nose and a soft
brown beard and moustache, and a good deal of a sense of humour.
Aged about 44 – she is a nice little creature a sort of piquant cross
between a mouse and Louie Penrose. She can't pwonounce her r's, but
is not any kind of an idiot, and is very easy going and cheery, and
anxious to let us all do what we like. The rest are all the Pinafore
company – viz. Mr. Lucien Powlett – conductor and general boss – very
musical amiable and friendly – "Ralph" a youth named, strange to say,
Smith. He looks 17 but is said to be 22. He has a sweet baritone and
pretty eyes, and is wholly inoffensive. Sir Joseph Porter – Ralph's
brother, a pale goodlooking-ish mixture of Harry Becher and Vernon
Thornton, rather a good actor and a reliable sort of person who knows
a good deal about acting and stage managing – "Dick Deadeye" is a
Mr Ward, in the 57th. A creature very like Mr. D'Avigdor in his youth,
with a dash of Gus Cramer and Hickman Morgan (the latter, I think
mainly eyeglass) He is extremely light hearted, and plays the fool mostly
all the time. He rather amuses me for a limited period, by dint of his
irrepressibility. He has Arthur Roberts on the brain and sings Killaloe

considerably. He did his best to get me into a row in church today. Mercifully I knew that the parson was an uncle of the House of Peirse. He is an old man like this [drawing] He gets fatter and fatter all the way down and having some curious malady of the throat, he begins all his sentences by saying "Purr – to this man was given – Purr – ten talents – er – purr"

Well my dear we were in three pews, the Dowager Peirse, Alice, Lady P and I in the middle, four in front of us, and Deadeye and Ralph behind – and directly the parson began to purr, Mr. Ward began to purr too, and gently poked me in the back to draw my attention to his successful imitation. Old Miss Peirse was next but one to me, and I did not dare to move, or do more [than] shake my hat and concentrate disapproval in the back of my neck. Poor Ralph says it was much worse for him, as Mrs. Peirse kept looking back every time Deadeye purred, and he did not venture to tell him to shut up for fear of being included in the condemnation. Captain Corcoran is a Mr. Hunter Blair, goodlooking, with a stutter, and lots to say – I like him very much, – in fact they are all a nice lot and the rehearsals are great fun. Alice and I had – until the men came – to help Mr. Powlett to drill the chorus. Nothing would induce the young ladies – superior milliners and young schoolmistresses and the like to have anything to say to the gentlemen – shopmen of sorts, most of them. We wanted them to be very loving, and at last in despair I plunged into the chorus and, my dear, wogged* a young auctioneer in a most abandoned way. I wish the squaws* could have heard me coyly murmur "I think you will have to put your arm around my waist" and still more, that they could have seen the minauderies* expended upon that hero – I broke in two in this way, and the next night Alice and I both went at them with such effect that they are now quite demoralised and hug each other nearly as much as Captain Corcoran and I. It is a demoralising pursuit. I wish you were here, as many things would amuse you – I nearly got into an awful mess at the first full dress rehearsal – I ought to have said "the poor bum-boat woman has gypsy blood in her veins etc – I had always funked the first epithet, and consequently, I suppose I said "the poor *gypsy* woman has" then I knew where I was, and with an effort that nearly made me sick I ended with "has fortune teller's blood in her veins". Alice says they didn't notice it, but an audience would, if I had by any awful chance, completed the reversion. We have an early dinner. Square tea at five thirty – rehearsal from 6.30 to 10.30 – more or less and then come home to supper – Alice says I am very good, and so I believe, do the others, but I am not really, and though I can now sing the songs well enough, my voice is foul. However my dress is very fine, and it is very good fun – though you are quite right in feeling that Dumb Crambo[1] is my strong suit – I don't know how to begin to act. Your ball must have been very good sport. I hope the races will be the same. We played golf all through yesterday afternoon. Sir Henry and Deadeye against Mr. Blair and I. We won at a canter or rather at a crawl. It is a deadly game, and consists in walking about three miles round a field at a foot's pace and now and then smacking a little ball with an iron stick . . . [*end of letter missing*]

Edith Somerville's birthday was on 2 May.

Finghall
Thursday May 3rd 88

My dear,
I daresay you will have understood why I did not write to you before, I literally and absolutely couldn't manage it, – anyhow, nothing better than a postcard – so I thought it would be best for thee and best for me to wait till I got back here. I wish you did not know about the painful anniversary which I commemorated yesterday and then you would not have an excuse for this thusness. It is awfully good of you – and a great deal too good of you, – and, in the matter of the cockade, wholly and entirely unjustifiable. The Chopins, I hope, we shall try before we are much older, and I trust you will sufficiently master your natural awe of me to be able to read them with the precision which you mention you displayed in connection with one of your Field Marshalls who sings – (this was a long and troublous sentence but I got there just the same.) I shall be more than delighted to share your couch at Connies if she is so hospitably disposed as to ask me to do so. I shall make no definite plans till I hear from you again – only bear in mind that, I should *like* to cross via Milford on or about Saturday week, and if Connie could stand me for two nights, I should be all the better pleased, as I am afraid the earliest hour I can get to town is 5 p.m. and I think the Milford boat train leaves Paddington at about 10.30 a.m. which would not, as you doubtless perceive, leave much time for the trans-actions of affairs. Fanny Currey has written to me to meet her in town before the 14th, as she wants to talk about Picture shows and the like. However all this must depend on your next letter. I hope you have not

1 *Dumb Crambo:* a mime game.

rechanged your plans, as I shall send this to Leinster Square. I am panting to hear what Edith thinks of the Shocker as mother wrote to me and said to me that Constance objected to it on the same grounds as she did – which was vague, but mainly meant objections to Nugent and general tone, and she said moreover that she thought "no publisher would accept it the way it is". I dont quite understand these objections, but you must talk to Con about it as mother is merely sketchily abusive. How about that Nugent chapter? I expect you have been as much harried and harrassed as I have, (I mean in a literary sense) if you could let me have it to look at before I leave this I should be very glad, and it might save time, as now that you are in town again you wont have further time for Shocking, and I have a comparatively peaceful week before me. Alice and I got back here about an hour ago, having left the Peirses' by the 11 train. Two of the company travelled down with us – Deadeye and the Captain, and the others came down to the station, and an average amount of noise was made. We have had a real good time, and we all grieved at having to break up the crowd, but as the Peirses themselves go to London today, of course the parting had got to be, bitter though it certainly was. The second night was the swagger one, but on all three the thing went awfully well, the only hitch was that poor Alice got a relaxed throat on the second morning – having sung right well the first night – and could only just croak her songs, and last night they had to be sung in the wings, but she was able to talk her part all right which was the most important part, and her acting was capital. Last night was the cheap one and we all played the fool as much as the Conductor and Sir Joseph Porter would allow. Deadeye and I were a good deal loved for various vulgarities, the culmination being when we sailed across stage, I supported by his arm while he tenderly waved a basin in front of me, besides other follies too numerous to mention – (only the last night, you understand –) After the show on each night we had a ripping good supper, and last night the Bedale Musical Society gave a ball in the Town Hall to which we were all invited – We went home first and washed our faces, but remained in our acting clothes, and after supper we set off en masse. It was immense sport; the BMS are mostly shopkeepers and the like, and the most elaborate and serious quadrille was just ending as we got in. The floor was splendid (it is the swagger ballroom hereabouts) and the music, – a band – exceedingly good. But the dresses, the manner, the customs, were too enchanting. After each dance the lady was formally deposited on one of the chairs which lined the walls, and the gentlemen herded together in the door and wiped their beaded brows and ate oranges – (strictly temperance principles.) A Pinafore Quadrille was got up in which we of course joined and danced with the chorus. I had a tall serious seaman, whose main object (I am thankful to say) was to keep me right, and thanks to his careful love I did not make one mistake. They have one most wild figure called Flirtation – the ladies fly round the room in a sort of gallop with each gentleman in turn, Deadeye and Corcoran kept up an incessant yelling and stamping – exactly like the Buffalo Bill Indians – and as I was being belted round by a small fat sailor (the one whom I had broken into hugging the girls at the rehearsals) he gasped in a sort of irrepresible way "Oh – isn't it jolly?". It was the last straw, and with that I burst. I should gladly have stayed all night, but Alice was tired, and it was not the right thing for the Quality to stay too long, so after another Lancers, of a most original type, which I trod with one of the chorus, a waltz, a *schottishe* (the steps of which I and my partner had to invent as we went along), and another waltz, we went home. The round dances we danced with our own lot, but the Squares were official and the various dresses looked fine, my bonnet and wig and the Captain's cocked hat being especially effective. I never met nicer people than the Peirses – they loved us all very much, and have bespoken us to go and stay with them again whenever we get the chance. I am too diffident to repeat the pretty things that have been said, but the glorified Dumb Crambo is just their form hereabouts. I am glad that you and other connoshures weren't there, except you had been on the stage when you should have had a noble time. *Lunch* – there is a whole gale of wind blowing but I believe we i.e. Aunt A, Alice, and I are going for a crawl this afternoon in spite of it. They are the very slowest walkers I ever came across, but fortunately it isn't cold, so I don't much mind. Mother is disgusted at your mother's renageing off to Ross, and no wonder – My sentiments will not bear being put on paper. By the bye, a dictionary word "*Poots*"* i.e. pretty – but always used in a disparaging sense as "she is *not* poots" or "not to say poots" – I have never heard it used in a positive sense. Constance has some fair copied sheets of the dictionary sent for her to try and get an estimate of the cost of printing. *Get them from her*. We might take them to Whiteley's, and ask. No time for more.

Farewell
Yours
E.Œ.S.

P.S. I am sending "Retrospect" to the Irish Show at Olympia. Have you read "the Deemster" Hall Caine – clever – too much terrific incident. Worth reading. You have heard of old Mrs. Wills death? Aunt Sydney says that two days before she died she repeated the whole of Chaucer from memory! This she says to show her vigour. I should rather call it an effort of nature to get it out of her system, which came too late to save her.

Ross was in an appalling state when Mrs Martin moved back in the summer of 1888. Funds were withheld by lawyers (who as a class grew rich upon the breakdown and dispersal of the old estates), so that at first Mrs Martin got by very much on the charity of old servants and tenants, a curious reversal of the usual image of the 'good' Anglo-Irish landlord's wife as a patronizing charity worker amongst her 'people'.

Mrs Martin had taken Martin to Dublin probably because it would enable her to be educated at Alexandra College. During Martin's school-days she and her mother had lived in a gruesome, gloomy North Dublin house. When school-days were over it was less important to be in the city, so that in order to help Robert put Ross back into repair Mrs Martin volunteered to head the first work-party. The tenant who had taken the fifteen-year lease from Robert in 1873 had stripped the estate – a common occurrence in those days, when gentry families were taking flight to England after driving the best bargain they could.

Great progress was being made with 'The Shocker'.

Ross
June 27 88

My dear Edith,
The first thing I would say is this – send me the potato cakes chapter – I am reading the Shocker to Mama, who is even more satisfactory than Rose – reiterates that it is thoroughly interesting, says comprehendingly "Hmmm" at every other paragraph – notes all points relating to the plot – altogether shows herself to be a woman of taste. This is encouraging. I have a very *dis*couraging divil tearing my Ross House so I shall in this letter be subject to phases of melancholy. I was very glad to find that you did not mock my misfortunes in getting back from the Irish Exhibition. They were very afflicting at the time and Mill Hall Park (there is no such place – it sprang into existence for that night) is written in fire on my brain. I can still feel the height of the stairs I rushed up and the length of the bridge I fled over to catch that last train – while behind me were smothered crowings and yelps from my wholly futile

companion[1] – who when furiously asked why he was laughing could give
no reason except that we were running to catch a train of importance –
and that emotion always took him that way – Idiot. However there *was*
something ludicrous about it. Honour the brave who in the 40 minute
midnight vigil at Turnham Green told the "Interpreter" – seeing that a
reaction in the spirits of the party were setting in – and told many other
tales which you have heard.

By the way Mr. St Leger has I think solved that which posed the best
intellects of the Buddhs* even the Mystery of the Furfur. He is an adorer
of English as she is spoke and I showed him this with the enlightenment
which *I* had thrown on it. He suggests this: Furfur is the Latin for grain
or rather *chaff*. This makes 'is not the meal more valuable than the
chaff'. Of course I put this in good English but turn to the place and
see how well it fits. Ha ha Miss, and Ha ha Herbert and the whole lot
of you. Is not the Cambridge man valuable better than the Oxford
scholar – who makes language his study? I do hope R. Tuck will take
those heads and subsequent ones, if you had as many as Hydra. Put by
a little of the spoil for coming here in the Autumn if he does. By that
time we may present a more seemly appearance than at present – though
indeed we are not altogether uncomfortable – I hope you have better
news of poor Fitzie who seems in evil case. Your account was as bad
as could be & it is too late now to think of moving him – at least one
would think so.

It is a curious thing to be at Ross – but it does not seem as if we were
– not yet. It takes a long time to patch the present Ross and the one I
remember on to each other. It is of course smaller and was I think
disappointing – but it is *deeply* interesting and as you can imagine it is
also heartrending. I do not know anything gives such desolation as the
loss of trees and shrubs and that *devil* who was our last tenant has laid
about him for pure spite. Every shrub about the house gone – just try
to imagine Drishane in that plight – and the stables here that it took
years to plant out are standing nakedly up without even a fig leaf to
hide them. In the garden the old apple trees were cut down by this brute
that he might have more room for planting his potatoes – and the
maddening thing is that he had no right to touch them. Simply there
was no one to say him nay – otherwise the place is pretty well but I do
mourn for the laurels which were in a small way celebrated – and I miss
some of the best trees – blown down, cut down, and what not. Everything looks ragged and unkempt – but it is a fine free feeling to sit up

1 Warham St Leger.

in this window and look abroad. There are plenty of trees left – and there is a wonderful Sleeping Beauty's Palace air about everything. Wildness & luxuriance and solitude – as to be lonely or anything like it – it does not enter my mind – The amount of work to be done would put an end to that pretty fast. There is literally everything to do except the tremendous pioneer sort of work that Mama got done in the garden which was as the people told me "the height of yerself in weeds" in fact not a walk was visible. The hot house is like the Durrus one – only more so. It is a sloping bank of vines. The melon pit rears a grove of nettles with great care. The yard is a meadow, but the stables only want paint. We inhabit 5 rooms in the house – the drawing room made for the present a kitchen! I could laugh and I could cry when I think of it. I am not gubbed,* as an empty house is not nearly as appalling in that way as a full one. Everything wants repairing, papering, painting – and there is no money to do it, at least there is – but the beastly attorney whom I had to battle with in Dublin says we must do it ourselves, that it can not be paid for out of the estate. I shall not be able to finish this now – as Mama and I are going to a tennis party given by some people called Vereker who have lately taken a house near Oughterard. Our horse is an old mare – very much the type of Con Sullivans and seems a charming animal – with a high character and a hollow back. I spent this morning in having her heels and mane and ears clipped. It took 2 men and myself to hold her while her ears were being done. I think the noise of the scissors frightened her. When she was finished Jimmy Connor said "I'll put her in the stable now till she'll loose that big ylleb¹ of grass she have before you take her out. Car or conveyance we have none, but for the present we have many offers of cars. I drive Mama on these extraordinary farmer's cars – and Oh could you but see the harness. Terrific – mouldy leather, interludes of twine in the reins – a sight for to see – but we hope to improve. I must before I forget it put down a conversation between Jimmy Connor and Paddy Griffy today. The latter is a very small man – a beloved of mine – I asked him about one Mat Kenealy. "Indeed he is the same way, and *indeed* Miss Wylett he's that ugly. He have a beard on him like that" (the mane of the mare, then under treatment). Here a look of scorn from Jimmy Connor to which Paddy "maybe if he had a red whishker on him like Jimmy he'd do betther". Then Jimmy after a pause "maybe Miss Wylett ye never heard of Paddy's wife – shure she's the height of the telegraph post, and one night she wanted to come at one of her childhren and it was Paddy she got, and

1 Ylleb: they used reversions frequently.

didn't she think twas the child she had all the time". Paddy retired to the cutting of the tail after that – and I heard him say – crouched on the ground – "I thought he wouldn't be aisy till he'd tell that" – I don't think this is a very funny story – but it was interesting at the time.

Thursday morning – Will you ask Violet to send me all the things of mine that are at Glen B. and will come by parcel post. I will send the stamps when I see what the parcel costs. One wants clothes here for tennis parties I see – People are more advanced in their ideas than one would suspect – there are a lot of small new people about Oughterard. The tennis party yesterday was pleasant – the Verekers are a young pair who have taken a farmhouse and are making it pretty – and are nice kindly people. The tennis is of the feeblest. I played *vilely* even for me, having a bad divil, but I was rather better than the others, not one of whom could hit a hard stroke. The afternoon was rather spoiled by an incident which though tedious in the telling will I am sure interest Minnie if you tell her. It appears the R.M. at Oughterard, Brady by name, and his large family have been for some time in the habit of sitting in our seat in church. Naturally when Mama came it was expected that they would turn out – but nothing of the kind – there they sat with Mama. The congregation were furious. Mama indifferent. The churchwardens then took it up – and the state of the case is this, on investigation. All seats in the church are free – but before the church was rebuilt we of course paid for our seats, and when it was rebuilt our present seat was made over to us in lieu of the old – but we ceased to pay for it. However there are our cushions, and it has always been ours – immutably – Last Sunday Mama and I went, and in came the Bradys, crowding us to suffocation and looking like thunder clouds. She is his second wife, and was his governess, and the whole pack are bounders, I may mention. The churchwardens who are gentlemen and nice people, then called on Mr. Brady and asked him to cease from troubling. Mama still remaining neutral, but *Mrs.* Brady replied that if Mrs. Martin wanted the seat she must come and ask *her* for it. Exit the churchwardens black with fury, and are about to consult the proper authorities as to the rights of it – I am sorry – as I hate a church row. But the upshot is that yesterday at the Verekers Mr. Brady was boycotted not by Mama who shook hands with all possible urbanity, but by everyone else. No one talked to her but Mrs. Vereker and everyone was discussing the thrilling topic in corners. It was rather a horrid feeling. After the tennis party Mr. Brady at once drove to the Rectory and told the Parson he would not have his wife sat upon – Whereat redoubled fury on the part of our lot. Mama now says she will not contest the point any longer but will go to the

Bob Martin seat, and leave them in possession of hers and of the detestation of all the people she was trying to be on the best of terms with. I think it is much the most dignified course, even though I know we are morally in the right – it is the height of bad taste on the Bradys' part and it will be disastrous to them. I hate rows and especially this sort of one – but it seemed thrust upon us, as Mama never contemplated the possibility of anyone disputing her seat and just swung in before the Bradys came. They are comparative newcomers and anyhow I can't see that they have any shadow of claim.

I delighted in the Piff and Morgan tales. "Matrimony is ripping" is incomparable – perfect. I say it to myself with the Morgan accent and find it most flavoursome. "Nature on the bellows" I implicitly believe, as Hildegarde tells it – she never exaggerates in recital (except when truckling) in a sort of way too I feel it to be Piffian.

It seems hopeless to think of doing anything here except just by tooth and nail to get the upper hand of the general decadence of all things. I see something new to be done every time I go into a room & then the next thing seems more imperative and so on – You have no idea how much is wanted in the way of paint. I must do as much as I can but I am ignorant. I wish you were here to show me. Can you tell me of anything that would take two old coats of paint off the stairs? I should like to stain them but can't on top of other stuff. The staircase wall was in the old days painted a sort of lavender blue, and I must get a dado on as new plastering has to be done low down. What colours will go with lavender I know not – give suggestions – My hand is shaking from working at the Avenue. I've been cutting the edges of it which will be my daily occupation for ever as by the time I get to the end I shall have to begin again. It is 5 furlongs, and both sides mean a mile and a quarter to keep right. By the bye how is the Glen B. Avenue getting along? Did those trees ever come out? I feel the greatest interest in it. I don't think I see anything here to beat the back of Drishane and the views up the harbour. I often think of these things, and think I did not say half the nice things I thought about them.

The tenants have been very good about coming and working here for nothing – except their dinners – and a great deal has been done by them. It is of course gratifying, but in a way very painful, and makes one want money more than anything. The son of Tom Walsh, the carpenter, has been making a sort of hanging cupboard for me, also all for love. He was a little embarrassing as he is a very smart person, went to America, and was conductor in a Pullman, then engine driver on the Grand Trunk and so on. He now keeps a pub in Galway and is a most dashing young

man with a curled moustache and a yachting cap. However he is still
the same Johnny Walsh whom Charley and I used to beat with sticks
till he was "near dead" as he himself says proudly. We have many visits
from the poor people about and the same compliments and lamentations
and finding of likenesses goes on. This takes up a lot of time and exhausts
one's powers of rejoinder. Added to this I don't know what to make of
the people, I know they are many of them blackguards, but they are the
devil to talk and jackact.[1] Of course some are really devoted but there
is a change and I can feel it.

I wish you had seen Paddy Griffy on Sunday night when he came
down to welcome Selina and me. After the usual hand-kissings on the
steps, he put his hands over his head and stood in the doorway, I suppose
invoking his Saint. He then rushed into the hall "Dance Paddy" screamed
Nurse Barrett, our maid-of-all work, and he did dance, and awfully well
too, to his own singing. Mama who was attired in a flowing pink
dressing-gown and a black hat trimmed with lilac, became suddenly
emulous, and with her spade under her arm joined in the jig. This lasted
for about a minute, and was a never-to-be forgotten sight. They skipped
round the hall, they changed sides, they swept up to each other and
back again, and finished with the deepest curtseys – Mama is indeed a
wonderful woman.

We have one man here, Tom Hynes by name who lives at the lodge
with his elderly bare-legged wife, and works in the garden, pumps and
tries to speak English. He and Nurse Barrett are our all in the way of
slaves, but we have handy people about. By the way a dog would be
almost impossible here, because of the traps – there are none now of
course, but later the rabbits are taken by the thousand – there are any
amount here now. The afternoon post just in and with it your letter and
praise be to goodness the summer number of the *Graphic*. My dear you
are very nice to me – and I am truly delighted to get it – to have and
to hold and to show to the people here – and I am proud to see how
you take the shine out of everything else in the number. There is nothing
to touch you – that is certain. I like your narrative, it is quiet and
interesting but I should have preferred sub-titles as in Paley Dabble.
However this is as right as rain whatever. The pictures look delicious
cool and strong and above all *fresh*. I see that "grandmother" who is I
should think in her dotage, gives a stimulating mention of the indecency
– and your name and address is close by. Why not try Williamson with
Carbery. He *might* – is it worth it? What are those other 12 sketches?

1 *Jackact*: fooling about.

As to Rivington and Sampson – It is certainly disappointing, but as you say perseverence is the only game. I see many small things in the Shocker which might have been omitted . . . [*end of letter missing*]

In order to help Martin place her articles with journals and newspapers, Robert introduced her to editors among his friends in London, many of whom were writers for Punch. *One of these was Warham St Leger who provided a rather low-gear and pastel-coloured romance in Martin's life. They shared the same sense of humour and tastes in reading; but although he wrote letters to her with sentimental and romantic overtones he does not seem to have proposed marriage.*

Marriage was a thing to be avoided if possible. Martin's views on marriage must have been severely blighted by her knowledge of the arranged marriages of her half-sisters. James Martin's first wife, Anne Higinbotham, had died at the birth of her fifth daughter. Her sister Jane had the daughters to stay with her as often as possible, to spare them the grim atmosphere of Ross. At the age of sixteen Emily Martin was staying with her Aunt Jane, at Inver near Larne in Antrim; she was seen at a dance by James McCalmont, the county's most eligible bachelor, who immediately turned to his companion to tell him that this was the girl he was going to marry. During the evening he danced with Emily twice, but made no particular impression on her. Out for a drive on the following day Emily failed to recognize him when he raised his hat as she passed by with her aunt.

On the next day James McCalmont sent a proposal of marriage to Emily's uncle. Emily was highly amused, saying that it could only be a joke as she would not be able to recognize the man if she saw him again. Emily's aunt and uncle were horrified at this levity and wrote to James Martin at Ross. He came at once and browbeat Emily into accepting the offer. McCalmont was very wealthy and James Martin had five daughters and an overdraft. Emily was taken back to Ross to prepare for her wedding. John Burke of St Clerans, a soldier, was already in love with Emily and on hearing of her plight he arranged an elopement. They were betrayed, however, by a servant who lived in fear of James Martin. Emily was then locked up in her room until she should consent to marry McCalmont. She was fed on bread and water. Her father visited her frequently to rage at her, but she would not give in. She became ill. At length James Martin persuaded his father, the charming Robert Martin, who was adored by Emily, to talk her into sense. She finally gave in at his plea, 'For my sake. Surely you won't break an old man's heart?'

Emily was married to James McCalmont on 27 April 1843 at the age of sixteen years and three months. She drove away from Ross 'howling' in tears. On her honeymoon with relations of her husband's, she spent her leisure time climbing trees and jumping hurdles with an eleven-year-old boy cousin who was nearer to her in age than anyone else. She bore two sons before she was twenty.

[*Page 2 is missing*]

Ross
Tuesday July 9th 88

My dear Edith,
Here I make a beginning in a spare half hour after a long afternoon's fishing – of which perhaps more anon – I was very glad to get that letter of yours. It is good of you to write so abundantly – when you have much on your hands – and now indeed they will be full when Emmie arrives and more than all when that dirty overflow meeting* is begun in the Purlieu* – As I suppose it will be on the 16th. Letters then will not be expected from you.

We had not heard of Fitzie's death till both you and Katie told us on Saturday afternoon. It was a shock – after all you had told me of him – He seemed a thoroughly alive and practical person. I don't know why it should be touching that he should rave of his sport to the end – but it is. I suppose any shred of ordinary interests is precious in a strange unnatural thing like dying. Poor Alice has a bad time to live through – Poor creature – I think often of a thing that a country woman here said to me the other day – apropos of her sons going away from her to America. "But what use it is to cry, even if ye dhragged the hair out o' yer head – ye might as well be singin' and dancin' ".[1] She was crying when she said it – and was a wild looking creature whom you would like to paint and the thing altogether stays in my mind.

This is bad weather for all concerned – very unconducive – and of course you have it the same. A grey morning, a few gleams at 12 o'clock, clouds and wind, and in all probability a wet evening, that is how we fare. Let us hope you will be better off with your visitors at Drishane.

---

1 Remark shortly to be put into the mouth of Norry the Boat in *The Real Charlotte*.

As to your late one I will not – as you told me not, trouble myself – as I do not think you are . . . [*missing page of letter*]

. . . for my room, it is a fitting abode for Mephistopheles and the rash gazer wipes his eye as he sees the hangings of the bed, the curtains, the dressing table, two other tables and an Ottoman and cupboard all alike – and me like Milton's sun "in bed, curtained in cloudy red". Poor Mama thinks it beautiful and I had not the heart to disagree or the money to alter. As for Gendie's comments on that letter from Mr. Rivington – they were funny enough to make Mama laugh so *excessively* – though she is ignorant of Gendie. But you have warmed up Mr. Rivington. It is magnificent – nay sometimes even terrible, as Ruskin says of the pine trees – and with Kenneth about to visit you, you have all the necessary scenario for a French play ready. I do not know why I am here reminded of an incident in boating at Kew this time. You would have felt it at the moment, but it does not sound much.

Someone asked if we had passed a certain drawbridge – on which Mr. St. Leger said "We passed the little drawbridge long ago" and then said it sounded like the first line of a sonnet – whereon we improvised one, line about – I gave a second line with something about standing at the gate, and my next had to rhyme with go, need I say that there was but one line in the language that suggested itself – and I began to giggle from sheer feebleness and stupefaction, while the others waited open-mouthed for the effort of poet number 2. I got through somehow and then came the last line of the octette – mine again, same rhyme – this time even more hopeless, and Mr. St. Leger divined my slackness and suppressed meaningless titter, of that I cannot doubt – from an answering or rather corresponding seizure which I observed – I lived through it, but if you had been there, or any squaw,* apoplexy would have supervened. It was one of the things which one can feel more than describe. Your letter spent two hours after its arrival on Saturday in Nurse Barrett's pocket – while they entertained some 30 of the children about here. Tea and bread and jam and barmbracks in the lawn and races afterwards – that was the class of fun – I had a very wearing day. Cutting up food in the morning, and then at luncheon time I received a great shock. I had told a girl who teaches a National School here to ask 12 of her best scholars, and to come with them herself – besides these we had only invited half a dozen or so being short of crockery – at luncheon on Saturday in comes the teacher's sister to say that the teacher had gone to Galway on business and that no children were coming. Boycotted – I thought at once – and Nurse Barrett told me the priest must have vetoed the thing – However I thought I would make an effort and sent a whip round to the nearest villages, which are loyal – and away I went myself to two more. I never had such a facer as thinking the children were to be kept away, and with that I nearly cried while I was pelting over the fields. It is an awful feeling to take trouble and to find it unappreciated. I could only find 6 children of whom 3 were too young to come, and one was a land leaguer's. However 2 were to be had and I pelted home again – very anxious – There I found half a dozen I knew would come and divil another. However I waited, and after I had begun to feel very low I saw a little throng on the back avenue – poor little things with their best frocks such as they were. I could have kissed them – It was such a relief – but gave them tea instead and before it was over another bunch of children, babes in arms and all, and there was great hilarity. Next time I shall do the asking personally – I never shall understand what was the matter about those National Schoolchildren and the teacher. She's a nice girl but they are all cowards and she may have thought she was running a risk, she was here today with a present of eggs and white cabbage which was to conciliate me of course. The presents are embarrassing and last week there was a great flow of them – in two days Selina, I and Mama received about 6 pounds of butter, about 4 dozen eggs, a chicken, a lot of white cabbage, and a bottle of port – all from different tenants, some very poor – and all have to be received with a due amount of conversation. Another experience of last week was going to see four sisters who work their father's farm in a place called Killannin. In the twinkling of an eye I was sitting "back in the room" with these 4 exhausting themselves in praise of my unparalleled beauty, and with a large glass of poteen before me which I knew had got to be taken somehow. It was much nicer than I expected and I got through a very respectable amount of it before handing it on with a flourish to one of my hostesses – which was looked on as the height of politeness. I wish I could remember some of the criticisms that went on all the time "I *assure* you Miss Wylett you are very handsome, I may say beautiful" – "I often read of beauty in books but indeed we never seen it till today – indeed you are a perfect creature". "All the young ladies in Connemara may go to bed now, sure they're nothing but upstarts". Many other precious things I lost as all the sisters talked together, yea, they answered one to another. Custom has taken the edge off the admiration now I am grieved to say – but still it exists – And the friend of my youth, Pat Connor is especially dogmatic in pronouncing on my loveliness. I am afraid all these flowers of speech will have faded before you get here – they will then begin on you. By the way ask Minnie if she remembers Johnnie Leonard coming to the drawing room door and saying to Mama "Hughie Jackson's ablow and wants the pan, and the Walshes is gone in to Sparrys". Mama declares that Minnie was present – Hughie was the Jackson's servant, always known by their name, and had come for the preserving pan, the Walshes were brothers, carpenters, who were wanted, but had gone to work for Mr. Sparrow, a neighbour of ours.

Violet has not yet sent the clothes, but I forgive her – I neither want the flannel shirt nor the hat – the former too small, the latter too big. I have a moderate sized hat, which has twice been submerged in the lake, but survives. I shall try the potash for the stairs, and then stain them with dark oak, but it is an undertaking. I think the bronze green would go with the lavender. I incline to an invisible purple blue but will see.

I fancy the idea of that Rineen sketch. I always liked that stream and it is very much your class of subject, more so than Hatta and the couch and the kitten, though the latter might be delightful to paint. What are you doing now, is it head or tale – the story or more children? I suppose it is nothing as a matter of fact, with Emmie and Aylmer. When you have time to write tell me faithfully of their comportment and of your mother's. When are they to be married, and which of you are to go over. Answer these things – I forgot that the beautiful Alfred Sykes also comes today – Tuesday. Throng as three in a bed[1] will Drishane be – literally perhaps. I hope you will take the conceit out of him over a few high stone gaps (he on Ballyhooley) but I am afraid he is within hail of wall country in Gloucestershire. I think I am within measureable distance of a saddle. Mr. Vereker has said something about lending his wife's – and he is a capital man – and she is a capital woman, not at present in a condition to ride I think. He has sent us over a punt which makes all the difference here – and I paddle about and get water lilies and enjoy it. Mr. Vereker is a tall pale youth with a white moustache and long white teeth – a good sportsman, and very wild and cracked, and with a good thorough brogue. He comes of the quality however. Yesterday he brought over Mr. Hanbury, one of the Oughterard soldiers, to fish for pike. They arrived at ten, full of excitement and with their trap loaded with bait. They trolled till lunchtime and came in hungry and a little less enthusiastic with one seven pound pike. I went out with them after luncheon and we trolled from end to end of the lake without success. Mr. Hanbury, who is a broad faced English youth with an opinion of himself I think, lost his temper a good deal, and finally took in his rod and said it was no use fishing in a place that was so full of

1 Used ten years later in *Poisson d'Avril*.

weeds. I must say the weeds *were* a nuisance – every other minute we had to haul in a line and free the hooks. I caught a perch be it said, and lost a big fish of some sort, and also lost a spoon bait, and a natural bait with the hooks – so I daresay it will be some time before they come out fishing here again. I was deeply bored for part of the time, and was very cold for the rest, and will try fishing next time with Pat Connor, who knows more about it, and is far more entertaining. The pew row has ended beautifully. On Sunday week Mama and I sat in another pew and the Bradys sat in ours. A few days afterwards Mr. B wrote to Mr. Hodgson, one of the churchwardens and said that rather than imperil the peace of the parish and in deference to Mrs. Martin's wishes he would give up the pew. So far so good, though it was rather late in the day, and a few days later came a letter from the ecclesiastical boss whom the churchwardens had appealed, saying that they had the right of it, and that Mama was to be reinstated – so Mr. Brady caved just in time – but not in time to avoid this tempest in the tea-pot that he has raised for himself – Last Sunday we resumed our old seat and moth-eaten cushion and all is well – except that Mama is rather implacable about the Bradys which is I think a pity.

The little puppet things – I can see them – I wish you could paint them and get that inimitable unsteady gait and mad glare of the eye – dear things – I suppose they will soon take their departure to Lough Ine, and with Aylmer when he goes – I suppose Emmie stays on for a good bit. Does she gush much? I know she will be nice anyhow.

I am much too busy just yet to write anything except letters. I make my own bed, I clean the silver, I do endless things out of doors, I have to drive or row Mama about a lot, I have to go and see the poor people. That is the way my time goes – and the staircase will be an awful piece of work.

The church practice is an unbelievable sort of thing – just the squaws* I suppose. I wish you played the organ here instead of Miss Roberts the parson's daughter – who is scarcely a success – but it is a vulgar little organ –

Yours

Martin

P.S. Remember me to Emmie.

Once Martin had settled at Ross, Edith and she began to exchange minutely detailed letters criticizing each other's writing. From this period comes Martin's criticism of a rondeau that Edith had written on lost love. This was later destroyed, so that all we have left is Martin's reaction to it. Martin set about trying to persuade Edith to visit Ross, her main line of attack being to stress the beauties of the landscapes about Ross as ideal for the painter.

Ross
July 26 1888
Thursday

My dear Edith —

Once more the critic dips his pen in gall and gets under weigh. You are a wonderful woman to invent these things. Faith you have a great power of attack, God spare your health, as is the custom to say here at the end of any personal remark. As I walked deviously up the Avenue yesterday in the reading of the rondeau, it seemed to me that you had put together some good lines, and how the mischief you did those rhymes I don't know. At the same time, me thought, this is not a correct rondeau — so I looked up the rondeau book, and found that a rondeau should have thirteen lines clear and two refrains extra. The refrain should not be the repetition of the entire first line but of half only, or even of only the first word. Your lines are not placed according to the usual form, but are allowable, and I think preferable to the other. So much for technicalities. I think the ideas of your first verse *awfully* good, and pluckily put. The best lines in it in my opinion are the second fourth and fifth. I am not sure that the sixth explains itself easily, and the third is too subservient to the rhyme exigency. It seemed to me also that "plucked" might be better than "picked" but I don't know. If I were you I should do this: make it a correct rondeau and re-write the second verse with some other misfortune than a thorn. That like many another true and beautiful simile has had its day I fear me — for instance "my false love stole the rose, and left the thorn with me." But you put it very tenderly and well and I should preserve three lines of the second verse down to "sunsets". They are good. Certainly you are very near a good rondeau and it is worth trying to perfect it. I understand that the great thing is to get your refrain in naturally and not as an exclamation. It must be the very divil to do, and I respect you from my heart, and wonder abjectly. If you finish it I should send it to Oscar if I were you. It would stir him about those others anyhow and rondeau are fashionable just now. I have very good hopes for Pierce Cormac which I am sure should have a *k* at the end. They have taken Uncle Loftus lately in *Temple Bar* (not appeared yet) and how much more should they take you. Anyhow this thing is bound to get a show somewhere. I feel you could do better if only you were not so thorough a Buddh.* This I can scarcely explain but I feel it all the same. You have given yourself your head a good deal more in Pierce than I expected you would, and please goodness will do so more and more. It will be a work of time to shake off the feeling given by the fact that there have been long letters from the Aunts in the morning and that your mother is calling like a lost spirit in the back hall, and that you have to write to the Chimp – or in fact any of your daily occurrences. This is mixed, but you know I don't mean that you are to write exclusively love-making and improprieties. It applies to everything. The family are clever and successful but they are unconducive in that way.

I tremble at the tale of the mad dog and had I been you and Hildegarde should have flown into the sick child's bed and burrowed there until the return of the slayers. Fancy how frightend Dick B and his tutor must have been when it passed them – and indeed I am thankful that any encounter with the little thing was spared. It might have meant that you or Hildegarde would have got a tooth in you – Oh Himmel, don't let us think of what we might all be feeling like today – God is good, as Mr. Sweeney said – which suggests divil a betther – and I may say that the two divils I have enjoyed since I came to Ross have transformed themselves into angels of light, and will soon be readmitted to paradise. It is a great comfort, as the last few before Ross had meant a dumb stupour of prostration. But this is wonderful air – everyone says so – and this leads me on to my next. Why not come and try it after the fatigues of the wedding. Bristol to Dublin is simple and cheap. Dublin to Galway 19 shillings second class and about 12 shillings third. It seems a good opportunity if you are not bankrupt by then. Keep it in your mind and mention it when you think advisable. I do want you to come here when there are still some leaves left, and the winter dreariness has not settled down. Going to Ethel en route might fit in. You know you would not like to go back from the festivities to the wet Sunday evening services, when the church steps are full of dead leaves and there is only Seafield to have tea at afterwards – so have a sickener of this place first, and then go home with avidity. I am delighted to say that Katie and Muriel come here next week to stay for all August and most of September. It puts a great backbone into me – I hate being more or less the managing and society daughter and having to keep my end up all the time – not that I mean that the society here is harrassing or that I am in the smallest way prominent therein, but even as regards Mama it will be a rest. Much work is towards in getting a room ready in the top of the house, into which I propose to stow myself. No one has slept in the top storey since we left 16 years ago, and the ghosts will undoubtedly eat me but the room is delightful, one window looking south over the lawn and lake and the other west over the top of the old sycamore to the lake and a brown hill, Croagh Keenane by name. Naturally it has every glint of sun. I must say that no window in the house faces north which would be a bad lookout for you painting – nor'east is about the best we can do. I shall be awfully gubbed* in the top of the house, as there is no one else there and there are four empty rooms for the ghosts to play in – but I daresay I shall get over it.

The school treat has had a lengthy scratch in the Galway paper – and also in the *Express* of Monday last – If you feel sufficiently interested you can look it up at Glen B. It is headed "Saint Nicholas' Temperance Society" and you will see how successful we must have been with the curates, and how elegantly they express their gratitude – If you can't find it I can send you one. I shall be very glad to hear the humours of the Penny reading – and any other humours. How rare it is to find people that it is a pleasure to hear from and a pleasure to write to. You may take this as you like . . . It is a fine thing that the *Graphic* has taken the Louvre pictures – and I hope they will pay decently. Think of more for them – Perhaps the Kerry Recruit *might* be in their line.

Mama was delighted at Madame O'D and the mustard – it is almost incredible – but deeply probable at the same time. *Never* again will I write you anything verging on backhair* if you treat Egerton and Aylmer to my tales. No – for the future my improprieties shall be so sooty that they cannot be passed on. I cannot see anything very funny in the Dowager lover expression but I am glad that others do. It slipped from my facile pen almost unconsciously.

Barbara is to be the name of Connie's kid – a family name – and good I think – but I like better Margery, which I rooted out in a thing of descents here. She might be both and be none the worse. The two Spanish names are Esmina and Zavara. I don't much care for either. This paper is a relic of Charlie's cramming days. Trigonometry I think. It is a fearful thing to be a bridesmaid but having Hildegarde with you will be a great comfort. It is really delightful that Emmie is what she is. I am awfully glad for Aylmer's sake and all of your sakes. Curious that last Sunday when you were late for 6 o'clock service so were we. Through a mistake in the clock we did not get in until near 7 in the *sermon*.

Yours
Martin

[*Note by Sir Patrick Coghill:* 'Page 2 missing']

The bed
August 4th 88
Ross

Dear Edith Œnone

It is all very well to talk of your beautiful bed writing. You have sight and can put your book in any position – whereas here am I scraping it with my nose – and digging the corner of the thing into my manly bosom. These are not the small hours, but the breakfast hours – and here am I having disconsolately taken the early tea and toast of the invalid – meditating on many things in your letter of yesterday afternoon. The vague lassitudes and neuralgia bouts of last week turned into a sudden whirl of headache and nausea on Sunday night – and having got up yesterday I was driven back to bed before lunch by a return of the same with much disposal to cast off. A midday sleep disposed of that, but the headache was bad, and this morning it is lying in wait somewhere, stretching mesmeric claws at me but not grabbing so far – and I have the most romantic delicate fatigue, and inability to get up, so here I stay – quite well to all intents and purposes – but much afraid of the return of the mysterious sickness, and consequently eating next to nothing – That is the line of me at present and so I pass to other themes. Of course I meant you to keep that *World* – I did not think it worth inscribing your name on it – but you can do so if you feel disposed and you generally *do* take chances of the kind. It shows the hero spirit in you that you tell Mr. Rivington of your fellow Shocker's good luck. There is an opportunity too of keeping him alive about the Shocker itself. I have anxious thoughts about that; could we at some time revise the Shocker? I am sure it wants it.

Mama wrote to *your* Mama on Sunday, and I have no doubt told her of Charlie's homecoming – which ought to happen in the next fortnight – minus the wife and child – which in confidence I may say is a great relief. The poor wife appears to have other occupation on hands and stays with her mother – and Charlie comes direct to Ross and delighted I am at the prospect. Even if he were not coming I am afraid I could not manage Castle T. for reasons of sorts – though indeed there is nothing I should like better – your doings read delightfully and temptingly – It has been a summer of many humours and Ethel is the crowning one – in her grass widowhood. I always feel that Ethel is as the squeeze of pineapple to the mint julep (an American drink, dear) that Castle T.

is short of its full flavour without her – but I need not tell you that –
you need not . . . [*missing page*]

. . . – and 88 is a lucky year. By the way that *Birthday book*[1] is
standing to you in a very solid way. I must get a copy and push it in
these parts. It will be the very thing for the people round about, notably
Mr. Vereker. We have had a curious visitor for the last three days – On
Saturday evening up drove a car through the mist and off it lept an agile
figure, and walked into the house – followed by a portmanteau. With
the breeding of the old noblesse Geraldine and I waited till he was in
converse with Mama and then listened at the door. We heard an American accent and a fluent harangue of some sort, and finally Selina was
sent out from the ark to tell us that the visitor was one Archer Martin
a descendant of the Ballinahinch people, who had come all the way from
America to write a book about the family, as it might be Howard Coghill
– I bundled out of my room and gave it to him, and here he has been
ever since, rooting out all kinds of things. We had heard of his being in
Galway, at the same game, and he already has a thick manuscript
compiled – deeply interesting to most people, I should say, except for a
few wild tales of bloodshed – and the like – He is not a very near relative
– his great grandfather was Humanity Dick (the Martin's Act Man,
whom I am in the future going to erect in opposition to the Chief[2]) and
Humanity Dick's great grandfather was younger brother of the Ross
man of that date which makes the relationship a trifle distant. This youth
is not the least like us – but a little like both Hildegarde and Hugh –
only fairish neither tall nor small, right well made – awfully well put on
head and ears, *beautiful* feet, and hands more like mine than I thought
possible, only a great deal better, and not much larger. His accent is
detestable, his manner alert and American beyond telling, his ways those
of a gentleman – his intelligence immense. He is moreover a person who
has read and travelled, and taken in all he saw and read and can repeat
Longfellow and Edgar Allan Poe by heart, does not much care for
Howells, thinks "Tennessee's partner" magnificent and is wholly in
earnest on all subjects. I alternate between dislike and affection, hatred
of his odious smart Americanisms, and respect for his candour and self
reliance. He is a barrister in Manitoba, but his people have always lived
in Hamilton, in Canada somewhere – and from a photograph of their
house they seem to be very rich. There is a pertinacity and an energy

---

1 The *Mark Twain Birthday Book*: a compilation of quotations for each day of the
   year from an author that Edith obviously knew like the back of her hand.
2 *The Chief*: Lord Chief Justice Charles Kendal Bushe.

about him which are incredible and refreshing. On Sunday he just hiked up on to the roof top of the house and began to wage war with the jackdaws, standing on a place that makes me giddy to think of. Yesterday he was up there again, and also I, and he sent loads of soot and jackdaws nests thundering down the chimneys with a long pole – a thing that many sweeps have failed to do. Today he has given Mama and Geraldine a lively time with examinations as to Martin marriages and the like and leaves this afternoon for Oughterard and finally Ballinahinch. He has fought with Burke, has extorted an apology from Froude for some mis-statements in his "English in Ireland" as to some ancestor or other and I think the epitome of him is that he spent an hour at the top of a ladder in a crowded Galway Street, composedly taking a rubbing of the coat of arms over a door, with about 200 people gaping at him.

Eileen is kneeling on the bed, curling my hair with a hammer – very gently she assures me – but I know better – she is a nice little thing, and as clever as your life without being precocious – There is a dance at the O'Flaherties on Thursday I shall if possible get out of going – it is not worth the candle to go and dance with your neighbour's husband all the time, and even Mr. Hanbury has gone away. But who can tell where the excuse is to come from – I have seldom been at a pleasanter dance than the Liss Ard one last year, and hope the next will be as good and that you and Hildegarde will look as nice as you did at the other. This is the afternoon, and I have been all day at intervals toiling over an article for the *World* anent Dublin and the horse show and I simply can't get the hang of it and *loathe* it. I doubt I shall send it if I finish it. I don't want to disgust Edmund[1] all at once, and it is very foul. I think my head is bothered – but if I send it at all it should be tomorrow – and accordingly try to add a line or so as I can – Robert has I believe sent a scratch of "Olympia" into the *Pink 'Un*!! I shall be curious to see it, and whether I am called Miss Ballyhooley. I have in the last few minutes had my hair finally curled on the hammer and with a wet brush, and next an extra pair of jet bracelets and a necklace of Mama's . . . [*last page missing*]

---

1 Edmund Yates, editor of *The World*.

Drishane
Sunday afternoon
August 5th 88

My dear Martin
I shall probably fall into sleep before I get very far, but your letter of
this morning persuades me to make a start. I have most of the rest of
the day clear before me. In letter writing I can never quite make up my
mind if it is better to begin on your own facts, or to review the letter
which you are about to answer. In this case however, as you begin on
the subject of the dance, I will do the same and combine both schemes.
It came off on Friday night, I suppose the simplest thing is to tell you
first who were there, and then to give details. From this house: Aylmer,
Emmie, the two boys, H. and I – Glen B: the Bart, Egerton, V. B. and
Herbert – Seafield: Harry, Minnie, S. and Arthur – Minnie, Nelly, Bock,
and Phil (a brother) Pork – Mrs King, Dick Brougham, Miss Powell,
Mr. Stewart – (a good youth, tutor to Dick) and Mr and Mrs. Lloyd.
That was the crowd. The floor was good, the supper was *admirable*, the
music very moderate, the entire show as far as I was concerned, exceedingly dull. To begin with there was not one man who could dance. In
the second place, there was not one man. I may be vitiated, but I like
men at a dance. Harry tried to get Cameronians. But failed. The Bechers
had no men, nor the Flemings, nor the Morgans, so we asked none of
them. Even the Agile and the Gordon were away. They would have been
invaluable but were unattainable. Herbert came, but cant dance, and
though I would have gladly have humped somewhere with him – as I
did for two or three dances – I could not desert the show, and he went
home at eleven thirty. I had worked pretty hard, and had a nasty sort
of nervous headache that smote me in whirling throbs after each dance
and took away all power of food. (However thank goodness it cleared
off towards the end). Poor Aylmer also had a baddish sun headache that
made him rather a wreck, but he danced away with Emmie in spite of
it. She looked smarter than paint, in an awfully neat white frock with
huge black and white sash. She dances very nicely and looks well going.
I had a turn with her, but she felt too much like a swift smooth little
planchette, easily steered – but unemotional – I like to feel the music in
my partner. I am bound to say that mother played indifferently. She
wont take the trouble to play well, and talks all the time, to the extreme
detriment of her bass. H. and I did as much playing as we could, but
the small boys were mad to dance and resented our playing bitterly. I
was disappointed in both my little King man and Phil Somerville's

dancing, of which the Porks had said great things. The former is just medium while Phil is dull, and reverses. Of Phil I don't quite know what shall be said. He is small and rather good looking, rather like Grace with a moustache. I don't like his manner at all (he has been a practical working engineer and has had no chances – be it understood) – it is common and uneasy with a certain assumption of familiarity. I am sorry for him, as he is a good steady creature, but I don't care for him. However to Hildegarde's and my great amusement, we detected an illicit liebarcation* between him and Violet – Violet striving to appear unconscious as with purple cheeks she led him forth to the conservatory. We have since mentioned the subject to her with characteristic gentleness, but she only rubbed herself deeper in among the pillows of H.'s bed, (on which she had temporarily retired to rest) and looking at us over the edge of her shoulder with a gleaming eye, she bishy wizhed something which was quite unintelligible. My dear little King man was a good deal sealed to Nelly and Bock – (I believe Grace is his real love, but her recent measles kept her at home) but I had some converse with him – he is a nice little sort, and I hear, has a deep appreciation of the Buddhs.* In this connection let me tell you what Connell said to Jack – "Well now master Jack, I suppose Miss Edith knows every language – Latin and Greek and Spanish and French and all of them?" The faithful Jack admitted that in a general way, I did – to whom Dick Connell, in a tone of pensive reflection – "Well now – I'd like to hear Miss Edith talking Greek"! – Hugh (who has just been appointed to the Monarch) looked delightful in his white waist coat and brass buttons. It was pretty to see the Bunny's infantine pleasure at taking the floor with him, and Hugh's politeness of the ancient régime was beyond praise. (More especially as he said to me afterwards that "really the Bunny was very hard to get on with, and she stuck her knee between mine when we were dancing – I assure you I could hardly get her round".) Hugh will be the typical young man who talks of "the ladies", and begs you to "get on your bonnet and shawl". He asked me to put the studs into the front of his shirt for him – "as Ladies' fingers are the things for neat work". – "But Heow," I said "you know sailors are supposed to be very neat fingered people". "Yes, perhaps," says Heow "in *strong* things, but we haven't pointed tops to our fingers like you – ". Mrs Harris would have loved him – indeed we missed her very much. She had some great qualities. Sylvia's hands were quite full with Dick Brougham, Mr Stewart and Hugh. The latter she treats with a certain scorn, as a mere child; Dick is valuable from the sincere quality of his de*voti*on, but Mr Stewart who is about 21 is the leading favourite. Sylvia is not in a good stage now,

being wholly given over to the pursuit of liebarcations,* not even scorn-
ing to hold converse with the younger policeman. She sulks if Hildegarde
talks to her, and is left by Minnie to follow her own untramelled devices.
It is a great pity but I think she will outgrow it – or will work her
amusement in a less crude and vulgar manner. She would remind me of
Bess (and does in many things) only that she has a certain servant maid
quality, and a self-consciousness that our good Bess never had. There
was a fine free simplicity about Bess's woggings* that had always a
disarming effect on me. Harry is loud in his praises of the dance and all
at it, and it was almost impossible to get him out of the house at 2 a.m.
– when it died off. (Fancy one of our dances having fairly worn itself
out at 2. Ichabod.[1]) I am glad you were not there: tho I think you would
have got as much pleasure as I did at dancing with Jack and Hugh.
Their keenness was delightful, and they don't go at all badly. Jack has
an enchanting innocence and is in no way ashamed, with the usual
schoolboy shame, of being fond of his female relatives. The Dowagers
are I think, a good deal set up about Bourget. The Bart started for
London, and it all begins to look very like it – but until the money (Vide
Goschen's new bill[2]) is paid to enable them to start a new company, I
shall not believe in it. Have you heard that Seymour and the Lady
Kathleen are now in Devonshire? He has been sent a most pressing
invitation to go back to the Irish Bar, by the members thereof, and I
believe he is going – I am delighted – I hated to think of him being
wasted out in those heathen countries. I know she was a beast, but if I
were the family I would call upon them – if for no higher reason, at
least to avoid the misery of having to cut Seymour if one met him in
the Street. Anyhow I think his two years of wandering has been penance
enough, without his own people making it worse for him.

. . . Apropos of nothing Harry told me of a man in the Court House,
up for drunkenness, who on being asked how much he had to drink,
said he had had "eight glasses of whisky, and two at-tempts".

They will be home from church in a moment, so I will say no more.
In fact I have no more to say. Emmie and Aylmer go on Wednesday –
I am sorry to say. Daily we like her more and more – I hope Aylmer is
good enough for her. Boyle ought to get away by the 21st. He says they
are having a mighty hard time of it. He has given Hildegarde a bale of
sumptuous brocade to make her wedding dress – I think you saw the

1 *Ichabod*: from I Samuel, 4:21 'And she named the child I-chabod saying, The glory
   is departed . . .'
2 Rt. Hon. G. J. Goshen, Chancellor of the Exchequer, brought forward the
   Consolidated Fund (No. 2) Bill this summer.

pattern. It is very noble of him – as he has not the riches of the Chimp – or of you – those gloves you gave her were the best I have ever seen – you slut –

The dear horses are back from Cork, and look right well – Papa had over a fortnight of it, and I believe . . . [*end of letter missing*]

The Morrises at Spiddal
Mass was said at Ross throughout Martin's childhood, and the angelus bell sounded to call the servants in to prayer twice daily. Her grandfather Robert had married a Catholic, and all of the Ross servants were Catholic. The Martins had suffered by holding to their Catholicism during the Cromwellian period. Some gentry families managed to avoid Protestantism, or shrug it off as soon as convenient. As a result of O'Connell's campaigning and the removal of disabilities against them, great progress was made by Catholics – in the practice of law particularly – by the middle of the nineteenth century.

When Martin talks of the neighbouring families in County Galway, friends and relations, she is referring to a Catholic as well as a Protestant gentry. The O'Haras were relations of her great-grandmother, and the Morrises were old friends of the family. Lord Morris became Lord Killanin of Galway in 1900. His career in the Law was splendid: Gold Medal, T.C.D. 1847, called to the bar 1849; QC 1863; Recorder of Galway 1857–65; Solicitor General for Ireland 1866; Judge 1867; Lord Chief Justice 1887; created a baronet in 1885.

[Note *by Sir P. Coghill*: 'Page two missing']

Ross
Tuesday, August 7th 88

My Dear Edith.
I write in haste and indignation with Robinson. I paid him that bill of your mother's that time that I went up from Glen B. to Dublin, in January. Mama was by and corroborates, so my memory is not playing me a trick. I desired him to forward the receipt by that post to your mother which is where I made the mistake, though he swore to do so. I should have waited for it. I think it was 7 or 8 shillings, and it had got into a bill of mine somehow. There may be some confusion in this way, (though indeed I was lucid and eloquent at the time) he discovered an ancient entry against me at the time, some three or four shillings,

which not having the money with me I did not then pay – nor indeed since then. This I shall send to him tomorrow and remind him of the transaction with some emphasis. I remember well saying at the time. "Now Mrs. Somerville has paid up for everything". It appears from the Diary that that was on the 6th or 10th of January. So far in one breath of indignation . . . This evening all the time that I was working at the Avenue a woman was standing there and telling me of how her father had two evenings before turned her out of his house – at night too, and she had to go and beg a shelter. I believe Nurse Barrett found her crying about this house when it was past ten o'clock. What on earth is one to do with these creatures. As it is we are weighed down with giving a little work and a little wages to people who are too old for field work. There is a terrible, bitter spirit. The young are prosperous, the old get left, and no one cares a button for anything but their own gain . . . [page missing]

. . . a power of good money and haven't much to show for it, or much satisfaction in thinking of it. How much better if we had never left Ross. There would be some pleasure in looking back to years of keeping the Avenue in order and looking after the sick people. These reflections come of writing at night. I am going to try the effect of posting before 8 a.m. which I accomplish by creeping out on to the awful ghost walked landing and laying my letter on the ground outside Nurse Barrett's door. She is up at awful hours and sends it by Tom Hynes who is even earlier.

Mama has laughed for a fortnight in mad outbursts at the Oughterard parson saying in the course of one of his excited extempore sermons, and in connection with a high and sacred subject "this my beloved was the brightest feather – in His – in His *crown*". She and I heard him say it. Of course you understand that "cap" had merely slipped out. We did not laugh at the time, but since then I often hear Mama in the dead of night in her own room, in strong convulsions.

Yesterday was given over to our expedition to Spiddal. Nothing could explain the length of those 11 Irish miles, or the loneliness of the road. It was like mid ocean and a slight mist tended to increase the unboundedness of the stretches of moor and bog. The road is very bad with dykes each side, in parts you couldn't pass anything on it – and we might have had a bad accident from the only car we met getting its step locked into ours (I *was not* driving). The wind blew tremendously up in those altitudes and it and the grey hilly country and the mist were at last a sort of intolerable nightmare. We descended at last to the coast and behold a sluttish large village spread along the shore, a fine black looking salmon river, young trees, and finally the Morrises house or fishing lodge. Civilisation in Siberia could not be more surprising. They are pleasant people – you know what he is as to agreeability and to brogue and she shrewd and kind – she is Protestant – He and all the children are RCs. We sat up in a perfectly orthodox bow window and hungered for our lunch for a bit – when up there drove what I took for our old Ross omnibus. The very ditto of it – with three on the roof, one beside the coachman and thousands inside just as we used to do. These were the O'Haras, distant cousins (my great grandmother was O'Hara) come all the way from Galway – and in they marched with their visitor people all young lovely and beautifully attired – exactly Pilotelli's idea of young ladies in the country with the exception of a very wonderful apparition who strode in last of all – A girl more hugely fat than anyone I know of her age, rather tall, her pouter pigeon front emphasised by a broad white striped waist coat, and then suddenly, short hair hanging down below her shoulders – the inflated Sylvia – on top of all a white sailor hat such as Violet wears in winter – no better than that, and a large high coloured face – in short a Monster. . . We lunched to the number of sixteen – and in the height of luxury – still the feeling of Russian magnificence in Siberia – and it was very pleasant. Mama and the Monster shared the Chief J. & I and a nice English strange youth shared his lady – and all was interesting and soothing – I never heard people talk as they all did – it was deafening and the Chief J.'s slow firm brogue penetrated it all like a broom handle. The Monster showed uncanny abnormal intelligence Mama said, – and could have made Gladstone look foolish. It was a strange gathering of Galway people – O'Haras, Lynches, Morrises and Martins and no brogues among them except the Morrises, and of course ourselves. Of Miss Morris I am much enamoured – not very pretty, but a taking short sighted way with her head (which *indeed* I haven't got) not very anything except nice. We walked by the beach and river in the afternoon and I had some interesting talk with her – she has a delicious accent only enough to be emphatic – and is as clever as you want – if she were not too humble to know it. I never met better company. I bore you about her but I know something about her which makes me take a great interest in her – as a study – I can't tell it but it is a melancholy thing. Personally I know her very little. There was tennis on a first rate concrete ground, and I played with one of the officers against the Monster and another soldier. The Monster is just as nippy as Sylvia where a man is concerned I may mention – she was reputed a wonder at tennis, and is not within points of Violet, except in a furious violence of stroke. We were handsomely licked, but it was a small satisfaction to know that our only two games were got by my service which came off for once, and knocked sparks out of the Monster.

We found a letter from Geraldine when we got home saying that she and hers propose coming here for a few days on their way through to view Connemara – I shall believe nothing now till they come, after that sell about Katie.

I cannot believe Bourget even yet . . . but it will keep the Bart in great humour – Katie says she hears almost daily from him in a sort of crescendo – I am sure I should love Mr. Gay – and I hope you will get some good of his criticisms – encourage him in the purlieu* and ask him deep questions of life and death. The candle is burnt out almost and I have no time to talk of Seymour, of the dear Sorcerer, of many things – but I must mention that beautiful fact, that the Spanish Armada procession, with Queen Mary, Lord Bacon and all, marched to 'Bally-hooley' through Plymouth. Robert has yet another song having as its ending "the blackest hearted ruffian that ever whirled a stick, was a man that brought a bath to Donegal" must finish tomorrow – blow the early post – I am too frightened to go out of my room –

[later] . . . but it does catch the early post after all – and by so deplorable a chance as the death of a poor cur dog. When I was writing to you last night I thought I heard a curious yelp under my window, but supposed it was one of the strange sounds of this place at night. Just now when I was soddenly asleep (6.45 a.m.) came a shot that took its place in my dreams at once. Then yells from a dog – the most heartrending, just outside – I was awake in 2 seconds, then came another shot, and then merciful dead silence next a chorus of laughter – "he's finished now" from Nurse Barrett "Brutes" says I lepping out of bed and flying to the staircase, down the well of which I had the pleasure of repeating the expression to Nurse herself. This poor dog, a white common cad, got into the area last night, and was there caught in one of the traps set for rats. That was the squawk I heard. He endured what way he could till the people got up and then Jim shot him – and quite right too – but why laugh? Jim didn't – he has shot too many things but I was disgusted with the other two. "I never slep a wink" says Nurse, "with his dhraggin the thrap along and yelping and sure when Tom Hynes went near him he grunted at him to bite him." Grunted I have heard before, it means snarled. Does it not make you sick to think of the poor hurt thing putting a good face on it, and showing its teeth after a night in the trap. Perhaps it was a maddy – and do take care of yourselves and your dogs – talking of that – the poor little puppet one and the little son, stealing out for the walk – and then the cough and your picture recalled his little face of misery and question. You really are very noble about writing. In

your place I never should write to anyone, as I ever find time here a difficulty.

Captain Acton and the wife with the cork leg come out today. He with a pike rod and I must fish with him. The Jacksons are camping at Killaguile (two miles off and further). J comes fishing too. He is a *very* nice boy – we had tea at Killaguile yesterday a wonderful meal – a rustic garden seat with the cushions of the car upon it – the kitchen table half covered with a cloth and huge cups and not enough of them; and Madeleine herself looking beautiful and serene in a holland nightgown and wielding a black kettle. Her paintings of wild flowers are good – a little weak in colour but full of feeling – It was a pleasant afternoon whatever. Let me know if this gets to you tomorrow – Thursday morning – Goodbye and good luck –

Martin

What are the bridesmaids to wear?

A good example of minute criticism of Martin's work by Edith. In several letters of this period they refer to the Irish Exhibition at Olympia, and both reveal their Irish nationality in their aghast comments on the 'Saxon' and his reaction to Ireland.

Edith took careful note of the comments of Minnie Townshend, the mother of Sylvia and Arthur at Seafield, and here we see her pass on to Minnie the article by Martin that later appeared reworked in consequence of this criticism.

Drishane
Bed 11 p.m.
August 15th Wednesday 88

My dear Martin
The post office fools kept your parcel of M.S. and I did not get it till past three o'clock, so found it impossible to answer you today. I have read your paper twice – once to myself – once to Hildegarde, and – as you want my candid opinion I think it is *awfully good* – full of ideas, and well and originally-applied adjectives, and the real feeling and sense of and for things. What struck me when I read it first, was a certain tightness and want of the ideas being expanded. It read too strong. Like over-strong tea. It felt a little crowded and compressed in style, and *perhaps* now and then – (that *I* should say it to *you*) – a superfluously

ingenious adjective – entirely expressive and well applied, but still its very ingenuity tending to load the sense, and task the reader's strength of appreciation. It just feels, as I said, a little too strong – compressed into cakes for exportation, or pills for the waist coat pocket. But it seems to me alive with thoughts and originality – (This sounds the most desperate puke, but I can't help it.) One paragraph – the second from the beginning – is not very well expressed, or punctuated, or something. "A gratifying recollection, which (?) finally perhaps" etc – and again from "True in the main these life pictures are" the sentence seems to me thick and awkward. I think I would try and spread it a bit thinner. The pickle bottle is a delightful idea. In the next paragraph I think if you repeated the noun – "life pictures" or a synonym would be clearer than "they", tho of course "they" is all right.

I cant stop at the bits I like – they are too numerous – (all the boat bit is full of sympathy and comprehension) I don't quite like, on page three the way you begin the paragraph "It would appear then that the Irish Cry etc". It reads a bit pedantically, but the idea is good enough to bear giving more simply. On page 5 ought the third paragraph to begin "startled question", or "*a* startled etc" or "questions"? And again "at this door", which door? Advancing age or subletting? That is not quite clear – (but anyhow it doesn't matter) On page six the suggestion of the old man's tragedy is very artistic, but would I think, bear expansion. I suppose the "traditional pig" is inevitable (on page 4) but I don't care for him – He always happens along in an Irish article, and by the bye is the "hereditary friend" the pig, or who? I don't quite see, (but I am a fool.) The old man and the ruin are very good, and the sentence is a very pleasant one to read and well finished. On page 8 would you say "to see tomorrow's *day* dying" etc instead of merely the possessive? The last little paragraph is like a bit of a sonnet and is simple and delightful. The whole paper is a triumphant proof to me of what I have always held, that if you have got the hang you can go it lively. You have style, and originality and sentiment, and I am blowed if I know what more you want. Write a story – don't waste yourself on topography. You are just bound to succeed if you put your back into it. When I read what you write and know how immeasurably superior it is to anything I could do, I feel it is ridiculous to pan on criticism, still, I know anything is a help – and better than nothing at all. I will try to get Minnie to read it, but her house and time are both choked up with visitors, and I doubt she will be able to give her mind to it. Hildegarde's jaw "dhropped that", at your talent, and she thought it very interesting. I have not yet garnered Mother's opinion, but the article is not much in her line. I think for *Temple Bar* you would want to pad and pan more. Give the Old Man more in extenso, and be a little bit descriptive and sarcastic about O'lympia – as *Punch* called it – Constance Bushe told me, she heard Saxons openly discussing the natives as if they were Central Africans who knew no word of English. Could you work a parallel case – Vide Theo at the Moycullen fair? – It now reads like a sympathetic and unusual news article but not a magazine one. Would the *Saint James Gazette* or even the *Saturday?* with a few more deep questions of life and death thrown in? You should hurry up as Olympia closes in September. I doubt you are too late for *Temple Bar* – or – happy thought – the *Graphic.* I will send it in for you if you will refix it a bit, and like the idea, I am sure Williamson would get it read, and I know they would give me an early reply and Mr. St Leger might work the *Globe* for you. I agree that it is not at all the *World*'s form: too serious, and not bitter enough. Two or three months ago *Temple Bar* might have done it but I know they fill up those Mags a long way in advance. I must go to sleep. I wish you were here, or I was there – it would save much time and trouble. I have had a taste of neuralgia (a bad tooth) . . . [*end of letter missing*]

Edith is planning a trip to Ross. She has sold a portrait of her cousin Hatta and thus has the funds for her rail fare and her keep at Ross. Financially neither of them was able to see further than a month or two into the future. Here we have an acknowledgement of the good effect of Edith's criticism on Martin: 'it has put a backbone into me'. She works hard at renovating Ross and she and her mother have decided to stay. They are pleased with the spaciousness of Ross after their gloomy rented house in North Dublin, and numerous sisters appear for summer holidays with their children and sometimes their husbands. This letter describes the return of Martin's sister Geraldine after sixteen years away from home.

Ross, Friday night.
August 17th 88

My dear Edith

These last two letters of yours have put a backbone into me – not that I wanted it – but a little to spare is no harm. First I am very glad about your October scheme for coming here. Long life to Hatta and the black cat – and to their patrons – Of course October will suit us, and Mama is very much pleased at the prospect – I think I should be more so only that I know you will write from the Sykes and say "Hang it – these infernal sights and Mother in conjunction wont let me come out of this, and as Boyle is going to stay on for an extra two months leave, it seems hard luck on him to go away. I am black with fury but what can one do." I think that might possibly be an extract from an October 1888 letter of yours. However we will hope otherwise – I wish of course that you were coming earlier, as ditch water will not be the word for the dullness, and the bare branches will make things look even worse than they now do. But clearly the Bristol & Dublin route is your chance – and you must try not to be later than the 20th. This is the place to cure you if you have got neuralgia, anyway. Mountain air is the thing – not that there exist any lofty peaks in the neighbourhood, but the hills stand about Ross, as about Jerusalem. You talk as if we were summer visitors here only, but such is not the case. The tap roots are down through the kitchen flags already, and Mama says that those who want to evict us must bring crow bars. It certainly is best in many ways to be here – more suitable and decent and there is room for such as the Hewsons. I have not been so perfectly sound and fit for ages as in these last 6 weeks (in a good hour etc.). I am getting round swollen cheeks the colour of peonies and my strength is as the strength of ten; and that is the reason of writing beef tea articles for unknown papers. You said a great deal too much as to that village thing – you did indeed. Neither it nor I deserve it at all – I have always felt that whatever you read you see more in than I do – perhaps even than the author does – I mean you are a curiously sympathetic reader. However let us be practical – I think the *Graphic* is a good idea and will do my best to loosen the article without lengthening it – I might leave out the old man altogether, for the matter of that, and pan more on the village. I know well what you mean about that tightness of style – it is always a temptation to make one ponderous word do instead of several light ones. But in writing that thing I was just shovelling it out in jerks; I had a kind of feeling that woe was unto me if I didn't make it an impression and nothing more – as I felt it – I did not mean any raison d'être – I hadn't one beyond just those ideas suggested by seeing the contrast very forcibly of the two villages – and taking the opportunity of describing one. As to setting about to describe Olympia at this time of day it would I think be superfluous. We see a heap of weekly papers here, and I assure you it has been described off the face of the earth. Everyone has seen it, and what on earth could one say of it. I think your idea of the animals at the zoo very good, and one that might easily enough be worked in. It is so hard not to be smart and pert, and that is the rock ahead in crabbing Olympia – but the visitor thereto is a good mark. As to that sentence about "a gratifying recollection;" I meant it to be with semi-colons – each clause detached – but no matter – I shall not fatigue you by going into these corrections, but shall act on them – but I *will* say that you might have known that the hereditary friend was the landlord. I will close the subject by reiterating that I felt somehow that I must be snatchy and cram down a sentence what ever end came up first or I should never get it down as I felt it – and naturally the result is obscurity and an affected strain.

As you were so stupid about the hereditary friend I think that the H.F. will inflict on you the tale of the old man concerned. I found him as therein stated, on the point of starvation – one fine afternoon – and on the next I went down to Killannin with foods of kinds from Mama, and felt more comfortable. He then came up twice a week for whatever garbage there was going and then strengthened – he came and gave us a day's work like the other tenants, and I am sure felt twice the man for that. Finally he said he would work for Mama for nothing but his food and it has ended in his getting the noble sum of 6 pence a day and two good meals anyhow – and he is here always! He is a fine looking chap, not so old as I made him out, and has renewed his youth and looks wonderfully since as he says "the misthriss put her hand over me". He never begs or says anything about his come down in the world. I had not heard, or rather had forgotten his domestic misfortunes and one day asked him how Johnny Connor's wife was – a woman who had just had a baby in Killannin. He said with surprising emphasis that he knew nothing about her – I reflected, and asked him if it were not Johnny Connor who had got his land from him. To my dismay he said with a sort of burst, and absolutely terrific look of fury and torment "wasn't it he that took my wife from me!" I just walked away. I couldn't say anything, and he was rushing into details – and I slunk out of the yard. It is quite true – the old fool married this young fool, and finally as Nurse Barrett told me "he bet her and threw her out" and now she is in the work house and Johnny Connor thrives, and is very friendly and pleasant to meet. And so the world goes round and round as Egerton has so many times expounded to us. I wonder if the next few turns will bring Bourget to London with his bags of money. Can these things be? I think it may end with his coming and borrowing a tenner from the Bart just to pay for the makings of the bags. But what is the use of mocking – as I say, when your father and the pope are shaking hands over it the mockers may hide themselves – till then it is a cheap amusement.

I am very glad about this good and industrious young man, this Mr. Gay, who works so nicely with you, and gives such deep attention to trivial remarks. Indeed it is a great thing to get a spell of useful work like this in the throngest days of the Buddhs,* and with Herbert requiring entertainment. His aspersions of you and that other are unworthy but inevitable I should say. At all events he is to be commended for "trumping Deaths ace" for you that time on the cliff. What with mad dogs about and windy weather and cliffs so prevalent I feel very anxious. I remember once being in a bad place on a cliff of a crumbly sort and not minding much at the time but nearly dying of it that night in bed. I am at this time a very tired woman. All yesterday I feverishly plastered a second coat of paint on my room – the Hewson quartet being expected in the afternoon, and got through with it just before they came. I then after many chargings down and pantings up of the 52 steps between this attic and the hall, retired to rest at a late hour and couldn't sleep from the strangeness of the room and the awful stench of the paint. You would have died long before daylight, with your heels touching your head. I survived, with the bed-clothes over my head, but it was not altogether enjoyable. Today the Hewsons went forth to lunch at the Hodgson's to see some men on an island in Loch Corrib, Edward being mad on such things; and I stayed home and cleaned the paint off my windows and put up curtains and many a thousand things including the careful reading of your letter. So I am stiff and tired and ought to go to bed – but there is a beastly bat in my room and I am too frightened to put out the candle or to catch him.

Geraldine looks pretty well but a good deal torn down. She is in excellent spirits and the unbunging* is very great. She felt this place more of a nightmare than I did not having seen it for 16 years, and I 9 years ago, when a good deal of harm had been done. I pitied her when she came up the steps – she couldn't say a word for a long time. There was a bonfire at the gate in her honour in the evening, a moderate one only, but built just as we described it in the Shocker – a heap of turf, glowing all through, and sticks on the top – Poor Geraldine was so tired I had to drive her down to it – but she went very gallant and remembered the people very well. There was no cheering or any demonstrativeness, and owing to a mistake many of them had gone away thinking that she was not coming, but there was a great deal of conversation, and subsequent drinking of porter. Edward was wonderful, in a trying position. In about 2 minutes he was holding a group of men in a deep converse, without any apparent effort – and he was much approved of "a fine respectable gentleman" – "the tallest man on the property" such were the comments. In the strictest privacy I may say that I felt all of a heap to see the bonfire blazing there just as it used to in my father's time – when he and the boys used to come down and all of us, and it was all the most natural thing in the world. It was very different to see Geraldine walk in front of us through the gates, with her white face and shabby clothes. Thady Connor (who is the bailiff and was the steward) met her at the gate, and not in any vice regal circles could be surpassed the way he took off his hat and came silently forward to her, while everyone else kept back in dead silence too. I know Thady is not what he ought to be, or any of them for the matter of that, but I think they felt seeing her – of course they had all known her well. What with that glare of the bonfire that *we* have described, and the welcome killed with memories for her, I wonder how she stood it. It was the attempt of the old times that was painful and wretched – at least I thought it so. Anyhow I have blathered enough about it.

Have I not many times told you that letters from here to you take 2 days, unless, as in this case, I post early in the morning. Be content then. In October we shall get the afternoon post about 2.30 at this house – not bad for the London letters. I have had a notion of a feeble kind for a little time and will try conscientiously to work it. But indeed I don't feel it my line – I feel more like writing pompous papers on emigration and such things, and even occasionally vex my soul with wonderings as to what germ of truth there is in Fenianism. I feel afraid of trying the story it would be so slight and so short, if anything, and one has always a horrible lurking fear that one is writing nonsense.

I am very glad that you are made to play tennis. Keep your form up, and if I can get the gravel court here into order before you come I shall invite the neighbourhood and display you – Let me know how Lilly Wee develops in tennis and all ways. But more than all do I pine to hear what you think of Boyle – don't forget that – Violet as the youngest and totally idle squaw* ought at present to be learning the ways of first cousins, a liberal education – Poor creature – I am sorry for that twisted foot – and can imagine the spartan smile of anguish with which she regarded her sympathisers. You do be saying nice things about my being an absentee from your revels. Don't do so anymore. It is really not good enough, or rather it is too good for such as I. I don't know why I drift into puke in this letter no matter what I do. It would make me sick to read it over so don't mind mistakes – "I therefore dismiss it with a frigid tranquillity" as Johnson says at the end of the preface to his Dictionary.

Read it by the way if you want an example of magnificent ponderous composition and ask Herbert if he knows it. How pleasing if he doesn't. Tell your sister who is called Hildegarde that I am deeply pleased that she liked Olympia – Robert's kid is to be Barbarah Xavara – I don't care for either within points of Margery –

    Yours
    Martin

How quickly Edith realized the value of Martin's letters as raw material is shown by her instant picking-up of Martin's splendid description of the welcome bonfire for Geraldine and her husband. The Coghill plans for the Bourget shares scheme seem more and more improbable and ill-fated. Edith and Martin's awareness that they were witnessing the loss of the last capital available to Egerton cast a blight on this period, as he and Hildegarde were deeply in love.

Hewitt Poole was one of the Pooles of Mayfield, near Bandon, and a cousin of Edith's. In the spring of 1878 he had had a flirtation with Edith; they exchanged poems and drawings. Edith already knew Martin's sister Geraldine, and by this stage Edith evidently thinks that she made a fool of herself. After staying at Drishane in September of that year (when he may have asked Colonel Somerville for Edith's hand in marriage) he departed and was never seen in Castletownshend again. He was unofficially engaged in 1878 to his cousin Mia Jellett whom he married in November 1880. This concealed real-life entanglement was used repeatedly as a plot in the fiction.

[From Edith to Martin]

Sunday evening
August 19th 88

I have some faint foolish idea of beginning to answer your letter which I got this morning, now; but I have no hopes of writing more than a few lines, as it is bed time and we shall all be hurooshed in a few minutes. Send along that paper for the *Graphic* as soon as convenient, I always have a dread that someone else will step down into the pool first. I will beg Williamson to get an early answer as the subject is one of temporary interest. I feel sure that some paper will have it. But please explain "the hereditary friend". It now only makes me think of the Divil. I am glad you have Geraldine. Give her my love, although I know I am

not in the least the same woman that she thinks she met in the year BC
77. Do not try and collate your edition with hers. It would not help
you, and I would rather you did not know how many parts of a fool I
was. I daresay I am just as many now, but they are different parts. I
should like to meet Geraldine again, but I would have a kind of envy
and dread of that shadowy idiot of 19 that was getting between her and
me all the time. It would be a fine thing to be back there again, and to
know better but I suppose anyway one would get there – i.e. into the
wrong place just the same. There are only a few people who know how
to get the best they can out of their time. Mr. Gay has come nearer it
than most. He chose his trade and has stuck to it for 11 years – just the
time I have wasted, by the way – and now he can paint anyhow. (In
bed) those sombre reflections have been, I think, mainly induced by the
fact that I have been making a very bad fist of a life sized head of Jack
that I have been trying to paint at Tally Ho. It is depressing to find how
soon you get to your limitations when you try for really serious work.
A torrentially wet Sunday also tends to gloom and the writing of three
uninteresting letters in the morning did not help me along. Before I
forget let me say that I don't think I would eliminate the old man from
your article: he is a fine tragic picturesque creature, and your further
facts about him are interesting and ghastly and well "dans le caractére
[*sic*]" – and by the way, (since I am a sympathetic reader,) I would like
to tell you how very well I realise that bonfire, and Thady Connor –
and – I say it seriously – you ought to make a sonnet, if only for the
sake of bringing in the phrase "a welcome killed by memories". It seemed
to give me the feeling of the whole thing. You are a big fool to sleep in
the smell of paint. I am surprised you are alive to write about it. I quite
admit that I shouldn't be. Cliffs and mad dogs are not in it with fresh
paint. The Bourget ferment has entered on a fresh phase, and today
came a letter from Uncle Kendal to Papa enjoining the strictest secrecy,
and saying that the name of the society of whom Bougie is the agent
must never be mentioned. This comes rather late after the Bart has been
proclaiming the length and breadth of it all to whomsoever he could get
to listen to him. However the Colonel seems much in earnest and would
not even write the word in his letter merely putting a dash, and begged
that the same might be instantly destroyed. I don't know what to think
of it all – I can only say that if it comes off it will be a great day for
the Dowagers, and also Papa, who is now to be a director. If he and
Egerton are summoned to town, we are to say they are on the board of
a bank, no more than that. I must say that these orders come rather
late, but we can't go beyond them. Moreover as everything is now on

a new footing, we are to say that the former schemes fell through – and – I conclude – the inference is that Bougie and his friends have tumbled through too. Communicate as much of this as you think fit to your Mother, in fact, if you follow Uncle Ken's orders you will only say that *"the original Bougie scheme is smashed and no more is known of it"*. This is to be told to everyone, and as it is in a way, true, perhaps you had better stick to it, and leave further possible developments alone for the present. After all, it is the Colonel's show, and he has a right to work it his own way (nevertheless, I bet the Bart will tell it all to Katie.) If you hear that Papa and Egerton have gone to town it will be about starting a new bank, and in no ostensible way connected with Bougie and will mean money for them both. It is all very wild, and the post is very interesting these times. You had better burn up this sheet at once, so that we shall be out of the condemnation. It seems to me rather absurd, but it isn't our affair, and it is best to obey the Colonel's orders – So only tell Geraldine and your mother what he has desired to have made known on the subject. In spite of your beastly insinuations I am quite set on coming to Ross when Boyle's leave is over, if your Mother is still of a mind to have me, and thank her kindly for asking me. The wedding is fixed for October 5th. The bridesmaids' attire is not decided upon, but they think of fine white cloth gowns and claret coloured hats, and Aylmer says he will give ostrich feather fans of the sort that Katie gave Beatrice. Nice things, and far more useful than a bangle or a brooch in the years to come. We are all going to a wonderful show in Skibbereen tomorrow night. I think you have been told of the Maggie Morton Dramatic Company who once played "The Private Secretary" there, concluding with a burlesque, (hurriedly put on in honour of all us) in which they pandered to the tastes of a vitiated aristocracy by taking off nearly all their clothes and standing unaffectedly before us trusting neither to song nor dance but to the mere pleasure which the sight of their huge crooked legs must afford us. This time they are to play "Romeo and Juliet", and though it seems a profane thing to do, we are going all the same . . . [*end of extract missing*]

[From Martin to Edith, August 1888: *first page missing; letter seems to start on page 3*]

. . . upper seams pretty well, and Geraldine, squatted in the bow, baled incessantly – with prophesies of destruction for us all – in fact she was in a funk – I rowed Stroke, Edward Bow. I do not pretend to great things at an oar, but I had some coaching this year on the river, and anyhow I can pull the same strength each stroke. Therefore it could hardly have been my fault that the boat progressed with the letter S movement, and that I received many mysterious blows on the back when least expecting them. We made Killannin in tolerably water-logged state, Geraldine announcing her intention of walking home, Mama wholly indifferent, Edward apologetic (I simply stiff with rage). Having got them all out of the boat I baled her dry and then rowed home peacefully alone, the boat not leaking a drop. Since then disaster has followed rapidly – Mama walked home from Killannin alone, and arrived dead beat and saying that Eileen had been attacked by stomach ache in Killannin and had to be doctored in a cottage – Later arrived Geraldine and one of the Leonards carrying Eileen – the latter white and flabby. Next morning (that awful wet Sunday, which was just as wet here) Geraldine and Mama were in their beds – victims to the mysterious grasps of pain in the waist, and to sickness. Selina crawled down very late saying that she had been violently sick in the night, and Edward and I from opposite ends of the table looked on each other with a wild surmise. But no, our withers were unwrung. The poor galled jades upstairs however had a very coarse time of it. Sunday and Monday Geraldine endured the grasping hand, but is today revived and up. Mama however has been and is very seedy. Perpetual pain, sickness and Turkish disease and everything makes her more sick and wretched. It is clearly caused by some raspberries that have been too long gathered and in Mama's case by over much fruit generally and cream. Anyhow this morning I drove off to a Mr. Kilkelly about 4 miles off – a friend of ours and a retired doctor to ask him what was to be done. He was consolatory and ordered mustard, and a concoction which Mama will not take because it has rhubarb in it. The Bushes are a strange people as to their insides and their perversity connected therewith. Of all afternoons the O'Flaherties chose this to descend upon us as also Mr. Kilkelly's son, champion bicyclist of Ireland me dear, and reeking of Trinity College Dublin (I am possessed of a violent devil but still) – forth to the wood of Annagh did Geraldine and I feebly lead our tribe, and the bicyclist was far above rubies in the appropriating of an O'Flahertie for the afternoon. The woods were delicious, and my portion was a Miss Guthrie, visitor of the O'Flaherties who spent her time in being rather ill natured and amusing about them. She was Scotch and rich and worldly, and yachts and goes to Ascot all the time – and I thought it beastly of her to give away her poor multitudinous O'Flaherties, one of whom was her school friend – sort of English Flemings they are. Edward, unhappy divine, made what sport he could for the dullest of the O'Flah-erties and has fallen into deepest dejection ever since. Perhaps he is sickening for the family disease.

You are now probably hearing "Romeo I come, this do I drink to thee" from the lips of Miss Maggie Morton. Do not be very funny about it it is almost too much. Just tell me quietly what it was like – and where you laughed most. I am awfully glad you are painting in this way and that Mr. Gay is so sound and so useful – it will be a lasting standby to you – and don't fall into gloomy reflections about Jack's head. Isn't he a difficult sort of subject? . . . All humours of the audience must be chronicled. Mama and Geraldine laugh loudly at the thought of the druidical idol and its Fleming and by the bye Geraldine saw in the *Spectator* an account of a cannibal with many wives, who in moments of ennui with any special one he gradually devoured . . . Where is Herbert's sonnet? And where is he mostly?

Martin

Boyle Somerville, Edith's favourite brother, was born 7 September 1863 and murdered by the IRA at his home in Castletownshend on 24 March 1936. He married Helen Mabel Allen in 1896. He was educated at the Royal Naval Academy and HMS Britannia. *He took part in the Chilean–Peruvian War in 1880 and the First Egyptian War in 1882. He served in China, Australia and the Pacific, the Persian Gulf, Ceylon and the Indian Ocean, taking his camera with him everywhere and amassing a photographic collection of great anthropological interest. He published dictionaries of the languages of the New Hebrides, New Georgia and the Solomon Islands;* A Catalogue of 1850 Stars for the Use of Seamen; Commodore Anson's World Voyage *(1934);* Will Mariner *(1936). A keen amateur archaeologist, he was the first to subject stone circles to mathematical surveys, and published his findings in antiquarian journals. He retired as Vice-Admiral in 1919.*

In this letter he reappears at Drishane after being away at sea for four years.

Drishane
Friday 24th August 88

My dear Martin
Your letter yesterday was a good deal of a disappointment to me. I had made myself believe that you would be able to come, and had plotted

out an admirable time. I would have liked you to come awfully. Next
– I think you might have done that much for me – it was so little – and
you knew how glad I would have been, whether you came here or no;
and I said you might let it depend on the Shocker. I know what you
mean and how you felt, but I think you might anyhow have kept it in
case a chance came of your coming here. Boyle is full of anxiety to see
you and is prepared to love you very much. He is curiously unchanged,
except in size. He is about 5 foot 11 inches, and his shoulders are like
those of a bull. In fact, I think he has a nice figure, and though not
good-looking he has an awfully nice face. He is full of art fads, and
theories which we assure him are Youngrot,* but he found no fault with
our decorations, which was a relief. His own boxes have not come yet,
he says that he has lots of nice things – which I can well believe as he
has excellent taste. I was really amazed to find that he is unaffectedly
keen about Rossetti's poems and sonnets and has a book of them. A
new edition of nearly the same collection as I gave you. He does not
seem to think it is any merit on his part to like nice books, but just does
it because he was built that way. He is excellently appreciative of any
sort of story and will soon have quite as good (and more intellectual) a
grasp of the squaw* jests and converse as Aylmer. From having lived
with the super correct Cameron girls, he was at first rather amazed and
scandalised, at the free mention of "Buddh-legs",* "decanting",* and
other kindred subjects, any of which caused the Camerons to faint,
actually and seriously. But he is very segashuative.* The first morning
he came – he arrived at 6.30 a.m., the Innishannon train – we took him
all around, and finally, at Herbert's instigation went in a boat up the
river and sat under a tree and talked. It was very interesting to see Boyle
sitting there silent, but quietly assimilating and placing himself – four
years makes a lot of difference in lingo and topics of conversation
generally. He has got a very square head, and can talk extremely well
and interestingly about his Japaneseries and their ways and customs. I
think you would like him very much. He is anything but "an overflow
meeting",* being singularly independent in his ideas and calmly determined in expressing and holding to them. You *must* come down here
before he goes; as goodness knows when there might be another chance
of your seeing him and I want you to do so more than I can say. I think
he is a dear boy and a fine fellow. Quite seriously. I have not much time
to write to you this morning, as I have promised to help him in refixing
those old rubbish cases in the anteroom, and will have to design shelves
of sorts and direct a carpenter, and many similar things. However I
daresay I will write again soon – as soon as I get Olympia (the which I

had rather hoped might come today) I am very sorry for the calamity which has descended upon your doomed household, and fervently hope you are not now in its – shall we say – grip(es)? [*end of letter missing*]

[From Martin to Edith, 29 August 1888: the Currarevagh Ball: *from page 5*]

Wednesday morning 5 o'clock a.m.

This was not sent yesterday morning – through a mistake – and now that I have just returned from the Hodgson's dance I am going to add to it in ghastly daylight, and without embellishments the adventures which befell us last night. Geraldine as you know, chaperoned me, our vehicle was an outside car, and Jim Connor our driver. We started at 9 in the pitch darkness just before moon rise, and as soon as we got into the road remembered with some apprehension that it was the night of the Oughterard races, and the roads would be full of carts with drunken drivers. We were scarcely quarter of a mile from the gate when some thing came lumbering along with shoutings. We shouted too, all we knew, and drew into the wall, and the next moment there was a thump and crash. Up went the car on my side, the mare backed, and I found myself clawing at the coping stones on top of the wall – in fact on my hands and knees on it. Looking round I saw Geraldine and Jim safely in the road, how they got there they don't know, but they were allright and the cart had passed on. We got the car down the bank without any trouble, and nothing daunted Geraldine and I got up, on the same side this time, giving Jim the brunt of everything we passed. With the dint of shouting and hiding in the ditch we passed innumerable cars and carts all parlattic,[1] and were nearing Oughterard on the top of a big hill, when we heard the rattling of a heavy cart trotting towards us. We as usual made for the ditch which in this instance was a bank with a very high wall on top, but before we could look crooked that cart just rushed straight into us. The car and mare spun completely round. Geraldine somehow jumped off, so did Jim, and I not seeing exactly where to jump got onto the well – the car all the time tilting forward – and my ears full of drunken screeches. I finally managed to precipitate myself on to the muddy bank and got clear. In the shouting and darkness we could just make out that the mare had fallen partly on her side and was

1 *Parlattic*: paralytic, i.e. drunkenly.

somehow caught in the cart. Then followed indescribable vituperation and we got the cart backed clear after much difficulty and talking ourselves hoarse. There lay the mare apparently stone dead – it was too dark to see a thing – and in the height of the confusion there came along an awful gang of roaring pedestrians. On this Geraldine and I applied ourselves to the task of climbing the wall in our ball dresses and wraps. We were not so much afraid of the drunkards as of their language, and having got up we hid behind the wall till they had passed. Emerging we found the mare on her feet without a scratch – apparently – the relief of which was enormous. The harness was in pieces, and no wonder – the shafts of the cart had gone between the belly band and the mare's body so she was lifted and swung round astride of the shaft. When the band broke – down she fell. How she was not killed is a miracle. We then made up our minds to walk on into Oughterard, about half a mile and to get a fresh harness, leaving Jim to follow with the mare. We got hold of a Ross man who was passing and made him protect us, but even with him we had a fearsome time from the drunken brutes we met – and from hobbling in thin shoes through the mud. It was a horrible walk, but once we got to Miss Murphy's hotel all was well. Jim brought in the car and mare, both perfectly uninjured and the fresh harness was jammed on and away we went for Curraghrevagh – feeling I must say a good deal battered but still undefeated – I cannot say how the whole situation was complicated by the darkness, and by my having on Mama's sealskin with a mackintosh on top of it. The feeling of suffocation when trying to climb that wall was near nightmare – and it is strange that I had a horrible dream the night before of trying to climb walls to save someone who had gone through the ice. We were of course very late at the dance arriving about number 7 but I had quite enough of it – I may say that I was tired and bored from beginning to end – though it was an awfully well done dance in every way. Somehow being knocked about tells on one, and I felt ready to subside into any corner available instead of which I dragged my weary bones through about 7 dances, and enjoyed my supper extremely – and we left as early as possible. There was no lack of people to dance with, but they were not enlivening with exception of Mr. Hanbury and another soldier of sorts – I thought the dance wanted go very much, or perhaps *I* did – Geraldine never lost the scared look, but otherwise was a highly creditable chaperone – Need I say that our accident was invaluable as conversation. One thing that made the evening seem interminable was occasional interludes of song from a little fat man with a Napoleon moustache. I started, when sitting in the drawing room, I heard "from the deserrrt I come to thee" in a strong vulgar baritone. I could have imagined myself at Drishane for a moment, but had to realise instead that I was talking of Trinity College to a youth with an unpleasant breath. I was somehow reminded of the Morgan's dance too – and could have found it in my heart to wish you were there – At intervals. The drive home was long and chilly but the dawn on Lough Corrib was worth looking at – I have discovered an inky bruise on my knee, another on my foot, and am generally stiff. How that Leigh over did these things I don't know.

Mama is only middling. I don't know quite what to say of her – but Philip will pronounce. The O'Flaherties have a dance this week – nothing will induce me to go – I don't know why dancing tires me so much these times – I think it is the want of the squaw* element – Does Boyle dance?

 Yours
 Martin

Martin re-immersed herself in the lives of the people that she had known as a young girl as tenants and servants, but who had now become small farmers and the like. She and her mother were both very attached to the man who had been the estate carpenter, Tom Walsh. Martin's account of his illness and death again shows the unexpected intimacy that grew up between Nationalist estate workers and their Unionist gentry.

[From Martin to Edith, August 1888: [*letter starts on page 2*]

. . . as to the Shocker it trembles in the possibilities much as Bourget does. It means I think that it will be read anyhow. I must say Mr. Rivington writes a good letter. Do you feel a sort of gentle disappointed way about him? A power of enthusiasm saddened and snubbed – (see how artfully I flatter the destroyer of Flora's peace) I am of course anxious to know about Bourget. When you have time let me know.

I send you that scratch[1] that Robert or his suborned one put in the *Pink' Un*. You may preserve it among your archives, (what are archives? ask Herbert) as I have another that Mr. Roberts sent me – I had the effrontery to tell our Edmund of it in my letter. I am glad Beatrice won that Tournament. She had written to me about it in much delight and indeed she has not so many successes that she will not appreciate this. I must write to Glen B. tomorrow. How does Violet fare? And how

---

1 *Scratch*: a favourable notice.

Willie Lee? I must say she is not to be pitied for that flop.* He seems a very nice creature and laziness is attractive to some people. Here things have been rather melancholy on account of the death of our carpenter that used to be. Tom Walsh – a man of about sixty – as clever and even brilliant a person that ever lived – with a face very like Carlyle – white hair, black eyebrows and a delightful swinging walk. He has been ill for some months, and Mama and I have been with him a good deal, and small trouble it was, it being a treat to talk to him. He died unexpectedly and on Friday last did not know anyone – not his own children – till Mama went in – "do you know me Tom" she said stooping over him, "Mrs. Martin" he said with a smile of the gentlest kind – and then relapsed into mutterings to himself. He died early next morning and I went up to see his wife, who was dreadfully quiet and took me in to see Tom, through a kitchen full of neighbours squatting about. There indeed was Tom, and such a sight that I shall not forget. I had not seen anyone dead since my grandfather, and I forget that. If I began to write about it I should not stop in a hurry, so I wont. On Saturday I was tired and wanted my luncheon and the sight of him took all the spirit out of me. I will only say that his expression was that of a person alive, not dead, a person who could speak if he liked but deliberately shut up his mouth – and the stillness gave the feeling of living tension and not dead inertness. That was the frightful feeling – and I made up my mind that if I had the misfortune to outlive the people that make life pleasant I shall not see them after they die. It is only running your head into a suffocating, intolerable mystery. On Monday he was buried and we all went to his funeral, despite the fact that he was a Delegate of the National League, at least we went a bit of the way – the funeral passed our gate and I waited there with a cross of white asters and ferns, while the others drove up to meet it. It was horrible when it did come – two or three hundred people straggling along – lots of them drunk – the coffin in a cart – and Tom's daughters sitting on the coffin – as is always done here – one of them was nearly distraught, with red hair flying about her. There was a sort of howl when the cart stopped at the gate, but the Irish cry was mostly done with by that time – I put the cross on the coffin and walked half a mile or so with Tom's son, and then we all came back and visitors descended and your letter came and I thought no more of it.

Does Aunt Adelaide know Kinsale people called Matthew? There is an English judge called Sir something Matthew, who has taken a place at Lough Corrib – at the ferry. Mama and I went over to call on them and found only two daughters at home – after some converse from them

of the civilest and thinnest my one informed me that she was a Land
Leaguer, as were also her sister and brother! Rabid leaguers. One of
them said with pride "Mr. Dillon says I go too far even for him." We
took them politely and as one would take the idiot baby, but they were
in deadly . . . [*end of letter missing*]

*Very little time was available in which to pursue a literary career. Edith
had some consolation in the good sales of one of her first literary efforts,*
The Mark Twain Birthday Book. *This letter illustrates the problem of
finding time in which to work, and the endlessness of the social functions
and charity events supported by the class in which they lived.*

Drishane
Monday September 10th 88

Dear Martin

I can't think why I am beginning a letter to you, as I feel deeply unlike
it, and have not even got time at that. I send you a Mark Twain, in
which I have caused several priceless autographs to be inserted. I beg
that you will take it to church with you every Sunday, and leave it in a
different pew every time. By this means its precious teachings may be
disseminated among the people. You will see it is in its fourth thousand.

This is a torn and broken day and the week does not promise to be
much better. Ethel and Jim went by the midday today. Tomorrow a
hideous tennis function at the Broughams – Wednesday Herbert goes –
some of us will probably be dragged to the Powells. Thursday, we have
a tennis party to which *every* bounder in the whole country is coming
and on Friday we have a dinner. My whole being heaves and curdles
alternately at the prospect. To attempt anything serious or demanding
steady work is just simply impossible here – and I feel sickened of even
trying. We are all so tied together – what ever is done must be done by
everyone in the whole place and as the majority prefer wasting their
time, that is the prevalent amusement. You may laugh if you like but it
is perfectly true – Boyle and Mr Gay are the only two who have a mind
to work, but although the latter can do as he likes, Boyle and I can't.

I feel a little better after this blaut.* I hope you are also better – you
gave a very poor account of yourself in your letter – I believe you have
been leaving off your tonics, or sitting up too late, or some blamed
foolishness of the sort. Don't.

This reminds me of those about to marry – Emmie says that the dresses are to be of some kind of white silk *gauze* with spots – and a good deal of white watered silk ribbon or sorts introduced – sash etc. The hats are high white straw, the brims turning up at the back and sticking out in front. Emmie says they are a very becoming shape – I hope so – but I don't care about the whole sound of the rig. Hildegarde and I see with prophetic vision, our huge amethyst faces under these coquettish little white hats, on a piercing October day, and shudder – but of course glorious old Rosie has fixed things as she likes them. Aylmer is giving little gold arrow brooches with pearls – A mournful lack of originality, and not half as good as his own original idea of big white feather fans. I expect G. O. R. has a big white feather fan already.

Is coming here really out of the question for you? We shall be leaving this for Bristol on about the 28th of this month so it seems to me that it would not be worth the expense of the long journey. This wedding comes at the most detestable time – and disarranges everything. Boyle's leave expires on the 20th of October. The wedding guests disperse on the 5th and what he is to do in the meantime is the question. We can't (and wont) stay at the Bideford woman for more than four or five days. The only question is, what is to be done with Boyle, who will have ten days to fool around in, and who has not got money to fly around backwards and forwards until Bourget comes – and goodness knows how soon or how long that may be – one has no idea what the family will do – Uncle Jos seems still to be in flourishing spirits over him – but these constant delays and put offs make one very sceptical in spite of the full and elaborate excuses and explanations which come along with each delay. I am now much amused by the conduct of the Uncles. They wrote to us, laying the direful injunctions of caution and secrecy on us, which I handed on to you, and now we find that they themselves tell the whole thing to anyone they meet. I have had no news from Belgravia.

I can write no more being distracted. I think I will keep this and finish it tonight and send on the book

Yours

E.Œ.S.

I shall say a few more words in bed – but not many – Boyle and I had a really peaceful afternoon. We drove to a cottage on the way to Rineen – sent the trap home, and then sketched till dark and walked back. The bonds fell from us for once – and we were temporarily free. I am looking forward to going to Ross. Are you *certain* you wont mind having me so late in the month? Ethel wants me to go on to her from you – I should like to – but it is all dark before me. I cannot ever explain our amusement at the notion of Archer Martin dropping from the skies and staying on to clean the chimneys. You certainly ought to marry him – I am sure he is very nice – I like his description immensely. But why do you call him American when he comes from Canada? We had a ripping choir last Sunday – Boyle is excellent, and comes to practice (confound your insolence) and learns his bars and doesn't think it any of a trouble.

[From Edith to Martin, September 1888: *fragment*]

. . . Mother has just said that she thought that chapter nine was excellent – "Most fiery love" – but she said that she was taken by surprise as she had not noticed "a stream of love leading up to it – only jealousy". This I think nonsense – & so I am sure do you. However I will talk no more Shocker & will look out for a letter on Tuesday. Send it on to Ethel as soon as you can. I am longing for her to see it. Tell Geraldine to send it straight to her – & if you will say where you want it to go afterwards I will tell E. to send it on. Minnie's entire & finished verdict is "good, interesting, & excellently life-like characters" I am in the stage of elation, but am going to try to forget it as I think it is a mistake to get it on the nerves. If you utterly disagree about Willy's wogging* speech – would you compromise upon "she's a nice little thing – But – " with a meaning I did not quite catch "I'll know better another time" . . . [*incomplete*]

An extraordinary outburst against An Irish Cousin *came from Edith's brother Boyle, at home on leave. He uses an odd family word, 'wog' to indicate the type of man or woman who revels in flirtatious behaviour (it was also used as a verb, 'wogging', and as a plural noun). Theo did not appeal to him, and it is amusing to read Martin's response to Boyle's criticism which reveals how much of a Buddh* type Theo really was.*

From Edith to Martin, September 1888 [*fragment*]

. . . I have been painting like mad these last 3 days at a life sized portrait of Papa – canvas 1′ 8″ x 2′ 3″ – which Aylmer asked me to give to him. Mother is pleased – which is a great deal – I think the likeness is good, in colour & form, but the painting "misses" somewhere. It has gone quickly – 1 day to draw, & 3 to paint (10 to 1.30) is good going. I have had no word of the Recruit or Pierce Cormac – or the Shocker – Boyle has taken an unlooked-for turn with regard to the last. After harkening many nights in silence, last night he announced that he thought it very well written & the people real & lifelike, but all were detestable. Theo "a beast – a perfect wog* – heartless, & leading Willy on, while in the most exciting moments she made remarks on the furniture. Willy, a vulgar uneducated lout. Nugent only just bearable. The common people the only ones he really liked – " etc etc in a wholly unexpected outburst, which must have been simmering in him for nearly a week . . . [*letter torn – section missing*]

. . . we had a truly Buddhic* episode last Saturday. We all, i.e. H.V.B. E. Boyle & I, walked to Myross Wood (from the bridge). It was so hot that V & I determined to take off 2 superfluous petticoats, & hide them till our return. Behind the Powells' gates we retired up, & took them off; & then, in a little coppice of willows, behind a low wall, we laid the petticoats, strewing boughs over them the better to conceal them. Coming back, the Townshends offered to walk part of the way with us. We could only beg them not to do so; I swept their 'leading gentleman', Mr Whitla (husband of Nora Myross) off ahead so as to give Boyle or Violet a chance to snatch the petticoats from their lair, while H & E tackled the 3 remaining Townshends, & this they could easily have done, only for the cussedness of those Townshends, who directed them to stop exactly opposite the lair, there to await the recall of Mr Whitla, by Boyle who came racing after us to send him back. Presently the others overtook Boyle & me & told us that at last, Egerton could bear it no longer but boldly strode into the thicket to fetch the coits;* unluckily they were so well hidden that he could not find them. His absence began to seem marked, & the great gommawn* Hildegarde made it much worse by saying with an apologetic deprecatory smile that he "had gone to look for a sketch" – a manifest lie, on a thick foggy evening at 6.30, when it was pitch dark. Then Violet, in despair, plunged in after him, & then – what the Townshends thought I cannot imagine – Egerton emerged looking like a bloated Russian hunchback, with one petticoat stuffed up the back of his coat while the other was laid upon his stomach, & Hildegarde's long fur boa hung round his neck by way of concealing his awful figure. Picture Hildegarde, with the cat-face, bright purple, silently wringing the hands of the Myrosses, while Violet eyed them with gleaming eyes to see if they had appreciated the backhair* side of the position – brought into such hopeless prominence by Hildegarde's lying excuses. I have written all this page at 5.20 on Thursday morning, having just come back from the Liss Ard dance. It was a very good one, & in spite of the lamented absence of our dear Joe Gubbins, I enjoyed it very much. They had hundreds of people & lots of men.

Morgan had imported Mr Bence Jones & 4 friends – one that big black curly haired bull-calf man, Stavely Hill, to whom I think you were introduced last year. The floor was *very* good, & the supper of the very best, ditto the champagne & the soup – Hildegarde had on a new pink silk gown, sent her by the Chimp, & looked exceedingly nice, & so did Violet in white with H.'s yellow chinese scarf. The latter is now wogging* Phil Pork – (we speak of it as a Phil-lirtation, in our funny way – & got on very well in the matter of dances – I loved Mr Hodson – he is strangely . . . [*end of fragment*]

It is perfectly clear from the way in which Edith and Martin recorded the pronunciation of their older relatives' sayings, that they did speak in a 'brogue'. We find references to the brogue of certain families within the Buddh* network, as in the 'Somervillio-Donovan brogue'; and the Martin brogue was a thing in itself. When Dick Martin, 'Humanity Dick', was MP for Galway, his fellow Members of Parliament in London fell about laughing at his brogue. Two generations later Edith and Martin were perfectly conscious, when they were staying in London, that they were country cousins with Irish brogues. It should be noted that although gentry children were punished for speaking in servants' brogue there was also a gentry brogue with distinctive variations by family, and it is gentry brogue that Martin labels as 'Somervillio-Donovan brogue'. It was a rich drawl with tonal changes noticeable in London drawing rooms, where the prevailing tone was a monotonous forte bray.

The family travelled to England for the wedding of Aylmer Somerville and Emmeline Sykes.

September 30th 88
Oaklands, Almondsbury

Dear Martin
This is a beast of a pen – A waving visitors bedroom quill, so I will only write a line . . . We, i.e. mother H. and I got here yesterday, leaving Boyle and Papa to go to Glandofan and follow us here tomorrow. We had a beautiful crossing and though there was a bit of a roll, cocaine fortified me. I wish you had seen our start – each of us had an average of four lap-passengers of the most flangey* and weighty kind. Mother and Papa both went off their heads completely with fuss – Mother's of the vociferous and rampageous variety. Papa's gloomy and scared – full

of the conviction that the train is a spiteful sentient thing that deliberately hurries away from its station without you, unless you can outwit it in some subtle way. The crowning shock was the discovery five minutes before the time at which we ought to start that there was but one jaunting car to hold us all – six people, and a man to drive – besides a picture-case from which I refused to be separated. (In this connection mother exclaimed, flinging wild eyes and arms to the sky "Oh! I *loathe* and *detest* artists of all breeds and generations!") Papa with an ashen face said he wouldn't go at all. Mother kept up a steady flow of impassioned blort* – Hildegarde, Mr Hodson and I laughed till we couldn't stand – Boyle alone kept his head and despatched Jeremiah for Hurley's car – (Egerton had gone on with most of the lap-passengers)

Then we set out to walk along the road till the car picked us up. It did so at the Pound, and welted into Skib, up and down hill as fast as the wretched horses could leg it, and when we got to the station, we had exactly quarter of an hour to wait. I think that is the epitome of Papa – we parted with deep regret from our good Eddie Hodson – (nate, grave and gay are curiously his adjectives) – and with promises on his part to come again. I discovered in him the rare qualities that constitute a Purlieu* Slut and on a wet day following the dance, Boyle and I employed him largely in that capacity.

E.H.B. and I stayed on deck, huddled in ulsters and rugs till 11.30 – and then slept peacefully all night. At Newport, Aylmer and Alfred Sykes met us – and there also we found that H.'s and E.'s boxes had been left at Milford. Much wiring ensued but as yet her boxes have not transpired. E. went straight to London. He wired last night to say that the Bourget business is in very good case. It has entered on what seems to me a very wholesome phase, I cant be bothered explaining it – but you may believe it. Here were Mrs. Sykes, Emmie, G. O. R., steady Norah and two Aunts of some 36 or 37 – sisters of Mrs Sykes. – Dealtry by name – and a waggish governess – (so H. says backed by Aylmer – I had not noticed it). I cant give any detailed account now of their humours – but will remember them. We were soon showed the presents . . .

Lack of money made Edith's proposed trip to Ross an impossibiity in 1888. Edith and Martin made a point of communicating on New Year's Day. At Ross there was traditionally a dance; in 1889, after only one year back at Ross, the Martins had not yet revived this. At Castletownshend, however, the traditional occupation was a hunt with the West Carbery. The one described here was a meet at Manch House, near

Bandon, home of the Connors. It is the lengthiest account of a hunt in Edith's letters and is a splendid example of her writing at flat-out pace.

Drishane
January 1st 89

My dear Martin

This is a filthy bit of paper, but I feel that the stirring events that I am going to write demand large sheets – and as I have no more here, I don't care. I am afraid I shall excite all your most evil passions in the course of my narration, but you must try and fight them down – Well – Aylmer and I rode the horses up to Skib, leaving this at 7.30. A lovely mild grey morning, and no rain for the two previous days. In Skib we met Mr Maxwell and Jack de Burgh, who were both boxing their horses up for the same meet. Sorcerer walked into the box like a station master, and Vesta followed him with equal calm. When we got to Ballineen we got them out and rode up to Manch House, the Connors' place. Mr Dan Connor and his father have always been friends of my grandfather's and of Papa's, but I had only once met the son – (who is in Dublin – married –) We had about one and a half miles to go and then we saw Mr Connor at a gateway – (he had been pointed out to me at a station.) A delightful hard bitten small cute-looking man with cut away grey whiskers and a nice old gentleman's brogue. He welcomed us with great delight and took us up to breakfast. No less than three Miss Connors of varying ages from about 32 to 35, and two old Mrs Connors (wife and mother of Dan) met us. Really awfully nice kind people, and very "good sort". One of the daughters was in a very trim little brown habit and hat; they were none of them goodlooking, exactly – but very pleasant and intelligent, and with lots to say for themselves. It was about 10 o'clock, so A. and I stuffed a hasty meal and then we mounted to meet Owld Bāāmish – who presently appeared with Woodboine and Waurrīor, and Saulamon, and Jāally, and all the rest of our old friends. He was most affectionate to A. and me and "hoped we would have sport." Mr Connor rode rather a goodlooking leggy young mare – he is a great owld jockey and used to have the hounds himself for years – and Miss C. was on a hideous black brute, but a thundering good jumper. She rides tremendously well, and is all there, and an awfully nice good little sort, only anxious that we should have the best possible place, and giving us all sorts of useful hints – as her Father said to A – "Oh, you're all right with Henrietta I thrained her up to know the country when she was a young thing, and she's as good as myself now – "

1. Edith Somerville and Martin Ross at work in the studio at Drishane.
(Photograph by Hildegarde Somerville, Lady Coghill)

2. Horse Island Picnic. (A bold contra-jour photograph by Boyle Somerville) The Stags, the rock formation on the horizon, were a useful mark for yachtsmen. Hildegarde and Martin are amongst the figures at the cliff top.

3. Edith Somerville at seventeen. (Photograph by her uncle Sir Joscelyn Coghill) This is one of two studies he made of Edith in the year before she put up her hair, 1876.

4. Martin Ross dressed for a Fancy Dress Ball in August 1887. She had been draped in a sheet by Hildegarde. Her companion is James Penrose, who married Ethel Coghill, Edith's 'Twin' and first cousin.

5. The West Carbery Hunt, a meet at Drishane in April 1892. Aylmer and Edith, Martin and Hildegarde, facing the camera, from the left.

6.7.8.9. Seascapes by Egerton Coghill. These were sold to tourists. Egerton
and Hildegarde made a small income in this way. Egerton refused no work.

10. Edith and Martin in Paris recuperating just after the publication of *The Real Charlotte* in 1894.

11. Herbert Greene, faithful lover of Edith Somerville. He was Fellow and Tutor in Classics at Magdalen College, Oxford, from 1888 to 1910, and prominent in the rowing world at Oxford. He proposed to Edith yearly over a number of decades. She made extraordinarily public jibes about marriage, despite his constancy. In *Irish Memories* – a volume of memoirs published in 1917 – she wrote of a visit to see wedding presents on the evening before the event: 'One critic said that to see them was like being in Paradise. Another declared that it was for all the world like a circus. Are things that are equal to the same thing equal to each other? It is a question for the Don of Magdalen to decide.'

12. Drishane in 1883.

13. Ross House, the front entrance.

14. *Retrospect*, a portrait by Edith Somerville of a servant, Mrs Norris.

15. Edith Somerville painting out of doors on holiday at Champex.

16. Hildegarde Somerville at a meet of the West Carbery Hunt.

17. The Somerville brothers and sisters in August 1924. From the left: Jack,
Aylmer, Edith, Cameron, Hildegarde, Boyle, Hugh. Aylmer died in 1928, Boyle
was murdered by the IRA in 1936. Edith lived until 1949.

18. The Castle at Castletownshend, home of the Townshends, showing Glenbarrahane Church above. Somerville and Ross are buried beside each other in the graveyard.

Of all the foul coverts to get a fox out of Manch takes the cake –
Liss Ard isn't in it, and it is worse than Liss Ard in being *absolutely*
impassable so that if the fox breaks on the wrong side you are done for
– and it is nearly a mile long. Well – we were fooling up and down,
waiting, to the South in the field – Well I saw the fox – a crōol brute,
as big as a calf – steal along to the east and in a minute the whole pack,
helter-skelter after him. We waited to let him break, when suddenly
there was silence. They had over run the scent in some mysterious
manner and some blug* had headed back the fox. Then ensued long
waiting and trying back. Mr Beamish creeping on foot among the jungle,
and no one knowing where the fox would break, but the wind being
west we all hoped he would break east and run down the wind. At last
after about half an hour, we heard very faint shrieks the *far side* of the
hill to the west. We belted round and found the fox had broke here
[map and drawing] and the whole pack got away a mile ahead of old
Beamish, who had however slipped off after them without giving a word
of warning to the field. We could see no sign of anything, but little
fringes of country fellows along the hills waved to us the way. It was a
horrid country – rotten fences and very high stone gaps. Our horses
went splendidly, over horrible ground, till we came to a boreen with a
low wall across it, on the other side a stream full of huge stones, and a
sort of bank – Sorcerer jumped it in the most able way, but the mare
wouldn't have it. It certainly was a very ugly place. A. licked and spurred
in vain. Then he shouted to me to go on – so, as we had made an
agreement to that effect I did so, following some other people up a road
for about half a mile. Then I saw Jack de Burgh and Mr Maxwell going
away to the north. I was just going after them when I thought it was
hard luck on Aylmer to leave him, so I waited and in about five or six
minutes he came up having lifted her over with the spurs. She refused
no more. Just then on a hill about a mile away to the north – going like
blazes, we saw the hounds and Mr Beamish. Between us and them was
a big turf bog with no sort of passage so A. and I made a hurried guess
by the look of things at the way he was running, and set off as hard as
we could lick round the bog, on a bog road – one local genius was with
us, but after we got round the bog he turned off to the east and we saw
him no more. We had a moment of agony as to whether we would
follow him, but decided to go our own way. And it was well for us. We
went on for about five minutes, best pace, when a country boy began
to roar to us, something about to the west (we were riding north west)
over the bog – we turned sharp off, Sorcerer nearly pulling my arms
out, he was so excited, when we heard something – My dear, about a

hundred yards back to the south we saw the *whole pack come* streaming down the hill, without a man within a mile of them! It was the fox only who had gone across to the west! When they got to the road they had just left, they checked – Then was our time. We rode down like mad, whipped them onto the line the fox had gone, and off they went again, full cry, with A. and I *alone* after them. It was almost too supreme a moment – I could not have spoken – except in a sort of mad howl to the hounds – to save my life, and I could hardly see. However they ran over a country where you had to see. Rather like the back of Lick, only worse bogs. We were just going as hard as the horses could leg it, but the hounds were racing with their heads up and the scent was red hot – It was all we could do to keep them in sight over that break-neck place, but we did somehow and in about 20 mins they checked round a huge cairn of stones. A. nipped off and climbed round to get the fox out, when suddenly before you could say knife, out jumped the fox into the very jaws of the whole pack. He had been in a tunnel and A. had started him out. The hounds were so taken by surprise that they hadn't time to nail him, and out *literally* between their legs, and away with him with the hounds, A. and me, all blue with passion, after him. But he knew what he was up to. In about two hundred yards there was a big rock, and he just wriggled into it as the leading hound made a snap at his brush, I couldn't have believed anything could have got away as he did. I am generally glad when a game fox gets off: but I must admit that A. and I could have cried. We thought we were sure of the brush. There we stood and stared at each other – (silent upon a peak, near Dunmanway) – while the hounds raved round the rock and tried to writhe through a place that only a fox in extremis or the blade of a knife could get into.

In about ten minutes Mr. Beamish came up. He was awfully nice to us, and regretted we hadn't killed. Then Mr and Miss Connor appeared and two or three blugs,* one of whom had given his horse the most awful cut I ever saw. His fetlock was nearly cut in two and the blood was simply flowing like a river. It was ghastly to see – and the poor blug was almost in tears – They tied it up and got it down to Manch about five miles off and when we left in the evening they said there was no danger of further bleeding. You might have tracked it the whole way there. The usual poking at the rocks then ensued, with the usual results, and at last we started back to draw Manch again. Mr Beamish and I had both cast hind shoes, so while they were being replaced we went up and had some admirable chicken pie at Manch – After that they began to draw the wood. Sorcerer had not returned and I heard Mr

Connor say to his daughter "I'll go on Henry,[1] and you can follow with Miss Somerville" I said to her "Oh please don't wait for me" Mr Connor thought I was speaking to him and said in a really Buddh* like way "Oh never fear *medear*, I'm not going to!"

Tumpany or no Tumpany,[2] I simpled howled and so did A. He is a most nice crabbed little owld chap, and the very essence of "themmishness" (i.e. one of the sort which Ethel and I most delight to love and honour. Derivation "one of them"* = one of the adored ones.) We then worried about without any further success – except that Sorcerer jumped so well that Mr Beamish remarked upon his cleverness – (owld Beamish and two blugs,* and the hounds and I had gone on a little fruitless excursion up and down and round a precipice). By this time it was nearly four and we had two or three miles to get back to Manch, and tea, and down to the station, so A, Miss C and I returned and as we were tay-drinking had the satisfaction of seeing Mr C return without having had a smell of a fox. They sent us down in a trap to the station, and put up the horses for the night, and Tom has gone up to bring them home by road. The whole thing cost us 17 shillings – apiece – which we could not have stood only that Mrs. Chave most nobly gave us one pound each at Christmas. Gladly would I spend it again in the same way if I had the chance, but I doubt we shall be let. A great point in our favour is not having touched the horses in any way. We were simply longing to have had you with us on Obadiah. I forgot to say that when we got back to the road we found Mr Maxwell and Jack de Burgh looking most awfully sick, they had seen nothing of the whole thing, and moodily set out to ride home as we started back for Manch. I am a bit stiff today, and very sore under my right knee from a vile garter that I put on to keep my stocking from slipping and rubbing, having cut into my leg, from being too tight when the muscle contracted for jumping. I have written this to you, partly because I promised and partly because you know and love owld Baimish and all his crew – and though that privilege has not been extended to Ethel I know she would like to hear of our adventures in these strange lands, so I would be thankful to you to send this on to her – "like a good child" – but answer it to me and not to her –

Yours ever

E.Œ.S.

1 Typical of the lack of real interest in gender in this society, Henrietta Connor was called Henry.
2 *Tumpany*: a child's mispronunciation of 'company'. Adopted after a small Coghill refused to spruce up for guests.

[From Martin to Edith, 1 January 1889: *fragment. Edith's note added later*: 'Paddy Griffy and Anne Kineary']

. . . at present I am in no want of society. My counsel to you is to go to Ethel as soon as you conveniently can, so as not to let any chance of the hunting slip. While there things will finally shape themselves about Paris, and if you cannot work *it*, come on here and do a bit of painting and a bit of writing – I am sure you want a change, and after Aylmer, Boyle and Hildegarde go things will not be very lively – This would be my programme if I were you – but I am not you –

Did you see on the papers that Miss Prittie was killed hunting in Tipperary – She was a great friend of Eva Vandeleur's – I have met her there – a big comely and cultivated creature. But she must have missed her tip badly to come off because the horse stumbled – and I suppose it was riding with her foot home in the stirrup that made it stick there. Anyhow it is an awful thing – and I am beginning to think that riding is a dangerous pursuit, and I hope you will be a good coward in Meath – A large bank with a tired horse is much more terrible than a shaky ceiling. The remarks about that ceiling still continue. Andy Welch and Paddy Griffy spent today in repairing it – "T'would kill her, if she was a *bull*" (to rhyme with gull) says Andy, viewing the bare patch – "T'would, or if she was an *ass*" which was Paddy Griffy's emendation – A very delicate compliment I consider – or perhaps a biting jest. However as he subsequently explained to me that the blessings of the pious were spread above me, (something like an umbrella), and as he remarked, when helping me to lift a table, that he loved ever the track of my feet in the gutter, I am sure he meant no harm – Anne Kineary (the post office woman) said a thing to me that amused me. Her children do not go to school, it being holiday time – and she is much distraught by having them under her feet all the time. As she talked she cast a vengeful eye on one child that was throwing a piece of bread under the bed to spite another one. Then she paused in her greasing of a horrid little boot and made a very unselfish use of her pocket hankerchief on a child with a squint, in a long gown of vivid blue – and said with emotion that what pained her was "that the people passing would hear me making peace between them" – I laughed in the most unfeeling way having a vision of what that peace-making consisted of – especially as when later on a little boy clawed at her with some request she immediately slapped him on the face without any other comment – Now I am going to bed – 88 brought some good luck anyhow – Let us not say anything agin it. But that was already a thing of last year and on this first of January 1889 the sunshine was lying purely and dreamily on sea and bog as we say in the Shocker. It is a hard frost, and a car full of shooters has just driven up to the door, and with their beaters have gone off to the wood of Annagh. I must say I think it is doubtful taste on their part to swagger about in front of the door as if the place belonged to them. But I believe they are not gentlemen — I feel an irrational hatred of them — not having seen a shoot here since the old days —

Slide 42[1] came this morning, but I cant send it off until you say what signature you want. Is it our names — or what? You once said you wanted Martin Somerville — *I* think our good names. I must take this up to the post —
Yours
Martin

Edith finally went to Ross, for a three-month stay, in mid-February 1889. This is a letter written to Edith after she had just left Ross to return to Drishane. This had been a disastrous visit as Edith's fox-terrier The Puppet had eaten poison laid for rats and died. Edith had great skill as a healer — the frequent references to 'The Mother' or 'The Mother of the Animals' are to her — and this small animal was the first to die under her hand. She had cleared its stomach and stayed up through a night to no avail; the poison had been in The Puppet's system for too long.

Ross
Saturday afternoon, May 11th 89

[*Edith's note added later:* 'Galway Hotel']

Dear Edith
Here is a dull letter that came for you this afternoon — So I take the opportunity of saying a little word or two — I felt much happier after the time I knew Hildegarde was with you — and happier still to think that now (5 o'clock) you are near the end. I felt very sick at having to walk away out of the station instead of steaming out of it — and can't forget the unhappy look you have had all the time lately. But we wont talk of that anymore — At least not now — my poor girl — I could — but I wont —

1 The short story that was later expanded into their second novel *Naboth's Vineyard*.

I had a most weird and varied time after you left. First of all I strode through the empty echoing streets to see where William Mac was going to put up his horse, and found that the yard was not open. We then went down past the old Martin House to knock up a sister of Anne Kineary's of whose overjoyedness of welcome William assured me, as also of the charms of her parlour One look at the house sufficed – I passed – leaving W. pounding at firmly barred doors and windows. All the Hotels were tight shut, and I wandered with clanking footsteps round Eyre Square, and finally to the station again. It was closed – I said a great curse and was inspired to discern a solitary speck moving towards me out of the infinite solitudes – a man – who finally showed me a back entrance to the station. Inside were seated in a row the porters, holding conclave with locked doors – and I made out the Ladies Waiting Room – After 5 minutes there in which a suddenly bestowed gift of tweesortir-ing* was a glorious dissipation, I became aware that my brain was giving way – there not being even a railway guide or an advertisement to look at – I left – passed the deeply comprehending row of porters, and went forth into Eyre Square again. This time I discerned that the outer door of a filthy hotel called the Imperial was open – and I boldly effected an entrance. There was a grimy hall with the sunshine blazing in on the dust and froust, and not a creature to be seen, but from the little parlour along the side came the most deep and manly snores. I crept in, and found the snores were from overhead, and could have wept for joy at seeing the *Family Herald* and *Titbits* on the table – Nothing could ever explain to you the dirt of that room – it was absolute slime – but I wallowed in it and read for at least an hour. There was not a sound in the house the whole time – till at last the post man came and banged till he got the boots up – while I remain perdue. Then my dear I made myself known and demanded tea – and was whisked upstairs to a foul coffee room and got good tea and bread and butter – and a dirty knife. By this time a waiter had arisen – evidently much scandalised at my having come so early – and I left and made for William Mac's yard. I found he had gone off shopping and accordingly I hung around Morrises till they took the shutters down and then bought gloves and things and finally went to my beloved Dominic Burke, where you bought a hammer, and there wrote a long and artful letter to Mama – and sent it by the early post. I explained the reason of the telegraphing and all the rest of it – and did not say a word as to urging her to come home. But I told her that two large borders in the garden were bursting into bloom and that the lily of the valley was in masses, that we should have gooseberry fool in a day or two, and last but not least, that on last Sunday Captain

Walker and Mr. Crosbie had come over for tea. I also recommended her to go at once to Aunt Marian, so as to make sure of seeing Philip whenever she wanted – and having done all this started for home at 10 o'clock. I made enquiries about the bullock on the house top, and found that he had actually managed to turn and get down as he came up. This is market day, and I have seldom had a more interesting drive from Galway – Nurse sat beside me and expounded the history of every cart we met. Endless were the varieties of salutations, as apparently every tenant in Ross was on the road, and I would have given anything for you to have seen them. Such fiery skulls, such old women, such screamings of Irish by Nurse and to Nurse. When I got in I found the telegram that we should have had last night. It was not sent from the Bray office till 8.20 and was not in Oughterard till 9.40 – thus missing the car. It just said "cannot come tomorrow – have written" that was of course the letter we read this morning.

There was no letter from her this afternoon – I had a line from Edith saying that she felt most heartily with you about the puppet – she understood how bad it must be – I got lovely shot silks from Hide – and have chosen one for the tea gown. [*large deletion*] Now I am sorry I said anything. You are such a brute – Never mind I have scratched it out, and I beg you will not apply your ingenuity to reading it – One sound sentiment I have left for you. It has turned into a horrid afternoon – rainy and grey – and my room feels horrible – I have not had the heart to unpack my things yet. One comfort is that William can take all my luggage on the car and I shall certainly make the early start. Curious to say I have *no* headache *or* neuralgia, and do not feel in the least sleepy. Moolah[1] has come up to be played cards with – so I make an end – Do try not to be so sorry – My heart aches for you when I think of you arriving at Drishane. – Goodbye – Edith my dear – Not for long I hope –

    Yours –
    Martin

---

1   Her niece Muriel Hamilton Currey, daughter of her sister Katie.

Ross
Monday, May 13th 89

[*Edith's note added later*: 'Tullywood']

Dear Edith –
I send you on Katie's letter by the early post. I know she feels all she says – I am longing to hear from you as to how you got home – and I am sure I shall by the second post – If I dont I shall tramp home with all the dark Spanish blood mounting to my forhead. I had a long letter from Mama today in which she said she had not as yet been able to get into Dublin, but she certainly would today. Her eyes seem very bad again, but she says she's almost sure that Philip will say the word go. Nannie Darley seems the person who is keeping her – saying that she will not hear of her taking the long drive from Galway till her eyes are better. My private impression is that Jubilee[1] does not agree with Mama, and that is what keeps the mucous membrane irritated. It was acute irritation of it that caused that heart attack at Jubilee so Philip told me. Mama says she is longing to get back – She wants to go hucksthering her green gooseberries in Oughterard, and Miss Carr, the flower shop woman in Dublin, is anxious to buy the lily of the valley – I had the proud distinction of being the only person in church yesterday who had a bit – Mama talks vaguely of "a few days more" at Jubilee. Owing to those accursed Houdans[2] she can only stay one night at Aunt Marian's as they cannot be taken out of the hamper (there being no place to keep them) – so Mama as their chaperone cannot be longer on the road from Jubilee to here than a night and a day – That is I believe the extreme limit of Houdan toleration of a hamper. If there were no question at all of her coming home I wish she would leave Jubilee. The long walks and the high teas and the bad manners of one of two of the inmates are the reverse of desirable for her.

All things go on as usual – Murray and I have held a council of war as to Moolah's meals, Murray at last making many songs about the way she is over-fed. She had a bilious headache yesterday, and so we are privately going to curtail the eggs and bacon at breakfast – and give her what seems fitting to us. I think an egg or bacon every second day would be ample. She has been better behaved, principally I think owing to my crossness – I naturally feel lonely especially at meals, and cannot tolerate

1 Jubilee Hall, Bray.
2 *Houdans*: a rare breed of fowl.

nonsense and greed. But I am not a bit cross to anyone else – I went up to the Verekers yesterday afternoon in lovely weather. They were really very kind and friendly – Mr. Vereker came down the Avenue to meet me and was awfully nice about the puppet. I shall always have a different feeling for him – Mrs. V. was also very nice about it, and comprehending – and says she has never been so sorry for anything in her own life as for a cat of hers. They wanted me to go up and stay at Killaguile, but of course that was not to be. I tried a short cut home across the bog. It was *awful*. I left Killaguile at 6 and was not home till past 8 and all the time was going in zig-zags trying to find a way over the *canals* that run in parallel lines across the bog – I took some jumps that frighten me now to think of – they really took all the pluck I possessed to try them and exhausted me so that I could scarcely crawl home. I kept a good line all the same and came out through Tully wood to Maria Connors house. I think the worst dykes were in Tully, or I was more tired. I had one or two perilous crossings there on little trees laid across with awful black profundities underneath. Never again, either with or without you, will I try that way. But as Thady said I was "grinding my teeth" that I had not taken you into Tully – It is beautiful past telling, and weird. One part of it has a Carquinez woods effect – *very* big pines – and a soft dark walk winding in obscurity among them – there is nothing like it in Ross – or scarcely anywhere that I have seen – I was frightened by the solitude and stillness and the strength of everything. There are strange little glades of pallid sedge with little old firs in them – and I came on one perfect place for you to have painted. A little lake surrounded by trees, except on one side that opened beautifully to the hill behind Doone – and to the sunset – [sketch] – that was the scheme – You may not understand that scrawl, but I can assure you that it was beauteous – taken from the left hand side of the pond – which was a very good size. I must finish these foolish pratings – I have some most interesting Oughterard humours, which I shall probably give this evening –

Yours –
Martin

It took many months for Edith to recover from the death of her little dog The Puppet at Ross in the spring of 1889. They worked separately at articles while readers in London publishing firms considered An Irish Cousin. *The Martin family had previously taken no notice of Martin's ill health; but now, probably owing to the sympathetic suggestions of the Somerville family, Martin was taken to see various Dublin specialists.*

In the end she settled with Dr Stoker, the brother of Bram, author of Dracula.

Already we find that they are aware of their trade as a kind of intellectual cannibalism – that they are going to make an income out of their relations and acquaintances: 'Let us take Carbery and grind its bones to make our bread.'

The 'Luck' belonging to Edith that had been lost at Ross was a collection of silver odds and ends that she wore as a talisman, pinned to her coat or blouse.

Saturday, May 18th 89

My dear Edith

There has been no word from Mama as to going to England, but from her hoppings between Morehampton Road and Jubilee I think it possible she didn't get my letter suggesting it till last night. Anyhow I dont think there is the remotest chance of her going – I am going to write today and say I have settled to go to you on Thursday, as in the letter I got from her today she says "Hope I may be able to leave Jubilee on Tuesday". Which means that she will not be here till Wednesday at soonest. There is no reason now why she should delay.

You are broken in stamps for my letters – but you would be repaid if you knew how glad I am to get them – I think a great deal of how you miss your little dog – you needn't try to explain your forsaken feeling. It is long since comprehended even to painfulness. One must remember that the people at Castle T. have been accustomed for three months to his being gone – but still the specially coined little puppet words – your own property – I know how that must feel – I wonder you wouldn't hate the sight of me or anything connected with Ross.

I write with some difficulty, being laid on the bed. A mysterious pain in the bone of my back in between the shoulders, takes me if I sit up and write, or exert my back anyhow much. It feels like a remnant of the strain last winter, but is more capricious and more acute – I think it is liver – and Philip's medicine has even already begun to work in an undoubted way – so anything of the liver will be cured by that. It may also be the divil, who is nearly due – anyway it is unpleasant – I shall try Saint John Long[1] tonight – the divil is a consideration about my coming on Thursday – she is due I think on Tuesday – and I should be but a poor traveller on the third day. But we shall hope for the best.

1 Whiskey.

Hennie and Morgan must be on very good terms and before the summer is out there ought to be work out of it one way or other – Your Mother is a woman of courage – but I daresay Hennie did not much mind. Let us never forget in the press of other affairs what your mother said about Charlotte, and her rallying of her –

Lovely weather – but a few showers – I prance round the garden a good deal and give meat to my household as usual – I got a sort of grip of the "Education"[1] thing today, and I hope it may continue – but I am a fraud in the way of writing – I heap together descriptions with a few carefully constructed moralities interspersed, and hide behind them – so that no-one will discern my ignorance and hesitation – I think I believed in things more after that long summer here last year than I do now – you take the highfalutin' out of me I think – I feel you saying "Well, but I dont see" – and then I dont see either. But it is very good for me. Let us take Carbery and grind its bones to make our bread – Cut, my dear! – It would be new life to me to cut it – and we will – and we will serve it up to the spectator so that its mother wouldn't know it. Fancy 18 pages. Enough for two articles – those were our salad days – I hope the pretty little bookling gets on. To be pretty in black and white must be difficult. You never said what the subjects were – or what you think of the writing – The Roberts thought Moolah wonderfully like you
  Martin

Ross
Monday night, May 20th 89

My dear Edith
Here is your Luck – and much of it may you have – I am so glad I can scarcely write it. But I must tell you about it from the beginning. When driving home in the rain with Mr. Roberts we passed on the Avenue a cart with a punt in it coming from Killaguile. I heard when I got in that Mr. Vereker had sent down for the boat giving this in exchange for it – I was well pleased and sat down to read your letter – I was reading it for the second time, and was practically at Drishane, when Nurse Barrett came into the room and said with awful stillness "is this Miss Soomersfield's broach?" *It was* – we both got perfectly scarlet and then shook hands – It was all we could do – Peter, in cleaning the old boat before sending her back, found it among the muck; did not know whose

1 An article for *The World*.

or what it was, and gaily hung it on his steel chain – Nurse Barrett saw it as he came in and *flew* upon him – "Faith I think he thought I was going to ate him, the grip I took of him" –

Somehow you must have taken it out of your tie on that May day picnic in the Knockbane river – I feel in the greatest spirits on account of it – and hope it comes in time to have saved you confessing its loss to the Chimp. There is much superstition mingled with my joy – and I am sure there will be with yours. I nearly settled with myself to say nothing to you, so as to have the bliss of springing it on you when I arrived, but then thought it hard luck to keep your luck waiting. The pin was very rusty, but I have got most of it off with sandpaper. The Chimp must be a very housefilling and pleasing arrival, and I shall be delighted to see him. But he will hate Shockers – and me most of all. We now regard all our most cherished relatives through (or shall we not say, athwart) a web of sensationalism and countings of foolscap. It will make a very good summer of it to have him to go about with – and to play tennis with, and to play music with – It will be very enchanting to hear nice music things of all kinds – I don't think I could stand Oughterard church much longer in that way. In writing to Mama today I gave no hint that I was going to stay beyond Thursday – I just said nothing about it – so, bar accidents I think she will surely come on Wednesday.

I cant make out the Currey plans – what Katie is going to do after Castle T. Anyhow Murray is pretty sick at the idea of either losing Castle T. or losing her holiday – A dreadful alternative. Hamilton's letter was a nice one.

The Roberts luncheon was far preferable to the Roys. They are awfully cordial and hospitable – and that is a great thing – and the Cumings were there, Mr. C. quite all there and very nice, Mrs. C. also full of civility and askings to luncheon – fortunately a thing I was able to pass on to Mama – who glories in a luncheon. I had for shame's sake to ask the Cullens and the child over to tea, and they came on Thursday. The Roberts had a big, simple, and first rate luncheon and afterwards we played the piano and processed round the garden and had tea and I came home with Mr. R. and sympathised with him about the difficulties of his parish. I had an interesting drive in on the mailcar. There appeared at first to be no room, mostly from the huge amount of luggage – but two tourist men played up – and made room by one of them climbing on to the luggage. The one who climbed was inclined to be jocose – the other, beside whom I sat was nice – very like Egerton with whiskers, and we talked – not badinage, but with perfect gravity – as two men might under the circumstances. He was going up to fish at Ballinahinch he said, and asked many questions about it. Then perceiving I knew the country, he put many political questions to me – (he had never been in Ireland before) and I replied as you can imagine – and it was most interesting. The jocose man was frozen into awestruck silence, and the other seemed a little ashamed of him – explained casually "my brother-in-law and myself". He (the nice man) tried to draw me out as to myself – "Do you – ah – do you stay here for long?" I said most of the time, but gave no further information. Altogether I was sorry when we got to the rectory gate – as I was much amused by the frank intelligent ignor-ance of the Saxon. By the way in talking of Ballinahinch he asked if there were a "gentleman's seat" there – whereat I yearned for a squaw* eye. He asked of its ownership – I said with inward amusement it had belonged to people called Martin before the present owner. He said "Oh yes, he had read about them – and didn't they own all the country?" I said not quite, at present – at least so I believed – and more than ever longed for a squaw so as to have continued the conversation about the Martins – I was somehow ashamed to by myself –

The Roberts were awfully kind and sympathetic about the puppet. Mrs. R especially – She is a good creature. Much surprise was expressed that I should go away "Just as everything is beginning" –

Just think of beginning tennis now down here, and keeping at it till October. We got an invitation today to a tennis party on Saturday at Renmore Barracks – the Connaught Rangers depot. But as on that day I hope to be far, far away, a refusal must be sent . . .

Yours
Martin

Edmund Yates, 1831–94, was the literary man who did most for Edith and Martin's career at the very beginning. Well known in the 1890s as a novelist and founder of The World, *his early career had been in the theatre. In 1860 he became editor of* Temple Bar, *which was designed as a rival to the* Cornhill. *His novel* Broken to Harness: A Story of English Domestic Life *was a great success when published in 1864, and in 1867 he became editor of* Tinsley's Magazine. *On 8 July 1874 the first number of* The World: A Journal for Men and Women *was pub-lished; his staff included Miss Braddon, Mrs Lynn Linton and Wilkie Collins.* Edmund Yates: His Recollections and Experiences *came out in 1884.*

Yates died in the year that The Real Charlotte *was published, and his role as propagandist for Somerville and Ross was taken over by E. V.*

Lucas and C. L. Graves; but they always recalled his part in the birth
of their career with gratitude. Edith remembered him in Irish Memories
(1917): 'Mr Edmund Yates then had the World *at his feet, having created*
it not many years before, and that he possessed the flair *for good work*
was evident in the enthusiasm for her writing that, from the first, he did
not attempt to conceal from Martin.' The World *published the article*
'A Delegate of the National League' in July 1889 and 'Cheops in Conne-
mara' in October. These articles did not go down well with friends and
family. Edith thought: 'It is my mature conviction that they were horri-
fied by want of levity!' A cousin of Martin's snorted 'Potted Carlyle!'
The naming of the RM as Major Sinclair Yeates is a tribute to Edmund
Yates, and not to the poet W. B. Yeats.

Ross
Tuesday, August 20th 89

Dear Edith
Your letter came here yesterday, while I was in Oughterard. I was
weather bound, and had to spend last night there. Yours on my return
this morning was a welcome sight – as was also a letter from Robson,
the *World* printer, with the proofs of your two sonnets. They look very
well in print, except for having rather too many full stops. I got out my
copy of them, and ventured to put a semi-colon instead of a dash in one
place, as I saw you had done in the original, I mean you had not put
the dash. The dashes and full stops break up the run of the thing a bit
– but the two that are altered seem to make it all right. I of course put
"head" for "eyes". Now it will be a matter of great interest to see what
Edmund pays for them – and when they will appear. Very probably
next week. They are printed in succession and I should think will appear
together. I am awfully glad they are really in print. I think you are going
to be bloated with riches very soon – what with intimidating *London
Society*, and lifting cheques out of Mr. Langbridge – I deeply agree with
Fanny Currey as to illustrating being at present the way for you to make
money, and a pleasant way into the bargain. It would not interfere with
serious painting either, or rather you could do that sort of thing, tracing
etc, in thronging mornings in the Purlieu* when perhaps the other might
not be feasible. I am glad Canny[1] did not advise risking the *Kerry Recruit*.
It will keep – till a more propitious time. Is this the last illustration you
are doing for Mr. Langbridge. One of the £6 lot, or is it a separate

---

1 Fanny Currey was referred to as 'Canny'.

thing? I do think that – odious in many ways – Langbridge is going to mean a good lot of money for you, sooner or later. Are there any more ideas on the subject of your going to London next month? Rose wants me to go back with her but what with Edith coming and want of funds nothing is more improbable. Now I must dress and go to the Verekers, to meet the Helps party and others. The old mare is now in excellent case and Peter, attired in Cuthbert's, Hamilton's and Robert's clothes, is coachman – and drives abominably – slowly and feebly, but it is preferable to driving oneself – more anon.

It has been the most beautiful day – fresher and cleaner than seems possible, and all the hills as brown and purple and clear as – I dont know what – my complexion shall we say. Since I began I have been to Killaguile, and had really a very pleasant afternoon there – The three Helps, Miss Roberts, (very subdued) Th' officers, myself; and last of all, Mr. Vereker out fishing. We devoured tea and cake, we went round the garden, and the more swinish gnawed raw figs there, and then we had a dear little healthy walk up the hill above Killaguile, and saw a very charming view – which please goodness you shall also see some day. I like Captain Walker very much, I like Mr. Crosbie extremely, and yet both of these are going away, never to return, or practically that. They go back to Galway in two or three days, and strangers reign in their stead – creatures called Engelhart and Edwardes – the latter a Major, a brother to the Queen's Secretary, and married – wife charming Mr. Crosbie says, but she does not come here till January. Captain Walker is most sagashuating,* and spoke with truest feeling of his walk with you through the wood of Annagh, and the marvels of the primroses. Mr. Crosbie rode a grey pony over, and you may say that his breeks were a sight of glory, and his get up generally – Also it was apparent to the meanest observation how welcome to him was the pulling and bucketing of the pony as he rode away across the grass – he just adored holding him and bullying him, with a bit about a yard long and a martingale. All the same he can ride. Following him on this magnificent Lord Marmion exit came Captain Walker sitting decorously in the rectory dog cart, and driven by Miss Roberts, smiling quite peacefully at some . . . insinuations of Mrs. Vereker's – she is not trustworthy in these things, Dundrum and Rathgar ooze out between the joints of her harness – though she was on her very best behaviour today. Finally came the Helps and myself and then I walked home from the corner and thought how pretty things were, and what unworthy lamentations I had made about the bother of living here – and how more than nice you are to think about that.

I was of course interested and edified by Canny's critisisms. I am sure she is a good judge, though the only specimen I have seen of her style is very poor as far as literary brilliancy goes. I am much surprised at her kind suggestion about me. Perhaps some day you and I may take turns to read her to sleep, but I think she would not like me. I am a bad slave, except when taken judiciously, in the Purlieu.* What on earth did you want to go to Baltimore for? I bet she is writing about the fisheries there and there is a mystery about it – or she is starting another League. Anyhow you must have had a parlous long drive, and I hope Father Davis gave you luncheon.

What does Sarah do? Is she a barmaid or does she laugh at the tent door? Is it a big part? What do you wear, what does Hildegarde wear – and are you vẻr-ry frightenéd (you will observe the staccato marks to give Somervillio-Donovan brogue). I would give many things that I value to see the performance. I am sure you learn your part in bed, and meditate on it during the sermon. Altogether you are a busy woman and so, in other ways, am I. Mama and Selina come home tomorrow – Rose comes on Thursday, and I am afraid Edmund and Molly leave Oughterard on Friday. I spent Sunday and Monday with them. Sunday being wettish, Monday inexorable downpour . . .

For the *whole* of yesterday three Helps and I were shut up in one tiny sitting room, with nothing to see from the window but a green field and torrents of rain – and yet it was rather pleasant. We held much admirable converse – Edmund is an advanced but most philanthropic Radical till he talks of Ireland – and there he is depressing. Molly has certainly Radical tendencies, but is a fine creature. Knows everything, and more especially the lower grades of London slums, sweaters, Board Schools, and gives her opinion very squarely – but moderately. She is distinctly the fine woman's character in a book – clever and sensible, and womanly and motherly, as good as they are made, and as tender to wrong doing – I think she is far ahead of her husband, who has rather an effete assumed way of looking at things – or he gives one that idea. He and I had as you may imagine many combats over Home Rule and such things – conducted with heat not violence. I wish he could be here for a year. I am happy to say that I was able to tell him some few facts that he did not know – but I wished for your Mother and Fanny Currey and Robert. It seemed quite hopeless to convey to him that two holiday visits to Ireland were not enough to learn the Irish character in, and that he knows about as much of it as I do about the French character. It is also a sad thing to think that he is a very favourable specimen of his type. He is very advanced and indeed delightful on the subject of women –

he has an enormous opinion of them – and reviles their present social and legal conditions. By the way, I was sent the other day a paper to sign, by the National something or other for female franchise. Did you get one at Drishane? It was rather interesting to see the women who had signed, put down in different classes, doctors, heads of Education things (all the Girton professors signed) Art and Music, among which did I see Fanny Currey, Agnes Zimmerman and other familiar names. Authors and Journalists, under which head I propose to put my name, in very good company. I certainly think it is absurd that the people Mama employs should have a vote, and that she herself should not have one. After all most women who have to stand alone and manage their houses or places themselves are competent to give as intelligent a vote as Paddy Griffy or Sam Chard – I am really getting too dull for words. I think I was going on to say that when the day seemed hopeless yesterday I instigated a bold attack on the Barracks by Edmund, and with an invitation for tea – which the faithful soldiery accepted with avidity and came and made themselves as agreeable as they could – Mr. Crosbie told me that one of the most painful experiences of his life was when he saw Mrs. Hillyard at the tournament in Dublin fling down her racket and burst into tears in her sett with Miss Martin, when the latter had got the one sett and 5–1 in the second. He said it was *awful* and no one knew where to look, least of all Miss Martin.

It is now very late, and its in my bed I should be. I have not heard . . . Blazes. My candle is just out – Goodnight –
Yours
Martin

An Irish Cousin was issued in Bentley's autumn list of 1889. Martin showed a great facility for publicity and distribution; she had a great deal to do with the success of 'The Shocker' by bringing it to the notice of reviewers and literary men. This she did by pulling strings shamelessly, using the connections of her brother Robert in the London literary world. This letter is valuable for its revelation that Edith alone knew the story of the 'maniac' at Whitehall, that provided the plot for the novel. Later, in Irish Memories, *Edith blithely fictionalized the inspiration for the novel to include Martin.*

The Irish Cousin [*Edith's hand*]

Ross
Wednesday, August 21st 89

My Dear Edith
This is a go – I hope you got my telegram of this afternoon – I could
not get it into Oughterard earlier, though I saw the advertisement soon
after luncheon. It really took the sight out of my eyes. I was not looking
for Bentleys list even, but languidly reading the reviews when I saw it
by chance. It is *not* in the *Morning Post* of today. I am awfully disgusted
with Bentley for his meanness or carelessness in the matter of Viva
Graham – and said something to that effect in my letter to him today
– that I feared you would be much disappointed, and that we certainly
understood the name was to be Giles Logan – I do not regret the loss
of Giles, but Viva! It *is* hard luck, but if it be any consolation I mind it
as much as you do – I desired B. to send the leaflets to you and me
without delay. I should not be surprised if you heard from him tomorrow
or next day – in the natural course of things. I forgot to ask him about
presentation copies – will you? I think we ought to get two or three
apiece – I have already sent the fiery cross to Katie, Edith and the St.
Leger, and will not cease to do so. Mama did not come home today,
but she shall at once be set to work tomorrow. I go into Oughterard to
fetch Rose out in the afternoon and shall set Molly and Edmond on the
trail. In fact everyone I meet or can think of shall not be ignorant of the
Shocker. It comes at a bad time for you, just as you are rehearsing and
bothering about these plays. You will have to take to getting up early &
religiously writing a certain number of letters before breakfast. I am
afraid this is a baddish time for books to come out, but we must make
up for that by energy. What about Egerton's man on the *Saturday*? I
have incensed Edith about Willie Wilde and Desart, and must concoct
a discreet line or two to Edmund Yates – Edith is going up to the Horse
Show, and accordingly will see everyone she knows in Ireland, and can
go round the book shops – and the Gays are trusty people of large
acquaintance. I can't write much as it is bed time, and I have a headache.
I tried to make a start at an article today, and then all afternoon I was
writing letters and fussing, so feeling my head not the better for it I got
out the scythe and had a blissful hour with the thistles. It is a fine feeling
to swipe at strong groups of them and there certainly is no lack. You
can mow them like corn in some places. I seem to remember very much
the first beginnings of the Shocker just now – when as I was humping

over the Dumpy[1] and you were mucking with paints at the window you told me of the old maniac's face at the window over the White Hall door – and remember you were the person who suggested that we should try together to write a shocker or story of sorts on that foundation – and you also were the person who lifted us through the first chapters. But no matter. We little thought then that I, at Ross, should take the *World* with a view to seeing my own writing in it, and should see the Shocker in large type heading Bentley's list therein.

Goodnight whatever. Here's good luck to the Shocker and even if it doesn't do much to making our fortunes I do not think it was time wasted. It taught us a lot – in a literary way – and I dont think we shall ever forget it. And the long time that we fought over it, it was my fault – Isn't that true?

Yours ever

Martin – Goodnight again – you were a nice woman to write with.

Edith made the mistake of bowing to her mother's will and allowed the first novel to appear under a nom de plume: *Mrs Somerville had not wanted the good family name to be used in 'trade'. Early editions of* An Irish Cousin *were thus by Geilles Herring and Martin Ross, so that their first reviews hailed 'Messrs' Herring and Ross and speculated as to the background of 'the two gentlemen'. Edith was intensely irritated, and* infra dig. *or not, from then on she used her own initials and 'Somerville'. Confusion over her and Martin's gender has continued to this day.*

Ross
Saturday, August 24th '89

My dear Edith –

I am most truly glad that Geilles Herring it is to be – and am waiting with longing for the second post, and most probably the parcel of books, somehow parcels get through in a day from Castle T. to here. It is much better than we had hoped to have Geilles Herring, and it must have been the mistake of some underling to put Viva – or perhaps the dread fierce women have brought dissension and bitterness and wringing of hands as was foretold, and the house of Bentley is divided against itself. Yesterday in telling Rose the title of the book to put in one of her letters, I called it "an Irish Herring" and then laughed so interminably that Rose

1   The Studio stove.

nearly wept from boredom and fury. Your telegram of yesterday *just* caught the mail car – getting to Galway at 12. It was sent from Castle T. at 11.37 so one may roughly allow half an hour for transit between these points – As for Oughterard it is about an hour and a half.

I said in a letter to Robert that I relied on Carnegie[1] – I said well – today I heard from him "We subscribe tomorrow, and will ask him for your book, which we feel satisfied must be good. We will also recommend "Eason and Son" to get it, and have ordered a copy for ourselves from Messrs Hodges and Smith." Katie and I have always agreed that we should rather marry Carnegie than anyone we know. Were we not right. I shall send him six advertisment leaflets – Here is luncheon. I have much to say and am going to eat lobster – after which I shall not say it half so well – To resume – the books have come – I was a little disappointed with the first sight of them but have come to like them very much – the print and paper are certainly *excellent*. I have the pleasure of sending your one shilling and one and half pence for their postage. Black and green are of course fashionable, but at the same time it is a trifle funereal and gloomy. I do not know what to say about Minnie – *I* ought to give her a copy just as much as you – On the whole I think Ethel is the person – as she lives far from your mother's and your copies – and Minnie can of course see me anytime she wants. I know she deserves one if ever anyone did – but perhaps she would not really care for it as much as Ethel. I send the letter I have from Bentley – It is decidedly injured in tone – and I must smooth the ruffled dove in thanking him for the books. Molly Helps has been very kind about it – and said at once that she would write to Charlie Graves, who reviews the light literature for the *Spectator*, to give us a good word. Furthermore she said that she would recommend an article of mine to the Editor of the *Spectator* – who is a personal friend of hers. Now let us collect our newspaper friends – the *Saturday*, the *Spectator*, the *World* (?), the *Sunday Times, Vanity Fair* (Desart) and Willie Wilde who is I think the *Daily Telegraph*. I wrote the best letter I could to Edmund Yates today. Indeed I write letters all the time and Rose is very good about it too – Mama of course ploughs away, but her eyes come against her. I should make Aylmer ask for it at every station on the Underground if I were you. I am sure that your mother is magnificent in the matter of letters, and if the family really put their shoulders to a wheel they could do a great deal – I am also delighted that your mother likes the book now. I think it reads a little better than I expected – though here

1 Of the Carnegie Libraries.

and there I feel inclined to put the bedclothes over my head – Mama and Rose revel in it. You must be very hard put to it to keep everything going. That is wherein the soundness of your headpiece is testified. I feel very sick at missing the plays, and am not at all consoled by the fact that there is to be a dance at Lemonfield on the same night. I have just one little consolatory feeling that if I saw you in a cap and apron I might think you like Eliza Kidd – but never reveal it. I suppose you will dance at Drishane in honour of your soldiers – and I am sure you will have a truly enjoyable time, barring the hard work. I do not believe you are dull and noisy – I certainly should like most awfully to see you – but these things are not to be. I cannot write more – I must go out – though your admirable and most heartwarming letter deserves more than this poor and dull answer. I am stupid, and have no tennis or kind people who put on bad players to revive me – I will write again.

Yours ever
Martin

The very favourable reviews of 'The Shocker' immediately boosted the value of Somerville and Ross shares in the literary stock market. Martin understood this straight away, and it was she who took charge of the money side, holding out for the best possible price for their work. Their career was off to an excellent start, and they had the good fortune to be patronized by Edmund Yates.

From the time of the publication of An Irish Cousin *curiosity was intense: 'How did two women write as one?' Nevill Coghill knew more than most:*

The nature of their collaboration is as simple as any other miracle. Anybody can understand it at once and nobody can explain it. I once asked Dr. Edith which of them held the pen. She replied: 'I'm sick to death of that question! You're like the fox-terrier taken out shooting and convinced that the rabbits come out of the gun!'

As a matter of fact they talked their stories and their characters and their every sentence into being. As soon as anything was agreed it was written down and not a word was written down without agreement. So they would sit in the studio, or in a Railway carriage or wherever it might be; the two imaginations became one, working with the equal harmony of a pair of hands knitting a scarf.

Nº 3227, Aug. 31, '89

Messrs. Herring and Ross, "aut quocunque alio nomine gaudent," have accomplished a rare feat in writing an undoubtedly lifelike Irish story without a single reference to politics or polemical religion. The sensational climax is strong and original ; but the horrid tragedy at Poul (properly Poll ?) na Coppal, which closes the unhappy Dominick's days of remorse, is almost too sombre a consummation for the reader's comfort. Indeed, in spite of the light heart and straightforward honesty of the heroine, Theodora Sarsfield, who tells the story of her journey from America and her adventures among her Irish relations with much spirit, the gloom of the Celtic character and the tragic possibilities which underlie it are more prominent in these pages than its brighter side. The descriptions of the long, low house, the seat of her family, looking wan and ghostly in the moonlight, and the wild south-western coast near which it is situated ; of the breezy promontory and Myross churchyard, with the Irish funeral therein celebrated, are some of many pieces of excellent colouring. We think, apart from the question of cousinhood, we should have preferred our friend Theo to marry her cousin Willy, rather than the superior and Anglicized Nugent O'Neill ; but Willy had already compromised himself with pretty Anstey Brian, and it is well that circumstances compel him to be true to her. He is not very noble in any way, this Irish cousin ; but he has corners of his heart which are warm, after the fashion of his countrymen. The most interesting figure is Moll Hourihane, the mad woman, who, urged by a mixture of woman's passion and Celtic devotion to " the master," commits a crime for Dominick's sake, in which he is at least an accomplice, and which has the effect of destroying the attachment for which her guilt was incurred. In the end the male sinner also loses his reason, and mutual dread and fear become the Eriunyes that follow lawless love. It is a grim story, though it is lightened by many cheerful views of the oddities of rustic society in a distant district.

[*Edith's note added later*: 'Delegate']

Ross
September 4th 89, Wednesday.

My dear Edith

It is very much like a dream – that I should sit down and write about a flourishing critique of the Shocker in the *Athenaeum* – but there it is, in black and white. I will not send it back, as you have written for another copy. Keep yours – I have also sent for one, I should like to have it to send to Jim. Unless Edmund Yates has worked this highest of oracles it is a pure tribute of the charms of the Shocker. The one before is very amusing – but how sick that poor creature must feel – I send you back Mr. Langbridge's letter. I think a little more money might be skirmished out of him, or out of whoever he hands us onto. If he would say £20 down, it would be well worth it. I should not seem *too* keen about it, as it is certainly not a brilliant offer. Those two extra fivers seem remote. At the same time we might be very glad of the £15 even, by the time we got it – I know *I* should – and I should much enjoy writing with you – if it could be managed. A few more high class reviews might make him raise his price.

I am more than glad that the Chimp likes the Shocker. I expected it very little – so it is all the more pleasant. Thank him for his kind *naice* messages – and tell him I more than echo his wish that I could be at the show – I am of course most anxious to hear about that – but if the dress rehearsal went well the rest is safe. I hope the cheap night will not be like the second evening of the Primrose League penny reading. I am pining to hear Robert's account of it. I wonder if his dread of unduly exalting *me* will allow him to praise *your* acting. If so, you have understudied Violet to some effect, that is all I can say. Mama has laughed the *whole* evening, convulsively, because I told her of the way he flings his coat tails over his head when dancing – and says she cannot look at him at Oughterard. Poor woman, she required a little bucking up after the profound gloom in which she was plunged by a letter from Mrs. Connellan saying that she thought the "Delegate" was "high flown and verbose" – "merely of course the fault of young writing" – says Mrs. C. Mama was absolutely staggered, and has gone on about saying at intervals "kneebuckles to a Highlander"* by which she means to express her glorious contempt for Mrs. C.'s opinion of the classics.

I am keeping the "veiled Picture" as you said nothing about sending it back. I think it is excellent – especially the hand, which is very

RECENT NOVELS.

AN IRISH COUSIN.*

The authors have written an Irish story on entirely new lines, and which is lifelike and full of interest. Some distrust may at the first be inspired by the fact that it is in the form of a young girl's autobiography, a kind of literary production rather apt to excite apprehension in the mind of the experienced novel reader. Theodora Sarsfield, however, is saved by her American wit and Irish humour, from being either sentimental or gushing, and her experiences among her father's relations are told with bright vivacity. Not that there is much brightness about the tale itself. Mystery and gloom hang over Durrus, tho home of the Sarsfields, which the heroine, after the death of her parents in America, seeks half from youthful curiosity, half impelled by a natural desire to know her father's people. One of her strong points is description. Not only is her colouring good, but her word-pictures of these western wilds, from Durrus "looking wan and ghostly in the moonlight," to that of the old graveyard on the promontory, are impressive and vivid. There is much of poetical feeling in the sketch of Myross churchyard, "the forlornest and least frequented spot about Durrus," where the solitude of the dead—

"Who lay in crowded slumber within the narrow limits of the grey briar-covered walls, was ensured to them by the greater solitude of the sea, which on three sides surrounded them."

The *dénouement* of the tale is perhaps unnecessarily weird, but the authors understand the management of light and shade, so that tragical as are the main incidents of the book, it is frequently relieved by pages that would not be out of place in a purely humorous novel.

* An Irish Cousin. By Geilles Herring and Martin Ross. 2 vols. London : Richard Bentley and Son.

suggestive and good. The face is like Johnny Bushe – may I say that the nose seems impossible, "wants modelling", I daresay is the expression. But I thought the whole thing surprisingly good, and it is nicely engraved. Otherwise I cannot say the cover is pretty. I suppose you are now hard at "Pillycoddy"[1]. I wish I could imagine Ethel dancing – or any of you

1 *Pillycoddy*: theatrical sketch.

dancing. It is quite beyond me – tell me if you were very frightened. I should be dancing now but instead of that I am going to bed, and the house of Martin is represented at Lemonfield by thin silver – lent for the occasion. I have bad bad third day divil neuralgia and Mama is concocting a note to something that effect. No neuralgic creature could be expected to risk her life on an outside car at four in the morning, as I should have to do – and Rose had no ballgown, and besides goes away tomorrow by the 2.20. I go in to see her off, and to shop and to see Katie. Eleanor Geogheghan comes for Friday night – Robert on Saturday, Edith on Tuesday . . . [end of letter]

While Martin controlled their career from Ross, Edith was labouring over a charity theatrical performance given in the town hall at Skibbereen. Robert Martin acted with Edith, and performed several of his famous songs like 'Ballyhooley' and 'Killaloe'. Martin was able to play piano accompaniments on stage but hated the limelight of theatricals – at Castletownshend all the Buddhs* took to drama as soon as they could walk, and Edith was no exception.

September 5th 89
Drishane
Bed 1.15 a.m.

My dear Martin
At this unearthly hour I will say a few words to you. The second night of the play is over, and the whole show is done. It has been very successful. The first night was the very biggest house I have ever seen in Skib. That big town hall *packed*. We took between £27 and £30 – but don't know for certain – all the country was there. 112 three shilling seats alone! Egerton and Robert had worked like blacks with the most invaluable help from Percy's servant and a coast guard, and you cant think what a pretty stage they made. I was perfectly amazed – it really was as nice as possible. You must get Robert to describe it to you. In "Uncle's Will", Ethel wore that pretty blue and red tea gown, with plenty of old paste and her own hair. She looked awfully nice, as the rouge and the blackening of the eyes were very becoming; and I think – privately and confidentially – that, taken all round, she acted the best of the whole lot. Robert was certainly very good, but Ethel really *was* the part. In "Uncle's Will" Egerton was really poor; dull and heavy, and rather feeling for his words all the time, which made the prompting very

nervous work, but in "Pillycoddy" though not word perfect, he acted enchantingly, and was extremely funny, and his makeup was perfect. A photograph is going to be done of us all so you will see what it was like. As Mrs. Pillycoddy, Ethel wore a huge fair wig – (what Robert *would* call a "Totty wig") – my black sailor hat and a white dress, with a huge pink sash. H. had an immense red wig, a white bonnet with pink roses, a pink striped skirt, red silk body and my covert coat – She came on in Ethel's red coat, and carried a huge carpet bag and the giantess's parasol. She had a very amusing song to the tune of the "Pilgrim of Love" in which she had to wave and brandish the carpet bag and umbrella, after the manner of grand opera, and she did it *capitally*. You wouldn't have believed how well she did it; and the red wig gave her a terrific vulgar flahoola* prettiness that fetched the audience and her whole scene with Ethel went very well. Poor Robert's young man's wig as "Charles" was an awful dull brown mop-head. By dint of cutting it was made to look decent, but I must say it was a relief to see his bald pate again. The painting however gave him also a vulgar stagey good looks which went down with the people, and he is such a favorite in Skib that he could do whatever he liked. His acting was excellent – quiet and confident – and you know that he "never would get stuck for a word," and no matter how much he gagged he always got back to his cue right. You never heard anything like the encores for his songs in the concert. There was a perfect storm – Mrs. Morrogh sang "You sang to me" and "For you" as encore. Mrs H. Brougham sang very indifferently. Dully, and without any sympathy and no great display of voice. We vamped up an encore for her, and then found that her encore song had been left behind! She wouldn't sing the last verse of her song, (a second rate English song) again, so finally retired, I was sorry for the poor creature; it was very awkward, but if she was more amiable and less conceited about her singing, I would have had more pity for her. I was less nervous than you might have thought. I find that a curious kind of philosophical courage comes to me with the occasion, and I managed to worry along, and sang my song without any mishap. I cant act, but I can contrive a sort of imitation of acting that is good enough for a fifth rate audience. Robert sang the "Blatherumskite" and I sang the chorus with him and we danced round together, which fetched the crowd satisfactorily. "Pillycoddy" went awfully well tonight, far better than yesterday, which was a pity, as there was only a very small house, about two hundred at the outside. I was nearly broken down by laughing once – Robert and I were fooling. He pretends to forget the name of my master and says "Pilli – Pilly?" so I said "*Coddy*" (which was gag) with minauderings,* thereon Robert in the fattest of brogues said "Cāādy is it? Well go and tell Cāādy etc." which was also gag, and sounded so like Conny, said with a cold in the head, that I began to bellow with laughter. Moreover he looked the image of an appalling male Katie. It luckily was all right that I should laugh, but anyhow I couldn't have helped it. He had a reddish yellow scratch wig and a red beard, and he looked *too* like Katie after she has been washing her hair. I think you would have died of him. We have had a wearing day. Mrs. Morrogh came at twelve. Captain Ridley, Mr. Clark, (good-looking and pleasant) and Mr. Hibbert (rather unwholesome but a pleasant youth and a stout) all came at two and the moment afterwards in came Sissy Cholmondeley and Dick and Carrie Webb – having come from Derry on the chance of finding us in. Finally after lunch four from the Rectory. It was deeply provoking as I could see nothing of Sissy. It has struck two, and I am writing so dull and putrid a letter that I must stop and try to go to sleep – Goodnight – I *wish* you were here. Bed. 8.30 a.m. – Thursday. – I resume. The Chimp did band. V. was to have done it, but she was so badly wanted to prompt, and played so uncertainly from nervousness, that we ran the Chimp in, to his intense disgust, but he was a tower of strength and imparted a moral courage such as – for me – only he and Hildegarde inspire. She accompanied R in his songs and did it splendidly. I shall see him today, and will ask him what he shall sing at Oughterard. "Ballyhooley" and "Killaloe" and "Enniscorthy" and "O'Hara" were what he gave on the two nights here – I never saw any human being who took the stage as well as he does. It really is delightful to feel the atmosphere of affectionate swagger that he sheds upon the audience. (Don't tell him this) and he just got every last point out of those songs, they were as dry as lemons when he had done with them. You may well say that we shall be wrecks by the end of this week. Tonight we have a dinner for the Ronnies and tomorrow we have an "impromptu dance" and we shall have to *clear out the drawing room for it*. Jack is to take the men out shooting, so that they will be out from under our feet. I am faintly bored at this prospect. If only the dance were to be somewhere else it would be so far preferable but "Belial" Adams has no idea of getting one up for some time, and when she does there will be no one to dance with as these soldiers go off next Thursday. Cameron and Captain Ridley are deeply gratifying about the Shocker and have evidently read it with the greatest attention, and discussed the characters with much discrimination. I do think that the people in it are real people. Uncle Jos told mother that he thought it was extremely well written but that it bored him almost to tears from want of interest, though volume

two improved a little. It certainly does go a bit slower than the run –
you might say the rush – of his penny dreadfuls and French abominations. Old Grannums said she had sat up till 11.30 to finish it and was
very complimentary. She specially noticed the excellence of the brogue,
and commended "Ferretting". She has written to Melbourne for it,
besides many other places. All here, Mother and Ethel included, say they
notice no bad words, except O'Neill's Devil in the ball chapter re Mimi
– and we will *not* cut them out of Slide 42. You know Aunt Gig knows
a friend (or cousin) of Bentley's; this woman said that Bentley had taken
the Herring to a seaside place (appropriate) to read, and told her that
it was very clever. This is the best criticism we have had yet, as it means
he would look kindly on future work. If we ever get the chance of
writing together again. I am longing to see the *Sunday Times*. R was
speaking of him the other day and he was an extremely clever fellow
who hadn't yet got his chance. It is 9.15. I ought to get up, but I know
breakfast will be very late, and it is a wet day – and I don't want to
have any more of it than I can help. What we are to do with these awful
men heaven only knows. I trust you didn't go to that dance; it wouldn't
have been good enough. I hope Potter will send you the wrong "*Eagles*"[1].
I never knew anyone so forward and plenitudinous as you – Never . . .
Lunch time. The whole morning has been spent in prating to the Chimp
and his three men . . . They are all free "nice things" pleasant and ready
to be pleased, but it wēēries me to have to play up, but I know the
Chimp expects it. There is lunch – and here is post and no time to do
more than end up – I am not sorry about the saddle – I expect it would
never have fitted Sorcerer. But all the same Day is a fool. Don't expect
to hear from me for some time – too harassed

   Yours
   Edith

P.S. Love to "the dear old Sod"[2]

                                                              Ross
                                    Friday night – September 6th 89

My dear Edith –
I did find the letter I wanted when I got home this afternoon – and it

---

1   The Skibbereen *Eagle*, local newspaper.
2   Martin's Mama. A reference to the introduction of Robert Martin at a concert as 'a
    son of the Dear Old Sod'.

is very good of you to have written it, at night when you must have been *deadly tired*. It told all the things I wanted to hear, or as much anyhow as letters can tell. But you might have enlarged more on your own part, which I am sure was good. You are a modest person in some ways – not really so, but you want me to think you are. The photograph will be satisfactory anyhow, and if this comes in time let me implore you to blacken under your eyes before it is done. It makes all the difference to you, both in real life and in a photograph, as witnessed the fancy ball. I cannot help feeling very sick at not having been there, and seeing the whole ins and outs of it satisfactorily – but what is the use of talking – I am awfully glad Hildegarde did so well. I laughed much over the thought of the red wig – and over Robert's wig – and indeed over many things you noted. Robert certainly is a tower of strength on the stage. Making speeches brings out quite a new side to his character. Of course Ethel was the best of the lot – I can feel that about her. Skib will long remember this show and Robert's reputation is made. I am sure he might easily now be elected for South Cork, or whatever it is. The *Eagle* ought to be very filling – and I am extremely glad I ordered the copies. You have plenty to do and think of without that. I suppose you are now footing it – perhaps with Robert, who is sure to be melancholy and confidential – that is if he does not spend the whole evening in the conservatory with V., roaring crying. But the absence of Ynnoc must be bliss. I am sure R. will kiss you all – you must tell me if he does, and all particulars of his farewells – I dare say you will miss him, such is my self conceit – and I am quite sure he is very much the better in all ways (except one) for his summer with you. I shall be very anxious to hear what he has to say tomorrow night, about all things. It will be of deepest interest.

As to the Shocker – things certainly seem to flourish surprisingly – You may well say that Bentley's good opinion was well worth having. It is delightful, and you *shall* write another story with me or without me. It would be too bad to let go such an opening as we now have, and I am not man enough for a story by myself. Charlie Callwell wrote to his mother to say he had seen a most favourable review of it in some paper – He did not say what, which is provoking. However Bentley will send us all notices, or he says he will – and then we can blow ourselves out on them. I still get many letters from people, promising to read it, to advertise it, praising it before hand, and so on. The Bart's critisism passes by me as the idle wind – I dont know why – but so it is. I could almost have sworn that it wouldn't get at him anyway. And talking of books – I did last night a thing I feel ashamed of, and that I don't feel the worse of – I looked through *Nana*, Zola's book. I feel ashamed of having opened it, expecting it to be so very odious. But my humble verdict is that it is not as bad as Ouida or Swinburne. It is like an unvarnished police report, without any of the overlaying of mock refinement, or reiterations of female charms and seductiveness and finely balanced tempests of feelings that make you scarcely know your right hand from your left. He pitches his story straight into the lowest possible strata of humanity, and makes you feel nothing but how foul and terrific it is. As to making it attractive, I should say it was the last possible thing. As I said before I felt all the time ashamed of reading it, but not from any effect on me – and I could see the tremendous skill of the writing – I am sure you despise me a good deal, and I certainly think it is not a book to read, as there is no use in getting familiarised with bad things. But I should never want to read it through, or to read another – and I thought I should feel better if I told you. It was in Gerald Persse's room, which was the one I had at the Persse's. It was a very weird room – on the ground floor, with an earthy smell – I hate a bedroom on the ground floor. I get afraid of burglars. Besides there is a horrid long dark passage leading to the door and to nothing else, and in the top of the door two panels have been taken out and glass put in, to light the passage – so that the door and indeed the passage behind seem to stare with these square eyes. The final point of weirdness was rats. Mrs. Persse warned me about them, and assured me they couldn't get into the room, but the row they made was intolerable, and I slept very badly in consequence – I wasn't frightened, but just bored by them. The whole recollection of it is unpleasant. Neuralgia, the earthy smell, the distracting courses of the rats over the ceiling and down the walls, the hours that were so long and yet so far from morning, and Zola's dreadful facts steaming and reeking in one's mind. You can imagine very well that it was a detestable night – I got Gerald's Bible and read it, and thought it like cowslips and primroses and running water and the sky before sunrise, and felt more comfortable about things in general – and then wondered what you were doing and if you had got to bed, and planned out the 'Welt' Artikel and finally saw the blessed grey gleam where the shutter was open – and so to sleep – and have had a headache all day – or at least till the middle of it. I must go to bed now and indeed I do not see why I should have written of a night in the suburbs. I am content till Day has another saddle – if I then have the money. There is no hurry.

Your letter gave much delight to Mama – I think you are very white-headed in that quarter, and am glad – I have almost forgotten to say that Molly Helps tells me she could get us an introduction to Cook himself through a great friend of hers, an R.A. who painted Cook's portrait. I cant read his name. It might be Ansley or Horsely or Hurley? This would be a help to Robert. I have never heard from the St. Leger about "an Irish Cousin"! I hope he got my letter – He has been away on his holiday – Goodnight – dear Edith – I am sure you are having a pleasant evening with your soldiers,

    Martin

The family had taken much delight in ridiculing Edith and Martin's attempt to write a popular novel. 'That nonsense of the girls' had given rise to endless bad jokes; but now that there were excellent reviews to be read by all the world and cheques to be put in the bank, the atmosphere changed. In this letter, Mrs Somerville has even concocted a plan for Edith and Martin to work at Drishane and Ross turn and turn about for three-month periods, but they were never to be so fortunate.

Drishane
September 11th 89

My dear Martin
Confound *Temple Bar* anyway. Read their letter; it is conclusive, and whatever it would be a pity to muck at the story anymore. What do you think of *Blackwoods*? Some of their "Tales" are by no means wonderful. I wonder if it would be bad form to send them first all our best reviews and then follow up with a story? Read also Mrs. Langbridge. It is very kind of them to send us reviews. It is magnificent to have got a good show in the *Saturday Reviler*. Perhaps Egerton's man stood to us – I should prefer to think he did not. Shall we accept Mr. L's offer? I think it is good enough and though the pay isn't much, 170 pages isn't much either. Mother's last suggestion is that you and I should live three months about at each other's houses. I go to you for October November December and you come to us for January February March – I to you April May June. You here the next three and so on. Of course this is only a suggestion that she threw out to me with no very definite intention, but I think if your Mother had no objection she would be content to abide by it. It is the most feasible plan I have heard yet. I think I could go to you next month if you are sure your mother would not object to us writing, and *above all*, if you were well enough to let us write. I wont write with you until I hear what Philip has to say of

you. And if he denounces writing, you must just stop till you pull your strength together again. I am sure Edith would agree with me that you had better knock off work till you are quite strong. Mother says she thinks the writing for the *World* has been killing you, and I am not sure that she is not quite right. I lay it on your conscience not to run in debt at the bank but take that fiver from me, *who don't want it*, and you can pay it back out of the Langbridge show. I enclose Herbert's letter, or the interesting part of it, keep it and send it back as you have space in your envelopes. Answer to me about Mr. L. I think we might accept and chance it. I don't like letting seven pounds ten shillings go. I have been writing to Boyle and Herbert (and the *Saturday Review*) all the morning so don't feel up to a decent letter. I hope I shall hear from you soon. I was sick with rage that you didn't get that *Observer* notice on Monday. I had trusted it to H. to send to you. Mother talks of going to Aylmer's with Papa next month, and if I went to Ross H. could easily find a resting place somewhere. I would be glad to see Ross again. Do you notice that it is our own Bentley who writes for *Temple Bar*? I think they are wrong – However possibly they don't care for exclusively peasant stories – I have never seen one – except the "Village Tragedy" which is a long thing – It was a relief to find that Herbert liked the Shocker. I should have been sorry if he hadn't, and he has evidently read it with much attention. Cameron and his soldiery went away last night, and we are all lying back in our chairs panting. Four huge men were rather opulent, and the housekeeper especially rejoices at their departure. We had asked two Porks to lunch yesterday, but only one turned up – Grace – we asked for Bock – "Oh Violet said one or the other of us *must* stay and lunch with her, so we tossed up to which it should be". We naturally said "Who won?" – Grace wouldn't tell so one soldier waylaid Bock and found out that Grace had been the fortunate one. Poor Grace nearly lost her temper over it; but as she had lost her head to start with I didn't pity her much . . .

Martin was the guestmaster at Ross, and as she and her mother made Ross more habitable, more and more Martins turned up to inhabit it during the summer and early autumn. Robert's wife Connie drank, and their marriage was difficult owing to Robert's flirtations. A great deal of Martin's time was given to making things smooth in the household. This letter attempts to arrange Edith's next visit to Ross, and it was on this occasion that they had the idea for writing The Real Charlotte, *although it was to take three years to reach fruition. They knew they*

should write 'something big' but were distracted by the easy money to
be had for short amusing pieces, and by the lure of travel books.

Edith's faithful suitor, Herbert, irritated Martin, and this comes
through when Martin hears of Herbert's queries on An Irish Cousin.
Herbert was a rather pompous Oxford don and Martin was eventually
taking sarcastic swipes at him in her letters quite without provocation.
Knowing that Herbert was at Drishane with Edith on vacation, she
asked in a letter 'Is Herbert writing anything these times beyond Errata?'

Ross
September 12th 89

My dear Edith
In case I have no moment to write I do so now, on receipt of your letter
– I think *Temple Bar* has behaved most shabbily and scurvily. I feel like
writing to tell them so – dont you think *you* could write a dignified
acknowledgement of the M.S. I haven't time for writing of any kind. I
haven't touched or thought of an article for the *World* for a fortnight.
I may mention Mama is enchanted with the idea of your coming here
for any length of time – and desires me to say so – and you would be
able to paint a bit in October. I think Katie and Hamilton will be here
for most of the month, but that will not interfere with anything. Edith
and Cuthbert are here – arrived about 2 hours ago. He came to Galway
unexpectedly, so will stay till Sunday or Monday. We have fitted in
somehow. Edith and C. have the room you had first, and Edith dresses
in my room. Robert sleeps in the room outside mine, and all is quite
comfortable. We have another servant, *another Nurse*, for the time being
– the woman who was nurse to Muriel – all three Nursies are called
Mary – but the latest comer alone answers to that name – she herds
Lionel and helps all round and is an excellent creature and a clean. Edith
took the place most cheerfully though I could see she was a bit moved.
Still she did not show it – she looks right well – I have had no time as
yet to discuss things with her, but think I shall certainly try to go to
Dublin with her and get looked over – I am so glad it is such a glorious
day – It is really like July heat – and the place is looking its level best.
Robert has been the whole morning at that yew arch on the Avenue
with a couple of men, and has made it really awfully pretty – Heightened
it up three or four feet and trimmed it. He is awfully keen about
the place and is tramping about now with Cuthbert and showing him
everything. Herbert's letter is most satisfactory – but why will people
be such asses about "Anno Dominis" – we chose to put an English

plural to a Latin word – that is all – as Tennyson did when he spoke of "the cold Hic Jacets of the dead" – Do set H. right on this score and also remind him that there are on the River Thames other ladies eight-oared crews besides those of the Universities. The ladies eight is as well known at Cookham as anything can well be – and there is generally one at Henley – in a private capacity. It is very magnificent about the *Saturday*. I am *panting* to see it – I do not think £15 is enough for 170 pages. Why not do what they suggest and write it yourself. Of course I know what you will say – but you would really do it faster, and you would collar all the dollars and make it worth while to give your time to it. Of course I am quite ready to do it with you, and am only glad to have the chance. I think Mr. L ought to give us £20 down. Suppose we suggest doing without the added fiver for the 10 thousand – or for the 5,000 – and £20 down. I do think £15 is poor pay. They are very kind about reviews. You must indeed feel somewhat relieved by the departure of your crowd. I am now feeling something of what you felt all last week – what with concerts, picnics and dancing. I am awfully tired, leg tired, from standing about the arch when it was being settled, changing rooms, settling flowers etc but now there is a lull and I am going to lie down. I feel there is a most blissful ease in the sense of Edith being here – I am no longer the combatant daughter. The dance tonight should be enjoyable, from having our own little crowd. I wish you were going to be there. The neuralgia is much better – I think the porter drinking agrees with me.

I have had a letter from Violet, telling me many interesting things. I will answer it in a day or so. My final decisions about the Langbridge story are – Let us collar £20 if we can, and do without visionary fivers. I shall write it with you with pleasure and profit to myself – if you want me. And I think perhaps it would be better if we were at another book for Bentley. Robert pooh poohed the price offered by the little Langbridge –
  Yours Martin

[From Martin to Edith: *fragment: starts on page 2*] [early 1890]

. . . in the room sang – none quite atrociously – none well – with the curious effect on me that I was scarcely conscious that they were singing. All were sopranos – notably a Mrs. Hegarty, from the other side of the lake, whom I forgot to mention – who trilled and piped and sang tremendous songs and made a great appearence at singing like Patti. As I said, I sat in a sort of coma, till Edith O'F. lifted my teeth out of my

jaws with one or two Beatrice contralto notes, maddeningly out of tune
– she did that two or three times, and then the women were ended up
and Robert started with his new song "Through darkest Ireland" which
I like better than "Mullingar" in many respects. It has a very genuine
Irish turn about it – in the words. There was the usual audience in the
hall, of servants, car drivers, etc and everyone likes it very much – I
accompanied him in Mrs Riley, which was a huge success – especially
when R. dived into the hall and dragged one of the men outside to the
door and left him covered with confusion. We had a capital supper,
Burke O'F my portion, and cold pheasant my diet. I was grieved that I
had to wrest the former from Miss Roberts, and I am sure he was too.
However he was surprisingly interesting about his ostriches, and knew
Olive Schreiner's sister. It was typical of him and Oughterard that he
was not aware that Olive Schreiner had written a book. Mrs. Hegarty
was intelligent, and had read *Dorian Grey*. But I discerned that she had
read nothing else in the world – and didn't seem to think it advisable
to do so. It was past one o'clock before we got to bed, and then I sat
for ages over the fire reading your letter, and after that reading, "The
grey house on the hill" and thinking how admirable it is – I wore my
white dress – unadorned – and looked moderate – very – but clean and
simple . . . I am writing such a dull letter, but it is because of interruptions and discomforts. I heard from Mr. St. Leger – a New Year's letter,
sending a poem that was in *Punch* a couple of weeks ago and a magazine
called *Groombridges* that I had never heard of before – with a Christmas
poem of his, and articles by Mrs. Lynn Linton and others. He has given
up the *Sunday Times*, and is now sub-editor of *Black and White*. I am
going to ask him about our Mr. Williamson. We ought to be able to
place something there some day.

The entertainment last night was rather killing – not that I had anything to do with the outdoor business, but there was a good deal of
supper arrangement to be made when I got back from Currarevagh. The
poor people began to come at about 5 o'clock and were sent in at about
6.30, and immediately began to dance – headed by Murray and Allen,
in low cut dinner dresses. We went out about 10.30. Robert with Barbara, Ynnoc, Mama, Selina and myself. The place was packed and there
was terrific cheering when we came in. They made a little space for us,
and then Robert made a speech, very good – and telling – and every
point was cheered with frenzy – I felt a little chokey – at the allusions
to Papa and the reception they got. After the speech Jimmy Lee came
forward and proceeded to sing the song about Robert's "lovely fatures"
and his "honorable lady" etc. I felt bad again when it came to that end

part about the Colonels and good Majors and the rest of it. When it came to the word Martin there was a yell that you might have heard in Galway. After that Robert sang Ballyhooley, and then there was a jig, in which Robert and old Anne Connor, and Andy Welsh and I were the performers . . . [*page is torn off but letter continues overleaf*] . . . many humours – and besides I am too slack to write anything of interest. However I must say I never thought to see such a crowd and such enthusiasm at Ross again – even with restricted numbers from each house there were about 300 people there. Mr. Vereker and Robert had some fireworks, that looked lovely with the black sky and the white ground. The former and three of the railway engineers came into supper, and we did not get to bed till 2.30 – and slept till 10.30. The people stayed till about 4.00 o'clock. I will write again . . . [*end of fragment*]

For reasons not clear to the rest of his family Robert Martin had married a wealthy but uncultivated woman who, in her middle age, began to drink too much. She had neither subtlety nor wit and was completely at a loss with Martin and her mother. The problem of the mistressship of Ross became acute when Robert moved the whole of his family back to Ross in the summer of 1890. His wife Connie expected to be mistress, ignoring the fact that the woman who had been mistress of Ross since 1845 was still in residence. Edith and Martin toured Connemara this summer for the Lady's Pictorial.

[*Edith's note*: Prayers]

Monday, August 11th 90
Ross

My dear
Your letter was much looked out for but after all letters are poor things – I don't mean that yours was, but as a general reflection. I was glad to hear that you had accomplished that journey safely, with or without sandwiches. I must have imagined in my sleep that I was to take it too, as from before dawn on the morning you started I was awaking and wondering if it were near 6, and finally opened the shutters and wrote a bit of Ballinahinch and felt very sorry you had gone away out of Galway.

I have written to Katie, giving all particulars about the invasion, and she will tell them to you, don't ask me to write them all again – I am not equal to it – what with the fiend and general stupefaction. Broadly I may say that Mama says that the only possible plan is a separate establishment in this house. Separate kitchen, meals, and servants. For instance, we keep our present bedrooms, have the servant's hall for a kitchen, and the middle room to have meals in. It is loathsome of course, but better than having Connie at the head of everything, and in fact makes it possible for Mama to stay on here. I did pity her when she heard Connie was coming in a week, she was stunned into dead silence, on which Robert also fell into deepest gloom and asked whether Clareville was in the market. However they talked it out that night, after an evening during which no one opened their lips. Now things are most friendly and Robert thinks Mama and Connie will hit it off to a T. In the mean time Connie never makes the least allusion to Mama in her letters – never has from the first – However I wont write myself into a fury over it – the great thing is to keep one's temper and to sit tight here. Robert is having the room on the right hand of the top landing papered and painted for Barbara. He wrote to Bessy Ievers to send him paper – and such stuff as has come – probably the Storeys would think it very fashionable. By the way you may tell your people anything you like about the present crisis. There is nothing on earth to conceal, as far as I can see – in fact I should rather like our position to be known. Mama at once said she could not give up the idea of having you here to write with me, and of course with the separate establishment game it would be easy enough. She also said that she delighted in your being here – with other pleasing things – Nurse Davin was very sorry not to see you, so she told me today "Indeed that was a good gerr'il, sure wouldn't she put her hand to anything, and she a lady – Didn't I see her going up in the top of the house" – and didn't *we* hear her groans, when she had to carry up the water – Lastly let me tell you that Robert said he never in his life saw you look as well as that day at Merlin Park in health and otherwise – that you never looked healthy at Castle T. – so now – make for the tropics, for hot weather becomes you.

Robert is having all those old stumps between the yard gate and the garden cut away. He is the very newest of brooms, and would like to cut down everything. He wanted to cut down all the big tree laurels on the Avenue, so that they might sprout low down. I think the cows would see after that sprouting somehow. But Robert will do lots of good, and he pounds about in knickerbockers and takes great delight out of himself. Did you know that he has the most elegant legs – slender and shapely in a woollen stocking – but I don't think he knows it yet. He reads prayers – far more devoutly than Mama – On Sunday it was quite overpowering – a mixture of Irving and Beerbohm Tree – with a Broad Church I-assure-you-this-is-all-quite-simple-only-it-sounds-difficult sort of manner in the lessons, and then a sudden plunge into a fervid roll-your-periods, Lowest of the Low Church reading of the prayers. If you had been there I should have laughed, especially as on that solemn occasion the cat put on her tea gown for the first time and came down to lie on the sofa for a little while the children were asleep. At the kneeling down upheaval she stood and looked disgustedly about her for some time and then exactly as Robert began to declaim the general confession she uttered a series of the most heartrending wails, seemingly of contrition, and did not stop till it was over, when she jumped on Mama's back. The day was wet with us, as with you – I did not stir out.

. . . Ethel will indeed be an element of calm in the Castle T turmoil, and I am sure she will say a word in season to Violet about her goings on – she is a wondrous and far spreading hussy, but I really dont think she is aware of it, it is so ingrained in her. She will probably get to like Percy and then will be the ecstacies. But why should I talk platitudes to you – you know more than I do of Violet's goings on. Is Herbert writing anything these times beyond Errata? Is Constance painting? I have found the crocodile book – *in Mama's room* – and I will send it and your diary and *Blackwood*, for Katie, tomorrow . . . [*end of extract*]

Martin feels age creeping up on her. She works as hard as a man at manual labour about Ross, and the wear and tear is taking its toll. At this stage, she is not thirty years old. Edith has been on a painting holiday in Brittany, and a successful painting from this trip was hung in the Royal Hibernian Academy exhibition of 1891.

Ross
Thursday September 18th 90

My dear Edith
I am delighted to write to you again on British soil, and also to send you the *Literary World* with a notice of your "Paris Copyists" in it – Hildegarde sent me on the copy of September 5th without any comment or mark, so I dont think anyone can have seen it – It has quoted the phrase "a cold tribal friendship" which I always thought fortunate – so

now maybe – Nish cay dhier thu![1] I was delighted to get your letter and filled with a frenzy of resolve to go to S. Jacu*tt* and be hanged to it. You did write originally Jacu*b* – I can show you your letters. Before I forget it – Edith is much taken with the idea of Koko for the hair, and will have a bottle – but how is it managed – Do *you* send for it? Let me know. I think Betsy Moore is a very nice girl – why should anyone crab her? I also know her, so you needn't describe her to me. She and I figure side by side in a photograph done of the flower stall at the Masonic Bazaar which is still extant at Cranfield's I think. Then I was counted "one of the fairest flowers within the mossy barrier" by the *Lady's Pictorial*, now you wouldn't pick me out of an ashpit, or know me from one, with my filthy old clothes covered with the tracks of gorchings[2] many and fierce. Then the Chicken thought I was "a dear little thing", and now the Chicken is in his grave, and I am a grand old hag, as Nancy says, with an irritable temper and a growing interest in servants. I wonder how Louisa Moore feels – some parts of me feel like 18, others like 80. This is *very* interesting doubtless – but I think I shall turn to other topics. The procession of nuns through the convent garden[3] is lovely enough to soothe anyone to sleep. I see them, with their quiet faces, and you with your back to the sun dial, regarding them – and writing of them in your infuriatingly neat pencil hand – never mind – *Edith likes Hildegarde's hand better* – I wish I could truthfully say I did, just to spite you.

You ask a good many questions in your letter – and they shall be answered. There is no piano here, but there will be one immediately. If it will go into the Ronny's sitting room, it is to be there for Robert to compose with – if it wont turn at the end of the passage, as seems probable, I should think it will be in the drawing room. It will be the Ronnies piano anyhow. There is a sweet little punt on the lake, lent to R by Mr. Vereker which I hope we shall have many an afternoon in – and it is too crank to take Mama – Connie spends half an hour after dinner up with her kids – or rather with Allen, with whom she is on terms of nauseous familiarity. Then she comes down and has her glass, or glawss, as she calls it – while Robert either sleeps, or plays backgammon with Mama. However I believe she is going to use her own sitting room in the evening as soon as the chairs for it arrive. There will be the ecstacies then if Robert stays or comes, down stairs – and he will give

---

1 Irish phrase: 'Now what do you say?'
2 *Gorchings*: scorching tracks.
3 A painting of Edith's.

in about it – and snore up there all the evening. I dont think war will break out between Connie and Mama. The former knows it is her interest to stay here and save money, the latter just goes her own way, and a great politeness reigns between them. Anyhow whatever may be Mama's failings, she is seldom rude, and it takes two to raise a ruction. Robert's presence too is an admirable thing – I am sure you think you are coming into a cockatrice den, and it is awfully good of you to come at all – but it wont be what you think I am pretty sure. Don't be too hard on Hildegarde about going away – I have a sympathy with her on that point. But the sooner you can come, without seeming unkind to your family, the better. I *must* make money – so must you – and the Welsh Aunt[1] is an awful business – I wonder if the Chimp or Aylmer or Egerton would like to buy my half of the brewery share – I would sell it under the market price, whatever that may be, and they would have the coming dividend – I am of course hard up – but I do not mean that I *must* sell it, only that I want to sell it very much. Hang the old *Lady's Pictorial* – why wont they start these articles, or even answer my letter – Gibbons is a detestable creature, and I have always hated him.

I agree with you about Zoë being a doubtful element in Castle T. She has the spare time and the meddling instincts of the old maid – and she has the weight of matrimony to back her opinions in the family councils. Altogether there are a very few people one cares to contemplate as neighbours. Tell Aylmer that there is no Jubilee envelope at Rosscahill, but I will try in Oughterard tomorrow – I doubt that I should get it – I suppose you are now, seven o'clock, supping at Mont S. Michel, as calmly as if it were Mount S. Mitchell in Grafton Street – I know the look of the place from an old picture of my grandmother's. You shall tell me all about it soon – and it shall be great conversation for Connie – she knows it and S. Malo and all that country. On Monday I drove over to Spiddal to meet Mama, a sunny wild drive over that waste, and when I got there found Mama had not turned up. She thought it too rough a day. So I spent a long and most pleasant day with Lady Morris, a wholly unaffected person, who has by virtue of her office met every notoriety, and talks in a most interesting way about them, and with a comfortable sign of brogue. I actually played a game of tennis, a solo with Kathleen Morris, a nice and pretty girl, barely grown up, who beat me 2–1. I felt awfully out of it and puffy and stuffy, but think a day's play on that concrete court would make me get another four games from her, as she is only a very moderate steady player, not possessed of

1 *The Real Charlotte* was nicknamed 'The Welsh Aunt'.

a really hard stroke. However I am not man enough for that yet. I did
not get home till 8.15 after a drive against time as far as the storm was
concerned and just got in before it descended – Now write and tell me
how you got on – and whether you had seen the *Lit. World* – Goodbye
    Yours Ever
    Martin

                                                            Drishane
                                                    September 29th '90

Dear Martin

I wrote to Spiddal to you on Saturday, so I haven't an idea if you got
the letter or no, or if you ever will get it. With deepest reluctance I
herein enclose to you a cheque from Hildegarde for £6. When I was in
Bristol the price was from £11 to £12. So if you find that £12 is too
much you will have to give back ten bob, but I don't expect it is. I have
given her my half in part payment of my debt of £8 – so she has the
whole show now. Do hoard the £6 and *don't* buy things for the house
with it. Not even for your own room. I hate giving it to you, as I know
you will squander it. I also am very poor, only for the *Art Journal* – as
yet unpaid – I should be bankrupt. However it will float me, with a
small balance, and *all* my Christmas boxes will take the form of unsale-
able sketches (without frames). The money market may have brightened
by then, so I wont say this for black certain, but that is what I feel like
now. The Welsh Aunt is our best chance and will you honestly tell me
if you are able to work as we ought to work. Not if you are willing, I
know you are that, but genuinely *able*? I wont count the bilious attack
you spoke of in your last, as this was your own fault you say, but *before
that* were you fit to write all and every morning as of course we ought
to do. I would rather die in the work house than kill you by making
you work when you are not fit for it. The only thing that occurs to me
is that if you dont work with me you will be toiling about the vile house
and I don't know which is worse for you. Tell me the truth Aquilla – I
can't yet say "immutably" that I will come on Thursday week, only that
is a thing I will try to do. Thank you for the address of "aromatic
confections". Did you send it to Aylmer? If not I will do so. When is
the Phantom visit to Spiddal coming off? Why did you tell me to write
there and then never say if you went or no? Anyhow there is a letter of
mine care of "The Right Honourable Lord Morris" (is that right?)
waiting for you there now. Give my deepest sympathy to your mother

for her cramp seizure and accept the same for the fire alarm. I can see you whirling down to plunge yourself knee deep in flame. I am sure you were quite sorry that you couldn't damage yourself in any way. Would you ask Mary Mulloy or anyone if they know of a good Galway petticoat to be had – I want one, but don't think Hennessey's are good enough to send for. I remember that there was one to be had when I was at Ross last. We had our Harvest service yesterday. The church really looked very pretty, and the music wasn't so bad, a little Rectory friend, called Craig, came and sang tenor, and Sinnie and Carré were also there, and helped to swell the row. The Lloyd baby is better, I am glad to say; poor Kate hasn't been to bed for three nights or days, minding this tiny little ivory doll – that is what it looks like. They are trying to best Infant atrophy, which was brought on by sour milk in its feeding bottle, and the only thing that has hitherto done it really good is wrapping it in flannel steeped in codliver oil. However it was certainly better last night. The Roman Catholics prayed for it in the chapel (and of course it was also prayed for in the church) it shows real friendliness on Father Lyons's part. I never heard of it's being done before . . . It is blowing hard here, and all the leaves are falling, and I am thankful I haven't to cross the water again – all the same those four passages *were* good ones, good enough for you even, if you weren't such a little donkey. I am awfully glad the Poems from *Punch*[1] are going well – you might have told him so, with my love, only that I know you answered his letter by return of post. Ye slut. Alice Riddell has just had a daughter – a wire to Uncle Ken just announced it. She had a very bad time, the poor creature, but is doing well. The new coastguard man, Mr. Warren, was in church yesterday. He seems nice. Tall, clean shaved, devout, and the image of Mary the Boat. (Mrs Shaunapikeen's daughter) I hear he is going to keep three horses, so I augur the best. If only he and she will sing in the choir I ask for nothing more. His pew has been changed to the one just in front of the Bull, which may possibly have a good effect upon that brute. That was the object of the change. This is – it suddenly strikes me – highly typical of Buddh* ecclesiastical administration, but no one seems to think it at all funny. The Canon has had a fresh squozzums* for me because I stuffed thick masses of jungle in lumps on either side of the Chancel, made a cross for the pulpit, and played the psalms and Lohengrin. He flew at me and wowed forth adoration till I nearly dropped, and subsequently attacked Mother on the same subject. Uncle

1 *Ballads from 'Punch' and other poems*, ed. Warham St Leger (David Stott, London, 1890).

Jos now talks of going abroad about the end of November. I hope they wont. I must stop now. Write truth to me about your health of head and stomach.

Yours ever
Edith

[From Martin to Edith: Prayers at Ross. *Note by Sir Patrick Coghill*: 'A stray sheet']

. . . I unpacked your, or rather my picture last night, and that nice boy in the field is now regarding my door from the space above the cupboard camac,* and looks lovely – I feel ashamed when I see the gorgeous frame and the delicate colouring. It was too good a present for the likes of me. Your father put it up awfully well, wrapped it in an old curtain and put that class of boards on it [sketch] – and the most generous supply of blind cord. Katie said it was no trouble at all – quite a pleasure – and it is a real pleasure to me to have it – and to look at it.

None of us were fit for church today Katie being a trifle tired and Mama's eyes very bad – so we had prayers at home. Quite early in the morning Mama had strong convulsions at the very thought, and delegated and compelled Katie for the office of chaplain. Murray was surprised and before she came Mama stipulated that the Psalms should be read. Katie consented on condition that Mama should not try to read her verse, and after some resistance Mama gave in. In came Murray looking the picture of propriety, with a crimson nose – and Muriel armed with your Mother's *Childs Bible* – and Katie made a start. Will you believe that Mama could not refrain, but nipped in with a second verse, in a voice of the most majestic gravity. The fourth verse was her next, and in that I detected effort, and prepared for the worst. At the sixth came collapse and a stifled anguish of laughter. I said in tones of ice – "I'm afraid your eye is hurting" – "Yes" gasped Mama, and thus the situation was saved. I think Murray would consider laughter of the kind so incredible that she would prefer to believe that Mama always did this when her eye hurt her – Katie slew Mama hip and thigh afterwards I can tell you. I am finishing this in the afternoon and have been down to Killannin with Katie and Muriel and Murray. Need I say that the Leonards gave us a great reception, and there got out a donkey for Muriel to ride home on – which she did with bellowings of pride. I think it would have pleased you to have heard the Leonards fighting as to whether Katie or I was the handsomer. Ellin and my admirer Sonny

Lee stood firm for me but Bridget and Mary basely took Katie's part. Bridget however told me that till Katie came she considered me the most beautiful creature alive "The eyes and nose of you!!!! The lips and the little mouth!!!! Now just like when you dream of a pretty lady in a book." It pleases me very much to be considered a pretty lady. You can read this to Ethel in your best Galway brogue.

Katie had a huge letter from your Mother yesterday mostly lamentations over the loss of her, and abuse of Bourget. I don't think there was much news. Also letters from the Bart enclosing letters of Egerton's about Bourget – which were not in the least enlightening – Connie is very keen on the Castle and has made her offer to Mr. Fitzgerald, that dark and desperate man – who masquerades as a good young agent.

I suppose you will hunt someday soon, but I should rather not know what day. That is the class of idiot I am – quite suitable to "the pretty lady". This alarm about hunting. Give me every detail afterwards and stow all pretended modesty . . .

Of all the letters that Edith wrote to Martin from the midst of her family, the following best demonstrates the difficulties created by background noise, interruptions and the sheer inconsequentiality of home life.

Drishane
January 15th 91
Thursday evening

Dear Martin

Improbable though it may seem, I am going to try and write to you after dinner. The family are immersed in their books, and you may judge of my devotion to your interests when I tell you that I have plucked myself from the depths of a new American novel to write to you. Dhurode came exactly at the minute it was wanted. I enclose Spielmann's letter, and bill of fare. Keep the latter for me. I set to work and polished up the pictures, and made the miner-boy into an old miner-man. Quite worthy of the Mother Seigel syrup artist. I also re-did the Arum lilies, and made rather a pretty little blue grey one of it. I think your alterations are first class: I like them all, and one or two of them amounted to inspiration; however I am horribly afraid that it would be too long and literary for a beastly weekly, even with the St. L as subeditor. I likewise sent the "night journey to Paris" series; I had a set on ordinary paper, and by redoing one, and giving myself a changed and better looking face in the others I think they are within the bounds of possibility. The poor little thing;[1] it feels like ages since I was drawing them from him; I hated having to sit there and muck at them for filthy lucre. I wrote to Spielmann, (in a very friendly manner and tone) and said that either sketches – (Dhurode) or ditto article could sit up alone, each on its own totham;[2] I hope he will answer as he says, as soon as possible, (now they are all talking *and talking of books*, so you may imagine the row) [jagged line] this expresses my feelings of fury, I can hardly think . . . Does Robert know how the Balfour fund is to be got at? Widows are swarming in: three or four more came today; one was not a widow, and when taxed with the fact she said she had "nothing only a sort of owld man of a husband, that was fit for nothing only to stay in bed." On reflection I should not recite this story to Robert, except you stop at the comma . . . I hope also that our plans will soon begin to crystallize a bit. You may depend upon me to go to Ross, if only for a month, it would be better than wasting that month; and if Ross is to be shut up at the end of this month, you must either come here or we must meet at Ethel's – all the same, I don't care about that, as I think it is rough on Ethel, as you and I, when immersed in literature are more trouble than we are worth. I fear Paris is receding into the blue and heavenly distance – that fatal fact of four times five making twenty will be too many for us. Shall we go to the Glendalough Hotel, Recess, for a month? I wonder what they would charge? I never had a more frenzied morning than this; the drawings to fix, gum on, write letters about, and then the drawing room to arrange for a crowd of female tea drinkers, headed by Mrs. Warren, and continuing with the Myross Woods, Porks, Sylvia and Katie Lloyd and her ghastly Dullies of sisters-in-law and – Sinnie – the latter was the best value of the whole lot, and made herself very agreeable. Uncle Kendal had the rheumatics in his arm, and couldn't come and was a great loss. Percy was shooting at Lough Ine, but the Chimp, Egerton, and Jack, did their best, and Harry came in late and made himself very agreeable. I am finishing in bed at 11.30 p.m., after a fiery argument; the Chimp on one hand, and Mother and I on the other, re Richard Jeffries. I was longing for you to have been there, though you would have been deafened. Mother and I, from totally different points of view, held the same opinion, while the Chimp talked rot about Nature.

1 She is working from old sketches of the Puppet.
2 *Totham*: bottom

I made him produce the Eulogy and read to him some of our champion bits of twaddle, however he was as undefeated at the end of the row as we were, and poor Hildegarde was nearly mad with fury as she was trying to finish a very interesting, pathetic and religious novel called "Gloria" (translated from Spanish), and couldn't get forrad with it owing to the clanging of the heronry. My candle is burning down so I fear I must stop . . . Mrs Warren was as queer as ever, but I still maintain that she is a good sort, and not devoid of a certain humorous intention. The entertainment was not amusing. It began with walking Mrs Warren around the orchard, after which Egerton played a single with Grace Pork in a slight cold drizzle, and we sat in the drawing room and were meowed and quacked to by the Myross Woods and Mrs Warren.

The tea was *very* good, delicious cakes and quantities of thick cream. Everyone had two or three cups, and I was nearly dead from standing up and pouring out for them all. I am afraid Harry is not going to give me that copy of the poem, though he at first told me I might keep it for myself; he asked me today if I could give it back to him; I dont know what he will say when he sees my name written on it, but I shall try and make him let me keep it. It is strange that they should have come on it just at this time. It is just twelve o'clock and my candle has gone. [*end of letter*]

Lord Zetland had been appointed Lord Lieutenant of Ireland in 1889. This passage through Ross by him and his entourage must have been during his last tour of duty in Ireland as he retired in this year, 1891, after a troubled period of office. Robert Martin, as a service to his friend Arthur Balfour (Chief Secretary for Ireland), had offered to give a welcoming party to the Zetlands as they passed the gates of Ross; the organization devolved upon Martin as Robert was absent at the time.

Ross
Monday April 13th 91

Dear Edith –
I am stiff and tired but happy in the consciousness that Sunday is over, and all is well. Last night at 10.30 I sat with my feet in hot water, voiceless – but serenely happy in the thought that Lady Z was well on her way to Galway, and listening to the rain pelting against the window. I suppose I may as well tell you about things. They are interesting,

though I want to talk about "Cecilia".[1] It was as bad a night as I ever saw – wind and real awful rain. However we got the arch and everything finished and the fire lighted by 7 o'clock – then dinner – and there in buckets of rain Katie, Moolah and I set forth *in the van*! K and I laughed feebly the whole way, in spite of the torrents, as we huddled in hay and rugs. There was something trancendentally typical of Ross about it. We had a longish wait, however we had the gate house to sit in – where was Mrs. Vereker – mountainous in her grey ulster and a crowd of wet poor people – amongst them a railway official with an accordion of 50 horse power – which he played many times on and nearly deafened us. Peter Connor sang Ballyhooley and Mullingar in a tight small tenor, and with a faint imitation of Robert oozing through shyness. I was in and out like a dog at a fair, and slowly getting soaked about the petticoats and feet – as Mr. Vereker and I were organising a set of men to hold in their hands long sticks with sods of turf steeped in paraffin set on fire, on them. These proved the most shining success – as they were posted along the road, and looked fine. The carriage came so quietly in the high wind that they had only just time to light up. It pulled up under the arch. Lady Z. having stuck her head well out to see things. K and I were the wrong side of the bonfire, and Robert lepped down off the box without seeing us, and began rushing to and fro among the people, calling out for us – "They're here" howled Nurse in tones that would penetrate the ears of Johnny Franks. Robert speechlessly seized my hand, dragged me through the thickest of the smoke and sparks, with Katie and Moolah flying behind – and precipitated me at the carriage door – where I had to try and say what politenesses I could. Katie then came along, and Moolah handed up a huge and lovely bouquet of daffodils – while the man with the accordion played "God save the Queen" at the full blast of his infernal machine. Lady Z. could not get at Moolah to kiss her face, but kissed her hand over the edge of the window. She was *very* civil, praised the arch, said we had done too much ("Ah go on" says I) but she seemed a person of not many ideas – she is fair and pretty and kind and quiet – R. introduced me to Miss Balfour, but I couldn't see her well, she seemed dark, and she smiled very pleasantly, that was all there was to her. These things occupied only about a minute, and the people were all the time forming up each side of the carriage, the twelve men with the torches high up by the walls – and the effect was intensely brilliant and picturesque. The turf blazed beautifully, the bonfire glowed in the background, and all the faces shone in the light

1 A short story.

with the rain streaming down on them. They began to cheer them. For her Excellency – at R's bidding, then they themselves cheered for Balfour – for the Lord Leftnent and his Lady (Nurse screamed this above the row) for Mr. Martin and his family – and for the Queen. Such a row you never heard, I was astonished, both at the numbers, and at the noise – some of the men had walked up from the lake side in the deluge – and they were determined to have some shouting for their money – Robert then got a silence, and standing by the carriage with his hat off said about three sentences in excellent taste – nipped on to the box again – and off they went, to catch the night train in Galway – for which they had little enough time. Lady Z. stretched a slender paw over the door as she started and shook my hand effusively – we wished them a pleasant journey, and so farewell. The men with the torches ran for a bit alongside, and the railway huts were lighted up to show their beauties. Poor Selina, who was afraid to come to the bonfire, stayed at home, and had a light in every window for them to see as they went along Coolaghy. The fireworks did not come – and anyhow the rain would have done for them. There was a man in the carriage with his back to the horses, whether Lord Scarborough or the A.D.C. I did not know. He looked young, and grinned the whole time. After they were gone we and the Verekers returned into the gate house, where I had ordained tea, and in the twinkling of an eye Nurse and her two young ladies had got a cloth on a table and comfortable tea and bread and butter – which we had with closed doors, while the people yelled outside. I am glad to say that they cheered Mr. Vereker as he went home, no one ever deserved it more. He was invaluable, hustling and cajoling, and keeping a few who were [unreadable word], in order. Mrs. V. also gave much moral support – though not able to do anything beyond that, poor creature. We huddled into the van again being individually cheered as we tumbled headlong on the floor of it – and so full gallop back here – and to bed. I could scarcely speak by that time – but put my feet in hot water and went to bed – and today am nearly all right. The beastly *Irish Times* says nothing about our show, I wonder if the *Express* or *Freeman* do? Do you see them? However we had a line from Robert just now, before he started for England congratulating us on the success of everything, and saying that Lady Z. had desired him to convey her thanks to us and to all concerned – and that she thought it a splendid wind-up to her tour. Robert's face of delight was quite repayment enough for all the trouble – Now I must stop – Major Gaskell is coming here to tea and I must prepare – I return "Cecilia" with comments – I think the tuner a very good idea – go ahead. How *thankful* you must be that you didn't go hunting that day. Could you stay with Ethel till this Monday fortnight? It would I think suit me better all round. You might even go to the Curragh on the Saturday – but if you are in a hurry I will come. Of course I want to be off – but many things weigh on me. Let me know about this as soon as you can. My ideas will want shaping – Violet says I can come anytime –

Yours ever

Martin

THE WOMAN FOR GALWAY.

LADY ZETLAND's tour in Connemara for the inspection of distress and Government relief was thoroughly successful throughout, and ended last week in a manner typical of Galway and worthy of its best traditions. The last of many long drives taken by her Excellency and Miss Balfour was from the fishing-lodge at Screeb to the railway terminus at Galway, at which place they arrived at 11.30 P.M., having started at 3 o'clock. They dined at Oughterard, where the dinner-table at the little hotel was ablaze with red rhododendron blossoms; and they then set out on their last fourteen Irish miles in torrents of rain and pitch darkness. It was therefore a welcome break when, as the party neared Ross, the residence of Mr. "Ballyhooley" Martin, a brilliant light became visible, and they found at the gate a huge bonfire, an arch of evergreens with "Welcome" on it, and a large crowd of people, who ran to meet them, waving torches made of sods of turf steeped in paraffin oil and stuck on long sticks. The effect was intensely picturesque; the rain was powerless to damp the general fervour, and umbrellas, those raven-like and depressing objects, are scorned by the dwellers of Connemara. Cheers for "the Lord Left'nant and his lady," for the Queen, and for Mr. Balfour, were given with a "Galway" yell that must have warmed the hearts of the travellers; and the penetrating bray of an accordion, on which a local genius played "God save the Queen," *ohne Hast, ohne Rast*, blended happily with the din. Mr. Martin, who was himself accompanying the Viceregal party as one of the official distributors of the relief fund, improved the occasion by a few sentences of thanks to his tenantry for a demonstration which he had not been able in any way to help in preparing. Lady Zetland brightened up wonderfully during the short halt, and, having been given a bouquet of daffodils by Mr. Martin's little niece, Miss Muriel Currey, and having thanked Miss Martin for this effort to make her last experience of Connemara a pleasant one, she drove on to Galway, carrying with her a vision of wet, excited faces, waving hats, and blazing torches flinging wild light on everything as the people tossed them into the air. As she herself said afterwards, it was a splendid wind-up to the tour.

It is sixty years since Viceroyalty was at Ross, and then Lord Anglesey, who was Lord Lieutenant, and had a wooden leg into the bargain, nearly put an end to his tenure of office by falling headlong down a difficult staircase there. The only other story of his sojourn which has survived the lapse of time is of one of his *aides-de-camp*, who, in company with others of his retinue, had been relegated to some rooms near the stables. This young gentleman expressed himself at breakfast as having all but died from the unsavoury proximity, on which Mrs. Martin, a lady of much spirit, replied, "It's a thousand pities you didn't: we should have had such fun at the wake." Let us hope that Lady Zetland's recollections of Ross will be more cheerful than these.

LADY ZETLAND AND MISS BALFOUR IN THE WEST.

THE RETURN TO DUBLIN.

(FROM OUR SPECIAL REPORTER.)

Her Excellency the Countess of Zetland and Miss Balfour arrived in Dublin yesterday morning from the West of Ireland, accompanied by Viscount Scarborough, Capt the Hon O. V. Lumley, A.D.C.; and Mr Ulick Bourke, R.M. The party left Screeb Lodge on Sunday afternoon for Galway City, having first paid a visit to the well-known salmon fishery near Screeb, and inspected the salmon hatcheries in connexion with it. Some of the bonfires which had lighted up the countryside on Saturday night still smouldered, and here and there by the way groups of people had assembled to see her Excellency pass. The demeanour of the people was everywhere respectful. The day was bright, but there was a stiff breeze from the south-east, which raised great clouds of dust along the roads, and rendered travelling in an open vehicle very unpleasant. Oughterard was reached shortly after seven o'clock, and a halt was made of two hours at Miss Murphy's Hotel while the horses rested and the party dined. The evening became very wet and disagreeable before the journey was resumed. There was, nevertheless, a very striking demonstration of welcome, a few miles outside Oughterard, at the residence of Mr Robert Martin, of Ross, who, with Major Gaskill, had accompanied the party ever since their arrival in the county Galway. A number of Mr Martin's tenants, with a considerable contingent of people from adjacent estates, assembled near Ross, bearing blazing torches made of turf-sods steeped in oil, and stuck on the ends of sticks. Several large bonfires also lighted the way, and there was a scene of great enthusiasm as the four-in-hand dashed up to the entrance to Mr Martin's residence. A brief delay was made, and Mr Martin, by her Excellency's permission, said a few words to the people, congratulating them on the honour which had been conferred on them. Lady Zetland had now the gratification of seeing a Galway landlord and his tenants united to give a true Irish *caed mille failthe* to an illustrious visitor. Miss Martin was introduced to her Excellency, and then the party drove away to the City of the Tribes amid renewed cheers, while scores of blazing torches were thrown high into the air. Major Gaskill, Mr Martin, and Mr Brewn, R.E., took their leave of her Excellency and Miss Balfour at the Railway Hotel, Galway. Both Lady Zetland and Miss Balfour expressed themselves pleased at the amount of information which they had acquired during their tour concerning the condition of the people in the distressed districts, and the measures which had been adopted for their relief. They also appreciated highly the cordial manner in which they had been received at every place they had visited. The party travelled to Dublin in a saloon carriage, which was attached to the mail train leaving Galway at midnight, and arriving at the Broadstone at 6 a.m.

The Horse Fair at Dunmanway; marked and used in sections later.

[From Edith to Martin, winter 1891: *fragment*]

I have never seen a more perfect day than yesterday. The glass had fallen in the night, but its doing so had the most fortunate effect upon the weather. The party consisted of H. A. & I on our car, Herbert & Mrs Musgrave in the Judy cart & Hal & Harry from Seafield. Collins went in charge of Novelty, who walked into the box like a little lamb. We had to unship at Dunmanway, (though the line runs through the fair fields the Board of Trade wouldn't allow the platform to be used,) & drive thence on cars to the fair, about 3 miles off. It is a lovely country; our road way bordered with trees for half the way, & when we got out of them we looked out over a green plain with the river twisting across it & the most perfect coloured ridges of hills all round. We got off the car on the side of the hill above the fair fields & were in the thick of it at once. Such absurd young horses, such miserable old stags & such riders you never saw in your life. There were three *good* horses there. One a grey of Old Beamish's, a stout clever horse, a 4 year old brown – half brother of Novelty's who was bought by the Widgers for £100 & Novelty. There were a certain number of £25 to £35 horses, the rest were rubbish or screws of the rankest. Collins, dressed to perfection, & as sober as I was, presently rode down in to the "galloping field" which is below the line, & is the place where the classy animals go. In a very short time O'Connell the dealer was after her, with a fat vulgar man who wanted to buy her. Collins set her at the bank into the rough ground, & she jumped it to perfection, swinging out 12 feet over the ditch. Then the fat man got up & looked in a funk, & finally offered £60. A. said he wanted £90 – finally the fat man softened up *towards* £70 but as £75 "in its purity" was the last word, the fat man retired, & as it appeared he wanted to ride her himself I was delighted. Then Norcott – (a celebrated cross country man & a dealer) came up. He certainly is a pretty rider & the mare jumped like a bird with him; he & a Mrs Ivers (who wanted a young one unfortunately) said they had never ridden a better bank jumper, & Norcott offered £60 – A. said £90 or a bit under – N said she was worth it, but not to him & went off, but not right off.

Then Collins came up & said secretly that there was no money in the fair & Norcott could only give small prices as he always looked to clear £30 or £40. The Widgers didn't want her; they all thought her rather too fat, but that is no harm; there is time enough to get her down. Harry had brought his chestnut, but couldn't get an offer, except one of £10 from Widger & at about 1 o'clock said he was going to auction him! We all fought our way on to the top of a bank close to the tents – where biscuits, *crubeens*[1] & whisky were being freely partaken of) & a ring was formed, in the centre of which was the chestnut with an auctioneer on each side of his head, like blinkers, & Pat on his back in a most furious temper at the indignity. The first bid was £7 10s, but at last he was knocked down for £19 to a hotel keeper in Dunmanway, & as he has something badly wrong with one leg, I don't think that sportsman has much of a bargain. Then we all went to the top of the furzy hill & ate sandwiches, & watched the people. Such dresses as the country ladies wore; & such hats. One of them was clad in black satin from head to foot, & another had a vivid cinnamon brown with a green plush zouave jacket; they were past belief, & had mostly come from America. I heard one old man, in tears, telling another old man, also in tears, of how his daughter had sent him her likeness "she's fatter in the face than Mary, & broader in the shesht, but I dunno is she so healthy, & "Father" says she "dear Father, you wor a good Father to me" Begor when she says that to me I cried" at this affecting point he had to cry again & so had the friend, & as, when he began the story again, he took it up at precisely the same place, I went away. Down in the galloping field they had put up a very low mud bank, & as it had been ground to powder in about half an hour they had put a pole across the middle of it, it was about three feet high, & all the worst garrans[2] in the fair were jumped over it *incessantly*. Their riders tore up & down the field taking this thing on each journey, & falling off as often as not. There was a hulking country boy on a monstrous mare with a tail like the skirt of a dress, & with him tore a small boy in a red velvet smoking cap on a pony about as big as a rat. These two were perfectly undefeated: & the mare flounced first at full gallop & knocked the pole down & the pony scuttled with her nose at her heels & skipped through the debris. The little boy generally fell off, the big one fell out into the mare's mane & by clinging to it used to get back again into the saddle. The friends stood around hooting, & casting clods of the fence at the big mare to make her lep. We had two hair breadth escapes. We were sitting on the bank eating apples that old Dan Connor gave us, when a young mare ridden by a helpless countryman scattered down on to us, we fled up the bank, when she turned, & began to back right on to where Old Dan & Old Beam-

---

1 *Crubeens*: cold, boiled pig's trotters.
2 *Garrans*: a breed of horse related to the Scottish garron.

ish & others were feeding. It looked as if they had got to be trampled, but Old Beamish without rising from his lunch produced a huge whip & flailed the mare's fat totham with such fury, roaring at her as if she were a hound, that she took to her heels & ran to scatter death at the other side of the field. It was the funniest thing you ever saw, & Old Beamish treated the whole thing as calmly as if he had been attacked by a house fly & had brushed it off. Our other escape was from his grey horse: he had lent it to a fat little middle aged farmer, also a Beamish, to ride about, & this man, who must have been a little screwed, went thundering round & round the field, in each swoop coming nearer to us, & apparently losing a little more control over the horse. At last, when we had again had to skin up the bank to get out of the way, "Old Sta" called to him & demanded why was he using the horse in that way. To which the other Beamish who had a face like a turkey cock, fiery whiskers & moustache, & a huge stomach, replied in the voice of a dying Sunday School girl, "Ah, I was only coaxing him". I could never describe to you the absurdity of this little mincing voice coming out of the immense flaming face – & if you had only seen the "coaxing". With that we bursht. At about 3 o'clock A. & I came to the conclusion that it was no good waiting any longer, so we packed Collins off to Dunmanway to feed her & himself, & all set off for the same place, walking up the line. I can't hope to describe to you how lovely it was. The hills every colour, towering white clouds on the bluest sky, which was reflected in the river, & the bogs on either side of the line full of flowers. We were stopped twice by men who said we mustn't walk on the line (it was much the shortest way) so we said we'd get off it & didn't; Harry, who followed us, . . . [*end of letter missing*]

[From Martin to Edith: *fragment. Edith's note added later*: 'the cat in the oven']

. . . sink into H's establishment . . . I am tired of going down 75 steps to get my boots, of turning away my eyes from iniquity that I cannot rectify, of trying to get the servants up in the morning – but let me be thankful. I have done somewhat, and can leave with a clearer conscience – to get the kitchen chimney cleaned the pump mended and the kitchen thoroughly cleaned and white washed cost me close on £1 but it is done. And it is worth twice the money to me to go into a white kitchen where are no dirt holes and no smoke. I laugh foolishly when I think of the

NOVEMBER 28. 1891

BLACK AND WHITE

TWO new planets have of late swum into the ken of literary observers. A very happy collaboration was that of Geilles Herring and Martin Ross, to which the reading world was indebted for that very charming romance, "An Irish Cousin." The same authors have just produced a powerful story in one volume, called, "Naboth's Vineyard," in which the non-political aspects of "exclusive dealing" are turned to very striking account. The best traditions of Carleton and Lever are carried on by these new writers, and the splendid possibilities of Irish life and character have once more found apt and artistic interpretation. The names under which these writers took the floor were modest pseudonyms. The authors are two ladies, Miss Somerville, and her cousin, Miss Martin, of Ross, Galway. Miss Martin, a story from whose pen will shortly appear in *Black and White*, is a sister of Mr. "Bob" Martin, whose "Ballyhooly" and "Killaloe" are familiar as household words in the mouths of Greater Britain, and who, to a smaller circle, is known as an inimitable *raconteur* of the racy humours of his native land. Miss Somerville is not only an accomplished and observant writer, but a clever artist as well. A delightful series of letters, "Through Donegal in a Governess Cart," which, like the more serious works, was plentifully illuminated by gems of Irish speech and humour, lately appeared in a contemporary.

DAILY GRAPHIC,

IRISH FICTION.

The issue of a new story by the two clever ladies who gave us "An Irish Cousin" serves to remind us of the instructive fact that Irish fiction is practically in the hands of Irish women, and, let us hasten to add, in very safe hands too. Gerald Griffin and Samuel Lover, Charles Lever and Sheridan Lefanu have left no literary descendants in the male line. Mr. Rudyard Kipling, who, though he has Irish blood in his veins, has never set foot on Irish soil, has proved by his creation of Mulvaney that he possesses a real insight into Irish character. But for faithful pictures of Irish home life and Irish scenery we must go to the author of "Flitters, Tatters, and the Counsellor," to Miss Lawless's "Hurrish," and to the admirably vivid pages of "Naboth's Vineyard." What strikes one about all these writers is their impartiality, and, in the case of the joint authors of the last-named work, their keen sense of humour—qualities which many male critics deny to their literary sisters. There can be no question that the Home Rule agitation has exerted a sterilising influence on Irish humour—in men. It is, perhaps, then owing to the eternal law of compensation that we meet with a double portion of it in the writings of Irishwomen.

Herculaneum episode from which the cat and three kittens barely escaped with their lives. The cat, being in labour, selected as her refuge the old oven in the corner of the kitchen, a bricked cavern, warm, lofty, and secluded. Here among bottles, rags and other concealments she nourished and brought up her young in great calm till the day that Andy set to work at the kitchen chimney. No one knew that the oven had a special flue of its own, and it was down this flue that the soot elected to come. I was fortunately pervading space on that day, and came in time to see a dense black cloud issuing from the oven mouth. I yelled to a vague assembly of Bridgets in the servants hall, all of whom were sufficiently dirty to bear a little more without injury – and having rushed into the gloom they promptly slammed the oven door on the unfortunate family inside, on whom were raining without intermission soot, bricks, and jackdaws nests. Having with difficulty got the door open again the party was disinterred quite unhurt, but *black* and more entirely mortified than anything you could imagine. For the rest of the day Jubila cleaned herself with her children in the coldest parts of the house, with ostentatious fury and frump – she was offered the top turf box on the back stairs but instantly refused, and finally settled herself in a stone compartment of the wine cellar, a top berth this time, you bet! . . . [*end of fragment*]

Drishane
Skibbereen
County Cork
Sunday July 3rd 92

Dear Martin
After the whirl of political excitement, calm – A. has just come back from Cork; he would be given £250 and his expenses would come to about £500, so I need scarcely say it is off. I am not sorry, as we find that not a single man here is registered, and I expect it is the same all through the country – I mean among the Unionists. Not even Dick Connell so I expect he would have had awfully few votes and only had a lot of trouble and expense for nothing and made the "Unionist minority" a laughing stock. Those of the village who had heard of the idea were mad with excitement and lots of R.C.'s had announced they didn't care tuppence for the priests but would vote for Master Elmore. However as none of these enthusiasts were registered I fear they wouldn't have been much use. I am rather thankful after all, as the canvassing would

have nearly killed us and the horses and it might have come against the hounds. We are now seriously contemplating a revision of the registry, as if there is another election soon, as seems likely, it would be well to be prepared. I wish the whole thing was over. It is too exciting to be pleasant. I rode to church in a blue and white Mousseline de laine on Creole, with the old magenta Egyptian rug as housing to keep my dress from touching her, and Boyle, like Joseph marching beside me to open gates — we tied the old brute to the railings but she broke the string and after church, B, Mr. Warren and Dick Connell had a long and difficult chase, Creole flying before them like an Arab sheikh, dressed in her striped bournous — (which we had left on her to keep the flies off) . . . I agree with you deeply about David Grieve and the W.A. and everything and I am *thankful* about the trees by the lake and I am awfully glad that the stylograph was a good fit, but I must stop. I will write again in a day or two. The Cork Unionists are going to plump for Redmond — I fear that Kenny has withdrawm from Skib. Please tell E about Jack. Fifth Fusiliers. Cherat. Punjab — if he got leave he might go to Muriel and be near her —

Ever Yours

Edith

"Through Connemara in a Governess Cart," by the authors of "An Irish Cousin," is an amusing sketch of the adventures of two young Irish ladies during an independent excursion in the West of Ireland. Finding their visit to London insupportable owing to the continued downpour of rain, they rushed back to the more genial skies of their native land, where disappointment would no longer be possible. The tour in the governess cart, with all the adventures they met with, is described in a light and humorous manner. "Sibbie," the mule, plays first heroine, and a second "Irish Cousin" serves as a capital foil. Sketches of Irish life, the eccentricities of wandering Saxons, and descriptions of local scenery and events, are worked up in a manner which makes the book a pleasant companion for a spare half-hour. Mr. W. W. Russell has in his illustrations ably supported the writers. The publishers are Messrs. W. H. Allen and Co.

[From Martin to Edith, 1892: *fragment*]

I am full of business – Aspinall's enamel has set in with great fury. Everything in the house is slowly but decidedly becoming a sort of Persian red – baths, boxes, turf baskets, my face and clothes. The pea-green and turquoise blue are to follow – and after that it will be according to the supply kept by Madden in Oughterard – I have not succeeded in papering my room yet, and will probably reserve that as a rich treat for you. The tinkering at the chimney still goes on – Still does Andy Welsh pound up and down the stairs with mortar on his boots, still do I hear his muffled jackdaw voice in the chimneys, still does the kitchen placidly puff smoke in his disgruntled face.

Mama told me tonight to my extreme amusement, of an effort she made before I came home to get Selina out of bed, she having taken up her usual winter residence there. Selina at once announced with some heat that no one cared for her but Jim and fell to weeping with great violence. Mama was completely nonplussed, "but" she said with beautiful casualness "Kate Welsh happend to be within hearing, she had come down about something or other, and I think I had got her to sweep the stairs, and she with great cleverness came to the rescue." This meant, I found, that she came in and told Selina that she would rather have her than any young lady of the whole of them. The tide of tears began to abate, but was not completely checked till Johnny Welsh was called in – He in some other unexplained way had flown out from his situation in Galway and was probably at the moment making Mama's bed or lacing her stays. To Selina then, seated Niobe-like in bed behold the brave Johnny approached. He also roundly asserted that we were all but blackamoors compared with Selina . . . [*page missing*]

. . . in the tea room that she [Mama] had some strange red thing showing over her hips, which I thought might be a flannel vest showing through a slit in her dress, but some commotion made me forget it. When we got home, or rather at bedtime, I asked her what it could have been and put my hand under her shawl to look. It was a red kettle holder – clamming on to her side like a fly to the ceiling. "Oh" says Mama, interested but very little surprised, "that is the kettle holder that I bought for Selina. I searched everywhere for it and then they gave me another instead." She then immediately fell asleep in her chair, after her fashion. Selina then remembered having walked to Bray station with Mama, and been by when a woman came up and told Mama that her sponge *and* her sponge bag were hanging from her waist at the back. How they got there, or how Selina didn't notice them I cannot tell you.

Robert's political song "Ta-ra-ra-boom-de-ay" is good and a-taking but what a rotten little tune it is – He is *full* of scandal and gossip about interesting people. Mrs Grimwood for instance – who has evidently been going in for him. He thinks her second rate and larky. A very strange thing happened to her. Her mother ran away from her father with some other man – the father brought up this girl as best he could – and she came out – and almost at once she and a nice man fell awfully in love with each other somewhere she was staying. She came home to tell her father about it – "Good God" he said "He's your brother" – and so he was – her half brother, and he just took to his bed and died of it straight off. She recovered and married Frank Grimwood, for whom she did not care one brass farthing. That sort of thing sets one wondering if Nature or we ourselves are wrong – Fanny Shaw-Taylor has gone to pieces completely over this marriage of Mr. Crosbie's. They were engaged in a sort of a way – and her people said they would allow it when he got his company. He has now got his company – and there is Fanny Shaw-Taylor. She always had . . . [*end of fragment*]

Edith and Martin travelled extensively in 1893. In May they visited Herbert in Oxford, toured Wales in June and Denmark in September.

Tuesday
December 12th 93

Dear Martin

You will be surprised to get even this scrawl from me, but as I have the time you shall have the word – the weather changed last night and today was quite perfect. Brilliant sun and soft wind. A. Collins (on the Jennings black mare) H on *Marquise*, I on Novelty, and Mr. Warren formed the C.T. brigade and Zoë was on wheels – Papa drove Sorcerer to Skib. Very few of the Beamishes were out, Hosford on the grey and young Donovan on Cinderella, and one or two more whom I didn't know, Captain Welch, Dr. J., Sinny and Bennet were the only noticeable of our county. Well – we put in at the bottom of the Glen Tighe covert, and A asked me to go right to the top to view the fox – I went up and had the pleasure of seeing him on a hill in the covert, and hounds closing on him. Then, up came swarms of runners and riders. I tore at them and tried to hunt them but it was like hunting the rising tide, then A. came and damned and blasted, they retired while he was there and then back they came – A then went round to ride the covert, and after a long wait, stemming the tide as best I could, I saw three hounds come out

TWO MERRY MAIDENS.

"In the Vine Country." By E. Œ. Somerville and Martin Ross, Authors of "Through Connemara in a Governess Cart," &c. Illustrated by F. H. Townsend, from Sketches by E. Œ. Somerville. (London: W. H. Allen and Co.)

It is quite impossible in any sort of review to give a just idea of the vivacity and raciness of this delightful record of unimportant travel. If this be collaboration in journalism, let us have more of it. The authors made a little tour in Southern France in vintage time, and their entire ignorance of wine-making is the gain of the reader, who is spared the tedium of technical descriptions which he would not understand, and of statistics which he would not so much as glance at. Instead of these things we have the sunniest possible itinerary, exquisitely humorous at every turn, the commonest incidents of touring transformed into sparkling little episodes, and with touches not a few of the naïve unconventionality of the author of " A Girl in the Karpathians." Nothing escapes the ladies, and being deliciously conscious of their inability to weary us with the scientific or commercial details of their subject proper, they courageously fling their whole mission to the *vent d'Afrique*, and tell us—with detail enough now—how they did *not* do what they set out to do. We see them shopping for mosquito-nets and vainly trying to recall the French for mosquito; struggling with a kodak the manipulation of which was as baffling as the effort to comprehend the processes of the vineyard; dodging the greedy army of waiters and chambermaids in the hotel; making stealthy sketches of fellow-passengers on a steamboat which " made her way down the river on the principle of Billy Malowney's exit from the wake, when ' it wasn't so much the length of the road come agin him as the breadth '"; and cajoling a landlady, "built much on the lines of a cottage loaf." They got on pretty well with the mosquitoes, which were forbearing: "Perhaps we were caviare to their countrified tastes, or perhaps they missed the usual seasoning of garlic"; but they admit their humiliations in their perpetual wrastle with the French tongue. They have Mark Twain's knack of extracting a literary joke out of the most trivial *contretemps*, and a greater ease than Mark in presenting it. Here is a neat tip on how not to tip.—

near me and then heard a faint bugling by Glen Tighe – I belted down
with the hounds, no one followed me, and when I got to the brow above
where we once climbed up there did I see the two red coats and the
hounds off the other side of the valley beyond the hideous lodge, going
straight for Drishane! No one else was near – I tore down – passed Glen
Tighe down to the hideous lodge, jumped in just on this side of it and
off I set over the hill after them. They had half a mile start, but I saw
their hoof prints, and every hill had a boy stuck on it. At first the jumps
were small stones or fences – She never turned her head, then came a
whacking big bank, and three country boys yelled with joy at the prospect of my death and "the big lep". She refused once, I charged her at
it again, and she jumped it nobly and I belted her out over a biggish
hole on the far side. That gave me great courage, I crossed the road
where Stripes hunted the cow, got right across the top of Bludth, partly
by footprints, partly by men, and partly by one faithful hound, crossed
the long ring up through grass fields and out onto the short ring at Jack
Buckley's house – I was going of course for Uncle Harry's wood, when
a woman sent me South and at the corner of the two roads I caught
them. I had seen them several times but always a *long* way ahead. They
had checked at the road but they had hit it again, and went into the
wood at a good pace – Novelty was very hot, but not at all blown, and
though she had some *beastly* stone walls and bad rocky ground, I am
thankful to say she didn't get a scratch. Presently up came Sinnie and
Mr. Warren in a great fury (the latter) they had gone by *Laherdane*
wood, a mile out of their course at least, then Captain Welch via the
Rectory road – no one else – the colt had lost a shoe and couldn't go
on – Jennings' mare had two baddish overreaches, (how I can't think,
as she rises with her forefeet as a man using his arms when swimming)
but she jumped well (Collins said that Dr. Jennings had asked him to
be careful but he had said he "would do his best, but when hounds were
running he couldn't put her legs in his pocket"). It was then only 12.30,
but I didn't want to give Novelty any more, and A. was glad of the
excuse to save the colt – so Mr. Warren, who was very cross, said he
would take them back to Liss Ard and back they went with Collins and
him – Captain Welch would hunt no more and Sinnie came to lunch
with us. H came in at lunch and said Marquise had run away with her!
She then resolved to jump her, and she Tom Collins and Hosford came
across country from Laherdane to the Bohirneshall road and thence by
road home, it being hopeless to pick the hounds up. She says Marquise
jumped stone gaps of all sizes nobly, and without a lead – I am thankful
I didn't see her – Eddie, Percy, and the Colonel go out tomorrow. I hope

H. may get Bally. As Novelty was only out for two hours and her back is all right I will take her out too – the new idea is a hunt ball for the quality at Glen B! Seven and sixpenny tickets . . . [*end of letter missing*]

The West Carbery Hunt held a meet at the clock tower in Skibbereen every season to entertain the town. Edith's brother Aylmer was Master at this time. There was enthusiastic participation by town and country people alike.

[From Edith to Martin, 27 December 1893: *fragment*]

. . . Dick Connell and his buck. On Sunday morning Aylmer got a heartbroken note from Dick – "certain parties stole my *dear* last night. If I got them they would not enjoy their Christmas" – Soon after one of the police came to say that they had found the footmarks of two men. The door, which was nailed, had been burst open, and the buck's footmarks flying for the forest were plainly visible – "I wouldn't wish it for £10" says poor Dick. Dan Neil is darkly suspected of being the Liberator, as he has a grudge against Dick. I should not be a bit surprised if Gendie had secretly commanded him to do it. I must say I was sorry, as, for twelve miles round, the people were looking forward to the hunt & as the "dear" was in hard training it might have given us a good gallop. There was no time to try for a bagman, so A. wrote to Cullinagh to have the earths stopped and we met as usual at the Clock Tower. I think there were even more people than last year. About forty riders; no end of carriages, Zoë, very smart in her landau, and *hundreds* of men and boys and girls too. The shop windows all around were thronged with young ladies all of whom had donned monstrous hats and feathers in honour of the occasion, deep into the rooms you could see the phalanxes of nodding plumes. Collins was riding Dr. Jennings' black mare again, as he cut his own horse schooling the other day; he joined us at the Clock Tower, and entered upon the crowd full gallop and I believe, literally jumped over several people as he dashed through the throng up to the hounds. His entry was felt to be very spirited and suitable, by all save those whom he jumped. We then tore up North Street at full trot, with pistol shots from Collins and Aylmer's whips and *thunder* from the multitude. I never heard anything like it; it was quite alarming. We then jogged on for Cullinagh without going to Killnaroodhea, and put in at the east end of the hill (I entreat of you not to be stupid, but just to remember the points of the compass). Uncle

K was out on his young horse, in a fine double bridle my dear, (I was only allowed a snaffle) and in closest attendence on the Widow Currey. I can't think what he would do if Aunt Robson were to come back. She, Mrs. Currey, admits frankly that she is nervous about jumping her pony so she and the Colonel clung to each other down the road, and were no more seen. I headed the crowd at the path up the hill, and after due time let them up. We had hardly got to the flat at the top when from six women in red petticoats and about sixty country boys there rose a screech you might have heard at Ross. The fox! Neither Collins nor Aylmer were in sight, so I tore on for them and the hounds, met Collins or rather saw him being *hauled by the shoulders* up a precipice, up which he had somehow hunted the wretched Jennings mare, who was panting at the top, and we got the hounds on – A. was at the bottom but joined us at the head of the path. The fox just tried to go for Killnaroodhea, but was headed North, then he turned again and ran right along the North side of the hill towards the East. It was fairly good going. Several people got into bogs, A. amongst others, but Novelty and I were more wary and escaped. They went an awful pace, & till the first check, A, Collins, Mildred, Bennett and I were the only ones with them. Eddy's horse doesn't quite understand the country, but I think he will soon do all right. Novelty refused the first fence once, but after that never turned her head. We ran down off Cullinagh, crossed the road and went about a mile on over the next hill to abreast of Shepperton; there the brute doubled and took us down a baddish place where the hounds got away from us for a few minutes. Collins, Mildred and I got the best way down – the quickest anyhow, but it involved a long slipping scrambling drop of about 16 feet into a bohireen. It was wonderful how well and easily the three mares did it. The hounds had checked by a little lake with a covert on one side, and we cast and drew in vain. Then there were yells from a distant hill and we went on; afterwards we heard that the fox had swum out to a little island and lain there till we went, when he went happily home. There was very big jumping, but a lot of biggish rotten fences with drains on the far side. Novelty wants still a good deal of minding, and is rather apt not to jump out enough, and rather too keen to follow another horse, two faults of youth; she is however improving daily, and is jumping a little less big at stones. She did one very showy thing. Coming down a hillside through furze she was hopping and going delicately, and suddenly, when within about twelve or fourteen feet of the bottom, she rose like a swallow and jumped the rest of the furze brake into the field. Fortunately we weren't hunting, so we were well seen. Mrs. Welch actually jumped five times.

She told me so with much delight, and if her husband doesn't spoil her I shouldn't be surprised if she got her nerve – or some of it – back. We then went to Bunalun and drew the round covert blank, then the gorse. They hit on something low down before the firs – a hare I thought, – and were making for Hollybrook, but we stopped then and drew to the North; there was a fox there and they had one of the little rings peculiar to Bunalun, but it was getting wet and dark so we whipped off and went home. Jessie and a little Bantry boyfriend of hers, (who was out on a big grey mare) both came to grief at one of the Bunalun banks. The big mare "rared", so I heard the Bantry boy say, and fell into it, a near shave of breaking her back, then Jessie tumbled at it, and finally a farmer got into it, but no one was hurt. I am sorry to say I saw none of the casualties. Mr. Warren wasn't out as the Slug had a sore back which he had made worse the day before by bolting for two miles along the road with Mr. Warren sitting, helplessly hauling at a light snaffle, on his back. Now I have told you enough horse news. I will merely mention that I wont sell my share of Novelty next summer, and that H. had urgent business at home that prevented her from going out . . . [*end of fragment*]

Ward and Downey apparently made a bid for The Real Charlotte *before Edith and Martin had finished writing it. Of all their books it gave them the greatest anguish. The writing of it took three years of erratic spells at Ross and Drishane. As Nevill Coghill made clear in his BBC talk in 1948, some of the early chapters existed almost in final form at the end of 1890:*

> I have studied all their manuscripts carefully; almost every entry is dated. For instance Chapter II of The Real Charlotte in its first draft is dated October 29, 1890; Chapter III, November 4–8; Chapter IV November 10–15 and so forth. Delightful thumb-nail sketches evidently done like lightning while considering a point, decorate the margins here and there. I have found brief notes, two sentences long, containing the gist of a story, which in a later manuscript is expanded into a twenty-line synopsis, and later still into a full first draft, with corrections and insertions. Then at last the fair copy as sent to the printer.

However pressing the deadline with Ward and Downey, Edith cheerfully gave much of her time to organizing a hunt ball to raise funds for the West Carbery Hounds.

Drishane
Saturday
January 13th 1894

Dear Martin

I was awfully sorry I couldn't write to you yesterday, but – as I told H to tell you in her postcard – I literally couldn't have sent you more than a scrawl, and I prefer to wait till today. There has been more to do than you could believe, settling, re-settling, arranging, paying bills, etc etc. and as I undertook the charge of the bag, a great deal of it came to me, and I am now deadly tired. However thank goodness it is all over, and has proved very successful in spite of many lets and hindrances. I will first deal with your last letter. Has R. gone to Gib yet? W and D[1] are now well into Jan, but my firm belief is that they wont pay till they get the book and rope in a little money. I sent off the last revise yesterday. Wasn't it like them to send a volume and a half on the day of the ball to be done? I sent them off just the same. O. Crawford has taken no notice of my letter of remonstrance; what would you advise me to do? I haven't cashed their cheques; they owe me 25 shillings (to make eight pounds) but I suppose they think masterly inaction is their game, and I think they are right. If you can suggest a line of attack I wish you would. H. and E. go to the cottage on Monday, and H. is dreading having to deal with her new domestic – Lovett. She is said to be very good in all departments, and is the adored of the nuns, so I daresay she is respectable. Do you see any end to your abominable probate business? It is high time for you to be rousing yourself up out of that, though I grudge the thoughts of your going away to the cottage and not here. Reggums and Mrs. R come here on 31st and stay till February 6th. A hideous and unmitigated bore, but unavoidable. How are Edith and Cuthbert getting on? I have heard no word of them for ages and should much like to hear . . . Quadrille rages nightly and I dont know what mother will do when H. goes. You would hardly believe how successful Egerton is. There have been no blorts,* and pyrates flee, and even the Purlieu* fire is endured with complacence. Poor E. at first was, like you, scared by the incessant fightings through meals, but in mercy to him H. and I firmly withdrew from all contests, and Mother, failing two of her stoutest

---

1 Ward and Downey.

foes, lacks interest in the battles and they rage less than usual. I look forward with despair to H's departure. We keep up a semblance of shutting the door between our rooms when E. is there, but he really makes very little difference – as Mrs. R. Atkins said, he's the gentleman that's like a child, and nicer and gooder than you could believe. The evening of the dance was mercifully fine – or fine-ish, and all the women were on the spot of nine thirty. It was most interesting to see them, and most difficult to recognise them. Mrs. Warren's was by far the cleverest head there, as she had constructed a sort of Tie-wig [drawing] something like that, in shape, with wide black ribbon bows and beautifully pow-dered – Emmie's hair was quite modern in shape, but was also beautifully powdered, the rouge just gave her what she wanted and she looked like a little Dresden shepherdess in her pink gown – H. I thought one of the best looking people there, I did her hair – not very high at the front and coming out in big curls at the back, something like that [drawing] and mine was much the same only that I had a pad in front. I hear Mrs. Warren admired me very much, which pleases me. No one else attempted anything archaic, but they had most of them done the powdering awfully well. Kate Lloyd looked extremely pretty, young and bad, the widow was pretty but not bad. Bessy F. looked, as H. discovered exactly as Dr. Johnson. Ellie Piff and her tribe were very much improved. Ethel Morgan looked extraordinarily pretty. You wouldn't have known her – Aylmer thought her the best looking girl there. Fanny was painted like a clown and didn't look as well as usual, and the Porks were not interesting though they had done their hair very well. Henny looked very handsome and had a delightful patch in the shape of a fox, quite beating my two horse shoes, (which, nevertheless were more becoming a shape than a fox, which was rather straggling.) Sinny and Carré Powell weren't at all bad, and Mrs. Welch would have been pretty, only that she had made cakes on the top of her head with *salad oil and flour*! having been for four hours trying to whiten herself with violet powder. For the first half hour I thought the whole thing was going to be a failure for want of men. A. and E. were the only two till past 10, and the room looked like the stage of any theatre with an eighteenth century ballet on – rows of painted ladies in white and pink, and not a man to be seen. At last however they began to turn up, and though we were undermanned by about six, (six if not more) the thing went very well. A, Eddie, and Captain W wore hunt coats, and A looked extremely well, and really carried the whole thing on his shoulders, and kept it alive in a way that made me respect him. Egerton also danced with everyone as if he liked instead of loathed it, and as several of the girls had their own private friends – Ethel Morgan and Mr. Gape – The Piffs and a little "Aurora" sailor – and so on, they all seemed to enjoy themselves. The supper, which was mainly subscription from all the people round, was a splendid one. It looked awfully well, and tasted equally. We did not give champagne, only sherry, claret, soda water, claret cup and lemonade, and whiskies and sodas were sold by Collins – in full hunting kit – in the glass room. He had four constituents, and he sold them thirty six drinks! Disgusting brutes. They were Jack De B. Mr Symes of the bank, Captain Hand of the "Aurora", (a horrid looking man who was staying at the Warrens) and Bertie Morrogh, who was quite screwed by the time he went. A. says he came screwed, but I danced with him and did not find it out. It is a pity. One good thing was that Collins 'deludered' Jack de B, when in his cups, to lend him his big grey whenever he wanted a horse – I asked Collins next day when Mr. de B had made him the offer "*Lasht night*, Miss" says Collins with the eye of a devil – H. and I played and fiddled three or four dances with great effect (though our profesh. Mills of Bandon, played as well as anyone could wish) and we danced with women who could get no male partners and toiled and span in a way that would put any ordinary lily to shame. She and I had given Bessy and Isabel their tickets. Hence this conversation: *Izobel* – "Well Hildegarde I do really think I admire you more than anyone in the room" *Bessy* – (with a luscious sigh of loving remembrance) "Ah Hilde I *must* tell the truth, I admired you *greatly*, but still I *do* think that Eeedith was far the prittiest in the room!" The faithful Pethlums The amount of what H, in the language of Quadrille, called cross-roughs at the dance was very absurd. 1. Emmie and Kate Lloyd (with secondarily Mr. L and the widdy, the latter only faint) 2. Emmie and Henny, 3. Emmie and A, because A danced with Henny and was civil to her, 4. Grace and Aylmer A. asked her to dance, and she refused point blank, and Nelly (who was staying here) was mad with her, 5. the Porks and Sinny, 6. the Porks and Carré Powell because, in consequence of Sinny, the Porks haven't called on her, 7. and worst of all, though we only heard of it next day, our servants and Zoë's servants – I can't enter into it now, it is amusing and absurd, but too full of detail. H. and I steer a devious and cringing course amid all these ructions, and so far have kept out of trouble. I must say I think they are most degrading and servant-maidish. The Myross Woods neither came nor paid, which I think extremely mean. There was an extraordinary revival after supper – thanks to the claret and soda I suppose, and the Cotillon, led by H. and A went very well, though we badly wanted our own men, Jack, Claude, Boyle, the Chimp etc. to play the fool – Eddy did his best but it is not his line, and the others were the most consumate muffs. They went on dancing till three — which was pretty good and showed they liked it. Hildegarde and I strummed John Peel while A. blasted on the horn (four hands piano) till we were sick, then we tried God save the Queen, and were hissed back to John Peel, then we got into a groove, and though mad to play another tune, could think of nothing but John Peel. Then simultaneously, we burst into "Razors" and "Drink Puppy", you never heard such a row in your life, but they liked it. The piano notes have been lying down with their legs in bandages ever since, and I doubt they will ever be good for anything but light carting and Beatrice's accompaniments again. We gave the company the best of soup and we heard on all hands that it was considered a great success. The loss of the Liss Ard party was however irreparable, and though the outsiders enjoyed it I must admit that we all felt it to be rather a struggle. I forgot to say that Jessie came in a red cut away hunt coat, white tie, gold fox pin, white waistcoat and satin skirt, and a velvet hunting cap pinned to her hair. She looked nice and childish, and behaved very nicely. I danced the Lancers with her and I think most of the men gave her a turn and Mrs. Downs and "Mr. D." were enchanted with the whole show and told A so. We shall, I think, clear fifteen pounds and our exes were about ten pounds — so we have really done very well. There was such a lot of supper over that when we had given away the broken meats we decided to auction the rest. We had Sinny, the Porks, and all the village and having given them excellent tea, gratis, we sold the scraps and made two pounds. A. was an excellent auctioneer and got Mother and Zoë to bid against each other with the greatest success. On the whole it was worth the trouble, as fifteen pounds leaves only ten pounds to the bad over "Joe", Collins horse, poor Vixen having been paid for by Old Harry. The hunt breakfast was but meagrely attended but the usual lot (except Myross Wood) came, and about half a dozen went in and ate well. It was a lovely day, mild and bright; Novelty was very lively, owing to the frost-rest, and I rode her in a short double bridle-bit and bridoon; as I should have found her hard to hold in a snaffle; she doesn't exactly pull, but if she wanted to go you couldn't stop her easily, and she might have jumped on the hounds. They were put in at the usual place and H. (on Sorcerer, pulling *double*) and I went on to Dr. Jennings' gate and into the field to watch. We had hardly been there five minutes when we saw half a dozen hounds come out high up, and cast about in the furze, then they went back again and then the whole lot came out and went away over the hill towards the Poulavawn . . . [*end of extract*]

At this time the middle chapters of The Real Charlotte *are being written by post: 'Christopher's piteous renunciation' is a reference to Christopher Dysart. Much upheaval had taken place in the family. Egerton and Hildegarde began their married life in The Cottage, half-way down the village hill, with its distinctive diamond-paned windows. The windows at street level are still barred, a precaution of Egerton's to prevent Patrick (later Sir Patrick) and Nevill (later Professor Nevill Coghill) from tumbling out into the village street.*

Edith never threw anything away in case it might prove useful later, a form of economy that resulted in her living in squalor and deep litter. Here she refers to two stored items, one of them an inflatable rubber ring used as a swimming aid by Ethel Coghill in 1877. Edith had kept it carefully until 'its destiny . . . declared itself' seventeen years later. Some people found Edith's ways exasperating: Ethel Smyth was appalled by the accumulation of objects in the studio when she got to know Edith in the 1920s. By that stage food and dogs' hairs were being laid down in impacted layers.

Drishane
Tuesday evening
January 16th 94

My dear Martin

I have not had a comfortable time before this minute to acknowledge your letter of Sunday, and the book with No. 10. I think the latter is very good, and if I water it down here and there when the going strikes me as being rather heavy I hope you wont mind. I wont improve it, but I shall make it more meet for the intellects of fools. Before I forget, please send me as soon as may be that sheet of the revise wherein Christopher's piteous renunciation is set forth. I have given all the revise to H. to read, but it lacks that page, so send it along. I think of writing a friendly unbusiness-like letter to Otter, re advertisement cards, asking when it will come out, if it will be extensively advertised, and asking, as man to man, when they mean to pay us. Only if you approve – I don't see that employing Browning officially with W. and D., cuts us off from our favourite old pastime of Otter-baiting – but say what you think best and I will do as you wish. I have never, personally, written him a cross word, so I should not find it inconvenient now to write him a civil one. I will incorporate your beloved children in church according to your wish. Do you think it would be good to send the lot to Beard now and ask him how many words, and how many more illustrations they would want to make up a volume. My private belief is that three pictures to a chapter is too much, except in a big weekly. H. and E. went to the Cottage last night and H. is now engaged in fearfully breaking in a new Beanie* – Lovett is her respectable name, and she already speaks of E. as "The master" and calls H. "Mum". However, as, though Anglicised by long residence, she is of Skibbereen extraction, these grim formalities may wear off. I am very lone and lorn and thought of getting the Totthams[1] into my bed last night. I don't know what I shall do when she has to raise up grandchildren to her aunts (or foster mothers,) but no fitting spouse can be found. There are two projects on the horizon – 1. "£4.19s." on Patrick's Day. The races to be up in Ray, where Lambert will give the ground. A bank race, a hurdle, a flat, a trotting, and some other event – anyhow five altogether. It will be great fun. We will enter Novelty for the bank, and Aylmer will enter Curragirth for it, and Joe for the hurdle and the flat. We ought to stand a very good chance of winning if Welch of Bandon doesn't bring his grey over as she can certainly go better hunting than any other horse here, except Jack de B's big grey who, *with Collins up*, is very hard to beat. The other project is a Grand Bazaar early in August to build new kennels. It is to be a woman's show exclusively; no men on the committee and no male interference. This to square Mr. Warren who calls it infra dig. I said to him that much as I respected the hounds, I respected the church equally, and if it is not low to have a Bazaar to build a church – I didn't see why we shouldn't have one to build kennels. It will be a *fearful* nuisance. H. and I stipulate for public funerals the day after the bazaar. Novelty shall be led behind my bier with my brown boots on the saddle and H. will have Marquise and Robin with a boot apiece – I think with good side shows and a promenade concert in the evening, and a bit of a soldier band – half a dozen instruments – from Cork for the afternoon, we ought to do very well. They made a hundred pounds by a loathely little "sale of work" the other day in Skib! How *odious* it will be! But if we get the money I shan't care. I am sure you are much bored by all this and very anxious to hear about the hunting today so I will begin. It was a most threatening morning, and as I was sure it would pour (as it did yesterday) I waterproofed the right knee of my breeches with the india rubber inside of a save-life-from-drowning inflatable collar purchased for Ethel at the age of seventeen, thrown away by her in the following year, and nourished by me until now, when in the fullness of time its destiny has declared itself. It is a noble scheme, and as there

1   *Totthams*: here means a dog.

was not a drop of rain, I can confidently say that it kept me thoroughly dry ... We met at Cullinagh cross. A small field. A. was riding the farm mare, Dick's usual mount, the colt not being fit. H. drove Emmie with Marquise, Uncle K on his old chestnut, Percy, going with much flab on old Harry, Eddie on Mrs. Currey's pony, Sinny, Myross Woods, Tessy and Captain W. and two farmers were the field. We drew Cullinagh from end to end twice, with no success, and we fear that in their ardour of earth-closing the country boys boxed up the fox. I am glad to say that Novelty is quite temperate in bad places. She may fuss a little, but nothing to signify, and though she is very snubbing in the stable, she obeys the mother's voice in the field. After that we drew the whole of Keelnaroodha blank. It was strange, as they worked very well, and the country boys had been sure of a fox if not two, but a furious south west gale last night, and a good deal of the same this morning, had bellowsed them out of it. We had no great jumping, the only worst part was going down through the K. wood which was awful. We then went on to Bunalun. Driscoll, at Hollybrook has made *barricades* of timber all round his place. He must have spent a fortune doing it but his poisoning is costing him rather dear. On Stephen's Day he made sure we were going to Bunalun and he sent a man flying out to put down poison all over the place. As you know, we did go to Bunalun but not to Hollybrook, and the next day Driscoll sent a man out to bury the poison. He did not bury it deep enough. Driscoll's favourite collie dug it up, ate it, and was only recovered from death by giving him tobacco – (a thing I never knew before) – and he will be no more good; the unfortunate man who laid the poison got some into a cut in his hand, got erysipelas, and so died. This we heard today – and in this connexion I must tell you that Papa heard this morning from Father Fitz – "the Protestant Priest", a delightful old man and a great friend of Dr. Jim's – saying that in consequence of Papa's and Aylmer's having voted for his nephew McCarthy (who has just got the Workhouse clerkship) "all the McCarthies had bound themselves to see there should be no interference with the hunting, and if a fox was killed, let the guilty party look out for himself". As the Clan McCarthy is very strong in these parts this assurance is most promising, and fortunately they are not in the least likely to think that Papa and A voted for the McCarthy merely because they honestly thought him the best man for the post. We had to go into Bunalun for a sandwich and a drop of something. The Morgans wouldn't let us go on without it, and I am thankful to say that instead of the usual spread, they had nice little dishes of sandwiches on the sideboard, drinks, and nothing else. At this juncture Uncle K. Percy and Eddie went home which was both foolish and poor spirited. We then drew the round covert blank, and went on into the gorse. The bogs and mud were something appalling, and very soon we were belting though them full split after a fox. He ran up through the gorse to the east and made for that rotten fence where Creole fell with you. A. and I were ahead. I put Novelty at it to give Miss Connell a lead, she half refused and half slipped up in the mud and I thought she was cut to bits as she seemed to come right up against a murderous series of length-wise slabs which had been laid on top. I hardly dared to look, but *wonderful* to say, she hadn't a scratch, then I tried her a little lower down, equally bad, but she got over, very badly, but unhurt. A. took Miss Connell at the first place, she got across the slabs on her stomach, gruesome to see, and got across with a good big gash on one hind leg, below the hock inside, but not serious. The hounds were going hard, and the very next thing was a hideous stony thing, with a very bad take-off but the only possible. Collins who was riding Jack de B's big grey, got over. Novelty caught the top stone with her hind feet and came pretty well on her head. I thought we were both over, and so did Sinny, who was just behind, but in some astounding way she got onto her feet without rolling over. She is awfully active, and we arose in partnership, & though at one of the two places she had got a small cut on the outside of one knee, it was of no depth at all, and only made my young lady more careful, as after that she never put a foot wrong. They then ran over foul country about two miles to the east of Bunalun, Collins, Sinny, Mildred, and I, only with them – on the top of a hill they checked, and a good many of the others picked up. (Poor A. had to go back and stitch up Miss Dick's leg) I had heard at intervals Mildred wailing like a wet night wind, and it now transpired that she had broken her curb chain and couldn't hold the brute – in fact she *all but* jumped twice on Collins. By great luck I had some string in my pocket so she and Richard tied it up, and just then there was a holloa forward – Collins and I tore on, and found the fox had crossed down the valley, gone over the river and had run south. We lifted the hounds onto it, and having the legs of the party, (Mildred being mercifully occupied in tying up her bit) we got across the river miles ahead of the rest and had an unmolested gallop over good fields, with some really big fences, and a lot of big flies, (fences with stone coping,) always tending round south west in the Bunalun direction. Half way there the others cut in by the Lakelands road, and then the fox ran down to Bunalun. We crossed the river at the place where A. and old Harry got a roll, and then scent failed in the gorse, and we could do no more with him. It must have been a four or five mile ring, and there was only one check. There were some falls – Captain W. had one, so had Mat Swetenham, a regular head-over-heels-horse-over-man tumble, but somehow neither were hurt; later on however we met poor Captain W. leading his mare with a terrible gash just before the stifle. The sort of thing that makes you say that you will never jump anything but a sofa cushion; but indeed I mind her as much as is possible and you wouldn't like the sound parts. It was all that putrid Bunalun fence.

Yours ever
Edith

PS I forgot to tell you that N's bandage was made of an ex-surveying belt of Boyle's that I had stored even as the life-saving collar was stored.

One of the letters marked by Edith at the time of receipt as usable material, and containing Martin's own comment, 'It is the making of a story almost.' Edith supplemented her income by horse-coping, Gambler was one of her trainees.

[From Martin to Edith: *fragment, starting on page 3*]

. . . for two days probing that awful pond that is on your left just after you get into Annagh Pulleen-a-Fairla. His scapular and Agnus Di were found on the brink – and his purse. The police came today – but I don't think they got any tidings. They say there is thirty feet of water, and unknown depths of mud. He is either there or wants people to think he is – Mat told me "He took off the scafflin and the Agnus Di the ways he'd be dhrowned. No one could be dhrowned that had thim on him". The extraordinary thing is that last Sunday a young man in Coolaghy rushed to the lake and tried to drown himself. People saw him make the spring, and got there in time to save him – "He was lying on his back" says Mat and "the Agnus Di without the sign of wet on it – " Much more did Mat say, and it is all written down, and you shall hear it I hope soon. It is the making of a story almost. The children count me a great playboy. They are good little things, and hardy stumps, and nice and clean in their ways. Nurse D, when I gave her your Christmas messages, was overwhelmed with gratitude "and would ye please to wish her every sort of good luck and happiness, and the blessing of God on her. The crayture, indeed she was good and clane and quiet and sensible – and her little dog – so nice and so clever. She cried for him, the crayture. She couldn't do more." I am so glad Gambler is well sold.

It will be more to you than twenty quiver fulls when you speak with Mr. Warren in the gate.

Yours Ever
Martin

Martin's second letter on the Pouleen-na-Fearla drowning. The fate of the poor disturbed boy who drowns himself preyed on Martin's mind for some time: 'It fills my mind in its dramatic aspect mostly and perhaps after a talk with you it might take shape.'

[*Edith's note added later*: 'Drowning in Pouleen-A-Fearla']

Ross
January 3rd 94

Dear Edith

I had seen Colonel Adam's death in yesterdays paper – but did not know till I saw the Con.[1] how awful it had been for poor Melian – I feel very sorry for him personally. Wasn't it always known that his heart was weak or rather that he had heart disease? I am afraid that this must have rather dislocated your dance plans, in that it disposes of the Liss Ard contingent; or perhaps you will put off the whole thing – one has much sympathy for poor Melian. These sudden deaths are happy for the people who die them, but awful for the others, and I think she was very fond of him. Certainly it makes one feel that the thing to desire beyond most heavenly things is strength to face whatever dreadful thing there may be coming. One could wish for the passion for death that that young fellow had who disappeared on St. Stephen's day. They found him at last in Poulleen-a-Fearla last Sunday morning – hooked him up from among the branches of trees, by putting a boat into the middle of the pool – and staring down in all lights. They finally got a bauneen[2] and tied a big stone into it and dropped it in. They were just able to see where it went, and it placed things for them, so that they at last recognised some dim companion shadow as part of a body – and got it out – I avoided the place throughout, and did not look at the dismal procession that passed the yard gate with the body carried on poles. Need I say that Selina went out, and even permitted the face to be uncovered for her edification. I was at the pool yesterday – and could realise very

---

1 The *Cork Constitutional*, a newspaper.
2 *Bauneen*: white woollen garment.

well what happened on Saint Stephen's day. It turns out that what chiefly preyed on his mind was that they had one day called him from his work to come and shorten up the chain of the chapel bell in order that when Father Cowley the new priest came to hold mass the next Sunday the bell could not be rung. When he found what he had done he was miserable and ever since they watched him more or less. He tried to get away as they think to this pool a few days before, but as William Mac said, he felt them following him, and went back. On St Stephen's day he went out with his brother to cut a rope of ferns, and took an opportunity of escape when his brother's back was turned. They found the rope of ferns flung down and next the scapular on the bank, and finally himself. Never was a more bitter comment on a parish feud, and never was there a more innocent and godly life turned to active insanity by bad treatment. It fills my mind in its dramatic aspect mostly and perhaps after a talk with you it might take shape.

In spite of this gloomy diatribe I am well and most energetic – you would not know me. I make twice as good tea in the morning as you did – hotter, more brilliant in every way. I made tea in the middle of the night not long ago, having awakened on a hideous dream that the lake was level with my windows, that I was skating beautifully on it in twilight fraught with all panic, that I was jumping down banks on my skates, and finally that Johnny Hynes was lying on the end of my bed, very conversational. "This is mince pies," I said, "my heart, mince pies," and brewed a gallon of wash. The following night I took the most hideous mixture ever concocted by man, a monster Eno, with thirty drops of ginger in it. It is noble in its effects in a general way, but it is more disgusting than anyone would believe.

I was very glad to have your letter on New Year's Day, and the photographs. Except for the nose it is like you, but I cannot truthfully say that the nose is. It is like a sheep's. Anyhow I was delighted to have the picture – and to meditate thereon. Your family are very nasty to you about your pictures. They are admirable – Mama was full of admiration for them, and said "Oh how charming" quite spontaneously when she opened on Bullawn cave. Of course they are not as good as the originals, but I think that one of the two boys sitting side by side, Bruce with his arm over his face, is as good as anything could be. I am so glad the papers are off my mind. I sent on the proofs, and liked them better than anything so far. Unfortunately I fear that I have let soufflé go spelled soufflet, we must bear it in mind in the revise. I shan't be very sorry if Aylmer doesn't hunt Novelty, as she is hardly in fit condition – at the same time a good weight would be wholesome in her education and also a pair of spurs. You are very good about the *Daily Graphic*. It is much appreciated. We expect Geraldine and Eileen here about the 17th and I should like to be here for part of their visit anyhow. That is just what *you* would say, only it would be the whole of their visit. It is not very long, anyhow . . . I am toiling in number 10. I find it very hard to remember the road between Llanberis and Bettws[1], except in small spots. If we don't write Denmark soon we should have forgotten it all.

I am anxious to hear about the dance and what has happened and how your smothered cold has gone on.

Yours ever
Martin

The West Carbery Hunt was a ramshackle outfit compared with the smart Irish packs like the Blazers, the Ward Union or the Meath. Edith was given the opportunity to hunt with the Quorn – one of the top English hunts – and went in trepidation, but she and her hunter Novelty acquitted themselves splendidly.

Monday evening
November 25th 1894

Dear Martin

I was delighted to get your letter before I started out for the meet – (of the Quorn at Kettleby) – on Novelty. We went by train & so did the horses. Before embarking on the hunt I will discuss other things. I propose going to Constance's on Weds. – and can hardly cross to Paris before Friday. It is hard to go away, but it must be done . . . I am delighted that H. likes the hat, of course I will get you one, but you must tell me exactly what you want (and there wont be time!) I will do my best and chance it. Dark brown is the easiest to find in all shapes and would go best with your Paris gown, so most likely I shall go for that. I will say that it must be taken back if not approved of. If I see a nice grey to go with your homespun I might get that. *Why* didn't you give more definite instructions. I haven't heard from mother since I came here – (bar the letter you sent on) I have twice written since I left home. You might send this on to her, if it proves worth doing so. I am delighted you have felt Joker's jumping – I don't know any better. I feel all the same that unless he was well ridden over here he would not sell. We

1 They were writing up their tour in Wales.

The Real Charlotte. By E. Œ. Somerville and Martin Ross, authors of "An Irish Cousin," "Naboth's Vineyard," &c. In 3 vols. (Ward and Downey). The joint authors of this novel are well known to the readers of the LADY'S PICTORIAL, for they have contributed many a racy column to its pages. The book to which they have now appended their joint names is, in its way, clever and original, but the picture that it gives of lower middle class life in Ireland is not altogether agreeable ; the character drawing is, however, decidedly graphic, and there is abundant food for laughter in the first volume. The happy go-lucky mode of life, the curious mingling of shrewdness and childishness, the vulgarity which is offensive only when it becomes snobbish, and the irrepressible love of fun and frolic, are all so admirably hit off by the observant and clever collaborateurs, that we feel instinctively that they are drawing, for the most part, from life, and not merely giving fancy sketches in which imagination, not memory, plays the chief part.

But (there is always a "but"), the other side of the picture is not alluring, and I am sorry to be obliged to say that, as the story and the characters develop, and the seamy side of Miss Charlotte Mullen, Mr. Roddy Lambert, and others, is brought prominently into view, that my pleasure (I speak for myself only) in reading the book, gradually declined ; and not even the undoubted cleverness of the writers could reconcile me to the way in which the tale is worked out. The worst side of human nature has just now a strange fascination for novelists, and I fear that the power to make goodness attractive will become ere long, if our clever writers are not more careful, completely atrophied for want of use. English people who read this novel will be confirmed in their mistaken idea that Ireland is a nation of barbarians, for the authors have forgotten unfortunately, that without light and shade there is no real art, and as their story grew under their hands the light that glimmered in Vol. I. went out completely, and the book winds up in unrelieved gloom.

I am sorry that it is so, for the authors have the gift of delineating character very strongly developed, and, taken simply as specimens of clever character-drawing, nothing could be better than Miss Charlotte Mullen and her cats, "Norry the Boat," the Lamberts, and the foolish little heroine pretty Francie Fitzpatrick, who is allowed to make such a piteous muddle of her life. But was it worth while to expend such an amount of cleverness upon such a sorry crew ?

The next time that E. Œ. Somerville and Martin Ross combine to write a novel of Irish life I hope they will keep to the fun, with the undercurrent of sadness which is so typical of the Irish race, and devote their clever and graphic pens to the task of delineating men and women who are brave, generous, and noble, instead of wasting their powers upon elaborately finished pictures of the sordid-minded Charlotte Mullens and Roddy Lamberts, whose ill-spent lives need no historian.

Miss Charlotte snatched up the candle and held it close to her aunt's face. There was no mistaking what she saw there, and, putting the candle down again, she plucked a large silk handkerchief from her pocket, and with some hideous preliminary heavings of her shoulders, burst into transports of noisy grief.

A little later we see her walking in the garden. "The wrinkles in her forehead almost met the hair that grew so low down upon it as to seem like a wig that had been pulled too far over the turn of the brow, and she kept chewing at her heavy under lip, as was her habit during the processes of unobserved thought." And when she learns that her cousin is engaged to her lover, her colour "fades from red to dirty yellow," she tears his letter with her teeth, "moans like some furious feline creature," and after a scene of incredible frenzy, "staggered blindly to the sideboard, and, unlocking it, took out a bottle of brandy. She put the bottle to her mouth and took a long gulp from it while the tears ran down her face." Here is realism for those who like it, but for ourselves we find no fault with another character who calls her a "disgusting creature." Roddy Lambert, the object of her passion, and finally of her venge, is comparatively a civilised being, though a very great scoundrel. He marries a harmless, whimpering woman for her money, and spends his time in making love to Francie, Charlotte's cousin, who is a mere child. He persuades the child to marry him on the death of his first wife, and then delivers himself into the hands of his enemy by robbing his employer of £400. The child, on her part, is about to elope with another scoundrel, when her career is cut short by a fall from her horse. How the authors found the heart to invent so charming and innocent a character as Francie (when we first meet her) and then involve her in these sordid entanglements, we can hardly imagine. But the book is marked throughout by a persistent preference for ugly incident wherever possible. There is one gentleman in the story, and that is Christopher Dysart, who is drawn with considerable skill and perception, but even he must necessarily have a senile lunatic for a father. We should add, in fairness, that his sister and mother are admirably drawn, and that the scenes of country life in Irish Protestant circles are written with great knowledge if also with unfailing acidity. But take it for all in all, we can hardly imagine a book more calculated to depress and disgust even a hardened reader than "The Real Charlotte." The amours are mean, the people mostly repulsive, and the surroundings depressing.

went to a sale at Shepperd and Wade's on Saturday and saw *admirable* horses going for forty pounds – thirty seven pounds – and sixty one pounds – and one very smart brown mare for about twenty seven pounds – simply because they were not known. Hugh says it is always the way, a horse to sell well must be one of a string belonging to a well known man or woman – otherwise everyone buys from Hames the swagger dealer and gladly gives him a hundred pounds more than they would give anyone else. A Captain Burns Hartopp who was out today praised Novelty very much and thought her "a very good hunter". He thought she couldn't do with more than 12.7 and I think, in this killing country, he is right. He priced her at one hundred and twenty pounds, but said if I wanted to buy her from Hames he would ask two hundred pounds. Isn't it maddening? It is just Hames' reputation that enables him to ask what he likes. The meet was again a most extraordinary sight. About three hundred people nearly all well mounted and turned out to perfection. Nothing however strikes me more than the crowding and shoving at the gates on the way to the covert, and then when you hear "gone away" and are saying to yourself "How on earth shall I jam my way ahead", suddenly they have melted, and about fifty remain. I really don't think that more than fifty or sixty ride to the hounds. You see red coats on two hundred guinea horses *flying* to the nearest road and thundering along in a dense cloud, only confining themselves to the field when they know there are plenty of bridle roads, i.e. lines of reliable gates. This was what happened today when we found at a place called Welby Fishponds. It was a poor brute of a fox who ran in a big ring for two miles and back into covert again, being headed in all directions. At last he got away again, and we had some very hard going and good big jumping; Novelty went as well as if not better than the best. She never turned her head, or wanted to, I never saw anything like the way she will charge a thick place the like of which she never saw in her poor little life. Of course she generally had a lead, but it seemed to make very little difference to her. It seems to me that *most* of the falls that I have seen came from funk on either horse or rider's part. They check in front of the fence and then the horse slides into the gripe and stays there. Poor Mrs. Asquith got an awful fall, but it most surely was not from funk. Her horse took some timber with his knees and pitched neck and crop over. How she escaped was a marvel. Her hat was smashed, and the horse all but fell on her. She went on again as if nothing had happened.

I offered her to try Novelty, but she said she was too unlucky and wouldn't risk it. Mrs. Bunbury, sister to John Meath Watson, and said to be the hardest rider in Cheshire, was out, and has asked about the mare, and is I think to try her on Thursday or Friday. There was a lucky moment today. A check, and then Tom Firr cantered down to the foot of a hill and jumped a stile with a widish ditch on the far side; it was down hill, and a rather greasy take off. Sissy and I were close to him, and after waiting a minute or two we jogged on and went for the stile. Sissy's horse, Pilot, is a nailer, and made nothing of it, and I may say Novelty did it quite as well as he did. Hugh told us afterwards that Hames and several of these possible buyers watched the mare with much interest, and it was soon after that Mrs. Bunbury said she would like to try her. I fear Mrs. Asquith is no go. We had bad luck in the way of foxes, none of them would run straight rings more or less large, and back into the covert and the phalanx of roadsters. I saw the hounds chop one fox . . . if he had had a good heart and gone away he would have been all right as the scent was pretty bad. Tell A. that he and Collins don't scream half enough. Tom Firr and his whips utter long falsetto shrieks when the fox goes away, and all the whips have silver whistles and blow like mad and the row brings the hounds headlong out of covert. They have plenty of music and are perfectly lovely, and Tom Firr's casts are only equal to Aylmer's that day at Bunalun. At two thirty we started to ride about thirty miles home. It was no good staying, and we left them at the same old place where we had begun the day. We are going out tomorrow with the Cottesmore – I don't know what I'm going to ride. No one need expect a letter from me – possibly I may have time to write when I get to Constance's – I have just had a hot bath and am scrawling this before dinner – Mr. Giles, the horse painter has come. He is like a tall, fairly goodlooking Maurice Cave T. He was in an Indian cavalry regiment but chucked it for art. I enclose a line from Alice Penrose – Edith's letter was very interesting. How I should have roared crying if I had seen that V.C. presented. I must stop now as it is dinner time – love to all

    Ever yours
    Edith

[*Edith's note added later*: Liss Ard Hunt]

Drishane
December 5th 94
Wednesday

My dear Edith

I had this morning *another* cheque from B and W[1] for £4.4 shillings. Two guineas were for the literary matter of the last two of the Beggars.[2] Two for ditto of the first Quartier Latinity. The Beggars are now disposed of. I send the cheque as it is payable to you. There is £9 9 shillings altogether for us to divide – an almost impossible sum – It is I think £4 14 shillings and six pence each. Again, and in shame, I must ask to have my half. There are Crowley, Jerry, Collins and others to face before I go home. I will lodge the five guinea cheque in your bank straight away – and perhaps you will send me a cheque for my beastly moiety. It will find me here, as Mama has not been well, and has put off her journey. Your letter that came yesterday was full of interest to me – but you have yet things to tell. Where do you sit in the evenings, and *can* you

---

1 *B and W*: Black and White.
2 *Beggars*: Beggars on Horseback.

draw in the club, as you certainly couldn't in the game keeper's room.
Is it as small as the one H had. Does Kinkead improve on further
knowledge? I don't know what she is really. How nice of Leonard to
have breakfast for the poor traveller. How nasty of madame not to ask
for us. Is the Studio crammed? *Do you work too hard?* You do. Do you
take a little morning walk? You don't. What do you do in the evenings?
I want to know all these things. There has been a letter from Sissie C.
thanking H. for the violets, and saying she hoped Novelty would be all
right very soon — that your visit had been such a pleasure and that
Hugh was devoted to you. These things I grudgingly repeat, to avoid
forwarding the letter. Captain Welch told me yesterday that a thorn
took a fortnight to come out. This brings me to the fact that yesterday
Hildegarde, as a Christmas present, *insisted* on my riding Joker. His
back was not all that it ought to be, however the old white saddle fitted
him very well. The men say that your saddle is the only one that fits
every horse. The meet was Liss Ard — Eddy and Percy rode with me,
and on Carn Dhure the Cairns carriage met us. The young chestnut
suddenly whirled from it, nearly upset Joker into Shanacluan and fled
for home. Eddy held him to the Pound, where he ran into a donkey
cart, deposited E. on the road and galloped to Cross Street, where he
was stopped by Harry Becher. Eddie then mounted and came on, very
dusty and rather white about the gills. Percy abused the chestnut soundly
to me, and I hear that this turning suddenly is a trick of his. Creedon
told me so, after having said "Major Aylmer is separated from his horse"
— a very delicate phrase — At Lissard a good field of 14. Sinnie not out.
They drew the whole place blank! and it was a lovely soft grey day. It
then transpired that the trapper had carefully trapped two foxes the
night before — the brute. He produced one and wanted to be paid for
it! It was shaken in the top gorse and speedily killed in the top covert,
and the hounds gobbled him which I suppose was well. Joker was fidgety
but had no stirk.* We then drew Laherdan, blank, then went up onto
Bludth, at which juncture Eddy, Tessie Jennings, and Captain Welch
retired. We drew the whole way round Bludth without a sniff of anything
and came back to Lissard. The old Madam's gorse did not fail this time.
After great excitement and nearly chopping and much jumping of the
new bank back of the madam's he was got to run up to the Lissard
coverts. We lost him in the one above the target field then suddenly got
him away down to the furthest screens to the north. Then total silence
— and they seemed coming round the old ring. Mr. Warren, too cute,
went up to where the two avenues meet, and so did I and the rest. —
After some minutes of waiting the Myross Woods and I went to look

and distantly viewed Aylmer by the furthest screen flying for Lick – as it were. We rushed over the bounds ditch. I jumping well on top of the Slug, then much tearing, and we were sure the hounds, Aylmer and Collins were out of sight and going *north*. We could see nothing – at least I couldn't till at last there was another glimpse of Aylmer at the far side of Mahony's land, going like blazes, but for what point it was impossible to imagine. There were horrid blind fences, turnip fields, upright slates. Joker waltzed over all – at last a very bad place – country people waved us on. Joker jumped superbly a horrid stiley bank with an upright bayonet at the only feasible spot, and Mildred and Mr Warren were pounded for a bit. I flew on, awfully bewildered, but vaguely feeling direction – and got down by the left side of Mr. Goodman's Rectory to the Creagh road. There a screaming boy, too mad with excitement to answer for some time. He at last yelled "straight over the hill opposite" Mildred and Mr Warren picked me up at this instant – and we rushed for the railway crossing a little up towards Creagh – across the railway up a lane. "In to your right" roars Mr. Warren – I *inned* up a stile Mr. Warren again roaring it was too bad a place – Mildred followed – Richard and Mr. W had to try higher up. We thought we were pounded by a huge bank – unjumpable I now think, at which I crammed Joker and he very properly swerved away and over a side fence – one more, and then huge fields, and *very* big straight up splendid banks. From this juncture I may say with modest pride I cut out the work. I could see all right in those lovely great fields and just put in the north westerly direction, as I knew the fox couldn't run into Skib or into the river I had small hope of catching them, but anyhow, I knew it was my chance for pace and lepping. I crossed two enormous fields, the second fence a towering one – or so it seemed to me – Joker made nothing of it. Looking back I just saw someone in the distance picking up Mildred at the same fence, and was thankful someone was there. I was still more thankful when a cottage hove up in my line – belting and lepping I got within screech, the people pointed down below. I flew, and ecstasy – the note of a hound, the pack casting, and Aylmer and Collins in a ravine above the river – a good bit west of the bridge between the two roads. The next person up was Percy, who had had a much worse start even than me – then Mildred with her hat stove in, and Richard. The hounds were away again to the west in a moment, great lepping of lovely banks with ditches then down on to the road, a cast along by the river, then the hounds, hunting finely swung into the fields again, with the same kind of big honest fences and out onto the road about half a mile lower down than New Court. There the fox got into a gully by the river, it was getting dark and we chucked up. It was quite the best run I ever had except Meath – once we were out of the Lissard abominations – though there was misery and uncertainty. The pace was as good as I ever knew here. Joker is indeed a great horse. There were three times that he distinctly swerved from a jump, each time because a horse was refusing in front of him. When he got away by himself he was beyond praise – and each time that he had swerved he jumped the second try with a sort of fury. Percy rode a great hunt on Harry, to have picked us up as he did. He said "By George that little horse *did* carry you well. I *couldn't* get any nearer to you." Harry must have done wonders anyhow. Dairymaid was very good, but refused a few big things – only once. Aylmer and Collins say they never jumped bigger things than on that hill oposite the Rectory – and certainly they seemed to me very big – but it is hard to judge. Mildred belarded me with compliments, and was altogether friendly & very keen and plucky. I don't think I rode Joker at all well coming through Mahoney's land – but it wasn't quite my fault. I had to let Mildred or Mr. Warren choose the line as I couldn't tell what the right direction was – However Joker made up for my deficiencies. His back was a tiny bit rubbed on the bad place, but it is nothing I think – Joe is as stiff as a crutch. Dairymaid has a lump on her back, where a slightly sore place is but Aylmer thinks nothing of it. A sicker man than Mr. Warren you never saw. He couldn't get the Slug over the bank that Mildred fell at – not even by leading, and had to go right back to the lane – and then went away up to the Old Court, thinking that was our line – and never saw us again. I can't pity him. Why doesn't he buy a good horse?

Now this long and hysterical drivel must end. It is hysterical because I never thought to see the day where I would rush a fine horse through a fine country without a lead. You did much more when you belted Novelty out of Lissard to the short ring when she was as green as grass – but then I expect it from you and not from myself – Goodbye – and forgive much tediousness and bad writing –

Yours ever
Martin

A letter showing how Edith and Martin's reputation was spreading after the publication of The Real Charlotte. *It incidentally reveals Edith's expressive face; she would not have made a good poker player.*

[From Edith to Martin, winter 1894: *fragment*]

... Windle's? Ah I knew her very well in old days in Kingstown – the Maariner's Church y' know. Is that young lady yr sister? She's very like Mrs Windle" (H. at this moment was looking from heat & tea like a parboiled Martha Rix) "Yes, & poor Mr Windle too. Ah, he was a very clever man" (My countenance must have expressed dissent) "Well, he was very clever at religion. Oh, he was a wonderfully holy man. Now that's what I'd call him – holy. And he used to talk like that – nothing but religion: he certainly was most clever at it." Later on in the conversation, which lasted half an hour – "Are *you* the Miss Somerville who writes books with Miss Martin! Now! To think I should have been talking to you all this time! And is it you that do the story & Miss Martin the" (&c &c for some time –) "And do you put in every one you meet? No? only sometimes? And sometimes people you never met? Well, I declare, that's like direct inspiration!" Again "Do you travel much? I love it. I think Abroad's very pretty. Do you like Abroad?" And much more, which I forget. Preserve these reminiscences: if I meet her again I may glean more. She also told me that "Mr Coghill & his wife had just gone to Dublin – to see the great tree y' know!" By the aid of "direct inspiration" I guessed that she meant Beerbohm of that ilk, but as she had not mentioned a theatre, I think it was pretty good for me. It is going to be a lovely day & I must try & paint something. Have you any other Black & W. duplicate copies? I now have No 1, & two letter copies of No 2. Please send me the dates 3 & 4. I must absolutely stop.

    Goodbye.

    Yours ever,

    Edith

While Edith was once more away at her art studies, Martin went on a visit to St Andrews and had her first experience of being treated as a literary lioness. Here she made friends with Andrew Lang, who was to do much to further the partnership's career. Martin's initial pleasure at T. P. O'Connor's long and thoughtful review of The Real Charlotte *in the* Weekly Sun *turned to indignation when she fathomed that O'Connor took the authors for* shoneens *themselves. (Shoneen was an Irish term of abuse for those who aped things English; that is, as a Nationalist such as T. P. O'Connor would describe them, sycophantics who were traitors to Ireland) She had fallen down the stairs again at Ross.*

Kinburn West Saint Andrews
January 16th 95
Wednesday

Dear Edith

Your letter written on Sunday night walked in this morning, while yet
I lay beneath the eiderdown. There was hardly light to read it, so grey
and drizzly was the morning. You were good to write when your sleep
is so valuable to you and I never expected it. I had also a line from
Hildegarde, saying the Hunt Ball is knocked on the head for want of a
room – which is a pity not that it especially affects you or me. And here
I am – got in yesterday morning with a bad back, a cold, and the
beginning of a sore lip – but without headache or sickness. I had a very
good crossing, about five and a half hours and was neither sick nor
sorry. Small boats but awfully clean, and I had three sulphonals[1] laid
in. She rolled a bit, and I was frightened for a time, but finally got to
sleep. It was rather horrid turning out into a cold train but being stacked
with clothes I was all right – then an hour's belting to Glasgow. Then
an hour of waiting in the warm vestibule of the Central Station Hotel
– then on from another station at six a.m., a slow and reluctant daylight
appeared at eight. I changed for the last time at a place called Leuchars,
and so here at nine – a long journey I can tell you, by reason of the
many changings and cab drivings, and by reason of my back, which
gave me rather a poor time – I hurt it horribly two or three times in
getting in and out of carriages, – and was rather depressed about it
altogether – however it is pounds better today – quite a different feeling.
I am sure it was a bad bruise of the muscles and Elliman is serving it –
and so is sitting quietly in a warm room. I retired to bed for a good bit
yesterday, and came down to tea, rather rocky but still undefeated. And
with help was able to dress for dinner – I don't think I looked *too* bad
in spite of all. I was ladylike and somewhat hectic and hollow eyed. The
Langs have rooms in a large house – and their dinner party was fourteen.
Principal Donaldson and his wife – Sheriff Henderson and his wife – a
Mr and Mrs Everard, one or two others and an ugly nice youth who
was my portion. I was put at Andrew Lang's left and was not shy – but
anxious – A. L. is very curious to look at – tall, very thin, white hair
growing far down his forhead and shading dark eyebrows and piercing-
looking, charming brown eyes. He has a somewhat foxey profile a lemon
pale face and a black moustache. Altogether very quaint looks and

1 *Sulphonals*: drugs taken for seasickness. Edith used cocaine for the same purpose.

appropriate. I think he is shy – his age about 45 – He keeps his head down and often does not look at you when speaking, his voice is rather high, and indistinct, and he pitches his sentence out with a jerk. Anyhow I paid court to my own young man for soup and fish time – and found him most agreeable and clever – and I *did* talk of hunting, and he was mad about it so now. To me then Andrew L with a sort of offhand fling – "I suppose you're the one who did the writing – " I explained with some care that it was not so – He said he didn't know how any two people could equally evolve characters etc – that he had tried, and it was always he or the other that did it all – I said I didn't know how we managed, but anyhow that I knew little of bookmaking as a science. He said I must know a good deal – On which I had nothing to say – and talked of other things. I haven't the face to discuss *Charlotte* – I knew from the Jacksons that he admired the book very much and that was enough. He talked of Rhoda Broughton, Stephenson, Mrs. H. Ward and others, as personal friends – and exhibited at intervals a curious silent laugh up under his nose. He will be very nut crackery as an old man, though his nose is straight. He told me he pitched *David Grieve* out of the window of the train in almost ten minutes, and advised me not to read *Mariella* – He praised Mrs. Ward but deplored her total lack of humour. He was so interesting that I hardly noticed how ripping was the dinner – Just as well cooked as it could be – everything of the very best and quite regardless. I retired on my own man for a while, and Andrew upon Mrs. Donaldson then my youth and he and I had a long talk about Oscar Wilde and others. Altogether I have seldom been more entertained and at ease. After dinner the matrons were introduced and were very civil and praised *Charlotte* for its "delightful humour and freshness and newness of feeling" – and so on – one said that her son told her he would get anything else of ours he could lay his hands on – Long before she knew anything of me. Then the men again – I shared an unknown man with a matron – then the good and kind Andrew drew a chair up and discovered me, and told me how he is writing a life of Joan of Arc "the greatest human being since Jesus Christ". He seems *wonderfully* informed on all subjects – to hear him reel off the historical surroundings of the book of Esther would surprise you and also would slightly raise your back hair.* He offered to give me a lesson in golf, but I pleaded the 'eadache, and he said they would have a match for me to see. He and his wife dine here on Saturday next. Mrs. Jackson told me I was highly honoured as he very often wont talk to people and is rude. I must say I thought he was in his jerky unconventional way polite to everyone. Mrs. A. L. is a nice little woman, not unlike him, with a pile of grey hair drawn up from her forehead. She was awfully kind and friendly and very like an old miniature. That is so far my experience of the society here. Mrs. Boyd, wife of the country parson, comes here tomorrow to meet Miss V. Martin along with her daughter Mrs Granby Burke. It is a cultured place, and all the new books are here – I am into the *Raiders* already and many others lie around. It is a semi-detached suburban house, most comfortable and roomy, and has lovely Chip. and Sheraton things in the drawing room and old silver. My bed is luxurious, ditto my bath, and the food is excellent. I have seen nothing of the place as yet, it being wet, but a college boy hifling* by in his red gown was refreshing to see, and an old sportsman in a kilt. I found it very hard to understand the porters. One at Glasgow said, as I thought, "Is this only half" taking my bonnet box, after long pondering I realised he had said "is this oll ye hahf" I will further write of things as they arise – Don't tell Miss Studman anything about my version of the Langs except vague laudations. It would not be safe. She seems a nice creature and I am glad you have her next you this week. Big Mary Barnard must be a refreshment – with her extraordinary animal spirits and talent. Kinkead is well-bred, I said so the first day we went to see her – she is posée and has much intelligence besides. I wish I had been walking in the moonlight by the Seine. It is like a dream to think of it. Talking to Andrew Lang has made me feel that nothing I could write could be any good – He seems to have seen the end of perfection – I will take my stand on *Charlotte* I think and learn to make my own clothes – and so subside noiselessly into middle age. Thursday morning – I couldn't finish this yesterday having many letters to write. I must write to your mother now – having sworn to do so. Constance's letter was very amusing – the bonnet that the dogs ran away with amused me especially, and will all my life. I will keep it for you – *How* can I meet you in London on the first of March when I am hifling* straight back to Ross in a fortnight – there to stay indefinitely? But it is no use to talk of plans. It requires special firmness and hardihood to carry out any – and also money. As to that two pounds that is between us, I will if you like say no more – take it as a series of Christmas presents, to extend over thirty or forty years – but you know it is nonsense that you should pay my way to Castle T. Why shouldn't I pay your way to Ross the next time you go there? It is a very strange thing that I should be so much more successful at Drishane when you are not there – but it is a fact. A child might have played with your mother throughout – therefore I did so with a success that terrified myself. Everyone liked me much better, and I was much nicer to them. I cannot explain how or why, but it is so. I suppose people used to think that I only cared for your society, and I have always told you that I am at my worst when you are by. It is quite true. You make me shy and cross in some mysterious way – and I think your mother is like that too. She prefers your company to anyone's, but it seems over stimulating. So don't tell me again I don't get on well with your mother. I can get on with her forever when you aren't there. It is *you* who fight, and then my heart takes part with you and I turn horrible. It is a very intricate position, and has often made you justly angry with me, but believe me there is a basis of good feeling and always was, and it has often lately touched me to see how your mother has suppressed in talking to me the home truth that in early days would have flown from her lips, and would have roused the spirit of combat in me. This is a strange dissertation, and confused – but I thought of it all a good deal and I think I had better stay at Drishane only when you are away in Paris – and I am sure Hildegarde would agree with me. She used daily to cross herself regarding the Millenium harmony. But for all that your mother and I would rather fight and have you there – strange as it may appear ... Good-bye. Don't be killing yourself to write. It's not fair when you are so busy.

Yours ever
Martin

Kinburn West
St Andrews
January 23rd 95

My dear Edith.
Yesterday morning I heard the crackle of the foreign envelope in the hand of Jane as she came in. "Confound it," says I, "more letters from this bore", and I was very late for breakfast, – the Jacksons were too kind to say anything of blame. They are *very* kind – she transcends all I have known for her tenderness and nice friendly dealings. She wishes that you were here, and would gladly hike you over from Paris if she could – she says in her innocence, that we would be the most delightful pair to have in her house. Perhaps it conveys a little the simple and slightly old fashioned feeling about her to mention that in a prayer book lent me by Mr. Jackson last Sunday there was an inscription "To my dear husband", in her writing. Yet she is young, about forty I should say and she has a curious look now and then of that poor little Madame of the restaurant who has died in that pitiable way. I was very sorry to

hear of that. I am sure she was ill last spring. It must have been horrid to come in and find it all over, but I do hope you won't go to the funeral. It would be the best way in the world of catching cold – you might have to walk through the streets after the coffin too. I often wish you had seen someone dead. I should like to know how you felt about it, and I think it does one good, though it is excessively painful, but yet I should try to shield you from it when it came to the point. Mrs. Warren's letter was very strange and well worth the additional two pence hapenny. There but for something or other went a good and charming intellect. (Ha ha! She likes the Luxembourg article). Her little allusion to Novelty is very nice – and she is altogether a better lady than her husband – yet to appreciate her he must be nice. Her Christmas lines were wild and absurd. There is where the madness lurks – I will keep it for you. When shall I be able to give it to you in person. It seems a long way off – more than is good. If it means May we shall hardly know each other. *How* could I go to Paris – I should have no reason for such extravagance. But indeed I wish you could stay longer; now that you are going ahead so fast. The Chimp is coming at a most inconvenient time poor creature. He ought to be about home now, I suppose. I have writen a long letter to your mother, and hope for a return soon. Hildegarde has written me two frenzied sheets, in all, since I left – but she cannot help it. For some mysterious reason she has more letters to write than anyone in the world. I do trust that Joker is by this time carrying her across country – and that what you said about Old Harry has sunk in.

I am all right about money for the present, having had fifty pounds from Ross – I have paid some debts, and will pay more. You are – very much what you always have been, in offering to stand by. My dear – if it were not so awfully foolish I could put xxs in that place, like the children – You will understand that I have *not* done so because I don't want you to laugh at me.

Thursday morning. In bed before I am called. Do you know that even now the sun doesn't rise here till 8.30 and at the worst it is not seen till about a quarter to nine. It is the amazing cold of the wind makes one know that this is pretty far north yet I don't mind the cold. I have had that fur lined coat turned into a new one by Moore, a light colour this time, I wear it on all occasions. It has kept the life in me – and has been much applauded. Thank goodness I have finished the *Raiders* from about the middle it began to pall, and *Silver Sand* was extremely near becoming a bore. I have also read the *Dolly Dialogues*, which in parts is very amusing – very like *Dodo* in all ways, only far more amusing – I am reading *Barabbas* – which is stodgy and turgid, but not irreverent. I rejoice to hear of your reading Sterne. I never thought it of you, and I cannot believe that anything in his style is like mine – I have not read the *Sentimental Journey*, but have looked through it. Isn't it improper? In the fine old shameless gleeful way. Of course I remember all about Julia Cameron, and pity her very much. I never heard of any row between her and Connie but of course there may easily have been one. Nor was there any flirtation between her and Robert – but Robert admired her feet very much. That may of course have done it – or Connie may have been merely neglectful.

Since I last wrote various have been the dissipations. Afternoon teas, two dinners, an organ recital, a concert. It is very amusing. They are all, as people, more interesting than the average, being Scotch. And they have a high opinion of *Charlotte*. I am beginning to be accustomed to having people introduced to me, and feeling that they expect me to say something clever. I never do – I am merely very conversational, and feel in the highest spirits, which is the effect of the air. It is pleasant to hear Mrs. Jackson tell how she went into an assembly of women (among them Mrs. A. Lang, and a very clever woman who wears *a false nose*) and heard them raving of *Charlotte*. She then said "I know one of the authors and she is coming to stay with me". The Langs dined here on Saturday, also a Professor Purdie and Mr. Corbould, whom I had slight dealings with at Ross last summer. Andrew Lang took me in, but unfortunately Mr. Corbould was on my other hand, and had no lady, so that I had to talk to him a good deal. Considering also that I paid him every court last summer I couldn't go back on it so conversation was interrupted on both sides and Andrew talked to Mrs. Jackson who says she can't get on with him. Anyhow he found time to heap scorn upon Stainton Moses' books – I spoke of *Spirit Teachings* with caution and respect, and he gave one of his dreary crows of laughter and told me I mustn't mind all that stuff – I said I thought it seemed very like what Mrs. Humphrey Ward and many others had said. He said quite simply that it was stale and stupid, and obviously the unconscious outpouring of S. Moses' own mind. I must say I had thought that what are supposed to be S. Moses' sole struggles against Imperator were the feeblest and most leading remonstrances I had ever read, and A. L. said that Stainton Moses was an excellent man but he seemed unfeignedly amused when I said that I had several cousins who put *Spirit Teachings* above the Bible (your mother being one) and as literature.

In the evening Mr. Jackson showed some very good slides, (he is an excellent though quite unartistic photographer) mostly ruins, old churches and the like, being things Andrew is interested in. He ended with some statuary groups from outside South Kensington, I think, horrible blacks on the backs of camels etc. On the first glimpse of these Andrew, who had, I think been getting bored, shuddered and fled away into the next room – refusing to return till all was over. "If you had any Greek statues," he said feebly, but there was none. Then I was turned on to shriek like a dog, and he was bewildered and perturbed, but not amused. He asked me in an unhappy way how I did it, I said by main strength, the way the man played the fiddle. This was counted a good jest. On that the Langs left, he saying in a vague dejected way apropos of nothing "if you'd like me to take you around the town sights, I'll go – perhaps if Monday were fine" – He then faded out of the house. On Monday no sign of him – nor on Tuesday either. I withered in neglect though assured that he never kept appointments or did anything. On yesterday he sent word that he would come at 2.30 and he really did. The weather was furiously arctic – "Dr. Nansen, I presume" said I, coming in dressed and ready. He looked quite foolish, and admitted that it was a bad day for explorations. (Monday had been lovely) However we went. You will observe that I was keeping my tail very erect. In the *iron* blast we went down to South Street where most things are. It is a little like the High at Oxford, on a small, trimmed scale. He was immediately very nice and I think likes showing people around. Have I mentioned that he is a gentleman – it is worth mentioning – He was a most perished looking one with his white face, and his grey hair under a deer-stalker, but still he looks all that. I wont at this time tell you of all the churches and places he took me to. It was pleasant to hear him, in the middle of the leading Presbyterian church and before the pew opener call John Knox a scoundrel with intensest venom. In one little particular you will applaud me. He showed me a place where Lord Bute is scrabbling up the ruins of an old friary and building ugly red sandstone imitations on the foundations. I said with sufficient archness "the sacred keep of Ilion is rent". This is the first line of a sonnet by Andrew Lang in my Century book, mourning the modern prying into the story of Troy. It was successful. I also called him Saint Andrew Lang but this I fear has been done before. I was not at all afraid of him, and made him laugh very much by quoting "that carneying mass of affectations, the female dog". *He* also has written an attack on dogs – unaware of Stephenson's. He keeps and adores a cat, which he says hates him. I was quite intimate with him, yet don't know him in the least, and I *think* he is friendly towards me. He is so queer one cannot tell. While in the college library Dr. Boyd (the country parson) came in and spoke to him. I examined the nearest book case, but was aware of the C. P.'s china blue eye upon me – and he presently spoke to me. I think he knew who I was – but the conversation was not long or special, only about the library and so on. He is like a clean, rubicund priest, with a high nose – more than all he is like a creditable ancestor on the wall, and should have a choker and high coat collar. His wife (the barrel on castors) is now gloating over *Charlotte*, and I go to tea there tomorrow. *Why* aren't you here to take your share? I said to Andrew that I thought of going up to Edinburgh on Monday to see a few things, and he said he would be there, and would show me Holyrood. I have got his address and will write to him, he said in his resigned voice "I'll meet you anywhere you like," and wanted me to go to the house of the people they are going to stay with. Mr. Jackson comes up with me, so it is quite proper. I think Mrs. Lang is delighted to find anyone to amuse him. She doesn't I think care much about him, and he shrugs his shoulders and says he isn't his own master. I am going to write to Mr. Blackwood, who asked me to go and see him. It might be useful and I will ask him if he would like the Beggars. Andrew Lang wants to go there too. It will be very strange if we go there together. Now you must be sick of A. L. I will mention only two or three more things about him. He put a notice of *Charlotte* into some American Mag. for which he writes – before he knew me. I believe it is a good one – but am rather shy of asking about it. He told me that *Charlotte* treated of quite a new phase – and seemed to think that that was its chiefest merit. He would prefer our writing in future more of the sort of people one is likely to meet in everyday life. He put his name in the Mark Twain Birthday Book – March 31st. A not very remarkable text. Lastly I may remark that when he leaves Saint Andrews tomorrow all other men go with him – as far as I am concerned – or rather they stay, and they seem bourgeois and common place – all except my nice Mr. Jackson, who is always what one likes. Tonight Mrs. Jackson has ten people to dinner – among them a nice priest, Father Angus, who was once a soldier. I met him last night at Professor Knight's – and liked him very much – as much as I hated Professor Knight who is by way of being a literary boss. His breath was *pestilence* and his conversation purely perfunctory, and he described the scenery of Galway to me, having gone round with Mr. Greene, in the Fisheries yacht. He took the opportunity of telling me how he had written to Mr. Balfour and thus got Mr. Greene his appointment. He succeeded in making me sick, and in driving away Father Angus who was squatted on a milking stool at my left hand. Evidently Father A. detested him, as do most people here. He fortunately went off, finding me very dull, and my good little priest and Mr. Jackson at once flew to me, and were delightful for the rest of the evening. Father A. said he had just sent an article to the *Tablet* in which he said that something was as real as the *Real Charlotte*. He says he will send me the paper. We went to an organ recital two days ago given in the college chapel by Farmer, the Harrow organist lately removed to Oxford. I was disappointed. He played a big Beethoven sonata; quite correctly, and quite without power to move. How much should I have prefered to have heard one of the Nocturnes by a hand that I wot of very well. Yesterday a Miss Christie gave a concert in the hall of St. Leonard's Ladies' college here – a charming hall, and Miss C. had a good contralto, and sung Bois Epais and many nice things. She had huge sleeves and long black gloves and her arms looked like poodles' legs. She sang right through. We had tea on Sunday with Mr. Corbould, who has nice books and photographs, and has lent me a very interesting number of the *Art Journal*, devoted to Burne Jones.

Post has come, bringing a most unexpected tribute to the *Real Charlotte* from T. P. O'Connor, in the *Weekly Sun*. It is really one of the best & best-written notices we have ever had – and I read it with high gratification. Your mother sent it to me, with injunctions that it was to be sent on *today* to you. It was very wrong of her to send it to me at all, as it was sent to you. On it goes anyhow to you – and well you deserve it. I am going to send for copies, and to beg that your mother sends one round the Family. I do wish that one of the family could be here for a week. It would do them good. Armstrong of *Black and White* has written to say that he would like something about Saint Andrews, or Scotland from an Irish point of view. "But what about the artist?" says he – what indeed – and I don't know what to write about. Everyone has written about Saint Andrews. I saw them play the game of curling, which was very funny – like bowls played on ice, with big round stones that slide. With a photograph you might be able to do a picture. The friends of a stone tear in front of it as it skates, sweeping the ice with twigs – I mean brooms. So as to further its slide. When a good bowl is made they say "fine stone". It is in many ways absurd. I see that the hunt ball *is* to come off – and that the Chimp is in London – also that Egerton has applied for Lord Darnley's agency . . . Write to me on Sunday if you can. Goodbye. Tell me every little thing.

Yours ever

Martin

Kinburn West
Saint Andrews
January 29th
Tuesday

Dear Edith
As usual I am awake early therefore I will make a beginning. It is really
my only time for the kind of letter it pleases me to write to you. Although
the last time I did it I spilled ink on Mrs. Jacksons lovely sheet with a
drawn border. She has lovely linen. The legion of towels in my room
are borderd and garnished in every sort of way, & here is snow – that
of all Scotland we have been free from till now. It is an odious game.
Are you frozen? I studied the temperature lists in the *Standard*, and Paris
doesn't seem to bad. But I think of you on Sunday mornings, and wonder
whether your little stove manages to keep your little room warm as I
suppose the club fire is not lighted early. Are you getting any fatter? Do
try to. I feel a little fatter, but have been thrown back by something that
felt like turning to nettle rash, partly from the frost, partly from inward
acidity. Certainly it is a severe winter. This house is so very warm that
one doesn't mind it, and my gas fire is a joy. It is going this moment
like billyo, and the room glows with it. The dissipations have raged –
and I have been much courted by the Saint Andrew's ladies. I shall not
come back here again – having created an impression I shall retire on it
before they begin to find me out. It will be your turn next – though
Mrs. Jackson says she will not rest till she has had us here together. You
know that I had settled to meet Andrew Lang in Edinburgh. Mrs. Lang
wrote the day they got there to say that the Butchers, with whom they
were staying, wanted me and Mr. Jackson to lunch there – being proud
to be my compatriots. Mr. B is professor of Greek at Edinburgh university, and is a nephew of that Bishop of Meath who cut his throat. Mrs
B. was a Trench, of the Archbishop lot. Accordingly yesterday I hied
me forth *alone* to Edinburgh as neither of the Jacksons could or would
come. It was a lovely hard frost here, but by the time I was half way,
the ground began to be white – (it is about as far as going to Cork from
Skib) I may mention that I was well dressed – in new garments – a
smart black crepon skirt with big crinkles in the stuff, lavender silk
blouse with black lace, covert coat, big black felt hat with bunch of
heliotrope velvet – quite the lady – clothes sent by Mrs. Dawson. I have
a body for the crepon, trimmed with green broidery in the fashion
somewhat of a Norfolk jacket, beautifully fitting – a Holmes – so now.
I drove to the Butchers along Princes Street, all beastly with snow, but

my breath was taken away by the beauty of it. There is a deep fall of ground along one side where there was once a lake, then with one incredible lep up towers the crag – three hundred feet and the castle and the ramparts all along the top. It was foggy, with sun struggling through and to see that thing hump its great shoulder into the haze was fine. You know I affect Scott – so would you if you once saw Edinburgh. It was almost overwhelming to think of all that has happened there – However to resume – before you are bored. Andrew he received me so dacent and so pleasant, he's as nice a man in fayture as I ever seen before – He is indeed – a most correct and rather effeminate profile. No one else was in – He was as miserable about the snow as a cat, and huddled into a huge coat lined with sable. In state we drove up to the Castle by a long round, and how the horse got up that slippery hill I don't know. The Castle was very grand, snowy court yards with grey old walls and chapels and dining halls – most infinitely preferable to Frederiksborg. The view should have been noble, as it was one could only see Scott's monument – a very fine thing – and a very hazy town. My word, it is an awful thing to look over those parapets. The Black Watch was drilling in the outer court yard, very grand, and a piper went strutting like a turkey cock and skirling. It was wild – and I stood up by Mons Meg and was thrilled. Is it an insult to mention that Mons Meg is the huge historic old gun, and crouches like a she mastiff on the topmost crag, glaring forth over Edinburgh with the most concentrated defiance? You couldn't believe the expression of that gun. I asked Andrew L whether it was the same as Muckle-mouthed Meg, having vague memories of the name. He said in a dying gasp that Muckle-mouthed Meg was his great-great-grandmother. That was a bad miss, but I preserved my head just enough to enquire what had become of the Muckle mouth. (I may add that his own is admirable) He could only say with some slight embarrassment that it must have gone in the other line. We solemnly viewed the Regalia, of which he knew the history of every stone, and the room where James VI was born, a place about as big as a dinner table, and so on – and his information on all was petrifying. I wanted to buy a photograph or two, and he insisted on giving me half a dozen brown etching gravures – two and sixpence worth – not at all bad. Then it was all but lunch time, but we flew into Saint Giles' on the way home to see Montrose's tomb. A more beautiful and charming face than Montrose's you couldn't see – and the church is a very fine one. An old verger caught sight of us, and instantly flung to the winds a party he was taking round, and endeavoured to show us everything in spite of A.L.'s protests. I at length very firmly said "please show us the door out" knowing that luncheon was waiting. He smiled and led us to a door, which when opened led into an oaken and carven little room. He snatched a book from a shelf, and a pen and ink from somewhere else. "I know distinguished visitors when I see them" says he, showing us the signatures of all the royalties and distinguished people – about two on each page – "Please write your names." Andrew wrote his – and I mine – on a blank sheet – and there they remain for posterity. Andrew swears he didn't know him, and that it was all the fur coat – and that our names were a bitter disappointment. Why didn't I put "Princess of Connemara". Then to lunch – and the generous Andrew insisted on paying the cab that I had taken at the station and kept throughout. The Butchers were very nice. He is tall and thin with an ink black moustache. She short, about thirty five or more, and as pleasant and unconventional and easy as nice Irish people alone are – After lunch she and Mrs. Lang tackled me in the drawing room (it is a very nice house – opulent and tasty) about the original of the *Real Charlotte*. I gaily admitted that she was drawn from life – and that you had known her a thousand times better than I – none the less I told the tale of my interview with her. This revealed the fact that her name was Emily Herbert. "Oh yes" says Mrs. B in ecstacy, "she was my husband's cousin" I covered my face with my hands, and I swear that the blush trickled through my fingers – I then rose and attempted to fly the house in strong convulsions. Professor B. was called in, and said she was only a very distant cousin and that he had never seen her, and didn't care what I had said of her. They were *enchanted* about it and my confusion. But think of the Brigade-Surgeon[1] having been at that house in Edinburgh – that was the only time they ever saw him – I went away presently having discovered that Mr Butcher had in his youth been at Castle T and Glandore. They have a house at Killarney to which they go in summer and they have asked me to go there with delightful cordiality. (But he has not yet read the *Real Charlotte*.) Andrew L and I then walked forth to Blackwoods – a very fine old fashioned place with interesting pictures. We were instantly, and with respect shown upstairs, to a large pleasant room, and Mr. Blackwood greeted us in a pronounced Scotch accent. He is tall, sandy fair, rather bald, with a moustache, very plain, receding forehead and long shoehorn nose, but has a nice and kindly face, and is quite uneditorial. He did not expect A.L. and was rather taken aback, I think, at having to compete with us both. I broached the subject of the Beggars, while Andrew stuck his nose

1 Emily Herbert's brother.

into a book. Mr. Blackwood said he would like to see it, and seemed anxious to be on good terms. I exalted your artistic skill, he seemed impressed – and said they did much in the illustrated book line. I then tackled him about *Charlotte* – and he said that he would see that it was reviewed – Andrew L then spoke to him about an article on Junius that he is writing, and I put my nose into a book. We then left – There was no time to see Holyrood, as my only train was 4.30 but we went to an old picture shop and saw nice things in which you would have done better than I. Thus to the train and A.L. saw me off in the most approved manner. My most comfortable thought during the two hours journey home was that I had placed Emily Herbert on *your* shoulders. Andrew L was really very nice and told me that if ever I wanted anything done with Longmans to ask him to do it. This was quite his own idea. He said they wanted short stories or the like. I told him of Tay Pay[1] and he said at once that would be very useful to us – but treated us throughout as those who were arriveés – I mentioned T.P.'s suggestion that we were shoneens; and he said if there was one thing more obvious than another in the book it was that we were the reverse – I talked of E. Yates whom he *hated* on account of Thackeray – and told him how friendly he had been to me. A.L. was pleased to say that everyone had spots of sanity somewhere. He said we ought to employ Watts the agent to work with publishers, adding that he was only a man for people whose position was assured. My last impression of Andrew Lang is of his whipping out of the carriage as it moved on in the midst of an account of how Buddha died of eating roast pork to surfeit.

Now to your letter of this morning – of course I will send my photograph to Ward and Downey. It is a good advert, but how thankful I am that Shorter cannot interview us. I think the interview is one of the most pestilent forms of literature. It is a great thing that the cheap edition of *Charlotte* is soon to be out and I will reiterate about corrections and I think the photograph of you with Dot is fairly good and Hildegarde has, in the nick of time, sent me copies of mine. Perhaps you would send her as much of this letter as you think would interest her. I should like to tell her of Edinburgh as she has been there – and I have not much time for letters. My plans are – to sell to Mr. Jackson my return ticket via Belfast and to fly down third to London and see Edith and Katie. I propose doing this on Friday – 92 Warwick Street SW will find me. I want to stay there three or four days and so home to meet Robert at Ross. Mr. Jackson has several times asked me to stay on – but I

1 T. P. O'Connor.

haven't the time – though I adore Saint Andrews. Today we go to tea with Father Angus, that staunch supporter, and some people come to dinner – I hope you will tell me of the Wagner–Beethoven concert – Nothing could be more to my taste . . .

Yours Ever
Martin

Ross
Monday March 11th 95

Dear Edith
Here is the form for depositing the money. Reproach Hildegarde bitterly for not having deposited it before now – I was living in placid contentment in the assurance that it had been put in the first week in January – and that pennies were accruing thereon. It was originally three pounds I think – and there were nine shillings or thereabouts to be deducted from that for a piece of material. Armstrong is very nice, and may be a friend to us yet. All the ex-editors adore us – even Oswald Crawford. Four of them in all – Have you got back your photograph from the *Sketch*? I got back mine some time ago – I wonder they don't bring them out – and whether Ward and Downey ever sent them a copy of the book. I have got the *Yellow Book*, and am very glad you did not read aloud the Ballad of the Nun. It is disgraceful, to the point of spoiling a very beautiful thing – and the idea of the Virgin Mary coming down and being porteress while the young lady was off on the ramp like any dog or cat is almost noble in its novelty. But beautifully written it is, and I wish it were a little less degraded – I do wish people would give up making the central physical point of life its central point of happiness, of intellect, of interest, . . . [*end of letter missing*]

Martin delighted in ridiculous manifestations of snobbery such as she recounts here. The tale was told to her by the Somerville girls who were daughters of Dr Jim at Park Cottage in Union Hall (i.e. Edith's first cousins) and later incorporated in A Conspiracy of Silence.

[From Martin to Edith, 1895: *fragment*]

. . . the fir trees etched against the west and reflected through the last twig. It was satiating. The Porks told me strange tales of the Morris girls who live at Corran. They fly up when afternoon visitors come, and put on evening dresses, low necks & short sleeves, and come down crackling with paint. Little White swears this occurred, so do the Myross Woods on another occasion. They are quite young, and rather pretty, and they say that painting is their talent. "We spend the whole morning painting – we prefer painting solider's graves – and subjects of that kind". To someone who wanted their horse taken round they said that they would send for the groom, but that they didn't know where the stable was . . . *Beatrice* has taken to riding – is having lessons on Marquise from Uncle K. Did I tell you this – and of her breeches – Joe's were first tried. They would not go over her ankles. Then Violet's knickerbockers. She could get them on but not sit down. Finally the Bart's loosest knickerbockers. They just did – but are skin tight all over. H. and I ride to Innishbeg tomorrow. We both miss you awfully but don't admit it to each other. Good-bye and good luck to your journey

Yours ever

Martin

[From Martin to Edith: *fragment*]

. . . I believe two constituencies in England are open to him, and I do wish he could go in for one – instead of this rotten and humiliating game. In '72 Captain Trench, the conservative, polled six hundred votes against Nolan's three thousand and when one thinks of the altered franchise, and the complete loss of influence on the landlords' side I should say that if Robert got two hundred he would be lucky. If he has to stand he will be here in a fortnight of course, or less – and then will be the ecstacy. He talks of coming here in any case after the elections are over – but whether that means Connie I do not know. I am in hopes that they might take the house for August and September – and Mama would be very glad if they did It would be quite like my luck to come in for an election fuss. I always come in for hurrooshes* at Ross. William Mac's wife died suddenly two days ago, after producing a dead child – and was buried yesterday, up at the chapel on the hill – where a grave yard has lately been opened. I went up to the back gate and walked with it from there and saw the whole thing. It was *extraordinary*. The people who had relations buried there, roared and howled on the graves, and round Mrs. Mac's grave there was a perpetual whining and moaning, awfully like the tuning of fiddles in an orchestra the whole time. The drunken men staggered about, one or two smart relations from

Galway flaunted to and fro in their best clothes, occasionally crossing themselves and three keeners knelt together inside the inmost ring by the grave, with their hands locked, rocking and crying into each others hoods. Three awful witches, telling each other the full horrors that the other people were not competent to understand. There was no priest, but Mrs. Mac's brother read a kind of Litany, very like ours, at top speed, and all the people answered. Every saint in the calendar was called on to save her and to protect her, and there poor William stood with his head down and his hat over his eyes. It was impressive – very – and the view was so fresh and clear and delightful from that height. The thump of the clods and stones on the coffin was a sound that made one shudder – and all the people keened and cried at it. Cremation for *me* – and not this hiding away in the ground. There have been many enquiries for you since I came back Mat Kenealy thinks "he never seen a lady like you that would have that undherstanding of a man's work – and didn't I see her put her hand to thim palings and lep over them. Faith I thought there was no lady could be as supple as our own till I seen her. But indeed the both of ye proved very bad that ye didn't get marri'd, and all the places ye were in". Mary Mulloy thought I was thin – Anne Kineary thought I was fat. Nurse didn't say much. She thinks that you remind her of Mrs. Fox (my grandmother) you have that same way with you – and indeed she's as fond of poor Miss Somerville as if she was one o'yerselves.

Now I must take this to the post

Yours ever

Martin

[From Martin to Edith: *fragment*]

. . . I wonder whether you were hunting yesterday, or was Bocock too engrossing. Tell me about the horses. How my dear Dairymaid is going, and everything. You never told me how Mildred's pony was going – she was refusing a bit the last time I saw her out. I didn't tell you that Mr. Roberts in his sermon last Sunday on the Temptation said "No friends, that Temptation was a safety match, and would not strike on that box – there was no tender there for it" otherwise the sermon was a rather ingenious and wholly useless attack on the personality of the devil. Anyhow I prefer him to the High Church curates in London one of whom I heard say in a mellifluous tenor "But, dear people, we must not be too *hard* on the Apostles" Being called . . . [*end of fragment*]

The sons of Emily Martin and James McCalmont grew up to be Union-
ists and 'implacable' Orangemen. In this letter Martin has tea in the
House of Commons with her nephew James McCalmont, and feels
troubled by the conclusions that will be drawn by T. P. O'Connor –
editor of the Weekly Sun *and a Nationalist – when he sees her in such*
company.

[From Martin to Edith, 1895: *fragment. Edith's note added later* 'House
of Commons']

. . . Armstrong also wanted an amusing story for the Christmas number
which they are *already* thinking of. He told me that it was rumoured
that Pinker had gone into partnership with Williamson in this *Hour*
business – but he seemed to think it a dubious spec. I said Williamson
had made B and W what it was – A statement that met with small
enthusiasm. I also said the *Hour* wished us to travel for them. He said
that we must not be enticed away from B and W and proceeded to ask
if *I* could make any suggestions for the improvement of the paper. I
concealed my profane mirth, and said it was very good as it was. I told
him of the *Sketch* affair and of the *English Ill.* which had its due effect
– and so we parted. I took your photograph to *Sketch*, but Shorter was
out. I saw a new subordinate – quite the gentleman – really rather a
nice creature. I said I thought the one with The Dog was far the best –
and he at once agreed as had Edith and C previously "That's very jolly"
says he – so now my jolly tar – in you and The Dog go. I took away
the other. Cuthbert can't stand it, nor indeed Edith. I asked when he
thought the story was wanted for the *English Ill.* He said they had a lot
of material on hand, but if Mr. Shorter had asked for the story he would
probably put other stuff aside for it – and the sooner it was sent in the
better. You will admit that I have done some work among the editors
and made them toe the mark in style – I will send you tomorrow before
I start for Ireland patterns for your dress, and some cuttings H. sent me
on for you. I have been full of gadding – "The Ideal Husband" was
extremely amusing and quite proper – Fanny Brough inimitable but not
enough of her. The play dies into hopeless domesticity in the last act
and Oscar must have cussed as he wrote it. Then we dined deliciously
at the Metropole – and the Coopers took me to see the man come out
of the trance. He came with a painful struggle and pathetic bewildered
desperate eyes searching to get back his soul from Morrit's keeping –
while the sweat poured down his face. The milder word could not give
the feeling. Sunday was Hurlingham, a cold and rather dismal game I

thought, and I caught a cold there. Then tea and dinner at the Cavalry
Club – pleasant and warm – Last night a great thrate[1] – Jimmy McCalmont dined us at the House, and got us into the Ladies Gallery – Jimmy,
Edith, Cuthbert, myself, Captain Tattersall, and Dunbar Barton were
the party – for the third night the champagne flowed in rivers. Ladies
have to dine in little rooms underground and it was hot but comfortable
– at the next table was Justin MacCarthy, with Blake the Canadian, and
Ladies of sorts – at the other next table was our ally Tay Pay – and
Dunbar who was full of speeches about *Charlotte*, and had read it and
had read the *Weekly Sun* sent round a slip of paper to Tay Pay to say
that one of the Shoneens was there – and then I was adjured to pull
myself together and be stared at. Being blind I did not mind – and he
and Justin McC took stock I hope. I fear that being next to such an
implacable Orangeman as Jimmy will not do the Shoneens much good
with TP. Jimmy was furious with Dunbar for having any truck with the
unclean thing. We heard Saunderson, W. Redmond and Sir G. Clarke
speak, as well as others and saw the division on Redmond's amendment.
Of these things I will speak when I see you. I can't stay on till you come
– my ticket is up – but you must come to Ross – I have any amount to
say but must stop. How about your rocky interior? It is . . . [*end of
fragment*]

*On her mother's sudden death Edith became mistress of Drishane.
Although she was a capable woman and was satisfied to run the household and hold the family together, this accession to duty left her with
even less time to write with Martin. At this time Hildegarde was
pregnant.*

[From Edith to Martin, 4 December 1895: *fragment*]

. . . not know that however. The poultice did good and she seemed to
go to sleep so I went back to bed – at about 6 a.m. she woke me again.
Mother was very wild, feverish, and in great pain. We tried various
remedies, in vain – at dawn I sent a man riding post haste for Hadden
and morphia. I can't tell you the agony of waiting for him; she tried to
bear the pain and it would beat her. Then I sent for Uncle Kendal and
Egerton, and with mesmerism they soothed her a little. In the midst of
the worst she made me laugh by whispering that the nurse was "a little

1 *Thrate*: treat.

old bit of red tape", because she refused to try some unofficial remedy. At last came Hadden with the morphia. He said at once that she could not bear the pain, and injected a quarter of a grain of morphia. In five minutes the blessed relief came but soon the mucous from the lung began – in the inertia of the morphia sleep – to rise and rise in her chest. The breathing grew more and more oppressed. They got a great quantity of nourishment down, and we still hoped that she would wake relieved – we had wired for another nurse, as the first one was worn out. She never left the room from seven p.m. on Monday to 1 a.m. this morning. A nice woman came, and was of great help to the first. We also had Hadden's partner to spend the night in the house. They all frightened us by warnings, but all held out hope; at 2 (midday) Uncle Jim told us she could not live for quarter of an hour – but she seemed to rally, and many symptoms were good, and we believed in the Coghill constitution – at 10 they sent us to bed; Emmie and I went in order to make H. go too; at 11.15 Egerton called us. Her breathing then was peaceful. We did not stay long – Egerton and Aylmer took us away. Then Papa went in – you know he also has been ill. He tottered in between the two boys. Dear Martin, I think that was almost the worst moment, one could believe in that sorrow – the rest was inconceivable, and still is. He also was taken away. Soon – a few minutes afterwards her life went out in a light gentle breath. She had been unconscious throughout, and never even in her worst pain thought she was in any danger. I am so thankful now that we did not frighten her for nothing – she had too child like a soul to face death – it frightens (frightened) her – (It is hard to give up the present tense. Just now when a *truly* sympathetic telegram came from Gendie, I thought "I *must* tell mother"!) I must stop and make H. go out. She and E. will stay here for a while. The Chimp will be here tomorrow – we wired directly the doctor told us to and he might have been here by this but there was a hitch about it. In any case he would have been late. Poor Papa is wonderful – so gentle and good and so utterly and entirely heartbroken. It would wring your heart to see him. It was all so sudden – we had about eight hours in which to face it – and till the last we hoped. Everyone is more than kind. Keep well, be careful of yourself – Love from Hildegarde

Ever yours
Edith

I will try to write again tomorrow – Friday is the day fixed

Drishane
Friday night

Dear Martin

I can't go to sleep, I have tried but it is no use, so I have lighted my candle and will try to think that I am talking to you. Your letter came this morning, and the flowers came just in time. They came by train, with very many others; Cameron opened them and put them in the carriage that was full of flowers, then he came up to my room, where I was sitting with Hildegarde and Papa, and told me that they had come and gave me the note. I made him bring them up to me. It was late, but I could not let them go without seeing them. They were most beautiful and as fresh as if they had only just been gathered. I could not do as you asked me. I had only time to look at them and let Cameron hurry down with them, but I wrote the card as if it were to go on them. I don't know where to begin. It all feels like one continuous dream of pain that began on Tuesday morning. I don't know when it is going to end. I know you will tell me it is morbid and foolish but most of the things that come back to me are of words and actions that I was sorry for even at the time and now. – And then I feel as if I have never been a bit demonstrative to her or ever let her know how I felt – except indeed when I was angry or provoked. I know she took pleasure out of us all, but I feel now as if I might so easily have done so much more. That there were so many times ("like golden coins squandered, and still to pay") when I was snubbing or beastly – I dont say all of this for you to contradict me – but because I must get it out of my heart. I dont think I have told you anything. On Monday the doctor said her progress was perfectly satisfactory. On the afternoon she told us she felt she had turned the corner – (Yes I did tell you.) How could you ask me to run away down to the Cottage and let Aylmer bear all the brunt alone? It wasn't like you, and I can't think you wished me to do it. For one thing I should have gone mad there. It has been, up here, incessant arrangements and giving of orders and seeing that things were done and that H. didn't do them. Her pluck was quite splendid, but yesterday afternoon she broke down, (in health I mean) and Egerton and I drove her into bed in my room. Hadden was here – we had sent for him to *order* Papa not to go to the funeral; he said she was all right, but must keep quiet in bed and be spared strong emotion. I thanked God that I had persuaded her not to go in and see mother. She is much better this evening and has been in bed all day, a good thing, as we managed to keep Papa down here with her, and he was spared all the sights or rather *sounds*. He never knew when they took the coffin up last night or brought it down this morning – I went in on Wednesday to see her. She looked most beautiful, but so terribly, utterly, remote. I could not feel that it was she. It was a beautiful mask that her soul had worn, and now that it had been cast aside it had taken on a cold sort of serenity, a character of its own, quite apart from hers. In a curious way, seeing what had been her, reconciled me to leaving her alone in the cold half dark silent room. I felt that she was not there. I thought of her meeting Aunt Florry, and telling Minnie what a success the *Real Charlotte* had been and how, for her part, she had much preferred the Mad Dog Paris story. Aylmer and Emmie weren't with me. It is no use to try and tell you what they and Egerton and H. have been. Whenever A. gave himself time to think you could see how shattered he was by grief, but his pluck was beyond what I could possibly have believed. Boyle could not have been stronger or more reliable. As for Egerton I need not tell you of him. He has been everything – so helpful and tender and absolutely unselfish – and his and Aylmer's care for Papa was quite beautiful (it sounds trite but I can think of no other word.) On the night she died they sat up with him and sank all their own grief in trying to calm and comfort him. I could not cry that night – my heart felt like a hot stone and my mind was beating against the incredible truth, like the sea against those awful Arran cliffs. Emmie and H. and I all huddled together in E's room and the house was all alight and people going to and fro in the passages. We had got down a second nurse that day from Cork, a very nice woman too, and they did all that was necessary. I can remember that when at about half past eleven, we were taken in to see her for the last time, the two nurses were standing with tears running down their faces, one on each side of the bed, and I can see that young Doctor O'Mara's pitiful face as he held her pulse. I can't believe it now. I can see her stumping up from Glen B. to lunch, with her eyes on the ground, planning – "I'm an awful planner" she always used to say – or pinning us with her eyes as we told her of Mildred's latest enormity. I tell myself that she may have been taken away from possible calamity, and that for her it may be best, and all the rest of it, but when I think of her innocent joie de vivre and her unconquerable gaiety I find it a cruel fate that did not let her have a little more of this world that she was happy in. Poor Cameron only arrived by the early mail this morning. Everything was against him, the mail boat three hours late, etc. Luckily A. E, Emmie and I woke early and we had drugged H. and Papa with sulphonal so they did not stir. He was quite broken down. Even Egerton's pluck gave way and he sobbed with us like a baby. What else could we do? Would you have had me sneak down to the Cottage and cry there by myself? Martin, I know you wouldn't – H. and I have had a hard battle with Papa to keep him from going to see her. He is so broken down by his illness and misery that even his old obstinacy – ("he's the most obstinate man I know!" as mother used to say with a rolling eye –) has left him, and he does what we ask. I begged the same thing of the Chimp, and I am thankful to say he yielded also. Only when the coffin was shut and the violet cross, that was almost as long as it was, was fastened to it, he and Aylmer and I went in and knelt down by it, and said goodbye to her in our hearts. He saw her last in all her smart clothes, going radiantly off to Christine Morrough's wedding, that is a better memory than the pale serene severe presence that had nothing of her own gay self about it. We keep saying to one another how pleased she must be about all the letters and the flowers. Only a week ago she and H. had a most vigorous argument as to whether she or Aylmer were the most popular in the country – of course H. vowed that Aylmer was, and she fought for her own hand as usual. Now she will triumph. From all round the country, from all classes there is but one voice of grief. A. said that every man and woman in Skib. came up to him, Jack Buckley who had written daily to inquire for her was crying like a baby "your most affectionate and beloved mother, that with her own hands made a wreath to place upon my dear daughter". That was what he said in his letter of condolence. In the village they said every door and window was shut and not a sound in the street – "it was like there was death in each house," said Joanna. Papa had insisted on her being buried in Castle Haven, and we can never be grateful enough to Mr. Warren. He and his men went yesterday, opened the vault, cleaned and set everything in it in order, and then both lined and covered it all with moss and white chrysanthemums. Even Aylmer who had an unspeakable horror of taking her there, said that it was beautiful and all the dreadfulness gone out of it. They carried her, in relays of six men, our tenants for the most part, and some of the coastguards, and Jack Buckley and other farmers, who don't belong to us, but wish to do honour to her memory. The tenants and the Toe Head people got out early this morning and had swept the road as clean of mud and stones as if it were an avenue, I think it was most touching of them. Jim told Ethel he never saw so much or so genuine grief. There were seventy carriages and cars and hundreds of foot people. I do so hope she knows. Can you imagine how proud she would be? I must write and tell it to Mrs. Chave. I believe that would be her first wish. I cant help laughing at her even now with the tears running down my cheeks. Do you know that the nurse hadn't been in the house for half an hour when she started her in at "Naboth's Vinyard" and had told her all about Hildegarde, and shown her Jack's photographs? Jack Buckley was right in what he said of her – "your most affectionate mother" – oh, dear Martin, it is a comfort to write to you, but how Hildegarde and I wish you were here. After the two of us, no one knew her in and out as you do. I am thankful to think that you stayed with her this time last year, as she was so fond of you. She was always asking me when you were coming – I am so very grateful to you for writing to poor Kinkie. I literally hadn't time. There are forty or fifty letters still to be answered, and flowers still to be thanked for. Kinkie sent a lovely wreath and the most awfully nice letter. Nothing could have been more truly sympathetic and refined too. The Canon came down to read the service with Harry Becher. He broke down two or three times. The poor boys both broke down quite uncontrollably I believe. Men have hard things to do that women are spared. She always flirted with the boys, and they adored her. They were so far far nicer to her than I was – but it is no use saying so now. After it was all over the Canon and Harry B. came over and read some prayers to Papa and Emmie and the two boys and me and gave us the Communion. The Canon's face, like Stephen's was as the face of an angel. H. was in bed and in any case she could not have borne it. It was Aylmer's suggestion and wish. I think it was very nice of him. It is very nearly one o'clock, and my candle also is burned out, but I feel better and as if I should go to sleep now – and I hear Miss Dody[1] kicking like a little fury. I cannot praise Sylvia and Zoë and Grace enough I could never forget their kindness through it all especially Sylvia

Ever yours
Edith

H. is sleeping with me which is why I went to bed without writing to you. She is asleep now.

Drishane
Monday

Dear Martin
I haven't much time to write but I must send you a line. I am so glad you met poor Kinkie and I can imagine how glad she was to see you –

---

1 A horse in stable.

I know how much she will have felt it, and as none of her people knew mother, she must have felt very solitary. I am very glad you are so soon going away into Galway and are so much better but *do* be minding yourself. We are all better. Papa is sitting in his study, and as his accounts etc. had fallen into arrears he was well and wholesomely occupied in settling them. He is *wonderful*, and tries to be cheerful, and is so grateful for everything and so utterly uncomplaining. Harry Becher came up yesterday afternoon and read – (by his own suggestion) a much shortened afternoon service. It was kind of Harry, and he read very nicely, – only the second lesson; it was an extremely beautiful one and strangely appropriate. I have got beyond the stage of tears now, only now and then when some little foolish thing turns up unexpectedly, or I find myself quoting one of her absurd sayings from sheer force of habit then it is hard. You want to know how we are located. Egerton and H are in my room, E. dresses etc in the dressing room by the tank. I am in my old room – Emmie and A are in the nursery, Papa is in their old room, opposite. The Chimp is in his own room. We are going to make mother's old room the nursery. We could not bear the idea of Papa being there by himself. It was too lonely and miserable and the blue room was really his and mother's room for twenty years, so that he has only pleasant memories in connection with it. We all feel she would rather the children were there than it should be left empty or used for casual visitors and it will prevent that end of the house becoming dreary and neglected. Emmie and A. have given up all thoughts of Shana Court. I am more thankful than I can say. I don't know what I should have done without them. She has also given up the idea of going to England before January – but the babies go this week. No one could have written kinder or more delightful letters than Mrs Sykes – I could not have believed that she had such a gift of expression; I knew that she was sympathetic. I don't know what to say about you coming at once. You know that H. and I want you – I needn't say that, but till the Chimp is gone and the servants settle down I am afraid I ought not to ask you to come. The new woman, Margaret Hanlon, seems very nice, most reliable and quiet, and as tall as H. She is to be parlour maid. Mary is temporarily to be house maid. We rather like her personally, as she is a good kind little fool, but her vulgarity is *quite* intolerable and she is a vile servant or at least is vile here, but in a small house, under a good dragon I think she would do very well. She is most obliging and all the other servants are fond of her. Do you know anyone who needs such? I'm awfully glad your mother is better – perhaps in a fortnight you might be able to come. Don't think of me as moping, or the like o' that – I have more to do than I ever had in my life, but I am glad to go to sleep when I get into bed. You couldn't believe the amount of letters still unwritten that are before us. Father Lyons preached a long sermon about Mother in the chapel yesterday and "spoke most beautifully" they all say. He ended by saying the prayer for the repose of the Souls of the Dead from their Office. They say all the chapel was crying. It shows their powers of emotional sympathy. Half of them could hardly ever have seen her. I must stop. You think too well of me. Don't say the things you do – they only make me ashamed.

    Yours Ever
    Edith

Edith's letters now become a tremendous rush to dash down information in between duties. This letter begins with a description of a social event. Edith revelled in her country Irishness, and it is easy to imagine her emphatic shortness and tone when she responded to Madam de Bunsen's query on her blouse – 'May I ask, Paris or London?' – with 'Skibbereen.'

    Harry Plunket Greene, the singer, was another of Edith's cousins, and she was at a concert of his when this exchange took place. The day after the concert, Edith dashed to shop at Switzers and gave way to a huge explosion of temper. She then flew through Kingsbridge station to get back and organize Christmas revelries for the family. Cameron, her brother, 'The Chimp', was at home on leave this Christmas. The details given at the end of the letter show that each son was financially independent and left to his own devices to raise an income.

                       Christmas eve
                       after dinner

Dear Martin
. . . The 49 show was a *great* success: they had quite 250 people. Harry, Mrs. Scott Fennell, Miss Alex Elsner, and Miss Binger and Drummond Hamilton sang, and a Miss Lucy Guinness played the violin. We had cleared everything but a few chairs and a piano and a few tables for lamps, but the people were as thick in it as grass. Almost the first I met were Rose and Zara; the former looked *very* old and small and badly dressed, in a curious dowdy little boat shaped hat and ugly black coat. I could not and cannot now remember the quotation about "were these the eyes that set Egypt in a blaze" – (Do you even know what I mean? If so tell me what I *do* mean.) She was full of Arthur's leaving the army

and said "I know you will be very angry with me, but *I* think he is too good for the army!" Here Zara chimed in and said the army was a mere school for drinking and gambling. I said that Papa was a terrific example of both vices. We had a good deal of prate and they had a lot of food, so in all love we parted – Madam de Bunsen was there, but not the Cuckoo, who was in bed with a cold. Madam de Bunsen said, fingering my black and white velvetine blouse, "*May* I ask, Paris or London?" I said "Skibbereen", – "Ah, alors c'est le façon de le mettre!" It was highly gratifying. Harry really sang splendidly, and a great many songs. His voice is *astounding* in its power, after one of his big gorgeous shouts my head was really rattling, if you know the feeling after a cannon has gone off, yet it is all mellow sound without effort or roaring. One night at dinner they say he gave a great laugh and must just have hit the tonic note of one of the finger glasses, as they heard a sharp crack on the sideboard, and behold the glass was in two halves. His soft passages are equally admirable, and the way he can send a musical whisper to the end of the room is extraordinarily effective. I don't think I ever heard a more dramatic singer – he sang Maud V Whites "How do I love thee" quite perfectly; in fact he was like Tom Connell. Aunt Sylvia rose – out of bed – to the occasion and looked charming in a very smart gown. Consie played all the accompaniments most beautifully. Nothing would induce her to play a solo, which is a pity. She and Helen looked very nice in smart silk blouses, and Bess was stupendous but smart and amusing, and a tower of strength as an entertainer. It was almost impossible to get the people out of the house, they hung on and on in hopes of another song from Harry. He is quite unspoilt and unaffected, and his niceness to his father is delightful to see. Uncle Richard was going about purring with pride, it was a pleasure to see he had something left to him in his very sad life. The more I see him the more I like him. This is great enthusing but you brought it on yourself by asking silly questions. My habit came last night after dinner – (I was in agony lest it shouldn't come) – I tried it on and then tied it up again. Then I remembered that I had not seen my top boot and third crutch, (both of which I had left at Switzer's,) in the box! This hideous thought occurred to me about two in the morning, not long after I had got into bed and Bess had ceased talking. I swithered in anguish and rage. The next morning on my way to Kingsbridge I tore through Switzer's like a flame, searching and storming; no boot, no crutch. I left breathing out threatenings, while such of the staff as were out of bed were left sobbing apologies on their knees. This morning I found the boot and the crutch in the box, swaddled in tissue paper. The Greenes had written to say that they had been twice to blow up and were going again. I say these things calmly now, but the humiliation has seared my soul. I wired to Aunt Sylvia to grovel to Switzer, but I fear I was too late. Now, neither she nor I can comfortably cross again the threshold of Switzer. Mistletoe looks well and has been just clipped. Cruiskeen is much improved. A. tried her in a bridle the other Tuesday, they had a 20 minute run and she couldn't put a foot on a fence – as Crowley said "she fled them all" – which is I think a perfect expression – H. and C. saw Dodo and said she was looking grand and had a totham like a carthorse. Captain Boyce has been too ill to hunt her yet – he has been asked here for a bit next month. The Chimp has passed in all his subjects in his exam, and is incredulously thankful. It is the *greatest* matter for him, it puts three pounds in his pocket, and as he will be senior captain in a few weeks he now feels quite easy. He feared he would have to raise money and stew with a crammer, and all sorts of horrible things. He goes to Malta in September, which is a very hateful thought. Boyle is possibly coming over on January 2nd for a week. For many reasons I think it is a pity and I dont like his robbing poor Mab of a week when he only has six left. Please return the enclosed letter to me – I am going, after . . . [*end of letter missing*]

[From Martin to Edith, 1895: *fragment. Edith's note added later:* 'Thady']

. . . A beautiful day yesterday – fine and clear throughout. Today the storm stormeth as usual and the white mist people are rushing after each other across the lawn – sure sign of hopeless wet. If fine we go tomorrow to Galway to sign the papers – but it is a large if – and then the divil. But anyhow I can sign the day I go to the train, owing to the blessed fact of it starting at ten. If only it were warm weather I would come straight through, and save that much begrudged ten or eleven shillings at the Glentworth.

Poor Thady died on Thursday night, a very gallant quiet end – conscious and calm. Anne Kineary did not mean to say anthing remarkable when she told me that he died "as quiet, now as quiet as a little fish" but those were her words. I went up there on Thursday with Lucie to see old Anne – and coming into a house black with silent people was suddenly confronted with Thady's body, laid out in the kitchen. It was very awful – and Lucie got a good bit of a shock – she kept her head turned away but otherwise didn't make any sign, Andy Connor three parts drunk advanced and delivered a loud horrible harangue on Thady and the Martin family – the people sat like owls, listening – and we retired into a room where were whisky bottles galore, and the cream of the company – men from Galway, respectable, drunk and magnificent in speech. It was *quite* disgusting – and the funeral yesterday was only a shade better. At all events the pale tranced face was hidden, and the living people looked less brutal without that terrific purified creature . . . [*end of fragment*]

The fact that Edith and Martin had based the character of Charlotte Mullen upon Emily Herbert was common knowledge, and for years after, information was given to them about Emily's real life.

[*Note by Sir Patrick Coghill*: 'This fragment in ECES's writing was evidently addressed to VFM as it refers to "our inspired work" i.e. *The Real Charlotte*. Emily Herbert, who lived at The Point, Castle Townshend, County Cork was admittedly the character who inspired the creation of Charlotte Mullen. Mrs. F – who was Mrs Fleming of New Court, Skibbereen, County Cork, in her disclosures about Emily Herbert's past certainly shook ECES as neither she nor VFM had the slightest inkling of her affair with anyone at all.']

The letter, which is fragmentary, can safely be dated between late 1895 and early 1896.

. . . here yesterday. Big Mary is reading aloud *Connemara* to the New Court party, and gave it the height of praise. Then Mrs F took up the strain, and then began to speak of *The Real Charlotte* – "Tell me Edith, how did you know Emily Herbert had had a love affair?" I said we didn't know, but we had invented it, that I had often asked if she had had an amour but had always heard she was guiltless of anything of the kind – "Well Edith, all that you wrote is *pairfectly* true!" She then went on to say that there had been an attorney named Raymond, a Kerry man, of whom Emily was deeply enamoured. He was married to a good little nonentity (Mrs Lambert!!) and to her Emily paid high court till she died, and then siege was laid to Raymond, but, as in our inspired work, in vain, and so the matter ended. Isn't it extraordinary? Even awe-ful. Also they say it is an undoubted fact she steamed open letters that belonged to someone else! I believe her brother, Henry, the Brigade Surgeon, has not as yet heard of the book, but doubtless the day will come and no one will believe that we knew nothing of these transactions.

[From Martin to Edith, 1896: *fragment: starts on page 2*]

... why he should accuse you of being one of the people who discouraged the Irish language. Tell him of *The Real Charlotte* when you get a chance. My letter of Friday explained the position about Robert – I am now waiting to hear. Mama is very delightful in her reading of *The Face of the Waters* she turns a page, and in turning becomes apparently overwhelmed by the greatness of the world, lays the book in her lap and casts a gaze of passionate abstraction on the ceiling – she resumes the book, on the far page, skipping one completely. She is suddenly fascinated – glues her nose to the next turnover, reads two pages like the wind – then the fragrance of the pine (that Mat has hewn for the fire) becomes too much for her – and empress-like meditation falls upon her. It may end in sleep as sudden as everything else – but she is enjoying herself and the book very much. Displayed upon the eminences of her lap is a black apron broidered in white – dear as heart's blood. It was lost two days ago, and Bridget King on finding it told Mama it had been "waylaid" which you will perceive meant mislaid. It makes me laugh to look at the victim of the ambush ... [*end of fragment*]

[From Martin to Edith, ?1896: *fragment: starts on page 2*]

... Selina and I set forth to Oughterard on Sunday for the eleven o'clock service; we found the whole place full of people, with a vaguely threatening air about them. An election meeting – and the next thing we found was that the service was not to be till three. Two hours to wait. However was there not the meeting? As I said, the street was full of men, and fresh cars kept drawing up from Galway. Each man that drove up waved his hat and yelled "three cheers for Lynch!" which were given. Lynch I must tell you is the Parnellite candidate who was beaten last week by fifty votes for Galway Town by Pinkerton the A. P. and Galway is frenzied with fury about it. One or two cars drove slowly through in the midst of execrations – evidently with Anti-P's on them. I regarded all with ecstacy from the steps of the Church house. The thing was that Foley the Anti-P candidate for *West* Galway was about to hold a meeting down at the chapel, and the Parnellites who adore Joyce (an Oughterard publican) the Parnellite candidate, had formed up in opposition in the street. At last came a car with a beautiful gentleman in a tall hat, white waistcoat, and frock coat, exactly like any London stockbroker – and the row that greeted him was terrific – cheers, hoots, everything, blended in one yell. He drove straight down to the chapel, followed by a lot of the people – and by *me*! It could not be resisted – I took things easy as it was very hot, and I wanted the people to get ahead, and by the time I got to the chapel Mr. Foley was up on a tombstone haranguing. Nearly all his audience were standing on the tombstones in extraordinary clumps, holding on to each other. It was a mighty small gathering – not more than one hundred people – and the speech was also mighty small – what I heard of it was a very quiet dull attempt to explain to the people why he – Mr. Foley – lived in London instead of coming to Connemara. He said he could not afford to live anywhere but in London where his business was. He said he worked with a large number of English people, and had not a word to say against them – on the contrary he had the greatest respect for them – a remark which fell very flat. His chosen supporters stood around him on the tombstone, glaring into his face with delight and cheering at everything he said, but they were longing for blood and thunder but didn't get it. He was a man with a cheerful fat face and a big grey moustache – second class Londoner to the backbone. He really said nothing in the least remarkable, and the cynicism in the faces of some of the old men behind him was fine to see. The women tittered under their shawls all the time and evidently thought it a great spree – especially when they were called "Ladies" – old Father Kenny was up with Foley and evidently doing all he knew to keep the thing going. A great old chap he is – "You have a grand old man of your own here," says Foley ogling Father Kenny "Indeed I am old in thruth" says Father Kenny, "but I am not grand whatever. Be prayin' now gerrls for the success o' the meetin".' – that was as it broke up – and after a bit I straggled back to the street, where all the Joyce-ites were ramping with only two policemen to keep them in hand. It was entrancing. I got on to the doorstep again with a lot of girls and looked on while the crowd simmered about. All this time I must tell you Mrs Lisk, the keeper of the church, was dressing herself and doing her hair in and out of the little parlour and kitchen with Selina harrying her generally, and asking her what she would do if the people broke the windows. To Selina however be the credit of raising an excellent meal of tea and bread and butter at about two o'clock, by which time Mrs. Lisk had put on her company manners and the body of her dress. It was *very* strange as an experience – and most amusing. Selina was so wholly and unfeignedly and conventionally frightened. Mrs. Lisk was so devoured by propriety, and shame at having been caught in her flannel peticoat, and anxiety lest her children should get out into the row. A surpassing yell made me tear out from my excellent tea, and there did I see Foley on a car with Father Kenny coming up from the chapel. The McCarthyites formed round the car, and the shouting so great that not a word could be distinguished except "Joyce"! and "Foley!" Father Kenny with his hat kept waving down the people, and smiling anxiously, Foley gesticulating with his topper, bowed, smirked, and affected to think that everyone was delighted with him. The car got through, and disappeared under the trees, leaving the supporters shouting on the road, and then they turned and marched in a swaggering solid body down the street, dividing the crowd, and bellowing like a chant "To hell with Joyce". That was the only serious moment. The women all ran like hares, the Joyceites yelled "To hell with Foley" and I saw a stick or two go up. In a minute the two police began moving about, quite undismayed, and told the people to go home, separating, pushing and ordering, and there being no drink in anyone things quieted slowly. There were one or two more paradings, and flights of the women, and some mud was thrown – but they dispersed gradually, just in time for us to have our service. This consisted of Mr. Berry, the parson and Mrs. Berry, Selina, myself, Mrs. Lisk and her children. The youngest was a baby of a year old, and crowed, roared, squealed, and flung its toy on the floor incessantly throughout. It was like a long awful baptism – the poor meek parson reading steadily on through the howls. There is a harmonium, and Mrs. Berry and I had a duet in the Glorias, the Nunc, and that hymn "Jesu my Lord, my God, my all". Her voice was too awful. The extraordinary thing is, that I dreamed the night before that I was singing that very hymn – only instead of the last line "Oh let me love Thee more and more" one verse ended with something about the "Mo-ab-i-tish sow" which surprises me faintly in the dream – I thought it a rather violent reproach . . . [end of fragment]

Edith and Martin came to the attention of W. B. Yeats and Lady Gregory. Lady Gregory was a cousin of Martin's but little came of their interest in each other's work. To Edith and Martin, the Celtic Revival was a strange phenomenon; they did not really approve of something that had been brought back to life with so much artificial respiration.

[From Martin to Edith: *fragment. Note by Edith*: 'A Penny Reading at Spiddal']

. . . came yesterday by going early to Galway and being met. I am going to stay till Monday. I thought I should only stay a night, but have settled to wait. I think Ross is all right. Bridget K was nearly well before I left. They are all at home here, that is to say, Martin Morris and the two younger girls go away today. Did I tell you that Maud M, the eldest, is going to be married, to a Captain Wynne – a Sligo man – nice – not very rich – adjutant of all London volunteers. They are very much pleased with each other and entirely sensible. The concert was got up by Mr Tweedy, the police officer here, and the Morris's were the mainstay of it. They did a lot of skirt dancing, very well. Martin and his two younger brothers did the three old maids of Lee, whereat I wept and screeched disgracefully. The middle brother, one Edmund, with a long interesting white face, like Dante, was in black, with a tight bonnet & was a mixture of Mrs Breedin and Katty Atkins. He was *inimitable* – He simply was a woman. Martin's moustache, though soaped away made him ridiculous and the youngest, Charlie was plump and pretty. My heart was wholly given to Edmund and his long jesuit face. He is about nineteen and very clever I believe. The stage was quite a good size and very well got up and lighted. I suppose the room held two or three hundred, and it was full both nights. They took four pounds each time, at very low prices, and Spiddal is nothing like the size of Castle T. People came in from all around. Policemen and the schoolmaster eked out the programme – the latter recited hurriedly and with deepest passion a long stave out of Hiawatha – *Too* dreadful for those in the front rows. Every time he said Minnehaha – there was profuse giggling in the back benches. That at all events was a joke. The rest was quite inexplicable as indeed you can imagine. Later on he appeared again and chanted, off a bit of letter paper, a perfectly mysterious saga with a refrain of "twitter twitter little birds". There was nothing that you could call a tune but there was what might have been one – and birds from the north and from the south wandered through. He suddenly ceased and in tones of thunder said "three cheers for Miss Maud Morris and Captain Wynne!" and that was the end. It was no less than an ode on the engagement. Everything of course went with a yell from start to finish. Kathleen Morris accompanied all through. How, she alone knows. There was a policeman's wife called Mrs. Howard, who sang three dreadful songs with her front teeth tightly clenched. No attempt at tune or time, or anything. Kathleen said that she stopped playing several times in the hope that she *might* happen back on the right key – and Mrs. Howard went serenely on declaring that she'd "lawv tew roam in the green woods free." She looked as if she had never been out of Mrs. Power's workroom – and her breath would have felled an ox. I knew that the moment I looked at her. Mr. Tweedy sang McCarthy's widow – rather well – in a tidy small voice – not without humour and a policeman sang Enniscorthy – quite well – Eileen Morris's skirt dancing was charming – most classical, but poor girl, she did show her legs, being on a raised stage. I saw frilled drawers to half way above her knee. Maud also showed hers very handsomely in her horn pipe – and both were distraught by consciousness of it, as well they might. Mr. Tweedy came on at the end and told an Irish story, with local allusions, rather well – and sang a topical song – with verses about Lord Morris and Maud's engagement and was encored by the hour. Judge of my putrefaction* when he embarked on a verse beginning about being at a loss, and the rhyme to that was "Here's a health to Martin Ross" it went on with an allusion to *The Real Charlotte*, and recommended "all to read that book" – I have only met him twice for a moment – so was quite unprepared for notice – of course most of the audience were quite bewildered but the names Martin and Ross did all right and they hurroohed away. Everyone had been so covered with allusions throughout that it was not embarrassing – I wished you were there – Fitz O'Hara and Tom Blake came out from Galway for the show and they and the Tweedys had supper here afterwards. I drank champagne, of which I was in the want – and we rolled to bed, much exhausted.

It is pleasant to see the sea again – and the views are lovely. I walked a bit with Martin M yesterday and heard a lot about Yeats that was interesting. He is mad about his old legends and spirits, and if someone said "Thims fine lobsters" or anything, he would begin "There's a very curious tradition about lobsters" and then he was off. He is thinner than a lath – wears paltry little clothes wisped round his bones, and the prodigious and affected greenish tie. He is a *little* affected and knows it – He has a sense of humour and is a gentleman – hardly by birth I fancy – but by genius. Arthur Symons, who was here with him, was not much liked I think – just a smart little practical man of letters, who knows how and has no genius at all. Bad luck to him, he has written an account of Aran in this last number of the *Savoy* not badly at all – very culturedly – it is not illustrated, fortunately, and this is the very last number of the *Savoy*. It is a failure, and has ceased. There are one or two awfully good pictures by Aubrey B. in it – Yeats is writing a strange and mystic novel about the southernmost Island of Aran – how a very french young man . . . [*end of fragment*]

The sweep at Ross: material marked for use at the time of writing. Martin writes here in the highest good humour; only Edith called out *such a strain in Martin's writing. This incident re-appeared in one of the best RM stories:* Great Uncle McCarthy.

[From Martin to Edith, 1897: *fragment*]

. . . of it for ages. You will see that Augusta liked her pictures very much. "Robert" is Augusta's boy, not ours. You will see that her book is a great success. It is very ably done I think though her writing is not the very best. We propose an expedition to Spiddal tomorrow, where is Maud Wynne in a highly expectant condition I understand. My witticism about the precious ointment on the head, that ran down to the beard, meant that you can have too much of a good thing and you and Hildegarde are very innocent and silly not to understand it. You will never be able to write my biography at this rate.

We have had a sweep here – and as Cuthbert says, have in consequence lived every hour in the last 24. Cuthbert found him on the road, and Cuthbert got him up here on Friday evening. Edith at once said she wouldn't have him at all or certainly not next morning, as the Martins were coming out. The sweep then said he would have to return to Galway, seemingly an awful threat. Edith at once told him, in exactly these words that she didn't care if she never saw him again – with which she returned to her letters. He then settled to come yesterday morning. This meant that he arrived with the mail car at 2 a.m. and walked around the house all night, knocking at intervals and that Bridget spent the night in agony, believing it to be her mad brother come to look her up. At 4.30 he succeeded in awakening Tierney, who came up and in tones of thunder awakened Bridget, who is in the room opposite the one I am in – Bridget was on the point of wakening Cuthbert to ask for orders when I intervened, and in yells of laughter commanded that the sweep was to do nothing till Mat Kenealy came to watch him – Bridget and Tierney then went downstairs, and I suppose held high conclave with the sweep in the servants hall – Selina sleeps in the first room on the first landing with her door open, and in the thick dark I heard *her* take up her parable in high indignation, addressing the house in general. That went on in the stillness of half an hour during which I sobbed feebly and drowsily till my pillow was quite wet, then I dozed, and woke to giggle again. At breakfast time nothing had been accomplished except that Mat was saying in tones of bitterest fury "the divil roast the same sweep" and Bridget was saying, God forgive her, she'd "never seen anyone she'd hate as much as him." Then Andy arrived, and every fire in the house was put out. Mama in high frump and chill retired to the garden house and had a fire there with Wat Lee, loudly declaring that she much preferred chimneys on fire to a sweep. Things went a pace till lunchtime – the sweep and Mat and Andy on the roof, calling down the chimneys, bricks and stones avalanching down through the walls – the cook raging, the house black with filth, everyone perished with cold, except Cuthbert who clattered and tore up and down on the Bollée Voiturette.[1] However all is now well – but the memory of the sweep is accursed, through all grades of the household. In the afternoon I tore to Killaguile on the Bollée, down those awful hills in Doon and all. It is exciting, but chilly – but I much preferred riding home on a bicycle, which I did – Now I shall look out for a better account

Yours ever
Martin

[From Edith to Martin, 25 April 1897: *fragment*]

... sure he can place it – I had suggested B. & W – (at *yr* suggestion) for "Aran", but only in a letter, & I very stupidly forgot to speak of it; there was a good deal to say – He then asked me to come up to Lawrence & Bullen's, Henrietta St – Covent Garden, & took a hansom in the most dashing manner in spite of assurances that I preferred walking – En route he explained that the Art Editor & Sub-Editor of the Bad Mag[2] were combined in the person of a Mr Hedley Peek, who was also a sort of partner of L. & B.'S: he explained also that Mr Peek's position was rather delicate between L. & B & the Bad Mag people but that he might as a friend of both, buy serial rights for one & publication rights for the other – arrived at L. & B.'s we were marched into the usual rather dingy office & presently a tall frizzle-headed rather clever looking man of about 45 came in – Mr Bullen – followed by a short athletic-looking dark man, rather younger, with black hair, blue grey eyes, clean shaved very business-like – Very intelligent face, of a rather curious Egyptian type, & yet with a look of Boyle – Mr Hedley Peek – Both deadly civil & affectionate. We began about the Silver Fox – they say it is to be published immediately, & I have even now this minute, corrected the first lot of proofs – they are fixed on a 3/6 edition & have leaded out the type to run 250 pages. I urged a cheaper form, but they swear they don't sell better & quoted dodges of other publishers, in

1 *Bollée Voiturette*: an early, small motor car.
2 *Badminton Magazine*.

faking books of 1/- length with thick paper & other devices to look like 6/-. & it is supposed to lower the author if he is sold too cheap – I then asked of the Collected Works – they had not read them; they hinted at the idea that they ought to be all stories or all articles, but were not strong on the point. I said they were all Irish anyhow, & that we had often been asked to republish etc – They then raved of the Bad Mag stories – Hedley Peek had got them – especially the Grand Filly – by heart, & both attacked me to know wch of us wrote which parts – by chapters or how – the usual old thing. – I assured them that we did it all together – "Well" says H. P. "I have formed a theory, comparing these stories, & I think the person of these sentences "here he whirled to the G. F.," wrote these "& here to the 19th Cent. Mag." I was very arch & told him he was quite wrong, as they also were joint stock – or mainly so – & I said that tho' one story was signed by one & the other by both names that told nothing at all – They then all – including the little Pinker – swore we had got hold of a very good thing in this serio-comic hunting business – "To use literary slang" said Pinker, "this is *your own stuff*" & no one else does anything like it – " H.P said he liked immensely the start of Emily V. & Co, seemed to think if we could keep near that exalted level we shd do awfully well – "I hope you are going to put in plenty of love making" he said – I said we thought the pure Bad Mag etc – this he quite denied & said plenty of love & plenty of comic Irish business – He asked if it were exclusively hunting – I said we were having Country Races – He seemed relieved, & said that "No one on earth could write incessantly about hunting & keep it amusing & interesting" – He hunts himself, & said he was quite sure we knew of what we testified – He gave me to understand they will be glad of anything we write if we can keep to the G. Filly level and style. He said that as we propose to run the story serially we ought to arrange it to be not more than between 70 & 72,000 words, to be equally divided into 12 parts, not necessarily chapters,) & to arrange a curtain for each part – He wld like, if possible to have all the M.S. by Xmas – with 6 drawings to show quality, & to enable them to decide if they wld have more – If they liked the drawings they wld want about 70 (!!) & he wld – with great politeness – reserve the right to refuse or suggest corrections in any drawings sent in – He then gave me some very useful hints in connection with drawing for the Bad Mag, too technical to write now, & showed me some drawings to explain his meaning – I was very humble, sincerely so, & grateful to him; he is a nice man & is an artist himself & is also a writer so he understands things, & he has made a special study of the mysteries of "process" – Mr Bullen was very busy and fussed about in & out of the room & talked secretly to Pinker, & to red & glistening underlings, who come perspiring in at frequent intervals with proofs etc – I think from the way he spoke he wld be glad to bring out the short stories vol: he asked me if we had thought of a name – I said No – He said it was important – H. P. said something might occur to him & I said we would be thinking – the end of all was that Pinker told me he thought they would publish the *S. Fox* in a week or a fortnight, & that then they might take hold of the short stories & bring them out later in the autumn – H. P. said that as soon as ever he saw the M.S. of Emily & co that he wld make Pinker an offer, & that we could then decide – He said he liked the Royalty System – I said that we always liked it too, but that we should want a sum down, to wch he agreed) I really don't think there is any more to tell except that they begged me to come & see them again as soon as possible, & to bring you with me as they much desired the pleasure of yr acquaintance etc – The end of it all is My Lady Anne, that you must come back to Drishane or else meet me in a desert place as soon as possible, get yr insides tidied up by Willy S., & buckle to. Some other Irish Devil who can hunt and write will rise up & knock the wind out of our sails, & we can't afford to be jockeyed like that – The *S. Fox* money will make us fairly independent of course you take the usual proportion 3/5ths wasn't it? & that ought to give you a good lift, & you need be in no hurry to pay me that loan until after Xmas – I think on the whole it was satisfactory & worth the money, time & trouble of going up – I feel sure that you will remember heaps of things I forgot, but I done my best, & my check suit, white shirt, etc, etc, looked very ladylike & mildly sporting . . . I hope you will get the physic safely.

Yours Ever
Edith

[From Martin to Edith, 28 May 1898. Gladstone's lying in state.]

. . . – so many years of sighing and serving in the lout-hole may have had their uses. I long to see the Salons – in carpet slippers. Patent leather at the Academy was an experience not to be forgotten. We then lunched with E. at her club where were Cuthbert, and Connie. It was unfortunately Robert's *Pink 'Un* day – and he couldn't come. I hear Lord Morris lighted on my article in the *Sunday Times*, and spoke well of it to Robert "Sure it's what we all knew, and none of us ever thought of saying it like that". After lunch I went to the Morrises and found Kathleen &

Frances & Eileen just off to Boulogne for a week, with their bicycles. Provoking that they don't go a little later. They drove me to the Stores, and then, finding I hadn't enough with me to buy anything, I walked down to Westminster, and nothing daunted, joined the great procession of people that was passing through Westminster Hall to see Gladstone's coffin. It was rather a long business – and almost necessitates a picture [diagram]

The dotted lines are police. The crowds followed the arrow heads, a loose crowd at first, but at Westminster Bridge & Station it got tight. We had to keep the line of police always on the right. Some people tried to bolt through them, so as to cut off the long loop that had to be gone round, but they were always sent back. It was an eminently vulgar lower middle class crowd, dull beyond expression – and mostly up from the provinces – I should say – Little dowdy women and hideous girls and dingy men, mostly of that class. All most orderly – no one said anything the least interesting, and very little of any kind. I was struck by the small size of many, indeed most. I felt quite tall among them, and found that the little women had rather a tendency to cleave to me having observed that I was fairly clean, and took up little space – I saw some blue jackets, and a boy's cricket eleven with their bats and stumps. At no time was the crush worse than coming out of a London church, and though it was sometimes hot and odoriferous I didn't mind and there was no shoving allowed. Nearly everyone was in black of some kind but I must say that curiosity, and not concern or grief, was the temper of the crowd. There was a bit of a shove going in at the door of Westminster Hall, but the police managed it wonderfully, and the tide was cleft apart into two gangways, very wide ones, as you will see from the papers I sent you. I took the right, with the black cloth barrier up to my shoulder, and got along easily. You know the Hall I daresay, very lofty with oak arches in the roof, and a big stained window at one end and a big plain window at the other – Perfectly bare of everything but the coffin and the crowd. There was a black bier, raised about 6 feet draped very meagrely in black cloth that sort of way. [drawing] Over half of it was a white silk thing, worked in a few subdued colours. It was the Archbishop of Canterbury's pall or something and would have made a lovely bedspread. The coffin was dark panelled oak – unvarnished – with big brass rings. That and the big candles burning all around were the whole of the show. It was no doubt very impressive to think of what lay there, and also of Charles I tried for his life on that same spot or near it. But as a ceremonial it was too unadorned. One could see that the people looked flat, they wanted something more than all that blackness and bareness and angularity, though to anyone who had known him it must have been all that could be wished. Everyone looked respectful, but no one looked thrilled – and I was not thrilled either. As one mounted the steps at the far end, it was a strange sight – more imposing from there than anywhere else – The dark double flood of people, the island of light round the coffin, the faces turning up towards it, and over their heads the gothic arch of the far doorway framing a bit of Westminster Bridge station and the little vulgar shops by it. Then out I went and breathed a good many long breaths before the smell of the crowd was out of my system. It had taken nearly half an hour to do the whole thing. Let no one say again that I am unenterprising – and I continued my career by taking an electric cab up to the Cavalry Club. It was amusing, and it turned with extraordinary neatness in a block at Hyde Park Corner, but I should much rather have a hansom. This was like a little single brougham and through the front windows one viewed a driver turning a wheel and shoving a handle while a burring sound went quivering through all things, nothing unpleasant, but when I got out I felt my head a little uncomfortable. Being too early for Cuthbert I took a turn in the Row, where were a few much dressed and much bored people, and some gorgeous carriages and horses. I notice that lots of them have coloured favours on the bridles. I don't know if that is new. We had rather a pleasant tea at the Cavalry Club – all women except our hapless host. Edith Dawson, myself, Amy, a Mrs Sykes, (wife of a man in the Bays) and Kathleen Morris. Finally we met Pudgie Slacke and were taken over his charming little house in Piccadilly – like a house that Dodo would have lived in. With that Amy and I fled to the 7.5. at Charing Cross and got home here at nine. I certainly had not let the grass grow under my feet – and had been in most varieties of vehicle. Three buses, two trains, a landau, a hansom, an electric cab and finally a waggonette. As to my feet themselves, I tottered in and was just able to put on turkish slippers in which they were able to spread forth like seaweed in water – Otherwise I was no more than comfortably tired . . .

In November 1898 Martin was badly hurt in a hunting accident; the RM stories were written when she was an invalid, and Edith the nurse.

Thursday Evening. Oct 23/00

Dear Martin

I had to put you off with 2 postcards today & yesterday, so I will now try & write a letter on my studio block, (nothing else handy) Mab is sending Katie's address to Ethel Maxwell who will, she *thinks* be in Brighton while K. is there. I send herewith yr washing, (left in clothes basket) *Scribner*'s, & Aran, & I think there is nothing more. I also send Chandler's letter. *Could* we do anything for him? If you could apply yr heart to it, & plot, I wld try & fill in dry bones, & send on to you, but don't like hearing of yr stupified head again – I hope you aren't doing to much with yr tea parties & yr swaggering about roses – Did you ever hear of a little fable about a lion's skin? Never have I heard of such impudent fraud as your setting up as a gardener! I had always felt a good deal of a fraud myself, but you are an even more stupendous impostor – Merveille de Lyons is a very good white H.P. (Hybrid Perpetual, dear, perhaps you didn't know?) & Caroline Testout is a very good & free going pink. I will tomorrow look out that name of the big one you ask about – I *think* it is the Merveille de L – No, Madame Combat but can't be certain – Rodacanachi is a beautiful red, & has been going strong since June – Reiné Marie Henriette is a lovely climber. (Bright cherry red when in bud) You know William Allen Richardson of course – an E. aspect for it & not too much sun – Now you can continue yr career of Garden Expert – Chuck in Madame Falcot as an orange tea, & Laurette Messing as a China monthly, & you have enough to make yr poor lady sit up – I respect Edith for hiforing for Martin Morris – I can imagine her hard tenor screech – you wld give just such another – I spent yesterday morning at Rineen, trying to paint the bridge, & if this gorgeous weather lasts, hope to do so some more – Our glass is just sticking out at the top it is so high, & the heat is incredible for the time of year

Mab went out without her coat – no more can be said – she and I dined at Glen B last night to meet the Aylmers, Joe, and Capt Stokes, who departs tomorrow (Capt Ricketts arrives, with a wife and no children, said to be poor. Wants a cheap house. Sure to be dull I fear.) It was pleasant. I had Percy and tho my arm ached with wielding the pump handle, I got some few facts out of him. Eddy goes back next month – He looks rather perished, but is more talkative – He really is very nice – Joe was delightful and sang and jack-acted for, or rather to, Mab, with highest success. Capt Stokes broke forth in a species of swan song, *&, to his own accompaniment*, solemnly sang a horrid, stale, old sea-song, with a chorus about "jolly boys" & "folly boys" and a questionable verse about the chaplain with Bet Bowser on his knee, & the way to heaven being "why of course you young dog, in her arms"! a most unexpected development, & a most painful entertainment – I shd have written to you yesterday had not Mrs Myross & Nellie come in, just as I was sending off violets! Only for H. & Joe (who had arr'd in the very nick of the moment) all wld have been lost. Joe is really even nicer than Eddy in many ways – Far more useful. He drove me to Rineen, & will & can do any mortal thing he is asked – except tell a story in less than 20 minutes. He says a friend of his told him he had first read the R.M. "economically", a scrap every night – then he had gallopped thro' it, & then he just wallowed in it, & then, (& not till then, he was *thankful* to say,) he had been told it was written by two ladies! Mr Purdon today told me that whenever he was tired, & cross, & bored, he read it, to cheer him up! Are we really going to be bracketted with Sponge's *Sporting Tour*? It almost looks like it – and that brings me to the hunting today. H again lent me King, & I honestly think she wld have been dead, so I don't regret it or feel mean. Oh my dear, *did* I tell you? Mrs Honourable A. Bob Ridley, Veuve, wrote to me on Sunday to say that she would *buy* Caradil, and I had to write back and say that she wasn't fit – was ever, *ever* such rotten luck? – 6 weeks ago she was dead right, & now I had to say she wouldn't be fit for 3 weeks at least, & I suppose Mrs R. won't be bothered with her – But this is a digression – We met at Old Court Brig, 11 to the minute – Hugh & Mary – I am getting quite fond of them – biked – Dr Jennings, the Carsons, (whom I really adore,) Northridge on a mare he bought for £5, (*quite* a good one sold for incurable vice, & she is now like a sheep,) Henny & Elly B. & Mrs Purdon were out – We put in at the W. end of Creagh, & found at the far E – I was watching out, & suddenly the dear little fox face was developed, like a photograph, so stilly and like a breath do they come, in the middle of a hedge near me – he flicked across the open bit of the covert & across into the Old Court, & then for Lachareagh, hell for leather – King jumped right well, but wants kicking along – *one* field off the wood the fox twisted to the east – "the hounds was pinching him bloody tight" it was explained to me subsequently by an old countryman – and went away over nice grass & good bank to Lick, at the foot he turned & ran North – scent getting very bad, the sun like a furnace, my mouth salt with drouth, and ran as if for Lissard but turned and went to Kelleher's – there we were put wrong by a boy, & lost him – we picked him up again, but too late & schooled slowly back to the covert at Lachareagh – very good fun – about 4 miles – the first 3 very fast – only Mr Purdon, Carsons, Crowley & I in it – Mr Purdon goes like a mad thing, & has a good-jumped mare – I begin to think poor Henny B. is a fraud – She was on that huge 17 hand black mare – an ugly brute all over – she told me there was nothing in the county she wouldn't jump – there was one gap of about 3 feet high that she wouldn't, anyhow. & I don't think Henny asked her to jump anything else, or ever has – She talks too much – "Ah *that* mare" says Crowley, "sure she's like a pole Miss, she have no body at all – " It is a perfect description – she is just like a huge black telegraph pole, with Henny in a lump on the top of it – Henny had a long history of how she & Northridge & old Jennings were put wrong by country people – *Hugh & Mary* were knocking gaps for them! It is too amusing an idea, & Mary's slow little scorn for the party was most unexpected. We drew Lachareagh then, from end to end twice, but tho' I think there was a fox in it they couldn't get him out. The puppies were tired, having hunted most awfully well at first, so we went home, & I have enjoyed few things more than coming home from the kennels via Mary Dwyer's, and bucketting in across the Home Park. "Oh it was delicious" she said, & gave a brand new sensation to this aged frame. The a.f. aforesaid stood the racket wonderfully & is but mildly and agreeably fatigued. Mab is far more so, from having assisted at a massive infant tea at Hildegarde's, from wh Bubby returned, quite silent from pride, in a large paper cocked hat. I groan at the thought that B. will be sweeping off the whole party in little more than a fortnight – Do you know I am really trying to buy a pony – a good one to make a hunter and drive, and sell for polo – I suppose Edith does not know of one – I have scouts out here – Kootenays are to do it, & Ross. – lands will cover my retreat to the workhouse – Of course La Veuve Ridley *may* think it worth while to wait for Cara, but I shouldn't if I were she – I have, of course, told her the whole history – By the way you should have heard Miss Carson extolling your riding & your courage, & your success in the hunting field – I listened with ill-feigned acquiescence . . . [*end of extract*]

Champex
Monday – 15th/7/01

Dear Martin

Look on the other side of this, & see what you think of it – I have written to him – very politely, & apologetic, & saying that you have been ill, & I have been at Aix, &c &c & that we hope to get to work next month & thank you for yr kind letter. Shall I take him the article on Gardens? Just to stop his mouth – It isn't too bad – We hope to start on Wed. & get to town on Friday – Bolton Studios. Egerton crosses the following Tuesday. H. & I & the children on Thursday or Saturday. Master Jack goes to the *Hotel Cecil*, at Georgiana's charges! T'is well to be he! His hand[1] is really better, wh is something – I shall be thankful to be out of this, even tho it is just beginning to get tolerable, & I have found a place that I *could* paint – However it is not worth stopping for. The weather is very nice, & I keep wondering if it wld suit you – It is not the thing for me: I am dead tired at night, & not able for ¼ as much as I can do at home, or almost anywhere else – I sleep like a log, & hate getting up in the morning, wh is always a bad sign – (even tho the best time to paint here is from 5 to 8.30 a.m.) I enclose a letter from V. Don't read the "Private" part to anyone, as E. wouldn't like it – otherwise it is highly interesting – try & settle yr plans as quickly as possible, that I may do likewise – also try & stick to Ireland, because of Candy, but if you are keen on anywhere else say so – It wd. be cheaper to stay in Ireland – Hildegarde advocates Rathnew, on the Dublin & Wicklow line, about 1½ hours from Dublin – on a river – lovely garden of Walpole's to paint in – Very nice little hotel – but not as fine in all ways as Cushendall – & probably not so bracing – I was very glad to have yr letter the other day & to hear Good news of you – Do keep well and fit. Think of Mr Meredith, Mr Arnold, The Strand, Longmans, The foul Northern Syndicate!!!

Your ever,
Edith

[From Edward Arnold to Edith Somerville, 10 July 1901, included in her sequence of letters]

Dear Madam,
I hope you will excuse me for venturing to remind you how anxious I am to have the chance of securing some of your work. Have you not got something – anything, that you would allow me to see? Amusing books are so rare, that it is a positive duty for the few who have the power of writing them to continue doing so in the interests of the community.

I think Mr. Maxse was in communication with you about the article you mentioned to me some time ago. I think he told me he had offered

---

1 Jack Somerville was wounded in the Boer War.

to publish it without illustrations but had not then heard whether that would suit you.

Believe me,

Very faithfully yrs,

Edward Arnold

Glen B. 1901
Friday Aug 2

Dear Martin

The reason I don't write is that I have too much to say & no time to say it in.

Saturday Aug 3rd (& all soft were the skies, & it might be inferred I was going to rise, but it's scarce six o'clock, & a bath is a thing I despise −) Now try and scan that − I have the divil − I have just prowled downstairs, got these materials, met little Miss Oliver, & hinted an excellent cup of tea out of her, so now I can at last write to you as Bridget wont call me till 7.30 − The Mall as you have doubtless realised is the cause, it *is* the cause − my soul − I have, with the aid of Percy's frame, & the old Glen B. ottoman, & a mirror I bought in London, & other things, made a very successful over mantel − I won't now bore you with its details, as I will draw it for you when I see you, & please goodness that will be soon − Miss Candy emerges from seclusion today. Muck not for a week, (tho we have grave fears of one day when for 10 minutes she escaped from H., & came flying up from the point attended by Jerry & the coastguard dog −) Maria has just been immured. Egerton was, I hear, furious, because H. & I kept wondering "*where* poor old Maria could be", & being seriously anxious as to whether she had died in secret of her own surpassing stench. At last he very crossly told H. that Maria was shut up, & was made still more angry by H.'s uncontrollable amazement that it should still be thus with her − Personally, I should as soon expect Madame de Bunsen . . .

This letter provides a vivid description of W. B. Yeats by Martin when she was staying at Coole. Yeats had been aware of the importance of The Real Charlotte *from the moment of its publication. In a letter to Katharine Tynan (15 January 1895; given in* The Collected Letters of W. B. Yeats, Vol. I, 1865–1895, *eds. John Kelly and Eric Domville) he wrote: 'by the bye I wish you or someone else would do a general article*

in some monthly, either on the recent literature of Ireland, or on its
more popular past, the recent Irish stories – Miss Barlows and Miss
Lawlesses and O'Grady's books and such books as The Real Charlotte
– I have not read this but Henley praised it greatly to me . . .' He later
read enough to be able to refer to The Real Charlotte *as describing 'with*
unexampled grimness our middle-class life'.

[From Martin to Edith, 8 August 1901: *fragment. Edith's note added*
later: 'Yeats at Coole']

. . . The afternoon and night at Coole were very interesting – Augusta
Gregory, her son Robert (at Oxford) and W B Yeats were the party.
Kinkie left last week. I may mention that it is 20 years, or nearly, since
I was there – and I was in the same room, and the furniture was the
same. Yeats looks just what I expected. A cross between a Dominie
Sampson and a starved R.C. curate – in seedy black clothes – with a
large black bow at the root of his long naked throat. He is egregiously
the poet – mutters ends of verse to himself with a wild eye, bows over
your hand in dark silence – but poet he *is* – and very interesting indeed
– and somehow sympathetic to talk to – I liked him – in spite of various
things – and I got on well with him, so far. – He gave an opinion of
me to Augusta of which I feel inclined to repeat only the remarkable
adjective, "simple" – I didn't know that I was that nor perhaps did you.
It is strange to talk of "deep subjects of life and death" without any
selfconsciousness, and I must say he induces that, and does it himself.
He is not at all without a sense of humour, which surprised me. He
thinks *The Real Charlotte* very big in the only parts he has read, which
are merely quotations in reviews. He thinks we have the love of sincerity
which makes great novelists and that we should write a big novel without
delay, and if we did there would be no holding it. But he doesn't approve
of humour for humour's sake – (here Miss Martin said beautiful things
about humour being a high art) I will tell you more when we meet and
you will be awfully bored when I am done. Today Augusta made me
add my initials to a tree already decorated by Douglas Hyde, A E and
more of the literary crowd. It was most touching. WBY did the carving,
I smoked, and high literary conversation raged and the cigarette went
out and I couldn't make the matches light, and he held the little dingy
lappets of his coat out and I lighted the match in his bosom. No one
was there, and I trust no one saw, as it must have looked very funny.
Kinkie has I fear put her foot in it about crabbing Augusta's and his pet
artists, and looking in silence at pictures. She may be right in one way,

but she is foolish. Augusta spoke in annoyance about it. Yeats has a . . .
[*end of fragment*]

*Martin and Edith's coolness towards the Celtic Revival shows in their
comments on the novels of George Moore and the work of Edward
Martyn, and here in Martin's description of an Abbey Theatre play.*

Monday
October 28th 1901
21 Ely Place
Dublin

Dear Edith

In a spare half hour I may as well continue. I daresay I shall wire you
today to say that I am not going over till Wednesday morning – that is
the fact anyhow – I feel distressed about Geraldine who is anything but
well – a sort of English cholera; however she was going to have Mangan
to see her. I dont like either the sudden failures of strength, she almost
falls, and she drops things when the attack comes. However Mangan
can I daresay do a good deal for her. Her wan, worried face is before
me, not that I think she has anything to worry her at Ross, if Mama
keeps well, and if the servants go on as well as they have been doing.
My week is not up here till Thursday, so I may as well take as much
good as I can out of it. I was beginning to tell you of the Irish plays, to
which Eileen Hewson and I went on Friday night. There was rather a
thin house, but this was an unexpected night. It was to have been a
matinée. Mr and Mrs Benson's company did it, and I may say that a
more unattractive hero than Mr B I have seldom seen. In his love making
he moaned over Mrs B's face like a cat when a dog comes into the room.
I could have thrown up. I thought *Diarmid and Grania* a strange mix
of saga and modern French situations – George Moore and Yeats were
palpable throughout – the former in the situations the latter in the
beautiful writing here and there, and in the peculiar simplicities that
arose. It was hardly a play for Eileen I'm afraid – the biblical terms
being not shrunk from to describe the progress of the emotions of Grania
who was excessively French in her loves. In the first act she is on the verge
of an enforced marriage to Finn; she states without any contemptible
subterfuge her reasons for objecting to this, and finally deludes Finn's
friend Diarmid into falling in love with her and taking her away from
the marriage feast à la young Lochinvar. He only yields after much

lovering on her part – then curtain. The next act is sometime afterwards, and the really novel position is that she has become tired of Diarmid. I give George Moore some credit for that. Never was anything like her ecstacies of love for him in the first act. She then falls in love with Finn, which she might have done in the beginning and saved the writing of the play – and the curtain is Diarmid's discovery of them in howlts,[1] and his resolve to go and hunt an enchanted boar, which a family witch (a stout lady in a grey teagown and a conversational English accent) has prophesied out of her spinning wheel is to be the death of him. The last act is Grania's noble endeavours to dissuade him from the hunt, amid much thunder and lightening out in the woods. He makes one or two as backhairy* remarks to her on her conduct as George Moore would wish and retires to hunt the boar. After interludes there is a banging and roaring at the back, and Diarmid is carried in to make dying speeches to Finn and Grania and to be carried off to a funeral march, with Grania striking attitudes all round the place. Finally the court humourist, alone on the stage, says "grand will be the burning of Diarmid, but grander will be Grania's welcome to Finn". If this is the lofty purity of the Irish drama I am indeed mystified. But I believe Yeats and George Moore both believe that it is very grand to be the victim of a variety of fancies, – like Yeats' friend Symons who burst in to say that he had "never been in love before with a serpent charmer" – still there are great points in the play – and unusual moments. Saturday we went to the Royal Hospital concert; a poor show, except for the long old hall, hung thick with shining armour and the admirable tea (price one shilling) administered by beautiful flunkies in scarlet coats. The Duke of Connaught was there, also the Duchess and the daughters, and Lady Cadogan and all sorts worth looking at. Miss Elsner accompanied and was swept off in great glory to tea with the Royalties. She was amusing and nice about it afterwards. The band was indifferent, the songs common. Yesterday you may be sure I was at Dr. Carmichael's and heard a great sermon on Protestantism. I met Eileen Blakeny and her mother and heard from them that Lady Morris was in church listening to all the home truths about the R.C. religion. Saint Patrick's of course in the afternoon – passing pleasant and then tea at 49[2] – where I saw Aunt Sylvia, Consie, and the three uncles in a row. I thought Aunt S seemed fragile enough; and apparently Buxton baths have disagreed with her too – Consie looked so nice and charming – tell Jack that if he isn't in love with her

---

1 *In howlts*: locked together.
2 The Greene's home on St Stephen's Green.

he ought to be – I daresay she will have a good time at Oratava – better than Dublin, in a way – They were very keen to hear all the Castle T. news. Now I am off to Miss Manning's studio after this long and very heavy letter

  Yours ever
  Martin

[From Martin to Edith: *fragment*]

. . . Miss Elsner ceaselessly slips from Committee to Lecture, and Lecture to Meeting, and would hound me and Eileen to all. She is clever and energetic and unconventional, and is much wrapped up in the Feis Ceoil, of which a meeting, about village choral societies, was held in the Mansion House on Friday – I was begged by her to go – to look in at any time, and see the Lord Mayor beside, and hear much usefull information as to how to give Mat Kenealy and Honour Cady the ambition to sing tenor and alto – on the Tonic Solfa system. It was 5 o'clock before I approached, for the first time in my life, the portals of the Mansion House, and in the hall I could see nothing but a dirty bicycle and a little boy of about 10, who murmured that I was to write my name which I did with a greasy pencil from his own pocket. He told me that I was to make for the stairs and take the first to the left. I did so and found myself in a pitch dark drawingroom – I returned to the boy, who told me to go up the stairs and turn to my left – I climbed two flights, of homely appearance, and found a quite dark landing at the top. As I stood uncertain something moved in the dark, it was very low and dwarfish, and my flesh crept; it said nothing, but moved fast, no higher than my waist. It seemed, in the glimmer that came from the foot of the stairs, to be some awful little thing carrying a big bundle on its back or head. I shall never know more than this. There was light down the passage, and making for it I came to a room with little and big beds jammed up side by side, obviously a nursery. There was also a nurse – I murmured apologies and fled – The nurse took not the faintest notice – after various excursions round the landing, I went back to the nursery, and met a good little slut Tweeny without cap or apron who took me downstairs, and put me right for the meeting, which I entered in a state bordering on the zany. That died away very soon under the influence of a long and deadly speech about the hire of concert rooms and pianos, very practical – but deadly. The room was interesting, panelled, with portraits around and the audience was scanty. I recognised people who

I used to see years ago looking old and dingy, as I did myself – that is a lie for me – I had a scarlet face and a new white felt hat sent to me from Southsea and very smart. (Kathleen Bushe told me it couldn't have been bought in Dublin, it was that smart) . . . Yeats' father and M. Hone have an exhibition of pictures on now, but on hearing from Eileen that W B Yeats was incessantly there with Maud Gonne I thought I should stay away as likely as not I should have found myself mixed up in a conversation with her, and that would have involved my doing something rude – I saw her at the Irish play on Friday night, and thought her looks terrific. The features still handsome the nose salient and short but the badness of the expression was startling. A huge mop of curled yellow hair crowned her big fat body. One look at her would be enough for anyone to form an opinion. Yeats was with her in a box all the time, except when he was with I think Augusta Gregory in a box opposite. I never looked his way, I daresay the Irish Literary Revival was quite disastrously unaware of my presence in the shades at the back . . . [*end of fragment*]

[From Edith to Martin, October 1901: *fragment. Edith's note*: 'Jack's return after S. African war']

. . . to send it off before Maxse writes again, as I am sure he will – Don't knock yr head up; I think you may trust me not to do anything *very* awful; it wants so little, & I know that you aren't fit for hair-splittings & adjective-weighings, wh I shouldn't do, & wouldn't mind if I did – shall I say our terms are 4 guineas per 1000? or 5 – ? If we say the latter he might offer something over 4 – If we say 4 he will probably offer something over three – If he backs out we can send it to Pinker.

I find it hard to believe in yr lovely weather. Yesterday was the first really fine & lovely day, & tho' the glass went up to day the rain is coming down heavy and thick – it is most provoking – Jack & Cameron arrived last night, both together as C. waited in Cork for him. Jack had sent stringent orders that no one was to be told he was coming, but ordering his bedroom was enough & more than a notice in the *Times*, & all the village turned out. They had a bonfire at the gate, & wretched Jack had to get down & walk round & talk – It was rather silent & solemn; I think all concerned were a bit shy; then we walked on up the avenue, & behold, another tarbarrel in front of the house – more talking – then a trampling of many feet & up came the first tarbarrel from the gate, & they began to cheer – Then, while this was going on, down by the turn of the avenue a third light appeared, & a monster tarbarrel arrived at a gallop, belching flames as it swung on its garry, amid yells of excitement from a fresh crowd with it – It was exactly like some savage Queen-Dowager, or a bad Fairy at the Christening, rushing up, thinking she was late – Then the three roared and flamed together, & Jack went round & round shaking hands – A lot of the western people had come over, & almost all the village & there was much enthusiasm the barrels being belaboured at intervals to make them burn better – It was most wonderfully picturesque. All the faces lighted up, & the boughs and stems of the trees catching the light & the dark blue sky above. Old Mary Dwyer kept on saying "T'is he was the loving child! O t'is he was the loving child!" to which another old woman responded antiphonally, "And so homely!" Aylmer, Nat, her sister Toby, H. & Egerton, dined here which was pleasant. Jack is looking wonderfully well, & seems twice as hearty as when I saw him last – His hand is ever so much better & has a normal colour & consistency, tho' still very much shrunken – he can now pick up a ball, & last night he actually got a spoonful of soup up to his mouth, without disaster but that was a tour de force – It is most provoking that today is sopping & he can't be Sheba'd round the Gardens – He is not sure how long he can stay; the masseur fears another operation will be necessary to "break down" adhesions in the thumb – Cameron has till the 18th & Mrs Ridley is to arrive on the 9th & will, I fear, stay on till . . . [end of fragment]

Both Jack Somerville and Arthur Townshend served in the Boer War and had triumphs on their return to Castletownshend. This was the last war in which cavalry was able to take any considerable part (in The Irish RM Flurry Knox goes off to the Boer War). The South Irish Horse was one of the cavalry regiments to make its final appearance in the field in the early months of the First World War in which Arthur Townshend served, returning to Castletownshend to die of his wounds. He was unmarried, and so began the distressing complications of inheritance for the Seafield Townshends.

It was discovered that even the Boers were reading the RM. During the First World War The Times sent broadsheets of popular literature to the men in the trenches, and the RM was chosen for its 'cheering qualities'. Drishane had been let to the Warrens.

[From Edith to Martin: *fragment*]

. . . Arthur T. has just come back from being medalled, but I have hardly seen him at all – He has got quite a good moustache & and is *much* improved in looks. They say he is very interesting & will talk – One of his trophies is a large white flag of truce which he carried when going with messages to the Boer camp – It has a bullet hole in it, the honourable enemy having fired on him all the way back to Boshof! Mrs Purdon told H. that her son & his company came upon a dead Boer, & examined him for despatches &c – They found a copy of the R.M. – "He died of laughter – " (see advt.) They took the copy, & it became the camp bible, & was the thing they valued most highly – The widow Currey is here now: she also had her politesse to offer – A very smart lady going to Ireland for the first time said to a friend of the Widow's, "I have bought this book – I want to see how one should talk to the Irish" – ("Damn and blasht your soul" replied my friend Slipper, "may the divil crack the two legs under ye!" (see any page, anywhere, "Irish RM"))

Violet last night returned from a 3 days' rush to Birmingham to get her clothes, she had come straight here from Edinburgh, with no change of clothes beyond a tooth brush – she has now lost *the whole outfit,* on the way from Birmingham to Kingstown, & hasn't even got the tooth-brush – much less Ethel & Kitty, on whose wardrobes she has hitherto subsisted. H. & I are going to keep our doors locked. She has been sent a complimentary copy of what must be a fascinating little paper (one of the many new Society journals) – "*The Uric Acid Monthly*"!!! I say no more.

This village is reeking with whooping cough, & poor H. is in agonies about the babies – Their photographs, taken by Eva Le Mesurier, in London, have just come, & are, I think, not to be beat – H. is going to send them to you – There is one of Paddy in Chinese dress, sitting on the ground, that to my thinking is perfectly enchanting – The expression is so subtle & unexpected – I have not yet told you of that old country family, the Warrens of Drishane – It was a strange and *not* agreeable thing to ring the bell, & be asked by a scorbutic faced English maid "What name shall I say please?", but the Warrens themselves are nice, quiet people – So far they have consisted only of Mrs. Warren, slight, rather deaf, rather pleasant, rather like Mr. Baxter & me; Miss Neilson, her sister about 5 or 6 years younger than Mrs. W. – say 35 or so – and several plain children – I hear Mr. W. and a friend have now arrived, but we haven't seen them – They go on Sept. 2nd, & I want to be back here as soon as may be after that, as the garden and the hounds claim attention, & I don't see why we couldn't work here very comfortably. Sept. always suits you here, & is generally bright and dry, & if Nov. proved too bad you might go up to St. Andrews. Mrs. Coghill & I wish to say that if you find your health can't stand it, we will pay the cost of yr ticket here, as it is by *our* wish that you are coming – I have abandoned the thought of Cushendall – No time, & too late in the year, but I hope I may get to Ross about Monday or Tuesday week – But listen, *I won't go at all if I am made to play the organ* & you may tell them so –

The attitude of the poor people here about the Warrens is very amusing – Mrs Tim Crowley says "I'd *hate* to see them in it! I'd twice rather t'was empty!" Mrs Leary poses as Flora MacIvor to my Prince Charlie – "When are ye coming back? Send me up yer washin" – (in the blackest of whispers) "*I'll do it here for ye!*" This means, I know, an "alien's" soap and kitchen fire, but I ask no questions, & assume she does it at her own house . . . [*end of fragment*]

Christmas day
1901

Dear Edith

I snatch a moment between lunch and going up to tea at Killaguile to write to you. I got your letter of Saturday as I was going into Galway on Monday morning, and since then I may say I have never drawn bridle. Parcels, and always parcels, letters, cards. The worst is over now – I have left your letter upstairs, and am sure I shall neglect much that I want to say and answer. How good of you to think of Mama. She is writing – she is much bewildered over her Christmas letters and cards, and I only hope she will make no irreparable mistakes. I enclose a card from the Justin McCarthys. I found a lovely one in Galway, real shamrock, pressed, and a verse of decent poetry and a message "From old Galway" I wrote in it "with best wishes from the authors of an Irish RM." and despatched it – I also wrote a letter with it – so I think I did well – still many weigh on me – but so far my head has held out, with the dint, I think, of all the driving in the bitter winds and showers. Yesterday afternoon I had to drive over to the Oughterard workhouse to see about the workhouse tea that Edith gives every Christmas. It was twilight and murky moonlight as Mat and I drove back with the grey along that road that leads from the station to Oughterard – he was driving, on the right side – I saw three or four men coming towards us in the road – on my side – the nearest to me just in the centre of the road – Mat pulled away to the right, I called out to take care, but the man held on straight, and the wing of the car hit him bang in the chest, and he fell straight and hard as a baulk of timber, flat onto his back, and lay motionless – everybody shrieked and shouted, I jumped off and ran to him, – there he lay with his arms out, staring up, and the stink of whisky fumed up from him. At the same moment the 5 o'clock train came into the station, two or three yards away, and the other men took to their heels and ran to catch it, leaving me and Mat to deal with him – I may privately mention that Mat begged me to jump on the car and drive away. He was in a blue funk that the man was killed.[1] However instead of that he pulled into the side of the road, and I said I would drive for a policeman. With the greatest luck, just as I was starting a policeman came along the road. I told him, and he said I must stay there, he went to the man, who, to my great relief was beginning to grunt and groan, and pulled him about a bit. The next thing was a voice "Where's the man that knocked me down" – I then began to take heart. The policeman then asked me my name and address – and having heard it regarded me fixedly through the twilight and said "Were ye ever at a concert in Spiddal?" It appeared he had sung the song at the one I was at with the Morris's – so was all on velvet – before I left the man was staggering towards home – and as I have heard no further, I hope all is well. It was his own fault, but it was horrid to see him flung with such force – and fall with such a crash. Now I must away to Killaguile. Good luck my dear – You were in my mind today in church. I am sure you and H. are worn out with the Christmas doings – and there is much for you to contend with in your playing the organ. I know well how the hymns take you –

Yours ever
Martin

---

1   This incident was used in *Oweneen the Sprat*.

ST. PATRICK'S DAY IN THE MORNING.

A Patrick's Day Hunt. By Martin Ross and E. Œ. Somerville. (A. Constable and Co. 6s.)—"Poor William Sheehan" was the hero of the hunt, "and indeed poor William had great courage the same day." He escaped from the bondage of Anne Roche ("that's his wife"), though he knew, like the rest of the world, that if she heard of it "she'd tear iron." He mounted on his "yella harse" —'Shan Buie' was the local name for it and other duns with the black stripe on the back—and away with him. But whenever they met the first stone wall "the yella pony jumped it very crabbed," and got the fall of the ground before him, "and that was the time William was promising God that if he come safe out he'd howld to the side-car and not go huntin' again." Still and all, there was no fox coming out of the cover, though a woman of the Sullivans knew a nest in it and "seen himself and his pups walkin' in and out of it like young pigs." The dogs got a short spin after a cat, though, and ate her; and then another cover was tried: and in crossing country to it William Sheehan again distinguished himself. He coursed the yellow pony three turns about the field, "and when he thought he felt him jaded, it's then he faced him at the wall. But in spite of all he jumped it very sevare and ugly." "Meself," says the narrator, "I don't like them flippant leppers; I'd like a horse that will put his two forefeet into the butt o' the wall, and give ye time to say two Aves and a Pather before he leps out." (A horse is shown, by the way, in one of the illustrations in exactly this posture of meditation.) What else happened to poor William Sheehan after a drag with half a gallon of paraffin came to enliven the proceedings, and finally was run down in his own backyard, must be read in the chronicle. What passed between him and Anne Roche is left to imagination, but the narrator met her a full week after, and the dogs would not pick his bones after she was done with him. These flowers of style, it will be understood, are culled from the easy flow of the narrative, which describes a fox-hunt in County Cork with all the keen humour familiar already to readers of the "Experiences of an Irish R.M." It is very unlike the ideal thing, as shown in Lever and elsewhere; and it is vastly amusing, as one need hardly say. The illustrations are almost equal to the text, and, simply as illustrations, are not to be beaten.

Sylvia, Arthur Townshend's sister, was a woman of some resourcefulness. The next letter shows her confronting a domestic catastrophe and overcoming it in style.

[From Edith to Martin: *fragment: starts on page 2*]

Sylvia has formally and finally taken the Mall from the 1st January for a year! Reggie's people wired to say not to keep it for them, so she has it. I think the last spur, had one been needed, was given by the visit of Major Anderson, of "the Manchesters", which took place yesterday –

Harry wrote a long letter to Hildegarde about it. About a month ago the spirit moved him similarly & he wrote to her about the events in this place, exactly as if she were in England or in Australia. He said he never saw her & he wished to communicate with her sometimes. Today's letter was in parts truly delightful. I have sent it to Jim & told him to send it on to you, you are to send it on to Boyle, (having first shown it to Jack), Boyle to Cameron, & thence back to H. Sylvia came up this evening & gave us the history from her point of view, & it seems to me worth recording. The man Anderson was to come down by the 10.30 from Cork & return by what was believed to be the 7 p.m. He had very important affairs in Cork, a board of some kind, & could not possibly stay for the night. 4 chickens were slain & a turkey. Ham, tongue, lobsters, fish, (from Cork) were laid in, besides sweets innumerable. The Curreys were asked to lunch, the whole place to tea. There was to be boating &c &c. At 11 a.m. the rain began. At 1.30 the brave Manchester arrived & the worry began. Much-loved though he is, Sylvia admits that she never saw a man eat & drink as much; it seems to have been, tho' disillusioning, the brightest feature of the case. Bessie went a mucker & had 3 glasses of champagne & a wine glass of Benedictine, which had the result of making her talk incessantly & abusively of Sandys, selecting the widow Currey, Sandys' dearest friend, as confidante. Sylvia, coping with her man, heard such fragments as "Never forgiven me for marrying Harry" – "Never so insulted in my life" – and saw the widow getting more & more like a little drawing room poker. Then, to stop it, in spite of the rain, they all huddled on coats & went out to look at the view from the Castle T. avenue. Having admired the scenery sufficiently to give the kettle time to boil, they returned for tea. At tea Mrs Wilson seems to have been a great success, & they managed to keep going until 6.15 when Harry's brougham, with Dick Connell's horses came to remove the guest. He went away in heavy rain, & in 5 minutes the carriage was back at the gates. One of the horses had jibbed hard opposite Mal Maison, the other had pulled equally hard. Pat with difficulty averted a bad upset & turned back. They then went up the Glen B. avenue, but on arriving at the station found that the train had gone some time, being earlier on Sundays. So Pat drove him back once more – (I forgot to say that during the row on the hill the heroic Anderson had sat unmoved in the carriage, being under the impression that the abrupt turn for home was only a sharp corner on the outward road (I think the last whiskey & soda must have been rather severe –) His surprise at finding himself once more at Seafield must therefore have been considerable). It appears that Sylvia was not told of this first misadventure, & secure in the belief that he was off she had got into a dirty old white silk summer blouse, relaxed her stays, put on an ancient skirt, & was coming downstairs to take it easy, when upon the hall door there came a heavy knocking, as with a big stick. The parlour maid, who was in the cloakroom place, came out for one alarmed moment, & then darted back among the waterproofs, shrieking to Sylvia "The Lord protect us Ma'am, tis the Convict," – (i.e. the renowned Lynchahane, who is believed to be in these parts –) "Nonsense!" says Sylvia, "Open the door" – Major Anderson – who didn't know where the bell was, & had therefore to beat upon the panels like a man in a play.

It was then about 8 o'clock; Sylvia shoved him into the Starboard room for her father to deal with, & made a bee line for the kitchen. Mary the Monkey, secure, as she believed, in the calm of cold hashed party for dinner, was holding a levée. Two of her sisters, several old women, & a man or two – Sylvia says it was like a wake – "Mary!" she said with awful brevity, "Major Anderson has come back!"

"Lord God Almighty!" responded the Monkey, very appositely, flinging both her arms over her head. Then, & without another word, she faced the music – "Clear the kitchen!" she said, with a majestic sweep of one fat arm. In an instant the company had vanished, all but the two sisters, who were kept running like cockroaches in & through the house from that moment, till, as far as one knows, the following morning. There was soup, but there was nothing hot. "There *must* be a hot entrée", says Sylvia. "I have nothing in the place Ma'am" says the Monkey. "The Chicken pie!" said the inspired Sylvia. Its insides were clawed out of it & hurled into a bowl of curry, the lobster salad was similarly disembowelled, devilled, & sent in a savoury. It was a nice gentlemanlike little dinner, but in the middle of it Sylvia remembered that the guest had no sleeping kit, & that her father had only two sets of pyjamas – both incredibly old & decayed. Directly after dinner she wrote to Mrs Wilson for a pair of "Archdale's" – Mrs W. was in bed & asleep, it being then long past 10, but the faithful messenger would not leave without an answer – which took the form of pyjamas as thick as blankets & reeking of napthalene. S. hurried with them to the guest's room (the guest being steeped in whiskey & soda with Harry). This room had been got ready in the morning for him to wash his hands in, & to do him honour, its own dirty old cracked china had been removed & a smart new set of Sylvia's substituted. You may imagine her horror at finding that during the brief interval of his drive to Skibbereen the old set had been replaced, & all the little decorations carefully eliminated by the zealous Mary Anne, who felt, I suppose, that she was bound to assert herself as Sylvia's maid. At last, at some small hour, they all staggered to bed, & at day break S. received a note from Mrs Wilson – "Please do not think of sending Archdale's pyjamas to wash, as they are very special flannel & would shrink – &c &c" – S. wrote back to say that she would return them to Mrs Wilson as soon as they were cool, which, as Major Anderson had only just got out of them, they were not at present. He departed by the early train, & has not since returned.

You see I have told you the yarn at full length as there are things in it which might come in useful – but I think you had better keep it to yourself, as if, through Jack, the Pagets, & Zoë Cairns, a garbled version got back to Harry, I should get into row of the worst kind. Of course Harry's own letter is all right, but Sylvia's more intimate details might get us into a row, if repeated, as they might be. You may tell Edith if you like.

The rain has ceased & it is a very quiet night. I took Bridget out this afternoon & was drenched. She is as fat as three pigs – most unbecomingly so – Rayleen looks very smart – Goodbye. – Write & tell me how you like the stuff I sent you – I think "The Connemara Mare" would be a good & interesting name for the story – send on Harry's letter without delay to Boyle.

Yours ever
Edith

As Edith and Martin knew perfectly well that The Real Charlotte *was their best work, they were puzzled by its reception. Personal friends and some rather cutting reviews damned the book and it is almost as if they shrugged their shoulders and moved away into the safer territory of funny short stories. Certainly the invention of the* RM *rescued them financially and gave them what Martin called 'the large and swelling reputation'. When Martin or Edith visited editors now they were treated with reverence, as precious beings and celebrities.*

Saint Patricks Day
March 17th 1903

Dear Edith

How good of you to think of the shamrock. I found it here last night, quite fresh and all right, and I have a piece on for breakfast and hope to be hung with it this afternoon – as I am going to tea at the House of Commons – John Atkinson is the host, and Robert and Eileen and I are the guests – and the curse has come upon me, cried the Lady of Shalott – and I shall be stupid and headachy and nervous, and if you saw the things John Atkinson said about the R.M. in the letter you would feel for me. If only you were there, it would be all different – I daren't travel tonight so Eileen and I go tomorrow – I am just crawling (like a bird, that-a-way) down to Pinker – to talk of various things. Yesterday Cuthbert came up and went with me to the *Spectator* Office, where we had tea in Mr Strachey's room. There were there Mr S – large capable, Jewish looking, 43 years old – shaved except for a *tiny* black moustache, kind and all there – and modern – and stirring. There was Charlie Graves, and Eric Parker – a nice quiet young man now editor of *Country Gentleman*. Having had very strong tea out of breakfast cups (and some had two breakfast cups) Mr Strachey sat down before me and said that he owned the *Country Gentleman* as well as the *Spectator* – and would we allow them (him and Eric Parker) to make a bid for the serial rights of the new R.M. for the *Country Gentleman*. I was not to commit myself, or to think of taking a penny less than we were getting elsewhere – you can imagine that I temporised and said Pinker – on which Eric Parker brightend up and said he had the highest opinion of Pinker – and was delighted that we had an agent – Mr Strachey said resounding things of the R.M. – and said that the "Irish Problem" marked a new departure in humour. He raved of it – Cuthbert had his innings with him about the Automobile Club – satisfactory too – though of course all in the air – but I am sure Strachey would help – Mr Graves said he had a very nice letter from you (bother you – coming in behind me) and that you and I wrote very much alike. I do think of you, starting now for Skib – and I hope you have a nice day – It is blowing a lot here –

Yours
Martin

Priests were entertained as often as Church of Ireland clergymen at Ross, and in this fragment we have a glimpse of one of Martin's favourites, Father Connolly.

[From Martin to Edith, 9 August 1903: *fragment*]

... The run to Screeb on the motor was lovely – perfect weather – We lunched at the Saint Georges – at their fishing lodge on the edge of the

OF THE SOIL

"All on the Irish Shore. Irish Sketches." By E. Œ. Somerville and Martin Ross. With Illustrations by E. Œ. Somerville. London : Longmans. 6s.

FROM Lord Scamperdale's country or Handley Cross to those regions of Irish Ireland where they still hunt the fox in primitive fashion is a far cry. All the same, the spirit of the chase bears somewhat of a family likeness wherever they don the pink, and along with it comes naturally—inevitably it would almost seem— the breath of light-hearted spontaneous humour. It is not with any of the great Irish packs, famous everywhere for their perfect turn-out and the sport they can show, that the racy Somerville-Martin Ross sketches are concerned. We are introduced to squireens and buckeens, rub shoulders with sly horse-dealers and stable hands, and scrape acquaintance with blind beggars and village ruffians—quick-witted and engaging scapegraces all. And the quadrupeds ! Such horses ! Such dogs ! Long will memories be cherished of Miss Fanny Fitzroy's Connemara mare, the fiend-quadruped that wrought such diabolic yet mirth-moving mischief wherever it went. Or Freddy Alexander's remarkable pack— survivors of "the old Moynalty Baygles. Black dogs they were,

with red eyes ! Every one o' em as big as a yearling calf." The invasion by these "baygles" of the tinker's hut in company with Bismarck, the yellow dachshund, is the basis of perhaps the most rollicking short story in the book. Mrs. Alexander's dachshund mauls the tinker's dog, so the tinker calls next day :

"Me lady," began the tinker, "I ax yer ladyship's pardon, but me little dog is dead."

"Well ?" said Mrs. Alexander, fixing a gaze of clear grey rectitude upon him.

"Me lady," continued the tinker, reverentially but firmly, "'twas afther he was run by thim dogs yestherday, and 'twas your ladyship's dog finished him. . . . He was very wake, ma'am, afther he bein' hunted," urged the tinker. "I never slep' a wink the whole night, but helpin' sups o' milk to him and all sorts."

Finally, Willy Fennessy, the wheedling tinker, is told to "go round to the kitchen" ; and from that moment he becomes an incubus, a waking nightmare, on the Alexander household, with consequences that the delightful authors of "All on the Irish Shore" so brightly reveal. Except one—"The Bagman's Pony," in an Indian setting—all the eleven stories are racy of the soil. The fun, cunning, superstitions, and lovable qualities of the people are pictured to the life. We are made to feel the very atmosphere of the countryside ; the sense of rapid movement and the excitement of sport get into the blood in such descriptions as Mrs. Pat's pursuit of the hill fox over the heathery, boulder strewn fields ribbed with rocks. This story, by the way, "A Nineteenth-Century Miracle," turns on a curious case of healing, gravely narrated. Those who know previous results of the Somerville-Ross collaboration will naturally look for more of the characteristic illustrations. And they will not be disappointed.

sea. He is rather a rough diamond, who married an American girl, nearly six feet high – and full of money – chestnut hair – downright, blunt manners, good natured – very plain spoken and with a large and spreading reputation for rapidity – chiefly in the Harry Persse direction. Lord Dudley has been staying in the neighbourhood and finds her entertaining, but I have no wish to say there is anything in that – I never heard there was. She tops up by playing the harmonium in church – her huge long legs awfully in her way – but she gets through by mere force of character. We flew home from Maam cross. The other night Father Connolly dined here – very jovial – and he added thereto by three as fine pegs of whisky as you could wish to see – each about two inches deep, in a tumbler – Cuthbert said he would take him home in the motor which after demur Father C consented to – Cuthbert set forth with Victor and Stella to complete the party and whisked them all to the MacDermot's in Oughterarde at 10.30 p.m. where they were received with open arms – refreshment sprang forth, and finally Father C sang a song – unaccompanied – Cuthbert as the impressario took the hat round and received a penny, a used up half of a return ticket to Dublin, a picture postcard of a lovely creature labelled the "Yes or No series" – and for Father C in all seriousness, a two shilling piece, which was instantly snatched by Mrs. MacD. They then left for home, and reached Father C's house on the New Line at 12.30 – there they simply had to go in – a housekeeper had glasses and a black bottle on the table in a jiffy, and unhappy Stella had to sip some dreadful stuff which looked like sherry and was very sour – As she toyed with it, the sofa gave way under her – but nobody was the worse. A niece of about 17 then appeared, fully dressed, and also drank the awful stuff. They finally got back here before one. These things do not happen out of Galway.

To me, today, the diavolo – I may go to the Eglinton Hotel on Thursday, when Robert arrives. Give my love to Madge and my best respects to Miss Robertson. I shall be very anxious to hear about you and the journey and all things –

Yours ever

Martin

Aren't these photographs good. Keep them if you like. – (two photo's of Ross – first rate –)

[*Edith's note*: 'you might keep the part about the priest for me']

[From Martin to Edith, Newcastle upon Tyne, about 1904: *fragment*]

. . . Yesterday a Mr Orde took Muriel and me out in his Clement motor
– as I partly said. He has only driven since last October, and does not
know much of the machinery. We went very well to Whitley bay, – on
the sea – and he certainly drove very plucky and straight on slippery
roads. We were hideously near running over a child on a greasy down
grade – and he kept his head and saved the situation with a couple of
slithery swings. The child ran across at the last instant – and it was
awful. Soon afterwards the car, with volleys of "back firing" gave in –
and then the afternoon began. It broke down four times, and finally
dragged us somehow through deep black mud on a make-shift road to
Mr Orde's brick works at South Shields which happened to be near. It
was there, black to its axles, got into a brick kiln or something – and
after long and weird delays among inferno visions of brick furnaces we
walked and trammed to a station which we never found and consequently missed our train – among dark and nightmarish places where
they built ships – Finally we found another station – got a train and got
in, fainting for tea, at about 6.30 and I was not a bit tired today.
Thursday morning – I had to break off last night and go to a Miracle
Play done by amateurs at a Parish hall. A little better acting would have
it impressive, a little worse would have laid me on the floor in yelling
and screaming convulsions. As it was, I varied between aching boredom,
shrinking distaste for the materialising of sacred things, and torturing
shoots and thrills of inward laughter. Picture the Virgin Mary painted
and showing off her eyes, discoursing in early English with a hard
modern voice with a thing with dark red wings called Aungell Gabbriel-
le, about the mysteries that one would least wish to hear discussed. One
or two things and moments were faintly like what the poor things were
aiming for. The English audience sat spellbound in crowds – Katie
and I died many deaths. Muriel of course thought of nothing but the
technicalities, and said it was the birth of English drama – and so on.
Katie breathed in my ear "*can* we sit it out" and we did not – after the
kings and shepherds in wavering plain-song had left (I nearly died of
the Kings and had to remain weeping in my programme) which they did
at 10 p.m. We softly crept forth, to electric trams, to fois gras sandwiches, to whisky and soda – and the relief was great – I am so very
glad that I don't live in the early Christian period. [drawing] This is very
like the back view of the priests. They are capes . . . [*end of fragment*]

Among our recent literary productions there is one to which I feel bound to invite a special attention. It is a story called " All On the Irish Shore," and is the joint work of the two ladies who describe themselves in literature as Miss Ross and Miss Somerville. These ladies are the authors of " The Real Charlotte," a novel which won for them a sudden and well merited celebrity some years ago, and of many subsequent novels which well maintained the fame of that first effort. " All On the Irish Shore " does not perhaps make as high a claim to a place in the literature of fiction as " The Real Charlotte," but it is not too much to say that the light of genius is in it. It is a collection of intensely amusing and humorous sketches of certain fields in the Irish life of the present—chiefly, that is to say, in the life which has to do with horses, dogs and sport of all kinds—and it sparkles from first to last with genuine comedy, all the more genuine because it is here and there varied by some tender tones of pathos. I think I was one of the first to call the attention of THE INDEPENDENT and its readers to the writings of these gifted women, and I am glad to be able to say that this, their latest production, deserves the cordial welcome of all who can appreciate Irish humor.

While Edith was in charge of major structural alterations in the kitchen at Drishane, Hildegarde went to a ball at Castle Freke. This great house is now reduced to a shattered shell but is still worth visiting.

Drishane
Thursday July 21st 1904

Dear Martin,

Your two letters were grateful & comforting & now in a moment of comparative repose I will try & answer them. Don't expect too much as my head is not of the best. I am delighted to hear so good an account of the lady Edith Dawson. I should think however that the less she hobbled up or down stairs, or anywhere else, the better for her. The very day you went I sprung a muscle in my right calf when playing tennis – & went dead lame. V. says it is known as "tennis leg" & is very common. It is also a great nuisance, but by dint of keeping quiet on Tuesday I was fit for the show & now I hardly feel it. *Not* that I am keeping quiet. Far otherwise. The Japanese are in Port Arthur & have got the range of the citadel – ie the kitchen range, & all is in turmoil. Katie, Ellen & I are huddled into the dining room & study & the rest of the house is full of masons & carpenters, all in raging passions, & sending for me every five minutes to demand the head of Danny Boy on a charger. I have thought of sending K. & E. home to their Tower & fleeing to Tally Ho, but find that I *must* stay here so as to keep the peace & save Danny from dismemberment. You are well out of it. Added unto all these things were torrents of rain all the morning – now mercifully passed – & the divil. You might be sorry for me – I *must* dine out, as otherwise I couldn't dine at all – the dining room carpet is up & this room is part kitchen, part servants' hall – Ellen bears it like a saint. Katie has even laughed – so things might be worse. Hildegarde arrived from Castle Freke this morning at 6.30. She then went to bed in your room. I had left the tea equipage & my clock for her comfort. The former did well, but the clock, of its own damnable volition, loosed a shrill alarm at 7. H. having been asleep for 10 minutes. Why it acted thus it alone knows, but H. says she was asleep again in 3 minutes & remained so till 10.30. Then she *had* to be waked, as the bombardment had begun. As it was, her breakfast was cooked in the dining room. She says it was an excellent dance. Crowds of surplus men, perfect floor, band, supper, champagne – Lady C. had ordered an army of assistant hireling waiters from Cork, & every man of them arrived blind drunk & had to be put to bed instantly! However all went well. H.'s young charges, from Edie Whitla to Loo Loo, got on first rate & had all the dancing they wanted, & H. herself said that it was very good fun. There were some very wild Easterns there – Nevill Penrose heard a man say to the girl of his heart "Blasht yer soul, where were ye hiding that I couldn't find ye!" But all the decent people were there too; the incredibly kind Mrs Guinness had lent Bock a most lovely dress. *Hand painted chiffon* and silver spangles, H. says it must have cost about 20 guineas. It was amazingly good natured of her, & was far handsomer than the dress she had reserved for herself. H. says however, that Bock ruined her looks by wearing an awful "Juliet" net, (doubtless bought by Grace at Whitely's sale for ten pence three farthings) and having her hair in frouzy rings to her eyebrows – she looked, H. said, like a Gypsy in a Cave of Mystery at a fifth rate bazaar, but she seemed to have got on all right & had plenty of dancing – the lending of the dress should be before Mrs Guinness in heaven – if anything ever precedes anyone there.

Now as to the Show – I was out in the yard at quarter past seven to order the amazing yeomanry that were trooping there – "Danny Boy", upon Pixie, was the first to start, which he did with the speed of light, as he was hardly in the saddle when Pixie tore out of the yard as fast as she could lay legs to ground. Yells of laughter from all the men, shrieks from me to Danny to pick up his reins. He stopped her near the hall door, thank heaven, & then Dick McDonald on Joker, Jack Crowley on Moses, Danny Hayes on Bridget, (full of airs & graces) and Jerome on Loving Cup, ramped forth in various degrees of insecurity. Johnny brought up the rere on Lottery, & had started without the Show labels! when I happily remembered to yell after him & got him back. Poor little Mayfly had got a cut schooling, the day before & had to stay at home, but I wasn't sorry she didn't go, for reasons that I will unfold later. The day was perfect – one threat of rain at 9.30, & after that cloudless skies & no wind until 8.30 pm – (when the *heavens opened* in the worst rain I have ever known – The wretched drivers to Castle Freke!)

Post going. Must send this off – will finish later on – Bridget got 2nd in Hunter Class. Joker 2nd jumping – the 1st prize was his by right –

Yours ever

Edith

Frank and Willy Fay were the Dublin dramatists whose techniques in speech and drama training made the Abbey Theatre what it was. Martin's comments on the plays produced by the Fays are not admiring in the main, but she had the greatest respect for the Fay brothers themselves. In a letter to Edith dated 12 June 1906 Martin describes an occasion at the New Century Club where Frank Fay gave readings from Poisson d'Avril *and* A Patrick's Day Hunt.

April 29th 1905
101 Lower Baggot Street
Dublin

Dear Edith

. . . Of course I could hardly leave here on Tuesday, as Connie does not get to Ross till Wednesday. I have heard from her today that they all hope to get off on Monday night. Robert has been out for two drives. I enclose Katie's account of him – very good on the whole.

Mama gets on very well – I took her out to see Rosalie yesterday. It rained on and off most of the day – Emily has been in and out – and

MISS EDITH SOMERVILLE.

MISS EDITH Œ. SOMERVILLE was born in Corfu on May 2nd, and she is the daughter of Lieut.-Colonel T. H. Somerville, D.L., of Drishane, County Cork, and Adelaide, daughter of Admiral Sir J. Coghill, Bart. Miss Somerville has won first class honours in the Junior Examinations for Women, T.C.D. She is M.F.H. of the West Carbery Foxhounds. The books which Miss Somerville has written in collaboration with her cousin, Miss Violet Martin, are given in another paragraph. She and her cousin are working steadily at a further series of " The Experiences of an Irish R.M." She has drawn and painted since childhood, and has studied principally in Paris. Among other works, she has illustrated " Slipper's A.B.C. of Fox-Hunting," " A St. Patrick's Day Hunt " (of which Miss Martin did the letterpress) Dogs, horses, gardening, lawn tennis, and music are her chief recreative interests, and she is a member of the Ladies' Field, the Lyceum, the Women's International Art and the Belfast Art Clubs and the Irish Water Colour Society.

MISS VIOLET MARTIN.

MISS VIOLET MARTIN, who is the daughter of Mr. James Martin, D.L., of Ross, co. Galway, and Anna, daughter of Mr. Charles Fox of New Park, co. Longford, was born on June 11th, at Ross, County Galway. Under the nom-de-plume of " Martin Ross," she has written in collaboration with her cousin, Miss Edith Œ. Somerville, " An Irish Cousin," " Naboth's Vineyard," " Through Connemara in a Governess Cart," " In the Vine Country," " Beggars on Horseback," " The Real Charlotte," " The Silver Fox," " Some Experiences of an Irish R.M." and " All on the Irish Shore." Miss Martin's recreations are outdoor sports and music and literature.

is very good natured – and that nice George Brook came in and sat yesterday for a good bit and told one or two good stories. He is very sorry you did not come up to see his kennels, and hopes you yet may . . . Last night I whipped onto a car after dinner and sped to the Abbey Theatre to see Augusta's play. I can't go into it now – but it is well written – interestingly and artistically staged, and, with two exceptions, ill acted. But there was a refinement and earnestness through all. During the show I was greeted by Lord Killanin, who was with the George Morrises – and afterwards I was fallen on by Augusta who swept me and the Morris's and Killanin and others to tea afterwards, *on the stage*. A stranger thing I have seldom done – and Oh the discomfort of the sloping stage floor. How anyone acts on it I cannot think – I was introduced to the tragedy queen – who had swallowed a poker, in token of sovreignty – but had retained her brogue through all – and I was also introduced by Augusta (who swept me about as if I were blind and drunk) to Lord Monteagle, who was wholly uninterested in me and is a great rebel (Emily tells me) – I then talked very enjoyably to the leading comedian – Fay – a first rate little actor – and as common as a little Dublin cab man – but most agreeable to talk to. The Dermod O'Briens were also there – more conversation – then W B Yeats – and *very* highclass conversation – inspired by sips of black tea and a cheese cake. Robert would have had a bad relapse if he could have viewed me emerging from the stage door of the Abbey Theatre and escorted to a cab by W. B. Y. Augusta comes here this afternoon – so do Rosalie and Zara. The George Morrises any day or minute – ditto the O'Briens – and Carrie Gibb and Oliver Martin. Heaven preserve my reason – Farewell – tell me of the Chimp's shebas*

Yours ever
Martin

April 30th 1905
101 Lower Baggot Street

Dear Edith

I am concerned about your palpitations, and am glad you saw O'Meara though I did not suppose there was *really* anything wrong. But it is very difficult to believe that when they are going on. I have myself had a go of it lately, and these tall stairs were a trial at first. However that is passing off, and I am taking Quinine, with good effect. Anyhow I am sure that change will be the thing for us all, and in the meantime I do think riding will be capital for you – and for Miss Bridget. It invigorates you – and braces up the circulation and nerves. Give her gallops – she wants it. The palpitations don't have anything to say to exercise as far as you are concerned – Do they? I do feel sorry for Percy, but I trust he has taken it in time. It will be delightful if we can get Hildegarde to Aix. It ought to be a very entertaining party, and remote from interruptions. That odious *Strand* has not got our story in the May number. I don't suppose they will do anything more till we send them the whole lot – I must tell you that Augusta was here yesterday, and was rampant that I should write a play for the Abbey Street Theatre, protestations of total inadequacy were put by as the idle wind – want of time ditto – apparently they want what they are good enough to call a Shoneen play. I suppose that means middle class vulgarity. I couldn't face Edward Martyn – he is too idiotic a rebel – so I didn't come in for the tea party on the stage, for which Augusta told me she had cut 98 sandwiches – (I don't think '98 was intended) I also saw Yeats in the distance looking very like Kinkie! He had implored me to come and hear his play – and acknowledge that blank verse perfectly spoken, is the proper vehicle for poetry – and I was sorry not to be able to tell him that I thought it perfect for *acting* but that for reading to oneself the charm of metre and rhymes was as the power of different sorts of music – I had the pleasure of telling him that I thought it a sin to throw such beautiful weapons out of his armoury. He assured me his plays were full of lyrics. He does write well I must say – I am going to Saint Patrick's today with Mama and Flynn – It is the Easter music again

   Yours ever
   Martin

[*A possible postscript*]

It seems to me that they are very anxious now to rope in the upper classes, and to drop politics. When I divulged the fact that you had faint aspirations towards a play, and had written a children's one, Augusta was enraptured – "A week at Coole would do it. We could give you all the hints necessary for stage effects etc – even write a scenario for you – the characters and plot picked from your books – I will look through them at once – " I gave no further encouragement of any sort – and said we were full up. She wanted to insist on Mama going last night – and I wouldn't allow it. Mama was already tired from visitors. However I slipped out myself after dinner, and saw Yeats' beautiful little play "The King's Threshold" It quite took me away into another world – and was quite well acted on the whole – the quiet accessories, the absence of gesture, the magical and true delivery of the blank verse, and the real feeling made it a complete thing. It was followed by a peasant piece – a comedy – quite good, though not the best, and the principal part admirably done by my little friend Fay – with a *perfect* Dublin brogue – Augusta tells me he was a gas fitter. I was rather in the back of the stalls from which I saw Augusta in the distance in deep confab with someone very like Edward Martyn – and at the conclusion I slipped away.

[From Martin to Edith: *fragment*, Financial Relations and Martin Morris]

. . . I did enormous shoppings for Mama in Galway, had a cup of coffee, and then hied me off at 12 to the Financial Relations meeting in the Court House – Henry Hodgson had told Mama on the way in that Ladies could go, so I sailed up as bold as brass. Tom Blake came to me and got me in by a special door and up into the Grand Jury box, where the women were located. There I found Kathleen and Fanny Morris, come in to hear Martin speak – and I squeezed in between them and was very well placed, just at the corner by the Judge's canopy. Under it sat Lord Clonbrock, with on his left the R.C. Bishop of Galway, and on his right Captain Waithman – who was secretary of the meeting, and began by the usual reading of letters of apology. Then Lord Clonbrock made his opening speech – very well indeed – easy, and portentously grave, and with power of expressing himself well. After him came the Bishop of Galway – a shrewd and able harangue with the peasant cuteness and power of imagery, and innate Home Rule-ishness, that could hardly be hid. Sir Henry Bellew came next – an interesting looking man, rather like Jim Penrose. He spoke creditably, and made a few points – one I could hardly believe, that Denmark was for her size the next richest country to England. When Sir Henry was done with, someone who I couldn't see stepped up "This must be a Parnellite" said the Morrises – I heard a murmur in a familiar voice and spied poor Henry Hodgson making a low and confidential statement to Lord Clonbrock. He had been raked in at the last moment to propose a resolution, instead of Henry Persse, who was ill – and he was palpably almost paralysed by nervousness. He read the resolution, and there was a long and agonising pause – I thought he would have to get down again – but he managed to get through a few sentences about the reafforesting of Connemara. His sentences were all right when they came, but were almost inaudible. Sheehy, one of the members for the county spoke next – an interesting looking savage, and a very poor speaker – no fluency at all – but he said some useful things – Martin Morris then arose. His was by arrangement the speech of the day, and it was that by merit. It was admirable – a history of the Financial Relations since the Union – with many a biting truth about taxation. It had the slight academic brilliancy of youth, and all the Irish brightness, and it was given without the least affectation and with the greatest conviction and zest. Language was no trouble at all – and he had the Irish eye that takes the audience into its confidence at once – I admired the whole performance very much. After it was over we left – in high enthusiasm, and went and lunched. I think the two girls were awfully proud of their brother and they had a right to be. It was a most instructive speech, the only one that was so . . . [*end of fragment*]

> New Century Club
> Hay Hill
> Barclay Square
> June 12th

Dear Edith

Your letter has just come and gives a good account of you except for the waist pain. I suppose that gout is really at the root of that. Your foot seems to be doing as well as one can expect. You have had today sympathies and enquiries enough to make you better. Miss Woolf herself thought of sending you the wire, and did so – and I thought it very nice of her. The snow is over and that is my chief and happiest thought – I was there before 4 and met a luncheon to the Imperial Colonial Press visitors just emerging. I was introduced by Mrs Rentoul Esler to one or two Australians – all doosed civil. Then upstairs I met Miss Woolf – a kindly nice little thing – and two or three more of the authors, among them Beatrice Harriden; Dr Margaret Todd was to have been the boss of the show, but her sister was ill so Miss Mytton took it on – an immensely tall girl, or woman – and really awfully nice – good form and clever – she has written some sort of travel book about Burma. Little Fay was exactly up to time – a funny little tiny figure, with eye glasses and a turned down collar and our books under his arm. Him I introduced all round and to Katie Currey who had a long go in at him, and liked him so much. We were then admitted to the dining room which had a lot of seats, and a little Rostrum in the bow window, just as at the Franchise Meeting. There was a tea table near the door, and waiters circulated with trays of tea. Jack, Charlie Graves of the *Spectator* and *Punch*, Mrs Campbell and her sister, and Frannie Taylor had all turned up. It was a confused crowd, rather, and at last they all got seated – I put Katie between Alice Riddell and Alice Campbell in the front row, and that was all right. I had to sit in the front corner of the front row with the Board people. I was asked if I would say anything, and firmly replied that I should rather not – having discovered that there were appointed people to say all that was needed. Miss Mytton introduced Fay, in a very excellent little speech, full of praise of our

work and of Fay – with a sympathetic reference to your accident and
your absence. Fay then did the Patrick's Day Hunt, leaving out a short
bit in the middle. He was *excellent* – I could not have wished it better
done – the brogue of course perfect – it was a little too esoteric for some
of the audience, I think, but it read very well indeed to my ear and I
had to laugh secretly sometimes. There was a ripple of tittering went
on, and some bursts of laughter, but I should say that it was a little too
Irish in idiom for some of the audience. Then a pause of a few minutes,
and Fay went on at *Poisson d'Avril*. It reads much better in a general
way than the other – and was received with much laughter – but Fay
as Yates was not at his best, and his mispronunciation of several words
were rather trying. Of course he read with perfect understanding of the
humour, but "arroma" for "aroma" and several things of the kind were
very disquieting. Before it had started Jack had dragged me off to Lady
Florence Boyle, who was lurking in a back seat, and I fetched her up to
the front row where she laughed all the time. After Fay finished another
of the authors got up and proposed a vote of thanks to him – and an
extraordinary little Irishman who writes the critiques for the *Lady's
Pictorial* also murmured a few words – and there was an end – and
most people went off at once – Charlie Graves had to leave early. Then
polite speeches all around, and I thanked little Fay all I could. Jack was
delighted with him in the *Patrick's Day Hunt* – and certainly that, as a
piece of work, was quite delightful on his part. I must now cease, and
send him his cheque. He wanted to give us back the two books – but I
would not have that – and he is to send them over to you to write your
name in. I went off with Jack to see Gendie – who was not quite up to
coming. She seemed very fit and as amusing as ever. This is a dull letter
written at lightening speed. My clothes were most successful I am told,
H's hat and stole were the making of me and a great assistance throughout. Goodnight – I am so thankful it is all so well over –
    Yours ever
    Martin

*Robert Martin had suffered various illnesses during 1904/5 and died in
September of 1905. Shortly afterwards a group of his friends, many of
whom were in politics, decided to compile a memoir. The book was
organized by Sir Henniker Heaton. Martin was asked to write an account
of her brother and was invited to the House of Commons to discuss her
contribution. The meeting was a disaster.*

July 10th
Tuesday 1906
New Century Club
Barclay Square

Dear Edith

That I missed the post today was entirely the fault of Lily Severn – on whom I lighted when lunching at the Sesame with Emily. Too long to explain suffice it to say that she, her father, and her mother, were there and delayed me. It also made me forget to wire – till very late. Even now old Henniker has not said exactly that I shall not be wanted; but we are to have tea with him tomorrow at the House, and I feel sure that concludes matters – I may say that at once – to you, Hildegarde, and Edith – that I "never seen one I'd hate like the same sweep." He is common and unclean, self important, tactless, and vulgar. Goodhearted I am sure, and really devoted to Robert – but I dont wonder at Robert's feeling towards him. He has obviously force of character and an excellent opinion of himself. He has a stomach, and a large capable face, like a pale Falstaff – looks about fifty. I should say his literary sense was naught. Probably I was tired and captious, but he was abhorrent to me, in connection with Robert. The gist of it all is the book is to be crown octavo – and as well as I could make out, my part is to be about 15000 words! He said "about twelve columns of *The Times* – but you write all you like, and we can select what is wanted" – I at once said that I was too busy to write stuff that might not be wanted, and he seemed quite surprised – I dont think he at all realises the position, or that I am a professional writer. I shall not put you in a passion by telling more of his recommendations and advice; the upshot is that David Plunket, Lord Rathmore, is to oversee and really edit the book (I urged that, I can assure you) and that I am to have £20 for my expenses over the whole matter – I said I wanted no payment for such work, and that £20 was far too much for expenses – but he said the money was there, and he seemed quite determined about it, as about most things. John Corbett was ill on the way. Newnham Davis had another last moment hindrance (I was sorry for that) and the only other man was Mr Wolff, the Belfast MP, one of the trustees of the Carlton Fund. He shone beside H. H. and is really a very pleasant kind little man – and when Percy is old and has a short grey beard he will be like him. I have gathered at all events, that to go well inside the amount prescribed is my gain. Perhaps I have misunderstood, and H. H. may have meant that the *whole* biographical part is to be 15,000 words, not my part only – I shall find out tomorrow

– Rose and I liked him better as the evening went on, and he talked of Robert's political life – and told us much that we did not know of it. I am afraid David is in Paris, otherwise I think I should have had a hard try to see him. The book need not be ready till October – and there are to be only 100 copies – I fear old Henniker disliked me; it was so very hard to be in the least nice to him; Rose was wonderful, so polite and simple and tactful – though entirely of my camp – Emily did her best, and truckled to both me and him, and he likes *her* best of all. The champagne was of the best, and was in beakers – the Terrace quite lovely after dinner with the lines of reflections along tracts of perfectly quiet river and the fire fly lights flitting on Westminster Bridge – and the air was grey and warm. We looked in at the door of the House, and saw Birrell speaking; the image of his caricatures. Opposite to him Walter Long, Wyndham, Carson, Balfour lying on his shoulder blades almost – also the image of his caricatures. They were having divisions every half hour or so, and wild and forlorn cries to that effect wailed in the Terrace and dining room, followed by a rush of members from their food. H. H. had paired with Bryce for the evening. Mr Wolff with someone else. Please thank E for her letter – and Frannie Taylor's. I am electrified about Thyrza – and hope all will go well. I had tea with Flo Lambert, and nothing could have been nicer than she was – asked a lot about Edith and indeed about everyone. I suppose Lionel arrives tomorrow. I hope Edith's head is better.

Yours
Martin

Visits to health spas featured frequently in Edith's and Martin's lives after Martin's fall and injury in 1898. It might be thought that these spa visits were for her sake, but in fact Edith was beginning to suffer from the rheumatism that eventually crippled her. This letter, from Champex, describes a 'rest cure' with Hildegarde and Egerton that did nothing but depress and irritate her.

Champex
Friday July 12 /07

Dear Martin
I daresay I will send you some letters treating of Aylmer's wedding that will interest you – treat them – especially Cameron's – with discretion, &

"Some Irish Yesterdays."

It must be some six or seven years since some now famous experiences of an Irish R.M. first delighted the palates of those who knew enough to distinguish between the genuine and the counterfeit Irish literary product. But the flavour of that book (not to mention that of a subsequent volume or two) remains as fresh as ever in SOME IRISH YESTERDAYS (Longmans, 6s.) In one respect this delightful book is even better than that through which the names of E. Œ. Somerville and Martin Ross became a guarantee of good entertainment. The R.M. was kept far too busy to comment much upon all the brave and merry things that happened to him during his memorable magistracy. He told you about them, and left it at that. But here the authors range untrammelled up and down the west of Ireland and tell their stories in many guises. Now they are children in reminiscence children at picnics, or children happy and miserable by turns in the possession of a whole live stock of boon companions from dogs and monkeys to linnets. Now they appear *in propriis personis* as the lords of an establishment, recalling many a laughable tale of those who served them, or relate their experiences of "Hunting Mahatmas" so called, apparently, in virtue of their power of turning up by mysterious means in unexpected places. Or, again, undaunted by Lord Bacon, the Poet Laureate, and the very Elizabeth herself, they discourse with freshness upon Gardens. From gardens to scenery is but a leap over the hedge, and you may chance at almost any moment upon some soft Irish landscape or seascape rendered with the word that burns in the colour, to be diverted, perhaps, from its contemplation by the entrance of a joint author inimitably disguised as a sporting peasant, who hurries you off into the scrimmage of a "Patrick's Day Hunt." From this you will emerge with the impression that there is no parody of pathos in the world like that of the Irish hunting misadventure ; and though the drawing of horses is hardly E. Œ. Somerville's forte, those who already know "Slipper's A.B.C. of Foxhunting" may be glad to find these amusing sketches reproduced at the end of the book.

One may sum up the book as a happy blend wherein the grave and gay wit of the authors is interwoven amid th

humour that finds subtle expression in the brogue. How many of the uninitiated will notice, we wonder, that the brogue is not rendered here according to the English convention ("avs" and "uts" for "ofs" and "its," &c.) till the fact is pointed out to them in the last essay? "Children of the Captivity" might well be accepted as the *locus classicus* of what there is to be said upon this subject from the cultivated Irish point of view.

The Realism of Shakespeare and Meredith.

It would be as foolish, however, to imagine that the conversation in novels ought to be a mere imitation of the talk of ordinary people, as it would be to imagine that it ought always to be as brilliant as possible. Even Tolstoi, in his most realistic moments, suggests real life, rather than imitates it ; and the people we know do not talk like the characters in Meredith's books any more than they talk like the characters in the plays of Shakespeare. We feel, however, that the conversations in Shakespeare and Meredith are fundamentally true to life. They are refinements upon life, and are more real than reality. People in real life are usually inarticulate. They talk confusedly, melodramatically ; and their talk throws little light upon themselves. It is the duty of the novelist to make them articulate, to see that they always say what is dramatically the right thing. There are limits, however, beyond which the novelist must not go into the region of unreality. If he is writing in dialect, for instance, he ought not to follow some outworn and unreal convention, but to form a new and illuminating convention of his own. It is curious, as Miss Somerville and Martin Ross observe in " Some Irish Yesterdays," that the Irish brogue should be so universally mishandled by the novelists as it is.

Irish and English.

The brilliant writers in question mention a recent story in which an Irish Captain of Hussars, in a moment of emotion, exclaims : " Howly Mither av Hiven ! " English people, however, cling to certain notions of the Irish people with a bull-dog persistence. Like the old writer, they regard the Irish as " a merry people, and fond of pigs " ; and you cannot persuade them that the Irish peasant does not say " indade " for " indeed," " belave " for " believe," and so forth. The authors of " Some Irish Yesterdays " expose the imbecility of the brogue as used by both Thackeray and Mr. Kipling for artistic purposes. They do this, in Mr. Kipling's case, by simply spelling his words correctly and writing one of his sentences in ordinary English. The sentence—one of Mulvaney's—in its new form runs like this :—" Oh, boys, they were more lovely than the like of any loveliness in Heaven ; ay, their little bare feet were better than the white hands of a Lord's lady, and their mouths were like puckered roses, and their eyes were bigger and darker than the eyes of any living woman I've seen." As Miss Somerville and her collaborator remark, " Irish people do not say these things."

Mr. Kipling's Brogue.

Mr. Kipling's brogue is Wardour Street brogue. He has not realised that dialect is a matter, not of mispronunciation, but of idiom. The authors of " Some Irish Yesterdays " have not reached the heart of Ireland, but they have come nearer it than Mr. Kipling. They write rather from the point of view of the Irish upper classes, and the Irish upper classes are always something of foreigners in their own land. It is unquestionable, however, that they have captured in their sketches a great deal of the gusto and the comedy of Ireland. They have an abundance of good stories, too, as, for example, that of the butcher " who, when remonstrated with about his meat, on the ground that it had not been properly killed, replied unanswerably, ' I declare to ye, the one that had the killing of that cow was the Lord Almighty.' " Their defence of " bulls " is interesting. They regard the " bull " as " the effort of the true impressionist to create an effect regardless of the means," and give as an example, " Jerry was a grand man. When he'd be idle itself he'd be busy ! "

burn when read – we have laughed very much at the thought of Mrs Dietz flopping *to* the Chimp.

I am wondering when I shall hear from you as to our plans, & what you can do, & where you will go – H & I are simply counting the days till we get out of this place. It is too dull, & *too* unpaintable. Even Egerton can't find anything he wants to do, so you can imagine my forlorn case. The days are simply as long as weeks – weeks of Sundays, bar the clothes – I may admit that the weather is perfect, even tho I could do with it hotter, & the pine woods are admirable, tho not of the paintable quality of our dear little Etaples forest. We come out to them directly after breakfast & sit about, reading the *Daily Mail* to the bone, & – as now – writing letters, till 12.30, when we have dejeuner – then we drag the time out somehow till 2 when the 2nd post comes – Then all, save (hang it) I, (?) go to sleep on their beastly beds – I can't sleep by day unless I am overfed, or dying, or both, & I just hang about & get the tin mugs ready for tea – after tea we go for a walk – like flies round the inside of a tumbler – in this rotten little basin of a place, or it is possible, tho not exciting, to paddle round the tidy little lake, then comes dinner, at 7 – *after* it we either sit out on the terrace, or wait for a sunset effect on Cambin, or we have some singing. Unluckily H. brought no music, so she & E. have only the refuse of Jack's songs to sing – Jack & E. are in very good voice, wh is something, & Major Wilson has a few songs that he sings charmingly in spite of his wife's excruciatingly bad accompaniments – He is a very nice, queer, interesting creature "gey ill to live wi" by reason of nerves, but delightful in many ways, & I never heard a prettier voice – the sweetest & most fluting tenor possible, & he is *mad* to have a bass & sing bass songs! Mrs is a good creature but an *awful* talker – *Incessant* sometimes amusing, sometimes sensible, but more times just idiotic gabble – she reminds H. & me of Mrs Morrogh in her wild irresponsible babble, & the semi-asinine remarks about herself & her own capacity – all the same, she is a good kind creature, & is I think quite straight – she was a Miss Knyvett – a good family – & has all the English anxiety to let you know it. We had them to tea yesterday, & she nearly talked us off our heads – I write about them thus fully as I have really nothing else of local interest – I have finished copying the Garden article & will go & see Pinker with it – Madge & Jack get on excellently – she talks to him incessantly & he likes her, & she is certainly doing . . . [*end of letter missing*]

More than twenty years after Emily Herbert's death Edith was finally told the story of Aunt Fanny's will, and how Emily had destroyed it.

In the train from Kilmeadan to Mallow
Saturday July 27 08

Dear Martin

Hildegarde persuaded me to stop off & go to Hal & Isabel, so that she could see me through the tooth job in Cork. This we did, & we should have stayed there till Monday, but at dinner last night there came a wire from Egerton – "Violet wires Beatrice died suddenly this afternoon am leaving by 12 train tomorrow for Edinburgh" – we know no more. I suppose it was that she was not strong enough to stand the desperate high pressure at which she was living, or else that some clot became detached & went to the brain – (she had very bad varicose veins always.) It is best for her. Far better than dragging on in the Asylum, with possible lucid intervals when she would beg to be taken away, *& yet would have to be left in it.* (But what a pity that they could not have been silent as to all this wretched business, & not given it to Harry Townshend & his like to say that she died in an asylum.) Hildegarde feels it very much, & so indeed do I. Poor Beatrice was such an institution, that we have laughed at for so long – & was always a good fellow – no better – We shall meet Egerton in Cork, I hope, but I don't suppose he will know anything more. V., no doubt, has gone to Edinburgh & we shall hear no more till she can write. I have just said to H. that she had better write a notice for the papers, to which she assented. Saying that if Egerton did it he would most likely put "in Morningside Lunatic Asylum" &c. &c. & I believe he would. We were very sorry to have to leave Whitfield in such a hurry, more especially as the new Post Captain was there – (your wire was sent on to me by old Ward, & would have intrigued me considerably, only that B. himself just preceded it with the news. I may send you a wire today if I get the tusk out successfully. I was glad to get that word from you). B. had had a telegram from the Admiralty,[1] which has amazed him, as usually your first news is in the Official Gazette. How on earth did you hear or see it? We had the most *ideal* journey, & I bitterly regretted that you weren't with us. We slep' it out till 7, & then went on board the Argo & dug out Boyle. He might just as well have come on with us by the 8.10 to Kilmeadan, as it was very foggy, but he waited for it to clear & let him go out – which it

1 He was promoted to HMS *Research*, to survey in British waters.

didn't. However he got his telegrams all the sooner. He is radiant – poor fellow – it only makes me rage the more that he didn't get it years ago. He gave me a most learned article on the coastline of Ceylon, with plans &c. that he has just written for the Geographical Society, & they have published – I am *amazed* at his erudition. Whitfield *is* a most lovely place. I had no idea that it was so nice, & Hal's pair of greys, & his coachman, are fit for the Park. Old Mrs. Fleming was there & told us the distressing news that Aunt Fanny (of The Point) had left all her money to Jack & me – about £4,000 – Mrs. F. saw the will; Aunt Fanny *kept it in the drawer of her washstand*, & thence it was abstracted by our friend the Real Charlotte! Aunt F. wanted Mrs. Fleming to keep it for her, but she dreaded the responsibility. It was a murder she didn't take it, as it would have been easy to upset poor Aunt Fanny's later wills on "undue influence". She said Emily was an awful drunkard, & when she finally drank & cat-poisoned herself to death, they found her dead body in the bed with 14 cats sitting round it! There is a sordid tragedy for Yvette to sing about – & mighty well she would do it – that death song of her's of the Prisonnier & the Bells was as fine a thing as I could think of. Reckless & callous & deeply sentient of the tragedy.

You will be amused to hear that I now think of buying your dress from Hildegarde! She will be in black (& white) till Christmas. Of course I shall have to wear black for a time – but when we go to Sissy's I shall want a smart dress. Ogilvy will be amused. I have that black hat & will put feathers in it instead of the roses. I don't know what to do for a Sunday trowsher[1] in black. If you saw one of those black & white painted voiles – (I saw a beauty for 27/- in white with roses) with material for a body at sale prices, you might send it to me. I will write for Stagg & Mantle's list – wire if you get one for me – not more than 30/- The things I mean are like this [drawing] the pattern stained on to the stuff, not woven. Don't take trouble about it, as I shall write for a list today, but if you saw a nice one before Wednesday I should be thankful to you if you would send it to me. Don't forget to pay Miss Van Moloney for our grubbings on the last 2 or 3 days & send me the bill. It is *tremendously* hot here – as hot as London. We sat out on the steps at Whitfield till dinner time, & they were red hot under us – today is stifling. No sun & no wind. If you have *not* got a return ticket to Skib, try & settle to come down on Saturday & get an excursion ticket. The Agricultural Show is not till the 9th. We hope to go to it, & the return Firsts are 6/6 (or less). If O'Keeffe takes out my tooth I shall I

1 *Trowsher*: dress.

fear, have to go up again . . . No more now – the train is too rough –
I pray that you are not killing or bankrupting yourself, but I feel sure
you are – Goodbye dear
  Yours ever
  Edith

[*Edith's note*: 'Jack's Wedding' [to Vera Aston Key]]

November 1910
In the train to Bristol Saturday

Dear Martin,
I am very sleepy & dull after a week of continuous beltings, but will
just tell you that I hope to be able to stick to my plans & get home on
Thursday. I wish you could have a fitting for your habit on that day.
What you should have done was to get a weekend ticket, & go to
Lismore for Sunday – thus getting in 3 fittings on one ticket.

I don't know if I told you that I heard from Pinker, & went to see
him yesterday with Boyle. He was in very good spirits, & said he was
thoroughly delighted with the four chapters. I asked what he thought of
them, & said we didn't want compliments but criticisms. He said he
knew that, & still professed delight. He says he thinks he can serialise
it all right. I told him he could start in January. I think that ought to
be quite safe. He was much pleased with Longman's letter & was amazed
at the figures for the Further Exes. He said he would have expected the
big sales for the Old R.M. I couldn't quite make out why. He was full
of enquiries for you, of course, & was resolved on telling of his squire-
dom, the meet at his house on Tuesday next &c. &c. but I discovered
that the reason he had seemed apathetic about the Times Review was
that Maintop, having collared his beloved title ("Hounds Gentlemen
&c.") has then run the show himself, leaving Pinker outside! Rather
unfair I think.

The Wedding! The subject is vast for a fainting & anoemic pen. The
day began well, with frost & sun – *the whole house*, down to Gillham,[1]
went in by the 11. Hildegarde, Mary, & I, Katie, Ellen, & Joanna all
jammed in a fly, C. speeding a-wheel, Gillham I know not how, save
that when we were all on the platform, & the train in, there was no
sign of him. Then a sort of ball-like form shot along the farther side of

1 *Gillham*: a dog.

the station – I seized the guard in the act of whistling, & held him, & Gillham fell in a single impulse down the stair with a sound of thunder, & went to ground in Joanna's faithful bosom. When we got to London the rain had begun, & not an umbrella amongst us! Thank heaven, I had Ethel's dress in a box, & *had not as yet bought a hat.* To Harrods, top speed in a taxi, 1, to buy a fur neck-thing for H. 2, to get my hair done 3, to buy me a hat. H. got a long & handsome strip of one of those mythological animals called Sealsquashedconies, (or something like that) but not a hat under forty-nine & sixpence – Moddam – was forthcoming. H said there was a one-price-hat-shop near. Mary & I fled forth. We got into a little Robber's den quite near at hand, & only for Mary I should have run away, but she nailed me like a bad coin to the counter & she & the head bandit put a thing costing 34/3 on me & I had to keep it. It has had its admirers. We shall see if you like it.

Then to Harrods again. Hair done in 10 minutes, by a miracle of a man, dumb & swift – & on to the Club. We had a tiny room in the annexe for 2 hours only, & had to pay 5/- for it! A rank swindle but worth double the money. Ambrose & H. were ready when I got there, so Katie set-to at me & I believe I was all done in 5 minutes. *Nothing forgotten*! So to the church in a taxi. Red carpets, awnings, motors trumpetting in all the keys, whirling petticoats & long silk legs dashing into shelter – all the bridegroom's friends to the right, bride's to the left. It was then only 2, but already there were a crowd of people there both sheep & goats. I never saw so many of the family – (*not* Geraldine I am sorry to say – she had had a bad crossing.) Sophie Paget, looking about 40 & very handsome, Hildegarde's dumby, Vernon Thornton, David of Rathmore, the Japanese ambassador & his lady! These last were piled into our pew, (the first & grandest,) & Boyle had to yield his position as brother to their Excellencies. Then very bad organ music – a rotten selection, dribblingly delivered by a patently bored artist. He did one good thing. The Chimp, (best man,) was waiting, with his rigid, ashen charge, in the vestry, when to them came the inspiring strains of Tschaikovsky's *Chanson Triste* & poor John was charmed to a wan smile. Vera looked delightful. This is stale & conventional but true. She was literally snow white. Clear, waxen white, & it became her wonderfully. She had a beautiful old lace veil, hanging down her back, the end flat on her head in a Mary Stuart cap. A tulle veil in front, & a train about 4 yards long. Ambrose & his little fellow were perfect. They looked very nice, & stood as straight & slim as little peeled rods. Ambrose's back would make anyone (who didn't know him,) cry, it was so flat &

straight & good & he & the other little thing held each other's hands for comfort & to get courage. No one told them to. They (Jack & Vera) did the responses just rightly. Low, clear & firm, Jack getting obviously better as he went on. I am thankful to say I shed no tear, though when I saw him take the ring in his poor crooked thumb it was very moving. Nathalie not only wept but sobbed! Amazing being – I did not see her, but Mary & Alice Penrose did – (trust them both!) The singing was very good & the unaccompanied 7 fold amen at the end was really beautiful. Then they went to the Vestry & Mr. Aston Key came across to our pew & armed me in to sign the register. He, Cameron, Mrs. A. K., I, & the Japanese Ambassador were the high signatories, & then, with the wedding march blazing & fulminating – away with us in a huge Merton Motor to 18 Grosvenor Street. There were some of the Royal Artillery Band & the Wedding March again for all it was worth, & two *beaming* creatures all alone in a huge parquetted room. Such a change – the poor things. Mrs. Aston Key is the best. Courage of the highest. I never saw a finer case of pluck to the rescue. She was most beautifully dressed & looked immeasurably the handsomest & best class person there, & her manners could not be beat. Mary said she thought Mrs. A. K. was going to faint half way through – (you know she has been ill again –) but she held on, & mercifully nothing happened. The bridesmaids were not up to much. Plain. Their dresses also quite ineffective. Happily there were only 4 of them, & I will say Dora Key was a Trojan, & was on the spot all the time at the critical moments.

The enjoyable thing was to see the 3 Maguires & Joanna in the gallery – *beaming*, Joanna weeping, & praying like mad – (she told us so,) & at the end of the church Wilson & Michael,[1] who, like the coppersmith, did not cease to call upon Diana[2] in a voice only drowned by the music. The presents are beautiful – a wonderful lot of them & awfully good ones. Jack & V. slipped away unseen after cutting the cake. I don't know how it was managed. They have gone to Munich. Here is Thornbury.

Yours ever,
Edith.

P.S. Unless you hear again, send Curate, & tell dairy cart to get me & my things on Tuesday 6.30. I have sent trunk & King-cup's clothing on in advance at 6d.

---

1 and 2   Son and daughter of Boyle Somerville.

[*Edith's note*: 'The Coronation of George V']

June 23rd 1911

Dear Edith

Here while awaiting the procession I begin a letter – and the comfort is great of a seat here. I am up in the next room, remote from all disturbances – and I know that my seat is there, in front of the western-most drawing window – with an awning over it, and I have but to step into it, at ten o'clock or so. Yesterday morning I was away out of the house at 7 – and into the little electric railway from Battersea Park to Victoria, armed with my ticket for St. James' Palace, and the cherry brandy – and sandwiches – and opera glasses and a white striped coat and skirt, with the black collar that you don't like. It was then rough and cold and threatening. At Victoria I picked up Nora who is close beside there – and I was thankful to have her – as although the crowd was not great the motors and carriages were *streaming* to the Abbey – it was great and lasting fun to see the Peers and Peeresses therein – but too like the stage, only so much better than any stage. They looked so competent for their parts – sat, and held their heads rightly with their coronets in their laps as well as I could see. We worked on easily up Buckingham Palace Road and crossed the Mall just by Queen Victoria's memorial – I did not care for it on the whole. That big heavy circular base is, in my opinion, ugly – and out of proportion with the Victory at the top, and there is a feeling that the statuary is squeezed into it, and might fall out. What was very interesting was the ring of Malay and all sorts of native soldiers in unknown kits, formed up all around it. That was fine, in idea and fact. We got through by the Marlboro House way. Very easily on the whole. My ticket with the Chamberlain's name opened all routes, but there was no density anywhere, you could edge through the people, and the police were myriad – once at St. James's Palace you could circulate anywhere, as a space round it was kept clear. Here I went and viewed the Second Day Procession – of which more anon. I got in round the corner by the Ambassador's Court, and a winding stair took me to the roof of the chapel – a lovely place, all clean and white, and just beside the clock tower a stand was set forth to hold about thirty people – about as high up as the roof of Drishane – and a good high bulwark – I dont think even Hildegarde would have minded, though my seat was in the front row – it gave a good slanting view a bit down into Pall Mall – the chapel tower was a little in the way, and a good bit up St. James' Street. The sweep of the corner was perfect. There planted in her place, was McLeod who had got there at 7! Needling and worming by tube from Waterloo – I had a spare ticket, and as Kinkie had got one at the last moment, Hildegarde advised McLeod who, poor thing, was yearning for a sight of the fun. It was very cold and blustery up there, and a heavy shower descended at 8.30 – most depressing and also perishing – and the umbrellas dripped on the seats, and I felt very low for the sake of the poor royalties – all the time a ceaseless cataract of carriages passed down St. James' Street for the Abbey – with scarlet and ermine laps and fronts showing very gloriously – and the coronets in the laps – one could see the glint of them – (N.B. I had opera glasses) and perishing bare necks and chilly long white gloves – nothing can set forth the splendour of some of the Peers or semi-royalties' carriages. Hammer-cloths of every hue, heavy with gold, and coats of arms – footmen with long beatle backs, same as hammer-cloth – each coachman a ball of glory, in the hollow centre of his hammer-cloth. Three cornered hats, powder – and one knew it was all the genuine article – the carriages dug out and done up, the liveries "just so" – and such lovely colours – misty yellow, strawberry red – soft blue. It was like Fairyland. The horses were A1 – and their harnesses wonderful – all crusted with gold or silver and these old high carriages with tremendous coats of arms – I never thought to see the like. Those – and the King's Watermen, and the Beaf-eaters – and the band of the Lifeguards, were completely delightful as one could have wished – They were so genuine and easy – McLeod and I made an expedition into the Mall as the procession was leaving Buckingham Palace and of course could not get near, but a boy was holding up a mirror on the end of a long stick, and with a group of other scalliwags I saw the golden coach in the mirror exactly as I looked up into it. The rest was all cheering and "God save the King" all the way down the Mall. We then perambulated St. James' Street – behind the backs of the crowd really as much for warmth as for anything – everyone as pleasant and good as possible, some very sleepy having been there all night. St. James' Street was of course one mass of stands. Pall Mall ditto. The decorations spotty as usual – stupid and conventional – except for some pillars with baskets of flowers on the top. From the roof of the chapel we saw the towers of Westminster Abbey – and heard its joy bells crashing as if you dashed your hand across a harp – that was when the King went into it – about 12 came the cannon, announcing that he was crowned – and then they missed a chance – the soldiers should have presented arms and done things – at 1.30 the real excitement of the day came – a fire broke out a few houses down Pall Mall – in a big window of a first floor and smoke began to roll out. In about two minutes the police cleared the house – it was, thank heaven, a case of no panic anywhere – only the crowd bulged across the street – a man ran with a extinguisher up into the house like lightning, and with the glasses I saw the white stuff dart from the nozzle of the thing, up above his head – and almost at once the smoke began to die away – a great advertisement for the maker. In that gusty wind with the whole of the facade of the street waving with drapery, on top of wooden erections – and the pavements chock-a-block – it might have been an awful calamity. Before the smoke was finished, that is to say, in about two minutes, came the gallop of a fire escape – after it the greater gallop of a fire engine – with two white horses, along Pall Mall. You would have wept heavily – I did a little – Then a motor with the Chief of the Fire Brigade, another engine and then a grand one with a pair of greys coming hell for leather down St. James' Street with yet another fire escape behind it. The people cheered them all like mad. I believe the great fear was a fire and the engine simply flew to the place – all was right however – and the people even went back into the house nicely in time for the procession. It began with Lifeguards and Indian Princes and such. Kitchener and Roberts too. Then the red Watermen stepping most lightly in their red tights – the red Beef-eaters, the soft gold coats of the Lifeguards band – with the black velvet caps and the black horses and then the light cream ponies loaded with red and gold, and giving their riders and leaders quite enough to do – I could not see the King within the gold swaying coach; he was the far side from me and I was high up, but the Queen looked very noble, *very* white, but holding her head beautifully with its crown upon it – It was undoubtedly moving in some strange way. They certainly, in their helpless greatness, appeal to chivalry – I stood up and cheered and yelled and waved, and there was a fine roll of it went with them. Then the four children, poor little Princess Mary bowing with a good anxious and pale face, and her hair down her back under her coronet. The Prince of Wales beside her in his Garter Robes. After them many vague royalties and at 3.30 or so we got easily away in a large but loose crowd. This morning I started later – at 8 – and when I got to my little electric railway found that there was no train for half an hour – a perfectly strange female was in the same distraction as I – and she wanted to get to St. George's Hospital stand. We eventually found a fly – shared it at a cost of 2 and 6 pence each and got to near Hyde Park Corner near Belgrave Square – in much love. I got into the Lyceum – "Good morning Miss Martin" says the invincible porter in the hall, as I stepped in through the barricades. A great comfort then fell upon me – & breakfast – but by a stupidity I missed the first half

of the procession (and by writing to you) it was only the Colonial
Premiers however, and I could do without them. There were a lot of
soldiers – and Indian princes etc – and German and Austrian detach-
ments and blue jackets dragging their guns. And this time the King and
Queen were in an open carriage – lined with rose coloured satin – and
the cream horses as before – he was in Admiral's kit, and looked nice
and friendly. She was in cream colour with the blue garter ribbons across
– and a small hat with shaded blue ostrich feathers – she looked awfully
well – and one noticed again the admirable poise of her head. There
undoubtedly is a something about her. A cleverness and grace – and
pluck – one would imagine – I had a good look at Lord Roberts, and
his little young figure and the way he was *sewn* to the saddle. Now this
must go – I have just missed Hildegarde here which is annoying – in
the middle of the Coronation morning I pictured the Castle T scene –
and the organist and I knew that part at all events would be all right –
Farewell

Yours ever
Martin

*Dan Russel the Fox sold very well after some enthusiastic reviews, but
the staff at Methuen would not tell Martin how pleased they were with
it when she called in at their offices to sound off about misprints. In her
subtle way she found out various details which she then relayed to the
agent Pinker in the next street. Martin was quite a canny operator.*

October 25th 1911
New Century Club
Hay Hill
Barclay Square

Dear Edith
Please thank Hildegarde ever so much for the tabloids, not tried as yet.
The reviews also are very welcome – quite astounding – the *Standard*
one delightful – I tried to see Dodwell again today but he is still away,
seedy – so now it must be when I come back from Lowestoft – where
I go tomorrow. 17 Wellington Gardens Lowestoft, the address. (I really
stay in a comfortable lodging next door). But I think I shall be back on
Saturday, in fact feel fairly sure of it. McAlpine[1] has to reconstruct my

1 Their dentist.

lower plate, and is evidently in a fury over it all. But not with myself. He was anxious to know if I had heard from you how your plate was doing now. From him, just now, I went down to Essex Street and saw Webster, on the subject of misprints in *Dan Russel*. He has given me a copy to mark, and to send on to you to mark. He would like you to compare with the proofs – so as to know whose was the error – "the huntsman looses on the *moon*" is dreadful. It must be done as fast as possible – as the next edition is a-preparing. I gather that they have sold nearly seven thousand. He was so vulgar and cautious, like a man at a fair – began by telling me that they were afraid it was going to be a severe frost, but that now it was going well. I told him that the Stores were ordering 600 copies, and considered it pretty well the novel of the season – "*Hilda Lessways* sells better" says Webster very swiftly – thereby admitting that none of his other novels excelled it – Hesketh Pritchard, whose name I know was in there with another man – and Webster allowed himself to tell me of their frenzy of admiration for the R.M. They said, however, that America did not catch on about them (nuts and apples to Webster). With this I repaired to Pinker in the next street – and told him of the *Hilda Lessways* remark which interested him very much as he is agent for Arnold Bennett and is placing another book for him with Methuen, and found it excessively difficult to get the figures of *Hilda Lessways* out of him. We enjoyed ourselves over this, all round. Poor Marie Corelli is indignant over the want of excitement over her last book. The middle classes are getting a little beyond it and her. Pinker then confessed that he had only just read *Dan Russel* – (which I think was a mistake on his part) and proceeded to praise it in the heartiest and most genuine manner – assured me that he would tell me the truth, what ever way it was, that he really thought it quite first class, especially the writing. He was enthusiastic – I asked his advice about the next book. He still says that a short story volume would do just as well as anything else, but that whatever we wrote he was quite certain would be just right or thereabouts. We could take characters out of *Dan Russel* or anything else – "Do what you like; you are sure to do it well" was his cry – all very comforting indeed. He is still trying for an American publisher, and if he can't do it there he will sell to Longman. Now I think that is all my publishing news – and good it is – in spite of the ineffably second-rate Webster. I met today Miss West and Grace Caulfield, both of whom assured me of *Dan Russel*'s great success. Allowing for exaggeration I think it *must* be doing well. Rose Barton is moving to the Lyceum Club, and is better – she fancies the airiness there, and I think she is wise – I saw the Halcyon Club yesterday

– very small and rather bad – a nice little picture gallery – well lighted
– ditto little lecture room – but not for an instant could it shake anyone
of sense as to the Lyceum[1] and its beautiful rooms and good furniture.
No outlook – tiny hall, very small dining room – all done up in the bare
"studio" fashion. The back of my hand to it –

Yours ever
Martin

*Martin's description of Tyrone House shows that the great Anglo-Irish
houses, in their decoration and quality of building, had a grandeur which
survived long after the families who owned them had lost every last
shred of power and wealth. For those who know Tyrone as it is now,
a magnificent gutted shell, it stands – even though only a rookery – as
an indestructible monument to good taste and craftsmanship.*

*Martin's opinion of the St George family was highly coloured and
biased on account of a family dispute. The St Georges had once been
Frenches, who intermarried with the Martins of Ross, unhappily. A
fascinating and kindly account of the house and family is given by
Gordon St George Mark in the* Quarterly Bulletin of the Irish Georgian
Society, *Vol. XIX, nos. 3 and 4, July–December 1976.*

[*Edith's note added later*: 'Tyrone House: a possible subject for a book']

March 18th 1912
Kilcornan, Oranmore

Dear Edith
Your letter found me this morning – thanks for all the enclosures. I
return J. W. There is an unshakeable jocosity about him, and he feels it
to be especially suitable to ladies. However I daresay he may vote all
right; at all events he will not oppose – I have had a nice little time here
with these three kind people. They are hospitable, and know how to do
it – the comfort and the fires, and the imperceptable care in every detail
is wonderful. On Saturday we met Archer Martin[2] at Athenry, and drove
him straight on to the meet at Monivea – a big one – and also, it poured
in bitter floods from the South East. Amy and Archer and I sat in the

1 Clubs for women flourished at this period.
2 Martin's Canadian cousin became Mr Justice Archer Martin, Justice of Appeal,
   Victoria, BC.

house and talked, and the hounds battered one fox at least round the coverts, and we left them at it (Robert Gregory on Jim's mare) and got home for a late luncheon, and all drove over here in the afternoon. Archer and Tilly Redington (one 'd' please remember) were instantly deep in antiquarian things – each a great talker, and each finding it hard to get a word in. It was chiefly about a Martin and French marriage stone that is at Tyrone House, the St. Georges wonderful wreck of a place near here – (the St. Georges were originally Frenches –) Yesterday morning I was driven off to a little desolate awful church, to which the Ardrahan clergyman drives out. I have *never* been at anything so wretched – the little church quite well built, but coated with mildew and damp, the decaying old prayer books stuck to the seats with fungus. The clergyman came out and dusted a pew for me before he allowed me to sit in it – I, a young man, and a policeman were the congregation. The parson gave out a hymn, started it very well; I struck in, and he and I then sang a duet. When he found that I was well set he sang an *excellent* bass in a low baritone. The youth and the policeman listened reverently to this unique performance. In the afternoon Tilly Redington and I drove over to Tyrone House. A bigger and much grander edition of Ross – a great square cut stone house of three stories, with an area – perfectly empty – and such ceilings, architraves, teak doors and chimney pieces as one sees in old houses in Dublin. It is on a long promontory by the sea – and there *rioted* three or four generations of St. Georges – living with country women, occasionally marrying them, all illegitimate four times over. Not so long ago *eight* of these awful half peasant families roosted together in that lovely house and fought, and barricaded, and drank till the police had to intervene – about 150 years ago a very grand Lady Harriet St Lawrence married a St. George and lived there, and was so corroded with pride that she would not allow her two daughters to associate with the Galway people. She lived to see them marry two of the men in the yard. Yesterday as we left, an old Miss St. George daughter of the last owner was at the door in a donkey trap – she lives near, in a bit of the castle and since her people died she will not go into Tyrone House or into the enormous yard or the beautiful old garden. She was a strange mixture of distinction and commoness, like her breeding, and it was very sad to see her at the door of that great house – if we dare to write up that subject!

Yours ever

Martin

Martin's last surviving letter mentions the Conciliation Bill (the second reading of 1912). It was thought that Asquith was about to grant Home Rule to Ireland and that Irish members should not vote for women's suffrage in case this brought down the government. When the bill first came before Parliament in 1911 militant suffragettes suspended their activities, then renewed them when the bill was, as Lloyd George put it, 'torpedoed'. On the second reading the Irish members abandoned the cause of women's suffrage entirely, and the bill was defeated.

Careful fencing by Asquith kept women's suffrage at bay until the outbreak of the First World War, when the controversy went into abeyance in favour of the war effort. Chiefly in recognition of women's services during the war, the vote was granted to women over the age of thirty in 1918; but by this time Martin was dead.

As a result of the injury caused in 1898 by her horse rolling over her after a fall (or so her doctor thought), a tumour had formed at the back of the brain. Her final collapse and death were very rapid. She died in the Glen Vera Nursing Home in Cork City on 21 December 1915. Edith lived for a further thirty-four years, continuing to publish books under both their names.

March 20th 1912

Dear Edith

I was *very* glad to have your wire, as you said you were still feeling slack yesterday morning. I should think it was very probably the cigarette, as that has done it for you once or twice already. Anyhow the tonic will not do you any harm – and I think I should not fly out early, for a little bit – You will have seen that the Conciliation Bill has been "adjourned to some other Friday" by Asquith, on account of the Coal Bill. I daresay that it was inevitable – and I daresay it will stand a better chance when the crisis is over – but one can imagine the glee of Asquith and many another at finding the pretext – I suppose the Militants should now be delighted – did you *ever*, I ask, read a more vitriolically savagely spiteful article than the *Times* had about three days ago on "hysteria". They must have dug up their oldest and most bilious writer – you have had my letter abandoning Zoë Callwell. Let you do it – if you like – and speedily – I will not touch it – as I dont want to cavill and I don't want to praise. Anyhow I hope you will decide at once so that I may write to Strachey. Archer Martin sends you many apologies and much gratitude about Drishane but it could not be. He is bundling out of the country as fast as possible, for fear he might get hung up, as he must be back for his work. Yesterday he and I drove to Tillyra, and there we left him with Edward Martyn, who was very civil, interesting, and amusing – and very like George Moore's description and also like Bertie Windle – Tillyra beats all the houses I have seen here – rebuilt about 20 years ago – its splendid old keep embedded in a castellated grey limestone house – and I saw the study up in the tower and the chapel beside it. The staircase is quite away and beyond most. There are very good pictures in fact it is a thing to see. His mania now is the Marlboro' Street choir in Dublin on which he has spent 10,000 pounds and it is wonderful I hear. He even offered to take me to hear his choir sing madrigals and I was so taken back that I said nothing – so I shall not be asked again – and perhaps that is as well. He and Jim were both on the Grand Jury this week, and the resolution was passed calling on the Government to demand a high licence for fire arms, in view of the hideous state of affairs about Craughwell – Edward Martyn alone dissented – and I think Jim was a good deal disgusted. He and I did not get home till past eight – and had a narrow shave or two with Quinine[1] – Jim is a peculiar driver and Amy is even more so. Archer Martin crossed himself privately, & to me about his drive home with her from Kilcornan – "She does nothing till it is almost too late – drove bang up against a wall at a crossroad from not turning in time, and banged into a cart as well – " When I got back from Kilcornan on Monday I found an exquisitely empty house – all having gone in a motor to Ballynahinch (Archer's picnic) and they were not back till nearly 11 p.m. Archer is really a very good fellow – warm hearted and generous and I am rather horrified to find that he has sent for me – to Drishane – a dressing box – a gift! with some letters inside expressing the opinion of the favour that I confer on my family by belonging to it. He does not think they realise the magnitude of our work – they are very kind about it, but they do not understand – is what he says. He is a most faithful creature and a valuable friend to us all. Now I must catch my train. This is a new and fairly clean pot-house – Roxboro – Loughrea tomorrrow – till Saturday. Coole Park – Gort – till Monday

Yours ever

Martin

1 Quinine was a horse.

Glossary of Buddh words

It appears that Ethel Coghill, sister of Egerton, and Edith Somerville's 'Twin', was the first to search for a sufficiently grandiose term to define the Bushes and their far-spreading relations and fix upon 'Buddha-like' – suggestive of self-containment and self-satisfaction. In time and in use, the word eroded to the mysterious 'Buddh'.

To the people in Edith's and Martin's circle of relations, a very wide one, all descendants of Charles Kendal Bushe were called 'Buddhs' – those who were not Buddh were 'suburbans'. Edith and Martin thought it worthwhile to list all the words peculiar to Buddhs in the form of a Dictionary. The manuscript still exists and it is in their definitions of these words that Somerville and Ross began their writing career together.

Edith Somerville referred to Buddh terms as 'the froth on the surface of some hundreds of years of the conversation of a clan of violent, inventive, Anglo-Irish people, who generation after generation, found themselves faced with situations in which the English language failed to provide sufficient intensity, and they either snatched at alternatives from other tongues or invented them.'

Buddh words were sometimes very elegant euphemisms: for example, if one wished to explain that one had to leave the scene in order to empty one's bladder, the Buddh simply said 'I must decant'. Many of these private words were used in social situations as a protection against outsiders, 'the suburbans', gaining any personal information that might circulate as gossip, and were very effective as a protective device.

Backhair *adj.* Applied to conversations of a dubious sort. (Prob. deriv. foolish male tradition as to the topics discussed by 'the ladies' during the process of 'taking down their backhair'.)
Beany *n. fem.* 1. A female servant. 2. A small, mean woman.
Blaut/blort *v.i. and n.* Violently to express immoderate fury.
Blug *n. masc.* A low fellow.
Buddh Descendants of Charles Kendal Bushe and his wife Nancy Crampton. Edith and Martin had grandmothers who were sisters. This is beautifully encapsulated by Violet Powell:

Edith Œnone Somerville (1858–1949) was the eldest child of Colonel Thomas Somerville of Drishane, Castletownshend, County Cork. Her mother was Adelaide Coghill, daughter of Admiral Josiah Coghill, 3rd baronet, by his wife Anna Maria, daughter of Charles Kendal Bushe (1767–1843), Lord Chief Justice of Ireland.

Violet Martin, 'Martin Ross' (1862–1915), was the youngest child of James Martin of Ross, County Galway. Her mother was Anna Selina Fox, daughter of Charles Fox of New Park, County Longford, by his wife Katherine, daughter of Charles Kendal Bushe (1767–1843), Lord Chief Justice of Ireland.

Consequently E. Œ. Somerville and Martin Ross were second cousins.

Buddh or **Bush-leg** *n.* A limb of abnormal size. A racial characteristic. **B.P.** Buddh Pride.

Camac *n.* An equivalent for any known substantive. 1. Any unnecessarily complicated and costly contrivance for effecting a simple purpose. 2. Two men, clerics during the last century, by names Ryan and Camac, were hanged in Wexford for uttering false halfpennies. It became customary to speak of any valueless trifle as a 'camac', and the expression being adopted by the Buddhs rapidly acquired its rich comprehensiveness of meaning.

Carraway *n. masc. or fem.* Also spelled 'carroway'. The object of a temporary devotion.

Chastener *n.* 1. A portrait. 2. A tribute paid by the Buddh painter to Coghelian beauty, with painful and humiliating results. (Deriv. Moral effect on the victim.)

Chip *n. fem.* 1. The elder Buddh woman. 2. One who is erroneously supposed to be the sole prop of morality and order. (Deriv. Chaperone.)

Coghelian-sanguinity *n.* The inextinguishable optimism of the Coghills. (Deriv. Rev. J. Bushe.)

Coit *n.* A petticoat. See *Moy.*

Decanting *v.* to urinate [word in use but not included in the dictionary].

Dictionary Many early letters discuss the compilation of The Buddh Dictionary. It is written in three hands: Edith's, Martin's and Herbert Greene's. Herbert, a classics don at Magdalen College, Oxford, had worked on Liddell and Scott's Greek Lexicon and was one of the slip contributors to Murray's *OED*. When he was on vacation in Castletownshend he spent most of his time with Edith. At this date he had already proposed to Edith and been turned down, but in such a way as to remain hopeful. Herbert remained hopeful for years. The dictionary had to be compiled *à trois*.

Doldromise 'Doldromizing' *v.i. pres. p.* A state of mental inertia.

Dwam *n.* A heavy and half-unconscious state resembling coma.

Eggs as in 'Fresh egg, Good Egg, Egg, Eggling' – Terms applied to male partners in the dance, denoting their varying degrees of merit.

Epitome *n.* the immediate assumption of any newly acquired article of clothing. ('That's the very epitome of the character of you Coghills, to put on a thing before you've had it ten seconds.')

Family-hoof *n.* (to implant the –) The unerring selection by the blandly unconscious Buddh of the topic that will most effectually discompose his hearer. (Deriv. Putting one's foot in it.)

Flahoola *n. fem.* A large loud woman of a stupendous vulgarity.

This word is Irish in origin, like several others in the Dictionary. Although Martin, her brother Robert and Edith all came to Irish anew, learning through O'Growney's *Irish Primer*, several of the older generation used Irish in their daily lives. Edith's grandfather used Irish in his dealings with his hands and tenants, and his youngest brother, Dr Jim Somerville, the GP at Union Hall, was a fluent Irish speaker who used the language with most of his patients.

West Carbery was a noted centre for Irish. At Myross lived the poet Seán Ó Coileáin (1754–1817) the 'Silver Tongue of Munster' who wrote the beautiful Jacobite song 'An buachaill bán'. Much was recorded in this area by Canon Goodman, Rector of Skibbereen, who was a friend of the Somervilles. He was Professor of Irish at Trinity from 1884 until his death in 1896, spending six months of the year in Dublin and the rest in Skibbereen.

Flangey *adj.* Applied to an unwieldy and incoherent arrangement as of dress or headgear. (Deriv. Flange, a raised edge or flank, thence, anything which projects.)

Flop *n.* A lavish and unreserved depositing of the affections upon one whose reciprocity is wholly superfluous. (For the most part a feminine practice.)

One of the most remarkable aspects of life in Castletownshend to Martin was the easy physical affection shown at all times to intimates. The Coghills were particularly unembarrassed by physical contact, and we find Egerton Coghill and Kendal Coghill both using massage to help sick relatives who were 'laid up'.

Flusthration *n.* Extension of **Floosther** *n.* Fluster in a superlative degree.

Gammawn/gommawn *n. masc. or fem.* A common idiot.

Gub *n.* A vague pursuing horror, the embodiment of the terror of darkness. By the superstitious it is conceived capable of inflicting unimagineable injuries. The person enduring this pursuit or possession is said to be **gubbed**.

Gub was a word that changed its meaning during the 1890s. Buddhs had taken to spiritualism and seances from the very beginning and had become disciples of Stainton Moses, the author of *Spirit Teachings*. Edith, at this stage, did not take spiritualism seriously; she often refers in diaries and letters to Uncle Kendal's 'gubbing parties' at the Point. After Martin's death she became seriously interested in spiritualism and a believer, but in the early letters she is merely facetious.

Hifle *v.i.* Denoting the energetic progress of one who has some definite object in view.

Hurroosh *n.* An upsetting fuss.

Kamak see **Camac**.

Kenatiness Extension of **Kanat** *n.* An artful and dangerous person: capable of treacherous and flagitious acts.

Kneebuckles to a Highlander A wonderful explosive exclamation used by Buddhs frequently, though not included in the Dictionary. It implies that something is totally superfluous and useless. Highlanders wear kilts so therefore do not need the breeches kneebuckle.

Leebarkation *n.* Also spelled 'liebarcation'. A flirtation of a resolute character.

Little rawscal Phrase applied to those who have visited, or are about to visit foreign parts, notably Paris. It is used in a half-admiring sense, and implies a certain degree of light enviable vice. (Deriv. The remark of a proud mother to her son 'Chawles, Chawles, you little rawscal you're going to Pawris'.)

Lively Sarah *n.* Sal Volatile (facetious translation).

Marookish *adj.* Describing a condition of vague lassitude.

Microscopic-eye *n.* Term applied to the Squaw's superhuman keenness of mental vision when detecting in an ingenuous remark the latent elements of backhair.

Minaudering *pres. p.* of verb used to describe the transparent devices of hussies. (Deriv. from the Fr. 'minauder' translated as 'to mince, to simper, to smirk.')

Moy *n.* The unstamped envelope. (Deriv. literally 'me'. 'First comes me petticoit, then comes me pollydoodles, and then comes moy.' O.C.)

Nooden-afore *adv.* Ironical greeting addressed to the contrivances of ingenious poverty, e.g. an article of food or apparel which, having seen its first youth, still presents itself at table or on the person with an artificial assumption of novelty.

One of them *n.* A man, not necessarily young, good-looking or well born, who is endowed with a subtle attractiveness, imperceptible to grosser intelligences, though for the keenly sensitive possessing an over-mastering charm.

Overflow meeting *n.* Slang for the human dregs of any social event.
Outlying deer *n.* Meaning unknown.

Poots *adj.* Usually used in the negative and disparaging sense as 'Not poots me dear'. (Deriv. *Pooty*: pretty.)
Purlieu *n.* A receptacle for rubbish, literary, artistic, bestial and human. (Purlieu was in fact what Edith's studio was called by her mother.)
Putrified *v. past p.* Petrified. *Perv.* (Deriv. The mispronunciation of a German lady at once greedily adopted by the Buddhs.)

Re-cherch *adj.* Select, refined.

Segashuative *n.* A man who gives discreet and peaceful good company to women.
Sheba *n.* Any new and prized possession which is calculated to excite hopeless envy in those to whom it is displayed. (Deriv. Queen Sheba's despairing resentment at the sight of King Solomon's high class furniture. Rev. J. Bushe.)
Splay, or **Spladge** *n.* The hand. (Deriv. Splay, *adj.* applied to any large flat thing as splay-foot. Mod.)
a stoon of cold feet A **stoon** was 'A fit of pain so severe as to stupefy the mental faculties.'

Squaws *n.* Young unmarried Buddh women of the highest and most confidential type. (Deriv. Mod.)

Squozzums! *v. or interjection.* The exclamation of one who is suddenly seized with an insane desire to squash or break some soft or inflated object, such as a young kitten, an air balloon, or a baby. (Deriv. Apparently an attempt to construct the imperative of the verb 'to squeeze' the French manner.)

Stitchify *v.i.* The intransitive definite form of the verb to stitch. The sublimation and dematerializing, as it were, of the act of stitching.

Thousands me-dear – hundreds! Once said by Mrs Somerville when wishing to astonish her listeners by numbers.

Ti-W *n.* Reversion of wit. Pigmerry jesting, a form of humour prevalent among suburbans.

Too rich for my blood General expression of distaste and disapproval.

Touch of the crossroads *adj.* A disposition to gad about to places of public amusement of a dissolute sort. (Deriv. The dances held at Cross Roads on Sundays.)

Tweesortir *n.* A water closet (not written into Dictionary).

The two ways in her Descriptive of persons who are believed to be capable of double dealing, and a course of dissimulation.

Unbung *v.* To release the pent-up flow of Chip conversation, which from absence or other unavoidable cause has been temporarily checked.

Wog *n. fem.* A jealous and spiteful hussy. (Mod.) Often extended to 'wogging'. Often used of Sylvia Townshend to convey silly, flirting behaviour where a woman or a man tried to cut another in company.

Young-rot *n.* Term applied by sarcastic elders to youthful advocacy of those discoveries of Modern Science which seem to them superfluous and affected.

Index

Numbers in *italic* refer to illustration numbers